ABOUT THE AUTHOR

Ryan Jennings Peterson was born and raised in the south suburbs of Chicago. His debut novel, *On the Ladder of Humanity*, the first Jolene Hartley Novel and Book 1 of The Humanities Saga, was completed in 2012, followed months later by Book 2, *On the Edge of Greed*. The third in the series, *On the Road Through* Chaos, was completed two years later. Ryan currently resides in the suburbs of Chicago with his wife and two daughters.

ON THE EDGE
OF GREED

ON THE EDGE
OF GREED

THE HUMANITIES SAGA
BOOK TWO

A Jolene Hartley Novel

RYAN JENNINGS PETERSON

ASIN : B00ACMUNOO
ISBN-10 : 0615732062
ISBN-13 : 978-0615732060

Cover design by: Ryan Jennings Peterson

Cover photography from Pexels.com used under Pexels License.
https://www.pexels.com/@yungsaac
https://www.pexels.com/@alex-qian-1180283
https://www.pexels.com/@pixabay
https://www.pexels.com/@ivaoo

FOR

Billie. For Everything.

ON THE EDGE
OF GREED

PROLOGUE

The darkness of the night carried with it a coolness that had been all but forgotten, a reminder that the seasons were beginning their inevitable shift into autumn, bearing heavily upon the time when inhabitants of the city woke to the crisp, refreshing sting of below-freezing temperatures and frost-glazed windshields. Most would follow with an appropriate expletive as they reached into their frozen auto for the dreaded scraper, a tool that would no doubt cover their hands with ice chips while minimally clearing a line of sight.

That time had not yet arrived, however. The evening weatherman had stated tomorrow was set to be an incredible day, beautiful and sunny with temperatures reaching into the upper-seventies. Tonight, though, felt as if Mother Nature had decided to take a practice run, combining the biting air with a gale-force wind that zipped into the opened windows and cut right through the wool sweater Bartholomew Reed wore as he sat staring at his laptop perched atop his desk, the blue glow from the screen lighting up his home office in a hazy, dreary radiance.

He was not thinking about the upcoming atmospheric pleasantries, nor was he pondering the arctic blast that ripped through his home in an upscale community on the north side of the city, blowing loose papers and receipts to the wood floors. He did not care that the desk clock read 11:26 p.m. or that he was expected in the offices of his editor at six o'clock in the morning. No, these items did not matter much to a man who had the nagging feeling that his career — and life — were in serious jeopardy.

Bartholomew Reed, better known as "Reedy" by his fellow journalists throughout the offices of *State of Finance* and beyond, was nearing his mid-fifties and had long ago shelved the dream of becoming an attractive, well-aged individual. He had grown accustomed to the gray, thinning hair atop his large, round head as well as the weight that seemed to consistently add up even though he spent an hour a day on his workout bike.

Bart had married his college sweetheart, Melinda McCormick, shortly after graduating from Syracuse University, achieving his goals and leaving the state of New York with a Master's in Magazine Journalism, a minor in economics and an extremely attractive trophy wife, an accomplishment that, to this moment, he was proud of.

Yet as he sat there and stared intently at his computer monitor, it was his daughter, Kaley, that passed through his mind most. An energetic, young woman, Kaley, at age eighteen, showed more commitment to the area of journalism than he had shown in his entire life. That was not to say that Bart did not take what he did seriously. He did. And he was incredibly gifted at what he did. Yet Kaley, with her curly, brown hair and politician's smile, had taken a liking to her father's work and pursued it with vigor and determination, beginning a once-a-month school-wide article regarding the importance of a healthy hot-lunch menu and the need for exercise at recess. She had been in the second grade.

Bart sighed and rubbed his tired, aging eyes. When he opened them again he stared down to his appointment book, eyeing the initials and phrase he had written on today's date: DH — *Il Pescecane.* He leaned back into his plush, black leather office chair, aware of the absolute silence that had settled upon the house, the whisper of wind through the leaves outside quieting as if holding their collective breath in anticipation.

Bart leaned forward and flipped to the front of his appointment book, pulling a Post-it from under the inside flap and staring at the number printed onto the surface. He held the piece of paper in his hand and flicked the corner nervously with his index finger. He had to make up his mind. This was not something that was just going to go away.

Bart reached out and stuck the Post-it to his monitor, the blue glow of the screen buzzing around the obstruction like a halo. He pulled his desk drawer open and retrieved a pack of Marlboro cigarettes, a habit he picked up while in college to combat the long nights of research and worry. He had kicked the addiction long ago, yet still kept a pack within the confines of his office area just for that quick fix if the moment called for it.

And right now, it definitely called for it.

He lit the stick and sucked in deeply, cringing at the flavor of the smoke that passed over his tongue and swirled within his mouth. He always hated the first drag and the immediate heat that filled his lungs. It was the worst, but only for that one drag. The rest was pure heaven.

Bart stared to the Post-it again, inhaling another murderous cloud of eventual death as he ran the number over and over again in his mind. He reached out to the phone and brought the receiver to his ear, punching in the digits. The phone rang and his nervousness increased. On the other end someone picked up, though remained silent, the only sound sent across the wires a faint breathing.

"It's Reed," Bart said into the mouthpiece. "Give me the sign so I know it's you." From the other end the individual began pressing the keypad, sending a series of beeps into the conversation, releasing in total seven before silencing once more. Seven was the lucky number Bart was looking for. "My contact has agreed to meet. This story can't be swept under the rug, no matter what happens. Too many people are at stake to lose everything, and I can't let that happen." He paused, taking another drag from his cigarette, thinking about what else needed to be said. "I'm going to give him all that I have on my machine. The rest I need you to retrieve at the location we spoke about. I know this wasn't part of the deal, but in case my contact declines this, I need those documents to be within an ally's hands."

Bart held the phone to his ear for a few extra seconds before returning it to its base. He sucked deeply on the last bit of tobacco before throwing the butt in the crystal ashtray on the corner of his desk, reaching for the Post-it on his computer monitor and holding it extended in his hand. He brought the lighter to the corner of the paper and flicked his finger, an orange glow sparking to life and reaching up to massage the Post-it, its long, wispy fingers grasping for the numbers etched onto the surface. The paper caught fire as Bart tossed it into the receptacle next to the dying cigarette, watching with tense eyes as every last bit of the Post-it crumbled into a sooty, blackened ash.

It was done. He had made his decision. Now he needed to move.

Bart reached to the computer mouse and with several clicks shut down the programs and the machine itself, killing the blue glow as he closed the top and pulled out the power cable. He opened his black briefcase and tossed the cable in, placing his computer next to the wires before shutting the lid. He nervously looked around the room as a gust of wind came barreling through, rustling papers and sending a large bamboo planter crashing to the floor, the dirt spilling out onto the beige carpet his wife had just had installed two weeks prior.

He pushed himself from the desk and rose, reaching for the cigarettes and lighter and placing them in his interior breast pocket. It was going to be a long night, he thought to himself.

As he walked through the kitchen towards the garage, Reed halted near the refrigerator, pausing just long enough to uncap the dry-erase pen and draw a large heart onto the board. He kissed his fingertips and placed them in the center of the shape momentarily, a warm sentiment countered by the physical weight of the laptop resting inside the briefcase, as well as the figurative heftiness of its contents.

Bart Reed sighed deeply, gathering his car keys and wallet from the kitchen island before entering the garage and activating the lift, the light from overhead shining dimly onto the hood of his Subaru Outback as he walked around to the driver's side door, pausing briefly to gaze up and down his street.

Nothing seemed out of the ordinary as he backed his Subaru onto the pavement, pulling away from his house as the garage door shut and inching his way to the only man in the world that might help him: DH — *Il Pescecane*.

The roads were empty as Reed continued out of his neighborhood, winding down a side street adjacent to the park, the swing set and jungle gym standing tall in the clear, cool night. Ahead, the Chicago interior shined brightly, a welcoming beacon to Reed as he rounded a corner and came upon a stoplight. From behind him a car rounded the same curve, slowing and coming to rest to the left of Reed, its flasher indicating an upcoming left turn. Reed exhaled after several moments when the man behind the wheel continued his vigil on the overhead lights, seemingly waiting for the instance when the green arrow appeared and he could race off to whatever destination lie ahead.

Reed shook his head and retrieved his cigarettes from his breast pocket. In his nervousness, the lighter flew from his hand, falling to the floor and bouncing under the passenger seat. "Shit," he said aloud, pushing the lever into park as he bent to retrieve the item. He raised back up and put the cigarette to his lips, once again flicking the lighter to life, the flame dancing in the air —

The glass next to Reed's head shattered and he felt a sharp, heated pain sting the base of his neck, like someone had just jabbed a flaming hot poker into his throat. Reed reached up instinctively, simultaneously turning and raising his arm for protection as he saw the man in the car next to him pointing a gun in his direction.

The man fired several more times, each bullet embedding itself into the flesh of Bartholomew Reed or passing through and burying into the upholstery of his automobile. As he opened his mouth to scream, he heard one last pop, and then all went black.

Reed knew he was still alive, yet felt little and saw nothing. He could hear the near quiet outside of his broken window, the chirping of crickets clouding his mind as he desperately clung to life. He heard footsteps approaching, the crunch of glass beneath the weight followed by his driver's side door being pried open.

Reed opened his mouth but nothing came out. He felt a weight across his chest as the man reached into the car and retrieved the briefcase, yanking it from his nearly lifeless hand and placing it atop the car. Reed could hear the clicks of the locking mechanism pop open as the man rifled through the insides. "Where are the documents?" the man asked. Reed did not — could not — answer. "Are they back at your house?" Again the man paused. "You better hope your wife and kid are sleeping soundly tonight. If I get in there and they wake up, things are going to happen."

For the first time in a while, Reed was not worried. Melinda and Kaley were not home and would not be until the following afternoon as they made their way back by bus from one of Kaley's newly scouted universities.

Melinda and Kaley. The names resonated in Reed's head as his breathing slowed and he began to lose all sensation in his body. How he loved them. How he wished things were different. As Reed looked upon their beautiful faces in his mind, reliving experiences of his past in their arms, the man raised the gun towards the journalist one last time, aiming at his head and pulling the trigger, ending his life instantly.

The man lowered the weapon and remained fixated on Reed's lifeless body for several moments before snapping to. He placed the firearm in his zippered side pocket and reached into Reed's car, pulling the lever to drive as he stepped back. The Subaru rolled forward, passing through the red gleaming light and onto the road ahead, bouncing up the curb as the pavement swept to the right at nearly ninety degrees. Seconds later, as Reed's automobile slid down an embankment and rammed into a tree, the man turned his car around and began in the direction he had just come from, towards Bartholomew Reed's home and the documents that had to be there.

ONE

They repeatedly glanced over the candlelit table at one another, catching the other's gaze momentarily before averting their eyes to the white linen cloth draped across their knees. Their pleasantries outside the restaurant door had been quick and loaded with tension, forced smiles and a half-hearted hug that ended in her counterpart hanging on for just a split-second too long, making the embrace one of those awkward kinds that normally ended with someone making a b-line in the opposite direction. Neither one could make that exit, however, as their night had just begun, that anxiety-laden embrace at the entrance leading into what appeared to be the worst beginning to a date ever.

They had seen each other several times since the day on the pier, yet not one of those instances had been like this. For starters, this meeting was lacking the pens and papers, missing the formal line of questioning in the confines of the city precinct. Secondly, this time they were alone, save for the other patrons of the restaurant huddled over clean linen tablecloths and flickering candles, each smiling delightfully at their date as their fingers intertwined or grazed the other's hand.

Their table was not quite up to speed as the rest of the establishment, though in each of their minds they flirted with the idea, wanting badly to jump into the comfort of knowing that an errant hand graze or knee grasp would not result in a rapid, uncontrollable increase in heart rate that would lead to an early bathroom break or, worse yet, out-of-control perspiration.

However awkward this night seemed to each of them, Jolene Hartley and James Graiser could not deny the fact that each was attracted to the other. James was a uniquely handsome young man, with a warming smile and innocent eyes that peered from beneath a messy, brown mop. He sported facial hair that lacked a term, caught somewhere in-between five o'clock shadow and full-on beard. Yet, he wore it well. His personality was what drove him into people's hearts, however, his easy-going, lovable demeanor oozing friendliness that turned even the coldest shoulder into an adoring fan.

And then there was Detective Jolene Hartley.

Hartley was, as Graiser had confessed to Jolene's best friend, Kimberly Banneau, "a woman that made Aphrodite jealous." Her long, dark locks hugged her stunningly beautiful facial features: high cheekbones, exquisitely shaped lips and sharp, magnetic eyes that caught you with the slightest glance and turned your carefree night on the town into a race to woo this goddess before you. Tonight, Jolene's slim, supple neck jutted out of a satin black colored blouse, a short-sleeved top that revealed her toned arms as well as a little extra cleavage, a decision she had purposely made as the cab pulled to the curb in front of the restaurant and her fingers unbuttoned one final latch.

She looked up from her silverware to meet James's eyes once more before he shifted his own to his glass of water, raising the crystal to his lips and slowly downing half the available liquid as if her gaze evaporated all the moisture in his mouth. He set the glass back on the table and looked to Hartley with a grin, catching her gaze for a second before she followed in his wake and finished her drink. Needless to say, it was awkward.

"So," he said, clapping his hands in front of him and rubbing them together.

Jolene looked to him as she set her glass back in place, her eyebrows rising slightly as she tightened her lips. "So," she repeated, unsure how else to respond.

James waited for a moment before opening his mouth and raising a finger towards her. He was only allowed a grunt before being interrupted by their server, a young woman who looked no older than twenty. "Good evening," she said as she stepped to the table, James's mouth shutting abruptly as he lowered his hand and turned his attention to the girl. Jolene stared at him as she slowly tilted her head up to the waitress, a slight chuckle escaping her lips and stealing a glance from James. "Welcome to Von Trabor's. Have you two dined with us before?"

"No," James replied, looking to Hartley who shook her head in agreement.

"Okay, well, you're in for a treat. Tonight, in addition to our regular menu, we have several specials." She continued in a cheerful tone, reciting a lengthy list of appetizers, entrees and desserts with their signature wine selection to accompany the meal. "Would you like something to drink to start off?" she ended, looking rapidly from James to Hartley and back again.

James raised his hand to Jolene who nodded. "Glass of Merlot, please."

"Perfect," the girl responded. "And for you sir?"

"Gin and tonic?" James said with a quizzical inflection. Hartley chuckled again, bringing her hand to her lips as he shot her a grin.

"Great," the waitress said. "I'll go get those ready and come back for your order shortly."

"Thanks," James said. She left the area and James turned to Jolene. "Always laughing at me," he stated with a smile.

"Always so easy," she replied without hesitation.

They remained silent for a minute, losing themselves once again in the tension that surrounded the night. James, looking intently into her eyes, smiled and laughed, an action Jolene had grown accustomed to — and yearned for — during her recent investigation into a murdered ex-gang member, a case that had brought James into her life. It was the juvenile chuckle escaping his lips that had drawn her in, pulled her from the seriousness and vulgarity of her everyday job into a world of whimsical amusement and ease. "What?" she asked, grinning back to him.

He shook his head. "I see you a handful of times, talk to you on the phone quite a bit, and yet just because we don't have Kim parading on about who knows what, this seems difficult."

Jolene's eyes locked with his. "I know," she agreed. "I'm sorry."

"No," he hurried. "No reason to be sorry. I just thought it'd be easier, you know?"

She nodded. "Maybe because it being an official date, there's more pressure."

His eyes went wide. "An official date? Who said anything about —"

"Oh, God!" she sighed, wadding up her napkin and tossing it into his face. "Are you kidding me?" He laughed wildly and handed her back the cloth. "After all the shit you gave me with the Ochoa case, now I actually fulfill the end of my bargain and —"

"Fulfill?" he interrupted. "Makes it sound like you don't want to be here."

Jolene paused and stared to him, fighting the urge to jump across the table to either strangle him or plant a kiss on his lips. "If I didn't want to be here, I wouldn't be."

"I know," he answered. "I'm just teasing."

"I have a gun, you know?" she said. James brought his hands up in surrender.

Their waitress returned with their drinks. She took their orders and walked back to the kitchen with a cheerful grin, leaving the pair to sip at their beverages. "How's everything going?" James asked after a long pause.

"James, I just talked to you a couple days ago," she replied.

"I meant with your …" He halted and pointed to her side.

"Oh," she said, setting her glass of wine down. "Ah, a little sore still, but that's about it. I can move around pretty well." She paused as she breathed in deeply, feeling a slight twinge of pain from the broken ribs she had suffered whilst on the trail of Taylor Thames, a cold-blooded killer she eventually shot and killed on Navy Pier, an action that gained her a new degree of fame from the city's inhabitants and mayor. It was an action that had also saved James's life, which he was no doubt incredibly grateful for.

The two made random conversation over their meals, touching mainly upon her current cases and his next big adventure, James being of the mold to pick up and leave the country for extended periods of time. He was wealthy, an unwanted asset that had befallen him when his parents were brutally murdered nearly a decade ago. He did not touch his money much, however, choosing instead to earn his funds in whatever way he could when he landed at his destination. Prior to meeting Jolene, James had spent a month in Jamaica assisting a friend before returning to his apartment where he was immediately confronted by a masked Taylor Thames and a large, gleaming knife.

It was a fateful day that led him to his current situation, and he would not take it back no matter what, except for possibly the stab wound he had received. He looked across the table to Jolene Hartley, wondering what was going through her mind, pondering if she was feeling for him as much as he was for her, yet not wanting to push the matter and end things before they even had a chance to begin.

They exited the restaurant after finishing their meals and walked down the sidewalk to the left. Hartley had offered to help pay for the meal yet James refused, shaking his head and dodging the outstretched currency. "That would be nullifying the term *date*," he kept saying. "I'll be damned if you're going to steal my date with Jolene Hartley out from under me." They both had blushed at the statement, quickly changing the subject.

James flagged down a taxi for Jolene as she waited near the restaurant windows, her shawl clutched tightly around her shoulders in an effort to ward off the chill in the night air. She watched as James spoke briefly with the driver and handed him a wad of bills, evidently settling the playful dispute that would have arisen regarding the cab fare. She smiled as he approached and offered his arm to her, hooking hers through as they meandered slowly towards the waiting vehicle.

"I had a great time, Jo," James said as they stopped at the curb.

Jolene nodded her head. "Me too. Thank you for dinner."

"Maybe next time it'll be a little less nerve-wracking," he replied, stopping near the opened rear taxi door for an embrace.

She returned the hug momentarily before tilting her head back and looking into his eyes. "Who says there's going to be a next time? I believe you only helped me with one case, so technically we're even." She laughed loudly as his mouth dropped open in mock surprise. She leaned forward and placed her lips on his check, holding the kiss for several seconds before moving to the back seat, stopping with one foot in the vehicle to glance back to him. "Next time," she said, taking a seat and waving to James with a smile as the cab pulled away, an image of her large, plush bed forming in the forefront of her mind. "Next time," she whispered aloud.

TWO

Jolene woke the next morning before the sun had broken completely over the horizon, its young rays beginning their daunting task of heating the chilled city after what had felt like a blustery winter's night. She shuffled her way to the kitchen and made a cup of peppermint tea, her robe wrapped tightly around her frame as she held the mug in her hands and tried to extract the warmth from the vessel and into her fingers. She blinked away the residual sleep and peered into ever-brightening Chicago from her spot on the couch.

She could not help but smile as she thought of her date with James, even though it had started at an awkward snail's pace. Their paths had been set to cross the moment James's good friend, Alderman Daniel Vincent, had been viciously murdered five years prior to their meeting. The case, although going cold quickly, reignited when Benjamin Ochoa was shot through the head at a 51st Street bus stop overlooking the Dan Ryan expressway, sending Hartley and then partner, Anthony Barailles, headlong into the investigation.

It had also sent Barailles over the edge. While pursuing their suspect Barailles had been shot a number of times in an alleyway near James's apartment complex, an episode that led to an immediate surgery and his eventual resignation and departure from the police force. He had been lucky. Taylor Thames, the gunman, was a marksman with a military background. He could have killed Barailles with one shot, a tidbit Thames shared with Hartley during a close encounter.

Hartley missed Barailles from time to time, yet since his exodus a weight had been lifted from her shoulders, carrying with it a tension that had plagued her workplace for years. His longing and lust for Hartley, and their subsequent near-sexual actions towards one another the night before Ochoa's murder, had placed upon their partnership a strain that proved to be impassable, lasting from the moment she had started dating fellow detective Ronny Debarsi — four years prior — right up to Barailles's resignation. After being shot, however, Cynthia, Barailles's estranged wife, had tasted the bitterness of having come so close to losing the father of her children. They had decided to try and work things out, a decision that Hartley whole-heartedly agreed with.

He had a family and they needed him. He did not need to be pursuing gun-toting criminals around the city during the day and Hartley at night. She indeed did miss him, but mainly because of the familiarity she felt with him by her side in the interrogation room or pursuing a suspect down the crowded city sidewalks. Yet there was a definite thrill to being on the job by yourself, making the decisions without having to confer with your counterpart, not having to worry about another person's safety.

Jolene shook herself from her reveries and reached for the remote, flipping on the television and staring into the screen as it slowly came to life, the global news flashing across the display. "Earthquake in Malaysia kills 200 residents. Many more missing." "Five new panda cubs born in captivity in Chinese zoo." "Philadelphia bank robberies die down as autumn/winter approaches."

The last of these transported Jolene back two weeks ago when her ex-boyfriend and occasional lover, Ronny Debarsi, had shown up at her doorstep as she lay sprawled on her couch, enjoying her much needed vacation yet growing anxious as cabin fever began to set in. She had opened her door to him, learning he was back in town once more to accompany his mother while she underwent another round of cancer treatment. They had talked for quite a while, enjoying a delicious, homemade dinner and several bottles of wine, followed, inevitably, by a warm bath and an evening in bed.

Jolene had thought momentarily about James, yet only briefly. She was in no way bound to any one man, and, as bad as that sounded to her own ears, she was going to enjoy life to the fullest in whatever way she saw fit. That was, after all, what both she and Ronny had agreed upon during his last visit. She was just doing as she wanted — living life as she wanted — and if that meant sleeping with her ex-boyfriend who showed up at her door, then that was what she was going to do. The wine, by all means, had played a role in her decision-making, yet once again, she did not care. He left for Philadelphia the following day, calling his former squeeze from the road as she sat fixed over paperwork in the precinct. The good-bye would have crushed her months ago, yet this time she was okay with the proceedings.

Jolene stood from the couch and stretched her arms high over her head, the robe creeping up her legs as she shook the weariness from her muscles. She retrieved her cell phone and moved up the stairs and into the bathroom, cranking the shower lever up and jumping back as a stream of ice-cold water shot from the shower head and clipped the side of her face. She set her phone on top of the toilet and disrobed, looking into the mirror at her naked body as the cloth slid down her skin, eyes and fingers grazing her ribs from where Taylor Thames's bullet had impacted the Kevlar vest, knocking the wind out of her as well as cracking bones.

She was on the mend, returning a few weeks ago to the precinct gym and beginning her daily workout that consisted of a frantic cardio exercise followed immediately by sparring exercises. Although she had not been cleared yet to partake in actual hand-to-hand with another combatant, she was able to run through a series of punching bag exercises that would strengthen her bruised rib cage as well as work out any kinks she may be experiencing from the broken bones.

Jolene thought momentarily about cutting off the shower and heading into the station, yet decided against the morning workout, realizing that the steaming confines of her bathroom were exactly where she needed to be, not sweating it out with several other members of the police force.

She stepped into the tub and pulled the curtain shut, walking forward into the heated liquid as the dozens of tiny streams from the shower head began the rejuvenation process. The water soaked into her dark locks as she tilted her head skywards. Several miniature rivers began falling down the contours of her neck, cascading down her chest and stomach and into a pool near her feet.

Her mind drifted to James once more as she soaked in the warmth. Although the previous night had technically been their first date, she was happy with the way things were going. She did not feel pressured in any way by him, even with knowing full well he was interested in something more serious. She was interested in him as well, yet could not decide whether to pursue something further or not. Her relationship with Ronny had lasted four years and ended only months ago when he shipped off to Philadelphia and the FBI. Was she ready to dive back into a solid, committed relationship? Or was her mind telling her to test the waters, enjoy being single for a while, regardless of if that meant dating or not? She did not need to be rolling in the sack with someone to enjoy life, although it did help.

Her eyes bolted open as a sudden chiming resonated within the steamy bathroom. She stepped from the warm water and opened the curtain, reaching to the toilet tank and retrieving her cell phone.

"Hartley," she answered, licking the water from her lips.

"Jo," her boss, Captain Henry Nolan, replied. "Hope you're up and ready to go."

"Sir?" she responded.

"Patrol found a body in a car on the north side. I need you out there to head this up."

"Yes, sir," she said as she stepped from the tub, reaching back with her foot to switch the lever to the off position.

"Mac's on his way down there," Nolan continued, referring to Dr. Virgil "Mac" McLourey within the Forensics Services Section. "I got to run, but call him and get the whereabouts. I've called the station near you and arranged for you to borrow one of their cruisers."

"Thank you, sir."

"Do us proud, detective," he replied, the day's excitement noticeable in his tone.

"Always do, sir."

She placed the phone back on the tank and stood in the bathroom with her eyes closed and arms wide, her naked body dripping and the coolness of the hallway air beginning its circulation of the room. She shivered as the chilled wisps of air blew across her limbs and torso, raising goose bumps on her neck as she opened her eyes and stared out to the hallway.

Jolene was refreshed and ready to go. Her ribs, as of this moment, no longer ached as she twisted her shoulders to the left and right. She reached for the robe and placed it under her arm as she turned into the hall, the air immediately losing the humidity and warmth that had been trapped within the confines of the bathroom.

She was definitely ready, rejuvenated from the heat of the shower followed immediately by the crispness of her apartment. She walked into her bedroom and tossed the robe to the side, turning to her armoire and the lockbox within, placing her finger on the scanner and smiling as the mechanism unlocked. She opened the lid and pulled out her service piece, holding the cool metal in her palm as her naked body began to adjust to the temperature around her, her mind focusing on the task at hand: her victim and the person that took his life.

THREE

Hartley approached the precinct near her apartment confidently, having had met the majority of the officers that patrolled Lincoln Park and the neighborhoods surrounding it. "Detective!" they yelled to her as she strolled up with a coffee in her hand, hair pulled back into a ponytail that brushed the shoulders of her black leather jacket.

She glanced from side to side at the uniforms starting their shift, their eyes following the detective up the drive. "Hey guys," she answered with a smile.

"Please tell me you've decided to transfer here?" an officer she knew as Train asked.

"Not yet," Hartley responded. "Just stealing a car."

"Well, for you, I'd look the other way!"

Hartley laughed and raised her coffee in thanks. "Be safe out there, boys."

They waved their goodbyes and pulled away as Hartley entered the precinct doors. She was given the keys to an unmarked squad car that was quite possibly the nicest, cleanest cruiser she had ever sat in. No worn leather seats or tears in the vinyl. The windows looked as if they had just been Windexed minutes before her arrival. And to top it off there was no musty, mildew-y smell emanating from the back seat. The vehicle alone gave her serious thoughts about switching to Train's precinct.

She weaved effortlessly through Chicago's pre-traffic city streets, knowing in her mind the victim and Mac were going nowhere until she had taken a tally of the crime scene. Her cases rarely included the wealthier neighborhoods to the north where Mac had given her directions to, yet, in this day and age, anything was possible. With the downfall of the economy, the prosperous seemed to have been pulled with it, forced to sell off their pricey art collections, extensive assortment of jewelry or valuable, limited edition vehicles. Once-multimillion dollar corporations were now treading water like the rest of the world, fighting to stay afloat in a turbulent sea of uncertainty. And those behind the corporations had been brought to the brink of disaster and would do anything to survive.

Hartley turned on a winding road that overlooked Lakeshore Drive several hundred yards away, the brilliant view across the waving prairie grass and sporadically placed trees suddenly interrupted by a commotion near a grouping of large maples. Ahead, nearing the sharp curve to the left and the upcoming intersection, the forensics van sat parked in a cluster of patrol vehicles, uniforms standing at ease as they sipped coffee and directed the non-existent traffic flowing through the area.

Hartley parked her vehicle just before the curve and stepped out, turning in a complete circle while her eyes took in the surroundings. The intersection and approaching streets were empty. Traffic, if there was any in this neighborhood, was non-existent this morning. She had not seen any officers creating roadblocks on her trek to the scene, so she assumed this particular intersection was not heavily trafficked on any given day. The location put them directly in between LSD to their east and the communities to the west, a perfectly placed spot for a murder.

Hartley made her way around her cruiser, glancing at a group of officers standing several yards away. She nodded her greetings, each one in turn grinning back, several raising their paper cups in response to the beautiful detective. She stopped at the curb and stared down the hill to where her victim's vehicle had come to a stop, etching a wide path through the field of ornamental tall grasses.

From the front of the car Hartley saw Mac poke his head up, waving at her as she smiled and proceeded down the embankment. "Careful," Mac yelled up to her. "It's a bit slippery in some spots. Wouldn't want you to fall and hurt yourself."

"I think I got it. Thanks," she called back. Hartley worked her way down the slope, jumping from solid ground to rock and back, avoiding the areas where the chilled sediment appeared to be warming in the sun's rays. She reached the car just as Mac stepped to the back bumper with a pair of latex gloves. "What do we have?" she asked, sliding the blue gloves onto her hands.

He handed over a wallet. "Victim is forty-eight year old Bartholomew Baxter Reed. Cause of death: multiple gunshot wounds to the head and neck. Fatal shot appears to be a close range wound above the left ear. Got Julian pulling a slug from the passenger door now, but I'd say a .357. Good morning, by the way. How was the date last night?" Hartley looked up from the wallet she was sifting through. "Oh, come on now, Jo," he chided. "You think you can tell anything to Kim and not have it funnel through the rest of the precinct like a sieve?"

"Apparently not," Hartley answered, handing him back Reed's personals and looking to the car, her eyebrows furrowing to block out the rising sun. "It went … okay."

"Just okay?"

She glanced sideways at him. "Yeah. A little uncomfortable, but good." She paused momentarily before switching back to the business at hand. "I saw the address on the license is in the neighborhood up there. Anyone go to check out the home?"

"Doubtful," Mac said as he led her back to the car, motioning to the passenger side where Julian, his technician, was crouched. Hartley moved to him. "The gents up there on the hill were waiting for the lead detective to get on the scene." He pointed at Hartley as if to volunteer her.

"That's me," she responded with a laugh. "What else do we know about Mr. Bartholomew Reed?"

"Besides his name and that he probably should have stayed at home, not much," Mac said, crouching into the driver's side door and staring intently from a short distance at Bartholomew Reed's head.

"That's not entirely true," Julian said as he rose and plopped a crushed slug into a clear evidence bag. Julian was a twig of a man. By the looks of him he had spent the few years on the job surviving on Ramen noodles and cigarettes, rarely finding a barber to chop his overabundance of thick, curly hair. Mac stood up straight and stared over the roof at the technician. Hartley took a step back, remaining quiet.

"What do you mean by that?" Mac finally asked.

"Bart Reed is a writer for *State of Finance* magazine," Julian responded as he looked up to his boss, suddenly realizing he was the center of attention between the detective and his superior. "Well, *was* a writer. Uh, he did investigative reporting for the magazine. Stories about stocks and bonds and companies about to fold. That sort of thing."

Mac shrugged and raised his eyebrows to Hartley. "Man knows about stocks and bonds and instead decided to become a forensic lab rat. Go figure."

Hartley bent into the passenger door as Julian exited towards the rear of the vehicle. She glanced around as Mac appeared near the body on the opposite side. "Any reason why we think Mr. Reed was killed?"

"You know, you always ask these questions, yet I bet you have some sort of insight into things."

She flashed her smile. "I do, but I like to hear what you think."

"Want to know what I think?" came Julian's reply as he strode back towards Hartley.

"No one wants to hear what you think," Mac said loudly. Hartley suppressed a chuckle and glanced up to the technician, his face ashen as he quieted.

"What do you think?" Hartley asked him from her crouched stance.

"Why do you get his hopes up?" Mac said from across the car.

"Shush!" she said with a wave of her hand. "Go ahead."

"Well, I definitely think he was killed for something in the car," Julian responded.

"Why?" Hartley asked matter-of-factly.

"Well," he said, moving closer and leaning over her, his cologne wafting into her nostrils and making her giggle. *Guy looks like he hasn't showered in days, yet he wears cologne to a crime scene*, she thought. "You can't really see it from the driver's side, detective, but if you look under his right arm, there's a relatively clean section of the interior where the blood splatter didn't land." Hartley leaned into the car and looked at the described location, noticing that, indeed, there was a section of the front seat that was free of blood. Mac leaned in further and nodded his head approvingly. "I don't know what it was exactly, but there's nothing on the floor that looks like it could fit in that spot. Plus, there's no smear towards the front of the car that suggests the object slid."

"So you're thinking whatever was in that exact spot was taken out by our killer?" Hartley asked, egging the technician on.

He shrugged. "Either our killer or someone else."

Hartley looked past him to the surrounding fields. "Did you guys find any footprints in the area around the car?"

Mac shook his head. "Nothing down here. There's some glass fragments up by the intersection light that looked to be kicked around, but that's it."

She thought for a moment before standing and looking back to the intersection lights above. "If there's no footprints here then it had to be our killer. Whoever took the item from the car had to do it up there." She turned back to Mac. "You said no one checked the home? Do you know if the uniforms up there canvassed the neighborhood?"

"Not that I know of. They seemed content to just wait for the great Jolene Hartley to get on the scene." He laughed.

"Shut up," Hartley responded, rolling her eyes. She began towards the embankment again, yelling back to Mac, "Come get me if you find anything else."

She slipped twice while making it up the hill, the last time being saved by a uniform before she tumbled head over heels back to Mac and Julian. "Thanks," she said to the officer.

"No problem. Tim Newton," he replied, holding fast to her hand and shaking it gently.

Hartley smiled, not sure if yanking your hand away from the man who just saved you from rolling down a hill was kosher or not. "Jolene Hartley," she responded.

"It's tough terrain."

"Excuse me?" Hartley questioned.

"The hill," Officer Newton responded, pointing down to the car.

Hartley glanced over her shoulder to the vehicle and rubbed her hands together. "Right," she said to herself, although loud enough for the man to hear. "Listen, Officer Newton, when did you guys get here?"

Newton raised his arm and glanced at his watch. "We've probably been around for about thirty minutes."

"Thirty minutes?"

"Yeah. Give or take."

"In those thirty minutes, has anyone in your group over there even thought about canvassing the neighborhood?" Hartley pointed up the hill to a grouping of houses that made up the complex above, taking Newton's eyes with her.

He turned back to face her and cleared his throat. "We cleared the immediate area first. We thought it'd be best to wait for the lead detective to get here before setting anything into motion."

"Well, maybe next time we can at least send a couple of guys around the vicinity. While you and your buddies were waiting for me to get here, our killer could have been running rampant in that neighborhood." Her voice rose slightly, but it was the fierceness in her eyes that made the officer rethink his current situation. She shook her head and reached to her temples, rubbing them before lowering her fingers to the officer's forearm, his eyes shooting up to meet the detective's. "Sorry, Tim," she said sweetly.

"No, you're right," he replied. "We'll go up to see if anyone heard or saw anything."

Hartley smiled at him and nodded her thanks. Officer Newton spun on his heels and yelled to his brothers-in-arms, each retreating to their squad cars and heading towards the houses above. Hartley turned on her heels and laughed, knowing that her display of power would one day come back to bite her in the ass. She had enjoyed it though, as she always did.

As she made her way back down to the vehicle Mac stood clapping his hands. "Remember when I said you'd make some man incredibly happy one day?"

"Yeah?"

"I'm not sure about that anymore. I'm pretty sure you'll drive him nuts."

"You heard?"

Mac nodded. "Not everything, but I got the gist." He turned to the car once more before saying, "You're good."

Suddenly, from inside the vehicle a ringing began, starting low before rising steadily and speedily into a high-pitched chime. Hartley bolted to the passenger door as the ring faded, Mac reaching into the cabin and moving Reed's bloody jacket to the side. The sound began anew and Hartley bent to the floor, her eyes trying to adjust to the darkness that hid underneath the front seats. "Give me a flashlight," she said, reaching across the deceased man's lap to grab Mac's miniature

Maglite as the noise subsided once more. She clicked on the button and the light flared up, revealing a trash heap of coffee cups and papers.

The chiming filled the interior once more. Hartley brushed aside an ancient copy of *State of Finance* to reveal a small black cell phone. She flipped the earpiece up and held it near her head. "Hello?" Hartley said into the mouthpiece.

"Hello?" came the feminine reply from the other end. "Who is this? Is this Ann?"

"Ma'am," Hartley responded, "this is Detective Jolene Hartley with the Chicago Police Department."

"Detective?" came the reply. "Is everything all right? Where is my husband?"

Hartley moved away from the vehicle, spreading out the tall grasses that reached up to brush her waist. "Whom am I speaking with?" Hartley asked.

"This is Melinda Reed, Bart's wife. What's going on? Where is my husband?"

* * * * *

Hartley met Mac and Julian near the forensics van near the top of the embankment. The pair could see that Hartley was visibly drained, having just spent the last half hour explaining to Mrs. Reed of her husband's demise and the need for her to come into the precinct. Melinda Reed, although grief-stricken and in shock, had agreed to meet Hartley at the station in the afternoon, as she was returning with her daughter from visiting universities in Wisconsin. Hartley had expressed her condolences once again and hung up, taking a moment to collect herself and relax her nerves before turning and making her way to the men.

"How'd she take it?" Mac asked, grabbing the cell phone from Hartley's outstretched hand and placing it in an evidence box.

Hartley shrugged. "Like a woman who's stuck on a bus and just lost her husband." They remained silent for a minute before Hartley continued. "She's on her way back with her daughter. Said she'd come to you first to ID the body." Mac nodded as he closed the back end of the van. Hartley turned to Julian, who staggered backwards as the detective approached. "You said our vic wrote for a magazine?"

The lab technician nodded. "*State of Finance.*"

"How familiar are you with the magazine?"

"I don't get the question," he said after a moment deep in thought.

"Do you read the magazine often?"

"As often as it comes out. Why?"

"Just making sure that I won't look like an idiot going to their headquarters only to have the wrong guy."

Julian shook his head rapidly. "No," he replied. "It's definitely him. He's got his picture next to each of his articles."

Hartley looked to Mac who had removed the gurney from the rear of the vehicle. "When those uniforms get back from the neighborhoods, want to have them give me a buzz and let me know what they found?" Mac gave her a thumbs-up. "I gave Mrs. Reed your number too, just in case I'm not back from the magazine to bring her down there."

"Sounds good, Jo," Mac responded. "We're going to bag him up and head back. I'll call you if I find anything juicy."

Hartley removed herself from the scene, taking a seat behind the wheel of her impeccably clean car and punching in the *State of Finance* headquarters into the GPS. She needed to find what had been taken from Bart's car and why. And in the world of investigative journalism, Hartley knew that besides the reporter, the man that knew everything was his editor.

FOUR

The headquarters for *State of Finance* was situated downtown in the River North area in what was being called the Green Square, a highly developed technical complex that consisted of a half dozen structures that had either been recently built or recently renovated, each following the guidelines set forth by the environmental commission. The parking garages drew their energy from a mixture of solar panels lining the roof as well as wind turbines that hung from the façade, giving the structures an odd appearance, yet tagging it with a green sticker of approval.

It was in one of these garages Hartley parked the cruiser, exiting the car and making her way to ground level and the courtyard in front of *State of Finance*. The building was the smallest among the group, yet still rose up seven stories into the skyline. The glass walls gave the outsider a constant visual of the interior, the reporters and investigators and editors frantically running throughout the maze of offices and cubicles to further along their current projects in time for the presses.

The courtyard was set back from the street nearly thirty yards with stone benches and tables lining the walkways for that picnic-in-the-park feel while in the concrete jungle. Bushes and trees grew in abundance throughout and the committee overseeing the construction of the Square had installed a large, grass-covered mound to emulate the rolling hills of the suburbs, possibly envisioning the workers of *State of Finance* frolicking over the knoll and laying down a blanket and basket full of food.

Hartley made her way through the glass doors and into the building. She eyed the flat screen monitors to the left of the welcome desk, each displaying covers of recent *State of Finance* issues with the magazine's mission statement being narrated by a local celebrity. "May I help you?" the guard behind the desk asked as she approached.

Hartley held up her silver star to the man. "I'm on my way up to the *State of Finance* offices."

"Do you have an appointment?" Hartley stared at the man who, after a moment, shook his head in misunderstanding. "Let me rephrase that," he continued. "Is there someone I can call to tell them you're on your way up?"

She shook her head. "Just here on business. Maybe direct me to the reception area?"

"Sure," he said, grabbing a piece of paper from the desk and placing it before her. He wrote as he spoke. "What you're going to do is take the elevator to six. There's a receptionist there named Ann Carroll. She can direct you to whoever you need."

"Thank you," Hartley said, grabbing the paper from the man's outstretched hand. "How many floors does the magazine occupy?"

"They have the upper five floors," the guard answered. "The bottom two are leased by an ad agency and dentist office. There's also the printing press warehouse connected to the back of the building."

"Thanks." She walked to the elevator and rode it up to the sixth floor, exiting into a reception area occupied by a long, empty desk with the insignia for *State of Finance* magazine bolted into the wall. She ran her fingers across the desk surface as she waited, glancing at the doors to either side of her. The room contained two seating areas to her left and right, both identical copies of one another up to the number of magazines laid out on the wooden tables. The fluorescents above hummed deeply, bathing the area in a bright aura that Hartley thought unnecessary, especially for a company with the "green" tag.

"Good afternoon," came a greeting from her left. Hartley spun and watched as a woman in her late fifties stepped from the oversized doors. She was dressed casually in a pair of jeans and a pink blouse, though looked tired to Hartley, running on fumes. *The life of a reporter*, she thought to herself. "Can I help you?" Hartley raised her badge. "Police," the woman said with a smile. "Did one of our reporters cross the line again?" She continued smiling as she sat behind her computer monitor. Hartley remained fixed on her but said nothing. A moment passed before the woman looked up, this time with a fading grin. "I'm sorry. I didn't mean anything by that. We get a couple walk-ins a week it seems like. Being a reporter sometimes gets you in a little trouble if you're not careful. Really, I apologize."

"I'm Detective Jolene Hartley with Area One Homicide," Hartley replied. "Are you Ann Carroll?"

"Yes," the woman said slowly, the word *homicide* catching her attention. It was definitely not a term used within the confines of *State of Finance.* "Would you mind me asking you a few questions?"

"Sure," the woman said aloud. "Homicide? I don't know how I can be useful, but whatever you need."

"Great," Hartley said as the door to her left opened once more, pulling her eyes towards it. A man with a balding head and glasses stepped into the room, his brown polished shoes glistening from under his gray slacks.

"Ms. Carroll," the man said as he approached, nodding to Hartley in greetings. "Can you please call Mr. Reed again for me?"

"Sure, Mr. O'Dowd," Ms. Carroll answered. "But I just called him five minutes ago and left a message at his home."

"Well, try his cell. Again." Mr. O'Dowd answered quickly as he began towards the door once more.

"You won't get him on his cell either," Hartley interrupted sternly, ending whatever altercation was arising between the two. Mr. O'Dowd stopped abruptly and turned in place as Ms. Carroll hung the receiver over her shoulder.

"I'm sorry, miss," Mr. O'Dowd said. "May I ask who you are and how you know about my employees?"

Hartley held up her badge to the man who halted in front of her, leaning against the desk. "I'm Detective Jolene Hartley."

"I'm sorry," Mr. O'Dowd responded. "Didn't mean any disrespect. What's this all about? How do you know about Mr. Reed?"

Hartley glanced from Mr. O'Dowd to Ms. Carroll who now set the phone back on its base. "Bart Reed was found shot to death in his car near his neighborhood earlier this morning."

"Oh, God!" Ms. Carroll said aloud, slumping into her seat and raising a hand to her mouth.

Mr. O'Dowd's eyes went wide as his mouth dropped open, an eerie silence settling on the group, a silence Hartley let linger to gain an upper hand on the proceedings. "Mr. O'Dowd," she began.

"Seamus," he mumbled, his eyes falling to the floor slowly as if watching his past moments with Bart play before him.

"Excuse me?" Hartley said, not catching his comment.

He looked back up to her. "Seamus. Please, call me Seamus."

"Seamus," she replied, "what is your relationship to Mr. Reed?"

"I, uh," he stumbled, still lost in thought. He rubbed his forehead before continuing. "I'm Bart's editor. I oversee what he's working on."

"Is Bart really dead?" Ms. Carroll asked from her chair.

Hartley turned her head and nodded slowly. "I'm sorry. I need to ask you a few questions, if that's all right?" she asked, focusing once again on Seamus O'Dowd.

He nodded his head, slowly at first but gaining speed. "Absolutely. Please," he waved his arm wide to the door he had just passed through moments ago. "Come to my office. Ms. Carroll," he said, pulling the door open and looking to his receptionist. "Could you please call Kyle and have him meet me in my office?" She nodded and leaned forward, grabbing the phone and punching in a series of numbers.

Hartley passed through the door and entered onto a floor teeming with activity. Phones rang constantly, echoing throughout the office space as assistants and reporters moved on quick, nimble feet through rows and rows of cubicles, running to connect with their sources before the latter moved on to another customer.

She followed Seamus O'Dowd to the left, walking through an aisle and receiving several second glances from young, ambitious journalists who were caught up in their current actions, yet not so much to be oblivious to the specimen gracing their presence. Seamus and Hartley turned right at the far wall and walked to the corner office where they entered and closed the door behind them. Hartley waited in the middle of the enormous room, glancing at the trophies and plaques lining the wall, all of them awards for the agency and its evident hard work in the financial world.

"Please," Seamus said as he rounded his mahogany desk. "Have a seat." Hartley moved to the chair opposite him and fetched the notepad from her jacket pocket. She took a seat and sighed as the cushions took form around her frame, cradling her figure like no chair had ever done before. "Best on the market," Seamus said as she sank into the seat. "Ergonomically designed to support all of the right spots. Nice, isn't it?"

"Very," Hartley answered, shifting her weight and looking up to the editor. She flipped open the notebook. "You mentioned a Kyle before. Who is he?"

"Yes," Seamus began, shifting forward to rest his arms on the desk surface. "Kyle Walker. He's Assistant Editor of the magazine and my personal assistant as well."

"Does Mr. Walker also know what your employees are working on?"

"Probably better than me. We have many journalists on staff. Some freelancers, as well. I tend to take an interest in the writers that have proven themselves time and time again."

"Was Bart Reed one of those proven writers?"

Seamus smiled and nodded. "You don't read our magazine, do you, detective?" Hartley shook her head. "Reedy was — Reedy is his nickname around here. Reedy was a great journalist. He was the one guy who could get the information on a short notice."

"Why was that?"

"His character." Seamus leaned back and stared out the side window. "He was a good man. Had a way about him when on a story. He pushed you, but not enough where you wanted to never see him again, you know what I mean?" He waited for a response but Hartley remained quiet. "He always was able to come up with the story. I can't remember a time where he missed a deadline."

Just then the office door opened. Hartley turned to see a middle-aged man enter the room, his tie strung loosely about his neck, his glasses beginning their slow slide down the slope of his nose. He had piercing gray eyes that stared at the detective from under a full head of messy salt-and-pepper hair. "Kyle," Seamus said, extending his hand towards Hartley. "This is Detective Jolene Hartley."

Kyle smiled wide, the hardness of his face melting as his cheeks rose. "Detective," he said, reaching his hand to her as she rose from her seat.

"Mr. Walker," Hartley responded.

"Ann just told me on the phone about Bart. I can't believe it! That's such a shame. He was a great man." Kyle pulled a chair from a nearby round table and set it next to Hartley's, taking a seat and crossing his legs.

"We were just discussing how you were on top of what our reporters are working on," Seamus added as Hartley regained her chair.

"Yes," Kyle said. "The boss rides me pretty hard to know everything going on at *State of Finance*."

Hartley forced a smile. "And what was Mr. Reed working on?"

Kyle looked to his shoes and sighed, his cheeks puffing out as he thought. "Well, at the moment, not much. I know he was looking into some fluff pieces about budgeting your money for the holiday seasons coming up, but other than that, I hadn't heard of anything large on his plate."

Hartley thought for a moment. "Mr. O'Dowd, you said that Mr. Reed was a well-established journalist within the agency."

"Seamus," he corrected her, cradling his chin between his fingers. "Yes, he was one of the best."

"Why would one of your best reporters be looking into fluff pieces for the Christmas shopper? Isn't that somewhat of a beginner's job? I saw several young, hungry reporters on the way in that I'm sure would love a piece like that."

Seamus nodded his head and focused on her. "That's true," he said. "But Reedy was different. He liked to keep his beak wet with the smaller articles too. He was an award-winning journalist, but doing the fluff pieces kept him sane."

"Mismanagement of funds in a multi-billion dollar corporation," interjected Kyle, "is the good, juicy story, but the time and resources that go into researching such a piece can drain you quickly."

"The Christmas shopper article is a useful tool for the everyday consumer," Seamus added. "The article could be done in less than a couple hours. Little to no strain on the author."

Hartley glanced back and forth between the two men, her pen jotting frantic notes on the lined paper. "Being a journalist, I'm sure you can make plenty of enemies, am I right?"

"That's correct," Seamus answered.

"Did Bart have any enemies in the world that would want him dead?"

The two men looked at each other in thought. "I mean, enemies, sure," Kyle replied. "But people that wanted him dead — I can't see that."

"Why not?" Hartley asked.

Kyle shrugged. "I've worked in this business for a while and I've never seen anyone get that pissed off. I mean, heated discussions, shouting matches, maybe even the possible fistfight, sure. But never something as serious as killing."

"But some of your articles do bring businesses to the ground, correct?"

"That's right, but —"

"Mr. Walker, I've been doing my job for quite a while now too, and I've seen people murdered for a lot less than complete financial ruin. Just the other week a kid was killed for not giving his candy bar to a teenager." Hartley paused while her words sank in. "Now, do you think anyone wanted him dead?"

"From what I've seen around the office or heard through the grapevine, I'd have to say no. There was no hate mail with death threats of any kind. Reedy never said anything about getting flack outside of the office either. So to the best of my knowledge …" Walker let the phrase hang in the air, looking to the detective as she stared intently back.

Hartley scribbled some more before continuing. "Do you happen to have an appointment book for Mr. Reed? Something he used around the office?"

Seamus nodded, pointing to his computer monitor. "Yeah, we all use the same appointment system."

"Doesn't that kind of give away certain sources to other reporters?"

Seamus shook his head. "The program doesn't allow the journalists to view each other's calendars in that way. Only Kyle and myself are able to see whom someone is meeting with. The rest of the office only sees when someone is available or not."

"If you don't mind, I'd like to take a look at his appointments for the last two weeks."

"Sure —"

"I'm not sure we can allow that," Kyle interrupted. Hartley looked to him sternly. "Depending on sources and confidentiality, some of the contents could be sensitive in nature. I don't —"

"Mr. Walker," Hartley jumped in. "It's either I take a look at his appointment book now, or I get a warrant, in which case I'm sure another agency would love to pick up the story that *State of Finance* was uncooperative in an investigation into the murder of one of its own employees. Your choice."

Seamus held up a hand. "Kyle, please," he said. "This matter seems to be worth the risks." He turned back to Hartley. "Detective, I'll send a copy to Ann at the reception desk to print off for you."

"That would be fine," Hartley replied, finally looking away from Kyle.

A knock at the door turned all three of their heads. A group of journalists peered in through the window, one of the young men tapping his watch. Seamus held up a finger to them. "Detective, I hate to do this, but if there is nothing else pressing, I have to get to these guys."

Hartley shook her head and rose, reaching into her pocket and retrieving a card with her number etched onto the surface. "I understand," she said, handing the paper to a rising Seamus O'Dowd. "If you think of anything else, give me a call. I'm sure we'll be in touch again soon."

"Of course, detective. Thank you."

"Mr. Walker," Hartley said as she passed him.

"Detective," he responded, not rising from his seat as she exited the room.

FIVE

Hartley left *State of Finance* with more questions than she had when she arrived, mainly why was Bartholomew Reed, an award-winning, charismatic financial reporter, wasting his time with fluff pieces about saving accordingly around the holidays? His skill set seemed to warrant tackling the bigger issues, and the fact that he was working on a meaningless project did not sit well with her. It would have been like Captain Nolan assigning her for patrol: a blatant, obscene waste of resources.

She made a call to the precinct near her apartment to ask permission to keep the vehicle a little longer than intended. The officer on the other end assured her it was fine, understanding having the car at her disposal would save her critical minutes looking into her fresh investigation. It would also save her the out-of-pocket expenses of a cab fare, though she opted to keep that argument to herself.

She continued through the stop-and-go traffic of the early afternoon, cranking down the window and letting the city air blow across her skin, something Bart Reed would never feel again. Thinking of her victim brought a sense of dread to Hartley as she remembered Reed's family would soon be in the precinct looking for answers she did not have.

Hartley always hated meeting with the families. She knew it was an extremely important part of the process, yet it still took a toll on everyone involved, not to mention put a heavy burden upon the detective's shoulders. She was to become either the hero or scapegoat in the families' upcoming days, either bringing their fallen loved one's killer to justice or letting them slip through the cracks only to disappear into the seedy underbelly of the city.

It had gone both ways for Hartley, and many times. Cases that were solved brought tears of joy from the families. Hugs and kisses on the cheeks were not uncommon, and occasionally she would even have to decline a home-cooked meal, knowing that her job was to find murderers and allow the victim to speak one last time through her. She did not need to sit in their place and carve the Thanksgiving turkey.

And then there were the cases that remained unsolved. Those were the toughest to swallow for Hartley, knowing that through all of the diligent, careful investigation of following leads and scrounging up evidence, the perpetrator still remained at large. She then became just a reminder of the victim, a walking, breathing remembrance of their loved one. Hartley knew more about these individuals then she cared to, and their families understood that. Having someone that close to your brother or sister, mother or father, to know intimate details that no one else knew, was a hard aspect to handle and many of the individuals involved did the only thing they could: turned their back on her.

Hartley was not at fault in these situations, yet she realized why these people reacted as they had. Knowing your source into the case was closing the door on you to move on to another grieving family was difficult to grasp. Yet in the end, the families tended to forgive the detective, knowing in their minds that she had done everything in her power to shed light on what happened to the victim.

Her phone rang in her pocket and she reached for it, pulling the device out and staring at the screen. CAPTAIN. She answered. "Hartley."

"Jo," her superior said from his office in the precinct. "Where are you at?"

"I'm heading back from our vic's place of employment, sir," she answered. "Why? What's up?"

"Before you go anyplace else, why don't you stop back in here, okay?"

"Heading back there right now, sir. Is something wrong?"

"No, we, uh...We just got a transfer in here and I was hoping —"

"Sir, no," she interrupted.

"Jo, hear me out —"

"No, sir. Please," she pleaded

The captain laughed. "Are you really trying to tell me no?"

"Sir, please. Can't someone else —"

"There is no one else, Jo," he said quickly, the humor in his voice evident. "I need someone to show him the ropes around here, and not only are you my best, but you have no partner. So, to your no, I say too bad. Got it?"

She remained silent for a moment before responding. "Yes, sir. I got it."

"Good," he replied. "Now hold on a sec. Mac just walked in and he wants a word."

There was some rustling on the other end of the line while the phone was passed off, Hartley listening to it while grating her teeth at the recent occurrences. A partner? She had been getting so used to working on her own since Barailles left the force. She did not need to be carrying around extra weight at this moment, especially not weight that had no idea how things worked in Homicide. Baby weight. She —

"Hey, Jo," Mac's voice broke through her thoughts. "The wife and kid just got here. What do you want me to do?"

"How do they seem?" she questioned.

"Pretty broken up. Shocked."

Hartley thought for a minute. "Take them down to ID the body. I'll be back in about fifteen minutes."

"Okay," Mac said. "I also took a message from the officer at the scene. You know, the one who you made feel incredibly small?"

"Yeah, I remember."

"Said they talked to several of the people in the area and no one heard or saw a thing. The spot was just situated in the perfect location."

"Thanks, Mac. I figured as much."

"And it looks like I was right on the caliber of the bullet. . 357."

"Great," she replied. "I'll be back in a little bit."

"Hey, would you mind grabbing me a coffee on your way back?"

"From the usual spot?"

"Absolutely."

"Sure."

"Thanks. I'll see you when you get here. I'll bring the family up to you when I'm done."

"Thanks, Mac," she said as she hung up the phone, her mind racing not only with the idea of meeting Mrs. Reed and her daughter, but also her new partner. She cranked the radio on and continued driving, *Welcome to the Jungle* blasting through the speakers as the wheels rolled down the pavement and to the station.

SIX

Hartley stalled on the landing leading onto her floor of the precinct. She could not help but cringe at the idea of a new partner, not after everything her and Barailles had dealt with personally and professionally for the past number of years. She took a deep breath followed by a long sip of Mac's coffee and turned into the pit, nodding to several fellow detectives as she made her way to her desk — and the man sitting in her chair.

She walked up behind him slowly and clenched her teeth, her eyes becoming thin slits as she thought of removing the coffee lid and pouring the scalding hot liquid on top of the newly transferred officer's head. Captain Nolan must have witnessed the internal debate welling inside Hartley because he darted out of his office like a rocket and came to a stop in front of her desk with a forced grin. Hartley's eyes never left the man in her chair, even as he lifted his head to the captain.

"Hey, Cap," the man said with a strong, rich voice. "Anything I can do while I wait?"

The captain's eyes did not leave Hartley's as he said quickly and quietly, "Move, move, move, move."

"Excuse me?" the transfer asked.

"He said get the hell out of my seat!" Hartley said loudly from behind him, causing him to jump and her superior's eyes to roll.

"Jo!" Nolan said, slapping his hands to his legs.

"Cap?" she asked, mocking the pet name the new guy had for him.

The homicide rookie rolled back in the chair and stood, turning and locking stares with Hartley from a foot away as he began to exit her area. He stalled as he looked upon her, noticing the piercing, beautiful eyes staring into his soul, her lips parted and teeth grating as if she were to let loose another venomous growl. "Sorry, detective," he said, standing his ground, unblinking. "Cap told me to meet with you, so I thought I'd wait." He paused as he glanced from the captain and back. "Should have grabbed a different chair, I suppose."

He sidestepped passed Hartley, the scent of his cologne wafting into her nostrils as he reached the near wall and grabbed another chair. Hartley slowly moved into her seat and placed Mac's coffee on the corner of the desk, leaning back and staring up to the captain with a hint of pride.

Captain Nolan shook his head and moved closer. "Jo, this is Detective Jacoby Ratliff. Ratliff, Detective Jolene Hartley."

"Pleasure," Ratliff said, extending his hand to her.

"You always just make yourself at home like that?" Hartley asked, staring at his outstretched fingers.

"Jesus, Jo!" Captain Nolan said. "Really?"

"No, Cap," Ratliff said, retracting his arm. "It's cool. I shouldn't have made myself comfortable like that. My mistake. I'm sorry, detective."

The room remained silent for a moment, Nolan eyeing Hartley as she took another sip of Mac's coffee. She was having fun, he could see, yet he knew she was definitely not resigning herself to having a full-time partner on her hands. Hartley looked from the captain to Ratliff and nodded slowly, extending her hand to him. He reached out and grabbed hers, both squeezing firmly before releasing. "No worries, detective," she said finally, leaning into her desk and retrieving her phone.

As she listened to her voicemails, she glanced out of the corner of her eye at Jacoby Ratliff as he and the captain chatted. Hartley was less than happy at the idea of toting around this new detective, yet she was even more perturbed with herself at the current moment due to the fact that Jacoby Ratliff had now caught her eye and refused to let go. He was good looking — *No. Great looking*, she thought to herself — with light green eyes and short trimmed black hair. He was tall and athletically built, no doubt a product of the military or a youth spent within the gym. His ethnicity seemed to be mixed, possibly half-black, half-white, maybe a hint of American Indian. At the moment, it was a mystery, and would have to remain as such. The last thing Hartley wanted was to get caught eyeing up her new partner within the first five minutes of their meeting, especially since she was in full faux-bitch mode.

The captain patted Ratliff on the shoulder and turned away, leaving the transfer staring after him. He surprised Hartley by leaning back in his chair and looking up to her, sizing up his new partner in the silence between them. Most rookies would be in a state of anxiety with a new assignment, but then again, Ratliff was technically not new to the force, only to Homicide.

He waited patiently as Hartley zoned in to a message from Mac. "Hey, Jo," he began. "Family identified the body as Reed. They're in the lab taking some time with him. Give me a call when you're back in and I'll bring them up. Oh, and get my coffee." Hartley lifted the drink into the air, cringing at the fact that she had guzzled nearly a quarter of it since arriving.

She hung up the phone and reached into her jacket pocket, retrieving the notepad and printed appointments from her visit to *State of Finance*. She could see Ratliff sitting patiently, his eyes still on her as she tried to scan the papers. Hartley stopped and looked up to him, their eyes locking once more. "Is there anything I can help with?" he asked calmly.

"No," Hartley responded matter-of-factly.

"Maybe you can catch me up on the investigation?"

Hartley stared at him. "Detective —"

"Jacoby," he interrupted.

"Detective," Hartley repeated, letting the word linger in the air before them. "I'll get you caught up, but right now I've got to run through these papers before the family comes up here."

"If you let me know what to look for, I can run through them. You've already had a busy morning. I've got no problem taking some of the load off."

Hartley grinded her teeth together and squinted at him before continuing. "Look, detective —"

"Jacoby," he said again.

She waited and gave in. "Actually, I do have something for you."

"Great," he responded. "What is it?"

"Take a walk down to Virgil McLourey's lab and tell him I'm ready for the family." She laughed internally, knowing that the task was menial at best, something that would put him at the low end of the totem pole, just above fetching coffee.

He leaned forward and smiled. "No problem," he replied, shocking her as he stood and headed towards the elevators. Hartley watched after him, blushing as she caught herself checking out his backside. *Focus*, she thought to herself.

She shook the man's rear from her head and returned her gaze to the printouts Ann Carroll had given her. There were only a few sheets covering the previous couple weeks, an eternity to a journalist that should have been filled to the brim with meetings, notes or chunks of time Reed would have blocked off for assigned writing or research. Yet, besides random lunch meetings and conference calls with O'Dowd and Walker, Bart Reed looked as if he was the world's laziest journalist.

She tossed the papers to her desk and leaned into her chair, swiveling back and forth as she waited for the return of Ratliff and the family. Captain Nolan exited from his office and made his way towards her with a smile across his face, shaking his head. "You can be a real bitch sometimes, you know that? I heard from Mac what you did to that uniform at the scene. What's with you today?"

Hartley threw her arms wide. "Just doing my job," she responded.

"Yeah," Nolan said. "Doing your job and having a little too much fun. You may want to give this guy a break."

"Who? Ratliff?"

"Yeah, Ratliff. He's good. Got plenty of recommendations."

"Has he ever worked a homicide before?" Hartley questioned, staring intently at her superior.

He remained silent for a moment and then submitted. "No."

"Then I have to treat him like a rookie."

"Just keep in mind he cut his chops in Narcotics. He's a Homicide rookie, not an overall rookie. And he's your partner for this case, so keep that in mind before you go insulting people and sending them on errands." Hartley's eyes went wide and her mouth dropped open, mock surprise at the accusations from her beloved captain. "Don't give me that," he responded. "You've got a phone in front of you. You could've called Mac just as easily." He turned and began towards his office. "Just show him the ropes, Jo."

Hartley waved after him and then said, "Okay, sir. But I'm not bringing him in to interview the family with me." Captain

Nolan turned in his threshold and stared at her, a look of inquiry spreading across his face. "I don't know his style of interview and I'd rather not have someone I don't know in there with a family that could potentially give us something to go on. Not until I know he won't jeopardize anything."

They remained focused on one another as the elevator doors opened and Ratliff, Mac and the Reed family exited, the medical examiner taking the wife and daughter towards the break room. Ratliff walked to Hartley and remained silent, glancing from her to the captain as the stare down continued. Finally, after some thought, Nolan nodded his head. "Okay," he said.

"Okay," Hartley replied back, looking up to Ratliff as she stood, grabbing the notepad and appointment printouts as well as Mac's coffee. "I'll fill you in on everything, but I need you to stay out here for this interview."

"Jo —"

"It's either Detective or Hartley," she interjected. "Not Jo while we're on the job, got it?"

"Got it, detective," he responded. "You can still call me Jacoby if you want. And whatever hazing you have going on right now isn't necessary. I know how to interview people —"

"I'm sure you do," Hartley cut in. "And you will. But right now, in that break room, those aren't 'people' that need interrogating. Those are family members who just lost their husband and father. So until I get a little more acquainted with your style, I have to say no. Understood?"

She walked backwards from him, awaiting his answer. Ratliff nodded slowly and swallowed. "Understood, detective," he replied, taking a seat near her desk.

She continued several feet before the guilt set in and caused her to turn. "Ratliff," she said, pulling his eyes up to her. "It's Hartley. Call me Hartley." She held his gaze momentarily before entering the break room to the family within.

SEVEN

Hartley passed off the slightly empty coffee to Mac and took a seat in the break room with the distraught Reed family. She had barely gotten past the line, "Hi, I'm Detective Jolene Hartley," before each of the women burst into tears for what probably amounted to the hundredth time that day. Mrs. Reed hugged Kaley, resting her chin on her daughter's head as the tears ran down their cheeks, making twisting, winding rivers of black mascara to their chins.

Mac stepped close to Hartley and whispered in her ear. "All yours. I have to get back down there." She nodded her head. "And we'll discuss this later," he quickly added, shaking the coffee and its meager contents. He exited, leaving the detective with the grieving family.

Hartley, at the risk of being insensitive, began after a few minutes, needing to get the dialogue flowing and knowing with each passing second the killer moved further away. "Mrs. Reed, I'm truly sorry about your loss. I need to ask you a few questions if that's all right with you?" The woman nodded, wiping her dripping nose with a soaked tissue. Hartley reached into her pocket and retrieved the notepad and printed appointments. "When we talked earlier, you said you were on your way back."

"That's correct," Mrs. Reed concurred.

"Where exactly were you at?" Hartley asked, uncapping her pen.

"We went to a couple universities in Wisconsin," she answered. "Marquette. University of Wisconsin-Madison. Kaley has been trying to decide on where to attend next fall, and we wanted to get an early start on the potentials."

"How long was the trip?"

"We left three days ago. Took a bus up to Milwaukee first and rented a car to go between the two."

"Had you talked to your husband while you were gone?"

"Of course. Every night," she answered.

"And how did he seem?"

Mrs. Reed thought for a moment and glanced at her daughter. "Off," she replied.

"Off?" Hartley repeated. "How so?"

Kaley sniffed as she straightened up. "Preoccupied," she said. "A little jumpy, like he was nearing a deadline or something."

"Did your dad normally act that way when a deadline was coming up?"

"Not like that," she said, looking to her mother.

"He was supposed to come on the trip with us," Mrs. Reed continued, "but a couple days before he said something came up and he wouldn't be able to."

"What came up?"

"I don't know. I assumed it was something with work. The story he was working on possibly."

Hartley thought for a moment. "Was he working on a story?"

"Oh, yeah. Something big. That's all he would tell me though." The detective's eyebrows furrowed as she thought back to her meeting with O'Dowd and Walker. Mrs. Reed watched as Hartley drifted elsewhere. "Is something wrong?" she finally asked.

Hartley snapped back to the break room. "Mrs. Reed, I went to his magazine's headquarters and talked with his editor. Both Mr. O'Dowd and Mr. Walker told me your husband wasn't working on anything pressing at the moment. They stated Bart was looking into some fluff pieces." Mrs. Reed shook her head slowly. "Does that sound like something he would be looking into? Maybe for another company? Some freelance jobs perhaps?"

"No," she said. "Bart wasn't doing freelance. He hadn't for the last five or six years."

"You don't think he could have picked up some side jobs recently?"

Mrs. Reed continued shaking her head. "Bart was one hundred percent a *State of Finance* journalist. He got fed up with the freelance aspect of the job years ago. Always said he wouldn't go back to it. He liked the fact that there was a steady paycheck coming in."

Hartley handed the printed appointment sheets across the table. "These were given to me by O'Dowd's secretary before I left. I've gone through them and can't figure out why your husband wouldn't have anything in here?"

Mrs. Reed leaned forward and took hold of the sheets, flipping through the pages and skimming the contents before moving quickly on to the next. She shrugged. "I don't really know how he did things at the office," she replied, handing the pages back. "But he had a personal appointment book he kept at home."

"Did he use it for work matters?" Mrs. Reed nodded. "Would you mind if I had a look at that?"

"Of course," she said. "It's at the house, but anything you need."

"Thank you," Hartley said. They remained quiet for a moment before she continued. "Mrs. Reed —"

"Please, detective, call me Mel," she said.

"Okay. Mel, was your husband working in the office every day?"

"I guess."

"What do you mean by that?"

"Well, he had a spot in the office, but being a journalist he did a lot of traveling. So, I guess if he was in town he'd be at the office. Either there or at home."

"Did he have a laptop he used when on the road?"

"Of course," she said. "Took it with him wherever he went." She forced a smile as she stared at the detective. "You can have that too, if it helps."

"It may, thank you." Hartley looked down to Kaley who stared with damp eyes to the floor, lost in memories of the past. "Kaley," she said, reaching out to touch the young woman's knee. The girl slowly glanced up to the detective. "I've been doing this for a long time. I promise, I'll do everything in my power to find who did this."

Kaley nodded slowly, her eyes filling with tears. "Thank you," she said with a choked voice, Hartley's chest tightening as she looked to the now fatherless young woman before her.

"Come on," Hartley said, rising from the couch. "I think that's enough questions for now. I'll give you guys a ride back to your house."

The two women rose after her, each smoothing out their clothes and wiping their eyes. "Thank you, detective," Mel said. "Anything we can do to help, you let us know."

"A good start will be the laptop and appointment book," Hartley said as she led them out of the break room and into the pit, eyeing her new partner from across the way and beckoning him over. "We're going to give the Reeds a ride back to their house," she said as she pulled him to the side. "There's a laptop and Reed's personal appointment book we need to take a look at."

"Great," he said, holding up his finger and moving towards the desk nearest them. He ripped a page from a notebook and grabbed a pen, scribbling his name and phone number on the surface and turning to Mel and Kaley. He extended his hand to each. "Mrs. Reed … Kaley," he said in a soft tone. "If there's anything you need and you can't reach Detective Hartley, feel free to give me a call. That's my cell phone. You can reach me anytime. Day or night."

"Thank you, detective," Mrs. Reed said with a slight smile.

"Please, call me Jacoby," he said, tapping each on the shoulder before turning away and moving to his partner.

Hartley smiled as they began towards the elevators. "Smooth," she said.

"Just doing my job," he responded back. "Plus, this way you can focus on the case more. I can be the middleman for you if need be." The elevator doors opened and the group entered, Hartley glancing sideways at her new partner and feeling a tinge of pride. *Maybe this will be just fine*, she thought to herself as they descended to the ground floor. *A partner with confidence and charisma. Maybe this will be good.*

EIGHT

They rode in silence for a long while as she aimed the cruiser towards the Reed household with Ratliff taking in the outside world from the passenger seat. Hartley glanced from time to time at the man seated next to her, watching as he confidently dealt with the current situation in a calming manner that let the Reeds know he was there for them if need be.

The Reeds sat in the back seat, Melinda cradling her daughter in her arms with glassy eyes focused out the window to her left. Both mother and daughter were elsewhere mentally, their thoughts conjuring up a happier, more peaceful reflection of the husband and father they loved so much, a man that had been taken from them entirely too soon. Hartley could see the tragedy reflected in Kaley's eyes as she glanced at the girl in the rear-view mirror, her frame supported by her mother, eyes set to the vinyl backing of the detective's seat.

Hartley took in the differences between the women and their life experiences. On one hand was a young woman with all the potential in the world, a kid that, most likely, had never been confronted with a death such as this before. She had probably never experienced the numbing sensation of an unexpected loss followed immediately by the air being sucked from your lungs and replaced only by heaviness and helplessness. Kaley was lost. She did not seem to know what had hit her and, as a coping mechanism, had turned off her senses and floated someplace between her memories and reality.

Melinda, on the other hand, had put on a façade of control, an air of stability Hartley knew she needed to portray, if only for her daughter. Inside, just below the surface, was a woman screaming for her dead husband, begging for the universe to return him to her just the way she remembered him. She could not show her grieving, powerless side at the moment, however. She needed to be strong for both of them. Kaley needed to know that although this great tragedy had come into their lives, it would not be the end of them. Yes, their loved one was gone, but they would not forget him. They would not forget how close their family bonds were. They would remember forever the lessons Bart had taught each of them throughout their lives together.

As Hartley switched her focus between the women, she caught Mel's wavering, bloodshot gaze in the rear view. A tiny, forced smile crossed Mrs. Reed's face as she sniffled. "Thank you again for giving us a ride. You really didn't have to do this."

"Our pleasure," Hartley responded.

"Well, I guess you do need Bart's appointment book and computer. So …" She let the phrase hang in the air as she lost herself once more with her thoughts.

"Ma'am," Ratliff said, turning around as much as possible to look upon Mrs. Reed and her daughter with kind eyes and gentleness spread across his face. "Your husband was a good writer. I didn't read everything he did, but I did catch some of his articles from time to time. He was good."

Mel smiled. "Thank you," she responded with tired eyes and a forced smile. "He was good. He loved writing. It was his passion. Not many people get to work their dream job in the world, but Bart did. He was always writing."

"Did he write anything else besides magazine articles?" Ratliff asked.

"Oh, sure," she answered. "He had a couple books under his belt, as well as co-authored some material." She went silent for a minute and smiled to herself, lost in a thought, which, no doubt, included Bart. "Do you know what he really wanted to do before his career ended?"

"No, ma'am," Ratliff responded.

"He wanted to write a western novel."

"Really?" he said, a smile spreading across his face. "I love westerns."

"So did Bart."

"John Wayne. Clint Eastwood."

"Clint was Bart's favorite."

"Same here. Loved him in *Unforgiven*." Mrs. Reed smiled and nodded, bringing a hand to her mouth as the words failed her. Ratliff held her gaze from a moment longer before returning his eyes forward and leaving the Reed family to their reveries.

Although still uncertain about their impending partnership, Hartley was impressed with Ratliff. He seemed to have a quality about him that she found likable, a charisma and confidence that reminded her of Debarsi. He was a smooth talker, that much was certain. He had brought about smiles from the grieving family on two occasions thus far through what appeared to be genuine care and commitment. That was not to say Hartley did not genuinely care for the families' plights. She did. Yet she did not see herself passing out personal information and offering her assistance in the middle of the night. She did not need to be that close with the families.

They pulled into the driveway of the Reed household and exited the car, the detectives following the family up the concrete walkway leading to the front door. Hartley looked around the yard casually, noticing the well-maintained grass and trimmed hedges of the large plot of land. Part of her — although a minute part — yearned to have a life like the Reeds. She loved the idea of space: bushes surrounding an immense, wooden front porch; flowers framing the neatly trimmed grass; a trickling waterfall flowing into a pool of large goldfish. Yet that dream came with an enormous cost: lose the fast-paced life she had in Lincoln Park. She was not quite ready for that.

A collective gasp from Mrs. Reed and Kaley pulled Hartley's attention away from the pristine yard to the white, splintered doorjamb of the home. Mel glanced to the officers with wide eyes as they made their way past the family and to the entrance. "Stay here," Hartley said, reaching for her firearm and pulling it from its holster. Ratliff followed suit, stepping in line with his partner as they moved against the door. They locked eyes momentarily. Ratliff nodded to her and she hastily sprang to action, moving into the home with gun raised, sweeping through the large open rooms on nimble feet that fell silently as she made her way into the kitchen.

Ratliff moved in the opposite direction, slicing through the living room and den before meeting Hartley in the trashed office space located at the back right of the home. The detectives scanned the room, their eyes falling to the random stacks of books and papers thrown aimlessly about the floor. Hartley and Ratliff glanced to each other before turning towards the front door and the staircase leading to the second level.

The Reeds stood vigil outside the house on the walkway, Melinda holding her daughter as they stared to the front door, each fully in the present as the officers hurriedly climbed the steps and disappeared from view.

Upstairs Ratliff kept on Hartley's back as they walked room to room, clearing each before moving cautiously on to the next. They turned into each doorway with extreme care, knowing that a cornered intruder would act in desperation to make a hasty exit.

They cleared the last room and looked to each other with relief, both detectives holstering their weapons and moving back down the hallway and descending the steps. They exited the home, Ratliff heading to the family as Hartley pulled out her phone and called in the breaking-and-entering. She spoke with the dispatch operator briefly before returning to the group near the doorway. "Uniforms are on their way," she said.

"Do you think this has something to do with Bart?" Mel asked.

Hartley shrugged. "It could, yes," she answered. "But the officers have to look at the evidence they collect."

"But what are the odds that these two things happen like this?" Kaley questioned. "That can't be coincidence."

Hartley turned to her and shook her head. "Normally these types of things aren't coincidences. But we can't jump to conclusions. We have to treat this as a separate thing." Hartley turned back to Ratliff. "Stay out here and wait for patrol. I'll take them inside. Mel, I need you to take a look around and see if anything was taken."

"All right," Mel responded as she and Kaley entered the house.

Hartley turned to Ratliff as she followed the Reeds. "As soon as patrol gets here brief them on what's happened with the Reed family. I don't want them bombarding these two with a bunch of questions. Then get inside. Just like Kaley said, this can't be a coincidence."

"Got it," he responded, taking a step off the porch and heading towards their cruiser.

Hartley worked her way along the same path she had when first entering the house, heading straight into the kitchen and veering right into the office area. Kaley sat still at the kitchen counter, glancing at Hartley as she made her way towards Mel.

The space was a mess. The desk in the center of the room was void of drawers, each of the wooden compartments overturned and subsequently thrown into the area, one with such force it now housed a large chunk of plaster from where it had collided with the wall. Books from the oak shelves were strewn across the floor. A cushion from the corner reading chair was laying in the adjoining living room, leaning against a floor lamp that looked as if at any moment it would fall to the side and crash through the window overlooking the Reed vegetable garden.

Mel sifted through the mess, not quite knowing what to look for. At times she stood in the room with arms folded, balancing on one foot as the other flipped this book or rustled those papers. Finally, she turned and shrugged with arms wide. "I don't know. There's so much in here all the time. Bart kept all his work material in the desk or on those shelves." Hartley walked forward and stood next to her, a source of comfort in an otherwise chaotic day. "I don't see the laptop though," she said.

"Where does he usually keep it?" Hartley asked.

Mel pointed to the desk. "Always right on top," she stated. "But I don't see his briefcase either, so he must have had it with him when …" She let the phrase hang and put a hand to her mouth as the emotions came to the surface once more.

Hartley reached out and placed a comforting hand on her shoulder. She opened her mouth to speak yet nothing emerged.

"It's okay," or "Everything will be fine," were phrases she dared not utter, along with the ever-tempting, "We'll get whoever did this." She had learned throughout her career to not make promises she might not be able to keep.

She was saved from making any such comment as Ratliff approached, a uniformed officer on his heels. "Hartley, this is Officer Woodward. Officer, my partner, Detective Jolene Hartley."

Hartley nodded her greetings. "Officer."

"Detective Hartley," he responded with a smile, gazing upon the woman before him. "It's great to meet you. I followed you in the media on your previous case. The one that ended on Navy Pier. Great job handling that Thames guy."

Hartley forced a smile and took a step towards the officer. "Thank you, Officer Woodward, but do you really think this is the time for this?" She allowed the man to glance over her shoulder at the distraught Mrs. Reed before continuing. "I assume Detective Ratliff briefed you on what's occurred with the family?"

"Yes, detective. I'm sorry," Woodward replied, his eyes glancing to the floor in embarrassment.

"Maybe we can stick with what's going on now then?"

"You're right. Apologies." He cleared his throat and composed himself. "Have we gone through the house to see if anything is missing?"

Hartley shook her head. "Just started looking," she answered bluntly, her eyes remaining on the officer as he waited for more of a response.

When he realized it would not come he tried a different tactic, one that allowed him some freedom from the heated stare he was now receiving. "Well, I'm going to take a look around the outside of the home. See if I can find anything."

"Great," Hartley answered. "We'll let you know if we notice anything missing." She waited for the man to exit before turning again to Mrs. Reed. "Mel, did Bart always carry his laptop in the briefcase?"

Mel nodded her head, a questioning look spreading across her face. "Yes. Why?"

Hartley took a step closer to her. "The forensic team noticed something in the front seat of your husband's car had been removed after he was shot. I'm wondering if what they took could have been the briefcase and laptop."

"Had to be," she said, pointing to the reading chair. "Bart always kept the briefcase under the chair and it's gone too. My guess is he had the computer with him wherever he was going."

"And my guess is that whoever did this has your husband's laptop."

"But not his appointment book," came the voice of Kaley from behind them. They turned in time to watch the young woman bend over a pile of overturned books, reaching into the rubble and pulling out a thin black notepad.

Hartley walked to her and took the book from Kaley's extended hand. "May I?" she asked Mrs. Reed. Mel nodded her head and turned back to the room as Kaley came up to her side, mother and daughter wrapping their arms around each other. Hartley flipped the book open, eyeing the ink splotches and doodles in Bart's pen, everything from appointments with sources to drawings of Homer Simpson to movie quotes from recent flicks he had seen.

She stopped suddenly on the square displaying yesterday's date, the day of Bart Reed's murder. Amongst the scribbling, circled with what looked like an unsteady hand, were the initials DH, followed by the words *Il Pescecane*. Hartley's brow furrowed as Ratliff walked closer. "Jo?" he said, noticing his new partner's perturbed look.

"That can't be," she said aloud to no one in particular.

"Jo, is everything all right?" She handed him the book and slowly turned and walked to the window. "*Il Pescecane*," she heard Ratliff read. He looked up to her. "What does it mean? Do you know what this is?"

Hartley stared out the window into the enormous backyard, watching the trees blow in the breeze, the uniformed officer making his rounds of the premises. From the corner of her eye she saw Ratliff approach, his focus on her as he reached out and handed her the open appointment book opened to yesterday's page. "What is *Il Pescecane*?" he asked.

"DH. *Il Pescecane*," she said to him, turning. "It's an Italian phrase meaning 'the Shark.'" She paused before continuing. "It's a nickname we used to call my brother when we were younger. Dane Hartley. D-H." She stared at Ratliff as he processed the words. "It means that on the night of Bart Reed's murder, he had an appointment with my brother."

NINE

Hartley and Ratliff spent another five minutes on the scene, though the former had become perturbed in the eyes of the Reed family. Ratliff expressed to the grieving widow and her daughter that his partner was running the day's happenings through her head and was by all means on top of the case. He assured them the absolute best detective was on their side and then excused himself, walking with Hartley back to the cruiser just in time to meet with Officer Woodward and learn absolutely nothing of significance, other than the fact that the man seemed enamored by Jolene Hartley. The detectives had come to the conclusion that whoever had broken into the Reed household knew what they were looking for. The upstairs bedrooms appeared to be untouched, minus a drawer opened here or there with the contents hurriedly rifled through. The only room in the house that had been ransacked was Bart's office area. A forensics team was on their way to search for fingerprints, yet Ratliff figured nothing would be found. If this was indeed connected to Bart Reed's murder, the odds of finding a trail were slim.

The detectives hopped into the cruiser and raced through the busy streets toward the city interior, Ratliff glancing to his new partner from time to time with concern etched across his face. Hartley remained focused through the windshield with her mind racing and eyes searching.

"Why is your brother's name in a dead man's appointment book on the day of the murder?" Ratliff finally asked, receiving a quick, venom-laden glance from his counterpart. "Look, you just tell me what we need to be doing." Hartley shifted and fixed on the outside world. Ratliff, at the risk of digging a deeper hole, continued. "You need to give me something, Jo."

"Stop calling me Jo," she replied, brushing off his inquiry and returning to her thoughts.

"I'm going to keep calling you Jo until you at least fill me in on what's going on." He paused as Hartley ran her fingers through her hair. "Jo?"

"God damn it, Ratliff!" she exclaimed. "Give me a second to think!"

Ratliff held up a hand in surrender, turning his gaze out the window. Hartley's mind was working a million miles per hour, flashes of a deceased husband and father morphing into a stubborn, thirty-four year old man with a face she could not quite picture: Dane Hartley. *Il Pescecane*. Her brother. She had thought about him little over the past several years. Now, all of a sudden, he was thrown into her life as the sole lead in a homicide investigation she was heading up. Although their bond had been strained over the past decade, he was still her brother, and deserved to be treated as such. Yet she was still a homicide detective, and would act like one regardless of who was involved.

Hartley retrieved her cell phone from her jacket pocket and handed it to Ratliff who held it aloft in the palm of his hand, waiting for directions. When instructions failed to arise, he moved his attention from the phone to his partner, his gaze falling upon her steady, intense eyes. Hartley could feel his stare. She knew she was being unfair, yet, at the moment, she could do nothing about it.

Eventually, after several long minutes of silence, she glanced sideways to him. "What do you want me to do?" he asked calmly.

"Dane's an asshole," she said bluntly, a statement that caused a grin to form upon Ratliff's face.

"I agree," he said with a smirk. Hartley shook her head, surprised with the smile that had formed across her face, a smile Ratliff's calm demeanor had pulled from her. The tension within the vehicle dissipated enough for both detectives to relax slightly and open the line of communication once more. "Maybe before we get to your asshole brother you can fill me in on everything up till now. How about that?"

Hartley agreed, quickly summing up the events that had transpired thus far in her — their — investigation. She touched briefly on the crime scene: Reed's bloody body slouched in the driver's seat over a relatively clean patch of upholstery. "What are the ideas on that?" Ratliff asked.

"Mac and his team didn't know," Hartley answered, "but now that we think Reed had his laptop and briefcase with him, I'd put money on that."

"Makes sense. What else?"

"Well, before I came back to the station earlier I had a meeting with Reed's bosses who assured me our vic wasn't working on anything of importance."

He glanced at her, catching her tone that carried with it a hint of annoyance. "And you think he was?"

"I don't know," she replied. "I just think something isn't right. He's one of their best writers. Why is he producing pieces on saving pennies, you know?"

"Doesn't make much sense," Ratliff agreed. "And your brother?" he asked, daring to push the topic.

"Dane," she said, as much to herself as to him.

"Dane, right. What was the nickname?"

"*Il Pescecane.*"

"Right. How did that come about?"

"It was a name his little league coach gave him."

"The Shark?"

Hartley smirked and nodded. "I know. Weird, right? Completely bypassed Sport and Ace. But it fit the way he played. He was great at zoning in on the player with the ball and attacking. In high school it was the same way."

"And it just stuck with him till now?"

"Yeah, though I'm sure the meaning now stems from the way he goes about getting things. Last I knew, Dane's moral compass wasn't exactly pointing in the right direction."

"So how does he fit into this then?"

"Not sure, but if I had to guess, I'd say it was because he's also a journalist."

Ratliff raised his chin slowly in an *ah-ha* type of nod before asking, "And what type of journalist is he?"

"Last I remember: a dirty one," she replied. "Dane was always the type of guy who just didn't care, you know? He could be a sweet, funny, lovable guy, but there was this streak about him … He only looked out for himself. If you were in his way, watch out." She waved her hand in the air as if brushing thoughts aside.

"Seems like the opposite of our vic."

Hartley nodded. "Which is why I don't understand why there would be any contact between them. Reed, from what I gather, was an upstanding guy. Dane … Not so much. But who knows? Maybe our vic had some secrets." She paused before looking down to the phone in Ratliff's hand. "Do me a favor. Find Dane's number and send him a text."

Ratliff woke the phone with the press of a button, finding her contacts and the imageless listing of Dane Hartley. "What do you want me to say? I'm guessing 'Hey big bro!' is out of the question?"

Hartley tilted her head and eyed her partner with a grin. "Maybe a little less enthusiastic. Type in 'We need to meet. Now. 9-1-1.'" Ratliff did as directed and placed the phone on his lap.

They continued driving for several miles in silence, the constant hum of the tires on pavement the only sound within the cabin. Hartley's phone buzzed to life and Ratliff reached for it. "Grant Park. Thirty minutes," Ratliff read aloud, glancing to his partner.

Hartley remained focused on the road, weaving in and out of the city traffic as she made her way towards the large grounds of the park, an area known for its beautiful landscape, never-ending walking paths and the magnificent Buckingham Fountain. She shook her head as a memory popped into her mind. "Fucking asshole," she said, causing Ratliff to look her way with a quizzical gaze. "Grant Park," she began. "It's the last place I saw him years ago. He was giving me the bird as I walked away."

* * * * *

The detectives positioned themselves near a park bench overlooking the Clarence Buckingham Memorial Fountain, a stunningly mesmerizing display of water and lights dedicated in 1927 and representing Lake Michigan itself. Hartley had walked the Grant Park grounds hundreds of times, even remembering a few inebriated moments in college whilst rocking out at the annual Lollapalooza Music Festival. Her early career in narcotics had led her to focus on the park and an amateur drug ring that fed the tourists and city-dwellers with everything from marijuana to methamphetamines, and right from the front yard of Chicago.

Hartley paced back and forth near the bench where Ratliff had taken a seat, his eyes scanning the surroundings in hopes to see the approaching journalist. "When he gets here, give me a little space," Hartley said.

"Sure," Ratliff replied. "Whatever you need. I'll watch your back though." Hartley glanced to him and forced a smile, one that faded quickly. "What's the deal with you two?"

She looked down to her shoes before responding. "Do you have any siblings, Ratliff?"

"A brother and two sisters," he answered.

"How do you feel about them at this point in your life?"

He smiled. "They're great. I love them. They were pains in the ass when we were younger, but we're all pretty close now."

"Well, Dane and I are the opposite of that. We used to be close as kids up until about college. He got into journalism and just kind of put his family on the backburner. We've had some run-ins that didn't end too pretty. Ever since the last time I saw him, we've both somewhat agreed to just stay out of the other's life." She stopped as her eyes locked onto a figure approaching from a distance.

Ratliff followed her gaze to a man working his way down the twisting path, smoking a cigarette and staring at the ground before him. "That him?" Hartley nodded. "What happened? I mean between you two last time you saw each other."

"Our dad's heart attack happened. And he never came to visit. Met him here and he didn't say much about it. Apparently his story was bigger than our dad. I told him that if he couldn't even make it to see his father in the hospital, then don't come around again."

"What did he say to that?"

"Nothing," she responded, glancing to him. "He flipped me the bird as I walked away." The conversation stopped as Dane drew nearer, flicking the cigarette butt to the ground feet in front of the detectives and stopping. He was a handsome man in his mid-thirties, sporting jeans and a blazer that clung to his muscular frame.

Dane reached up and removed his sunglasses, exposing the same soul-searching eyes as his sister. "How you doing, Jo?"

"Good. You?" she asked coldly.

"Never better." He looked to Ratliff. "New guy, huh?"

Ratliff began to open his mouth but was interrupted by his partner. "You mind giving me a minute?" she asked to Ratliff. He nodded his head and walked to a nearby bench, taking a seat, his eyes never leaving her.

Hartley turned back to her brother. "New partner?" he asked.

"Yeah," she replied.

"What happened to Tony?"

"He quit."

"No shit? Why?"

"Took a couple while pursuing a suspect. He's got kids he wanted to see grow up." They remained silent for a moment, each eyeing up the other. Dane moved around the bench and took a seat, his elbows resting on his knees as he looked up to her. "I need to ask you a couple questions, Dane," Hartley continued.

Dane leaned back and held his arms wide. "Off the record?"

"Don't give me the 'off the record' routine, Dane. I need answers."

"And you think I can help?"

"Possibly."

He thought for a moment. "Shoot."

"How do you know Bart Reed?" she questioned, staring intently at his face as she tried to pick up on any emotion. He gave nothing away.

"He's a journalist," Dane answered. Hartley remained fixed on him. "He and I sometimes cross paths on stories. He has sources that he lets me pass information through and vice versa. Why?"

"When's the last time you spoke with him?" she pressed.

"Yesterday morning. Why?"

"What did —"

"Why?" he interrupted. She stalled and stared at him, his gaze matching hers. "We don't have that good of a relationship where I'm going to keep giving you information without knowing what this is about."

"Maybe you didn't see that badge on —"

"Maybe I don't give a shit."

The statement brought about another tension-filled silence that hovered just above their heads. Hartley glanced towards Ratliff and noticed he was still fixed on her. She turned back to her brother. "Reed was found murdered early this morning. He kept a personal appointment book in his home office that had your initials and nickname on last night's block." She halted to let the words sink in. "I need to know where you were between 11:00 last night and about 2:00 a.m."

"Are you actually considering me as a suspect?"

"Where were you?"

"Un-fucking-believable, Jo!" he yelled, standing to face her. Hartley kept her position, though from the corner of her eye she could see Ratliff did not. "You actually think I killed someone?"

"I'm hoping you didn't, but I need to know where you were. Your name in Reed's appointment book on yesterday's date puts you in this investigation. Tell me where you were and if it checks, I'll be happy to leave you be."

Dane thought for a moment before regaining his seat. "I got a call from Bart yesterday morning. He sounded in a panic. Said he had something huge that he needed out of his hands. Thought I was the guy to keep the story going."

"What was the story?"

"He didn't say. Told me to meet him around midnight at The Fairborne Club and he'd give me everything he had."

"What did he give you?"

"Nothing," Dane replied as Ratliff approached. "He never showed. I sat at the bar for about two hours before taking off."

"Can anyone confirm that?"

Dane looked from Ratliff back to his sister. "Try the bartender," he said with an air of contempt.

"I will. Until then, don't leave the city," Hartley said as she began to walk away, Ratliff falling in step with her and glancing back to the bench her brother still sat upon. Dane looked his way and raised his hand, his middle finger extending to the detectives as they turned a corner and disappeared from view.

TEN

Dane Hartley left his apartment building early the following morning with a cigarette resting between his lips, inhaling deeply as his eyes scanned the streets for an unoccupied taxi. He had a microscopic tinge of guilt as he thought about yesterday's meeting with his sister and her new partner in the park, yet that was it. He knew he had blatantly left out key information regarding what Bart Reed had actually given him. Yet the feeling passed quickly as a cab pulled to the curb and the day's agenda kicked into high gear. "Green Square," he chirped at the driver. "*State of Finance* building."

The driver kept his eyes to the rear view. "No smoking in here, sir."

"Come on," Dane said with a smile. "An extra twenty in your pocket if you let me." The cabbie thought about it for a split second before granting his approval. "There you go," Dane said, closing the rear door and cranking down the window.

"Might as well pass one to me then," the driver conceded, sliding the partition to the side and reaching back.

Dane shook his head and smiled, holding the pack up to the man. "You drive a hard bargain," he said. "Have at it, boss." The cab pulled away from the curb and into traffic, making its way slowly through the city streets and towards the *State of Finance* building and Bart Reed's editor, Mr. Seamus O'Dowd.

* * * * *

"Mr. Hartley, your reputation precedes you," Seamus O'Dowd said as he reached out his hand, grasping Dane's firmly as the journalist turned and smiled.

"Please, Mr. O'Dowd, call me Dane."

"Call me Seamus," the editor responded. Ann Carroll sat still in her seat with a grin across her face as she watched the pleasantries before her. "To what do we owe the honor?"

"I've got a story that might be right up your alley," Dane responded, stepping back from Ann's desk.

"Is that right?" Seamus asked, intrigued. "You've never written for us before, is that correct?"

"It is. Never followed the financial world all that much, to be honest."

"What makes you think you've got something we'd be interested in then?" Seamus smiled at him, enjoying the prodding of a prospective freelancer.

"Because you already were, according to my source." Dane smiled back, just as intrigued at the cat and mouse game.

"Is that right? And who is your source?"

"Bart Reed." Dane watched as Seamus's smile disappeared, his hand reaching up to itch his brow as he looked to Ann Carroll.

"I'm afraid I have some bad news —"

"I already know. Bart was murdered," Dane said bluntly. He watched as both Seamus and Ann glanced at one another, each with a quizzical look. "The lead detective on Bart's case is none other than my sister."

"Your sister? Detective Jolene Hartley," Seamus said aloud, though to no one in particular. "What are the odds?"

"You've met her then?"

"She stopped in yesterday asking some questions about Bart." Seamus paused as he thought about the detective. He turned his attention back to Dane. "Have you spoken to your sister about the case? Do they have any leads into the matter?"

Dane waved his hands in the air. "We're not really on speaking terms," he said. "She doesn't much like me and I don't much like her."

Seamus nodded his head in understanding. "Well, hopefully they catch whoever did this to Reedy. Please," he continued, grasping Dane's shoulder and leading him towards the doors. "Come into my office. Let's talk about what Bart's given you. Ann, please call Mr. Walker into my office as well."

They disappeared onto the floor, leaving Ann Carroll to stare after them, the demise of Bart Reed once again fresh in her mind as she picked up the receiver and dialed Kyle Walker's line.

* * * * *

"So how was the date with James?" Detective Kimberly Banneau asked as she bent forward to slurp up a noodle from her plate of chow mein. Her eyes peered out from under blonde bangs, a smile creeping across her pleasing face as she eyed Jolene in the opposite bench. Banneau was, according to Hartley, an oddball, yet she was also a good detective. She and her partner, Doc Hester, worked the kidnappings within the city limits, a role she took incredibly serious, especially when it came to the life or death of a child. She was good at what she did, her eccentricities flying out the proverbial window when on the hunt.

Yet she was wild and carefree when off the clock, living the life of a young, wealthy socialite in the evenings, though the wealth portion had not yet come her way. She pulled Jolene out with her whenever she could to cruise the restaurants and upscale bars of the city, dancing at the clubs in the pulsating red and blue lights of the numerous dance floors as her friend laughed and enjoyed the shamelessness Banneau always seemed to display. All in all, Kimberly Banneau was a riot, and Jolene loved her for it.

"Are you going to answer the question, or just stare out the window?" Kim pressed.

Jolene glanced her way and shook her head. She was tired today, having had a terrible night's sleep after yesterday's encounter with her brother in the park. "Sorry, what was the question?"

"James," Kim stated. "How was the date with James?"

"It was good. Okay. It was okay," Jolene waffled.

"Which was it? Good or okay?"

Jolene sighed and shrugged. "I like him. It was just too built up, I think."

"What went wrong?"

"Nothing," she replied quickly. "Nothing went wrong. I just don't know what I'm thinking. He's a nice guy."

"He's obviously into you."

"Right. And I think I'm into him. Like I said, I like him. I do."

"So what's the problem then?"

"I don't know. I just don't know if I want to get into anything serious. I like the freedom and ..." Jolene let the sentence fade as a mischievous grin passed across Kim's face. "What?"

"Have you been bringing home randoms?"

"No!" Jolene said loudly, drawing attention from nearby tables. She put an embarrassed hand to her face before mouthing *sorry* to the restaurant's patrons. "No," she whispered again to a laughing Banneau.

"You sure?" Kim prodded. "You should be. If I had a body like that I'd be pulling a lot of tail back to my place."

"Shut up," Jolene replied.

"How's the new guy?"

"Nothing gets past you, does it?" Kim shook her head. "He's … good, actually. He's proven pretty useful already."

"That's good. What does he look like?"

"Really, Kim? That's what you want to know?"

"Why not? Let's get to the important stuff."

Jolene tried to withhold her smile as she rolled her eyes. "He's younger than Barailles."

"I didn't ask how old. I asked how tasty." Jolene raised her glass of soda to her lips and stared back at her friend. "Oh, fine!" Kim exclaimed, waving her hand in the air. "I'll see him soon enough, I'm sure. Never wanting to give me the juicy details."

"You want details?"

"Absolutely!"

"How about this: guess who I met with yesterday afternoon?" Kim shrugged. "Dane," Jolene said, watching her friend's jaw drop.

"Dane? Your brother, Dane? No shit! Why?"

"For the case I'm working," she said, placing her glass back on the tabletop.

"When's the last time you talked to him?"

"It's been awhile."

"How'd he get wrapped up in this?"

"Went to our vic's residence to get his appointment book and Dane's initials and nickname were written on the day of the murder."

"No way! You don't think he had anything to do with it, do you?"

Hartley shrugged. "I don't know. But it's the only lead I have right now."

"Does he have an alibi?"

"Said he was at the Fairborne Club. We took a ride out there yesterday but it was a different bartender. I sent Ratliff out there again this morning to check it out." She paused and stared through the large pane of glass to the city outside. "I really hope it checks, but I wouldn't be surprised."

"Why's that?" Banneau asked. "I don't see Dane as being the murderous type. He may be a jerk at times, but I doubt he'd be able to kill anyone."

"We'll see," Hartley responded, glancing to the wall clock. "Look, I've got to head back. Ratliff's probably back by now and —"

"Go on," Banneau interrupted. "I'll pick this up. I'm going to hang out for a little bit."

"You sure?"

"Absolutely," she said as Jolene rose. "Plus me buying your meal means I can say I took you on a date." Hartley smiled wide and rolled her eyes once more. "I know," Kim added. "You haven't switched teams just yet. I'm working on it though."

"Good luck," Jolene said as she passed her, placing a hand on her shoulder and heading towards the door. "See you later, Kim."

"Bye, babe," came the response from the table as Jolene walked through the doors and headed back to the precinct and her new partner.

ELEVEN

Ratliff was in the process of moving to his new spot within the pit when Hartley walked onto the floor, catching his eye as the light pouring through the frosted glass running the length of the stairwell wall silhouetted her frame. He nodded his greeting and passed hurriedly in front of her towards his desk, a brown file box containing paper, pens, a stapler and other random office supplies balancing precariously in his hand. "Whoops," he said as he spun back towards her to retrieve his jacket hanging from her chair. The sudden movement shifted the heavy-duty stapler within the container, causing a catastrophic failure with the balancing act, the box beginning its inevitable slide and subsequent tumble to the floor.

Hartley reached up quickly, steadying the container and allowing her partner the time to throw his jacket near his chair before turning and grasping the box in both hands. "Thanks," he said, walking the few feet to his place and setting the box on the desk surface. He sat back in his chair and glanced to Hartley.

"No worries," she responded, following her partner's lead and taking a seat in her assigned spot. "You got everything you need over there?" she asked.

"I think so," he responded. "Well, everything but a computer. Cap said I could use yours for the time being —" He held the word for a split second longer than normal as Hartley raised her eyebrows to him. "But I figure I'd ask you before going off and making myself comfortable again."

She smiled at him mischievously, scrunching up her eyebrows. "You're learning."

"I pick things up quickly."

"How'd it go at the Fairborne Club?" she asked, crossing her legs and tilting her body into the armrest, swiveling to and fro as she awaited his response.

"He's clear," he said, leaning forward to retrieve a pad of paper from the corner of his desk and flipping it open. "Dane's alibi checks out. Met the bartender on duty two nights ago. Marvin Roselle. He's the head honcho over at the Club and he remembers talking to your brother the night of Reed's murder. And, better yet, the Fairborne Club's got cameras."

"Really? The bartender from yesterday said nothing about cameras."

"Yeah, well, apparently he's relatively new and Marvin didn't quite trust him enough to divulge their security situation. Anyway, Dane's accounted for from 11:52 p.m. to just before 2:00 a.m." He tossed the pad of paper back to the desk and turned to face her. "Dane's not our guy." Hartley titled back in her chair, putting both feet on the ground and locking her fingers behind her head, her eyes lifting to the ceiling as a deep sigh released from her lips. "Thought you'd be a little more excited about that," Ratliff said.

"No, I am," Hartley responded. "It's a relief, believe me."

"Then what's with the look?"

"What look are you talking about?"

"Careful how you answer that one," Captain Nolan said as he exited his office towards the kitchen.

"You're funny, sir," Hartley yelled after him, receiving a wave from her superior as he opened the refrigerator door.

They remained silent for a minute while Hartley sat forward, bringing her elbows to her knees and glancing up to Ratliff. "Well, with Dane being cleared, that puts us back to square one." Her fingers rose to cradle her chin as she zoned out, her foot tapping methodically on the pit floor. From the corner of her eye she watched as Ratliff waited patiently, his gaze never leaving her as the seconds ticked by. Finally she looked up to him. "Sorry. You'll get used to it."

"Take your time," he responded, grinning back.

"What keeps crossing through my mind is something isn't sitting well," she continued, noticing Ratliff's brow rising at her cryptic statements. "Okay. O'Dowd and Walker stated clearly that Bart Reed wasn't working on anything substantial for them. Yet Melinda said the exact opposite. She said he was definitely working on something. Something big."

"Seems like there's some inconsistencies here," Ratliff added. "Leads me to think Reed possibly was taking on outside work."

Hartley shook her head. "But Mrs. Reed said that he was done with freelance work. As she put it, he liked having the stability of a steady paycheck."

"He still had that steady paycheck, though," he replied quickly. "He was still employed by *State of Finance* so he was still getting that money. Seems like a perfect time to be doing some freelance work: when it's not your financial foundation. Everything is just money in your pocket."

"But why not tell your wife?" Hartley questioned. "What's the benefit in keeping it from her? Reed was a successful journalist. An award-winning one. There'd be no reason to keep information like that from her."

"People keep things from each other every day," Ratliff said. "Besides, we don't know what the topic was. Maybe it was top secret." Hartley sat back and rolled her eyes at him. "Seriously. Could've been."

"Let's reign in our theories here a little bit."

Ratliff smiled and continued. "Maybe he was working on something for some rival magazine to make a little extra dough."

"But why? He's got a steady income. That much we know. We know that he didn't like doing freelance work. It just seems like a waste of time. The money from *State of Finance* is good. He's got a large house in a good neighborhood with a daughter who most likely will get some sort of academic scholarship to a university of her choosing." She paused. "It all seems like a pretty big risk. He gets caught, he could get canned. Lose all of it."

Ratliff thought for a moment before conceding. "Good point," he said. "So what's the bottom line? Where do we go from here?"

"Well, if we assume that Melinda is right and he hadn't taken on anything outside of the magazine, then we need to get some answers from our inconsistent source. We need to go back to *State of Finance*."

* * * * *

As they walked to the *State of Finance* building Ratliff fell in line beside Hartley. He had learned over the last day and a half that his partner was different than most officers he knew, having an extremely soft, humorous side mirrored by an intensity that was rarely seen coming from someone that had been looking upon death for so long. He could tell she loved her job, and by the stories he had heard through the grapevine, she was one of the best detectives within the precinct.

And on top of it all, she was not bad to look at. He watched her as they made their way to the building doors, noticing the confident, sultry swing to her hips, the magnetic glare from her passionate eyes and the fierceness of her slightly parted lips. Her legs were long and toned, the movement of them pulling Ratliff's gaze and refusing to release it. She was, far and away, the best looking police officer he had ever laid eyes on.

They passed through the entrance and made their way across the lobby floor, Hartley raising her star to the guard who nodded his greeting and waved them through. They rode the elevator up to the fifth floor and exited into the waiting area where Ann Carroll sat staring at her computer screen. Both Seamus O'Dowd and Kyle Walker leaned into her desk and were conversing in low voices, smiles crossing their faces as the detectives came from behind.

Hartley cleared her throat and the men turned slowly as Ann pointed their way. "Ah, Detective Hartley," Seamus said, standing straight and moving away from the desk. Walker remained still. "I hope all is well?"

"Mr. O'Dowd, this is my partner, Detective Ratliff," Hartley responded. The editor extended his hand, her partner taking it in his.

"Pleasure," Seamus said, turning to his assistant. "Detective, this is my Assistant Editor, Mr. Kyle Walker." Ratliff nodded his greetings to the man stationed at the desk, eyeing the woman behind that computer monitor as she glanced from the detectives to her bosses nervously.

"What can I do for you today, detectives?" Seamus questioned. "Any new information regarding Reedy's killer?"

Hartley shook her head. "Unfortunately, no," she replied. "We're looking into a few leads at the moment, but nothing really solid." Seamus nodded. "I was wondering if we'd be able to take a look at Mr. Reed's station?" she continued. Kyle Walker pushed away from the counter and moved towards the group, an action not overlooked by the detectives. Hartley turned her attention to him. "Mr. Walker, before you ask: no, we don't have a warrant. But I'd be happy to get one. Just let me know."

Kyle smiled at the stern detective as he raised his eyebrows and hands high in defense. "No, please," he started. "That'll be fine. I actually wanted to apologize for my behavior the other day. Reed's murder just took me as a shock. Of course, you can have free reign over whatever may help you in the investigation."

Hartley remained silently staring at Kyle, her senses tingling, a red flag being thrown for reasons yet unknown. "Thank you," she responded as he and Seamus began towards the doors. Hartley shot Ratliff a look before the pair turned and followed.

The men led the detectives across the floor, past the bustling of young reporters scrounging for the day's juicier tidbits in a mass of overwhelmingly meager journalistic morsels. Reed's desk was the exact opposite of what Hartley was expecting. He was secluded against the far wall, his two connecting cube-mates non-existent, a third, at an angle, the sole inhabitant of the creative island. The clutter, which one assigns to a busy journalist, was missing, replaced instead by neatly piled stacks of paper and Post-its lining the outer edges of the desk.

Hartley pulled the office chair out from under the desk and sat, taking in everything before her as Ratliff moved into the cube. Seamus and Kyle spoke briefly in the aisle before the latter turned and vanished in the floor's chaos. O'Dowd moved into the vicinity with the detectives. "I apologize, but Kyle needs to fill in on a meeting for me. He'll be back on the floor in about a half hour, if you're still around."

Hartley answered without looking up to him. "No need to miss your meeting on our account. We just want to take a look and see if we can find anything that'll move us along in the investigation."

"It's no problem," Seamus said, leaning into the cubicle wall and crossing his arms. "Honestly, that meeting is the worst of the week. I'm glad to not go."

Hartley pulled on a pair of latex gloves, shifting papers and Post-its while Ratliff knelt down and opened the file cabinet. They continued like this for several long minutes, each calmly sifting through the material before them. Hartley stopped several times as she turned this page or flipped that Post-it, yet nothing caught her eye. She could feel Seamus O'Dowd behind her, could hear the wheezing of air passing through his nostrils as he silently sat vigil over the detectives.

She paused and looked to Ratliff next to her. "Anything?" she said quietly. He shook his head. "I just don't get how he has nothing here." She turned in the chair, backing it to the opposite side of the cubicle to face Seamus and give her partner more room. "How is it that Mr. Reed had nothing of significance here?"

Seamus lifted his eyes from his wristwatch. "Come again?"

"Mr. Reed," Hartley stated. "He's one of your best writers, yet he has nothing at this desk." She remained silent as he looked to her, obviously waiting for the oncoming question. "It would just make more sense if he had something here. A phone book. A list of sources that weren't confidential. Lists of potential stories." She shook her head and turned back to the drawers to her right, leaving Seamus at her back.

"You seem to know a lot about what a journalist needs," he replied.

"Yeah, well, I'm a detective," Hartley said quietly as she pulled a red notepad full of drawings from the upper drawer. "It's my job. Besides, my brother's a journalist."

"Is that so?" Seamus asked with surprise.

Hartley nodded, her eyes remaining on the pages before her. "Yep," she said. "Dane Hartley. Ever heard of him?"

Seamus thought for a moment before shaking his head. "Can't say that I have," he replied. "What sort of journalist is he?"

Hartley let the question go unanswered for a moment as she set the notepad on the desk and fished for a new target. "These days, I'm not sure."

"Is he any good?" Seamus asked, receiving a shrug from the detective.

"Yeah, he was. I haven't read anything of his in a while. But he was very good."

"Well, maybe I'll look him up in the future. We're always in need of good writers around here."

The conversation died down as the detectives moved through the cubicle. After nearly twenty minutes Hartley looked to Ratliff who stood, lifting his calf high to bring relief to his aching knee. "You okay?" she asked.

"Yeah," he responded. "Just kneeling too long over that drawer."

Hartley turned to Seamus. "Is this the computer Mr. Reed used?" He nodded. "You mind if I have one of tech guys come down here later today or tomorrow and check it out? We may want to bring it in to see if we can find anything that's useful."

"Absolutely," Seamus responded. "Anything you need."

"Great. Thank you again." Seamus walked them out, opening the door to the waiting room and pressing the elevator button. They remained silent as they waited, Ratliff glancing to the receptionist who stared back at him with anxiety-laden eyes. He smiled and turned as the lift doors opened.

"Please, feel free to send over your guy whenever you can," Seamus said. "Just give Mr. Walker or myself a call so we can let the guard downstairs know you are on your way."

"Thank you," Hartley said. "We'll be in touch." The elevator doors closed on *State of Finance* and the detectives rode down to the ground floor in silence, exiting the lift and building into the late afternoon air.

"So what do you think?" Ratliff asked.

"I think that entire desk was set up," Hartley responded.

Ratliff laughed. "Me too. There's no way a reporter is that tidy."

"Exactly. We'll get our tech team to take the computer. Hopefully something catches their eye, but I doubt there's anything there either."

The detectives entered the vehicle and began the drive back to the precinct, each relieved in their own way about what had transpired at the magazine. Although there was no smoking gun, both Hartley and Ratliff were aware that Bart Reed's employer was not telling them everything. Whether that was because of their current investigation or confidentiality for Reed's stories and sources, Mr. Seamus O'Dowd knew something more. He —

"What do you say about grabbing some dinner?" Jacoby asked, pulling Jolene from her thoughts. She glanced sideways to him, her hands tightening on the wheel as her heart fluttered at the impromptu invitation.

"I'm sorry?" she asked, a ploy that garnered a laugh from her partner.

"Dinner? You and me?" The car remained quiet as Jacoby focused on her, a grin crossing his face, his green eyes resting on her. Jolene's mouth opened and closed several times, her head flicked to the driver's side window and back as she tried to muster one simple word: no.

Yet she could not at that particular moment. She had plans with James, another dinner date that hopefully would go much better than the last, yet, for the life of her, Jolene could not say no. Instead, as the silence mounted and the seconds slipped by, she continued to think, continued to ponder the notion of her and Jacoby eating over a candlelight dinner, wine glasses raised as they eyed each other —

"You've got plans, don't you?" he interrupted. He smiled and turned his gaze to his window. "Maybe another time." Jolene nodded and continued down the road, wondering if she was destined to constantly confuse herself when it came to life away from her silver star.

TWELVE

It began to rain as Jolene exited her apartment and moved along the sidewalk towards the corner stoplight, her eyes searching through the droplets for a vacant taxi to take her to the restaurant. She and James had spoken briefly and both had agreed on a boisterous atmosphere filled with bright lights and juicy burgers, something that had started this date off on the right foot. Although Jolene Hartley's figure could have graced *Sports Illustrated Swimsuit Edition*, the detective had a sweet spot for greasy, fatty cheeseburgers. They were her guilty pleasure.

She caught a cab a block and a half down, giving directions to the driver on the easiest route to her destination, one that would bypass the construction and traffic of the early evening commute, thus relieving her of a hefty fare. The driver nodded, though his eyes revealed disapproval of the route, no doubt a reaction to the minimal tip he thought he would receive.

As the cab inched along towards the backstreets, Jolene watched the rainfall descend through the rear window, the illuminated droplets twinkling as they passed near streetlamps, the puddles shimmering adjacent to curbs like tiny lakes caught in a never-ending expanse of pavement. Water beading on the glass briefly distorted the external image before gaining weight and cutting diagonally across the surface only to be replaced by another moments later.

She rested her elbow on the door and her chin in her hand, her bright eyes sparkling as the vehicle turned onto an empty street and away from the evening commute. The driver glanced to the back seat and nodded his approval. Hartley caught the glance in her periphery and smiled, though remained focused on the outside world, her thoughts jumping from face to face as James and Ratliff fought for her attention. *What am I doing?* she thought to herself. *Focus.*

She cast her attention to James, his charismatic youthfulness, the charm and demeanor that pulled Jolene's humorous side to the forefront whenever he was around and relieved her of the stress that seemed to blanket her when working a tough investigation. Their first date, the beginning of which had been miserably uncomfortable, had been turned around by James's attitude, leaving Jolene feeling sure that she wanted another rendezvous.

Yet she could not help but feel awful as James's face turned into Jacoby Ratliff's, her new, smoldering partner on the job, his tanned complexion and short-trimmed dark hair accentuating the glowing green eyes that gazed into her soul. She shook her head, wondering what her fascination was with this man. Was it just because he was her partner? Was she replacing one lustful, unsteady work relationship with another?

No, she answered herself. *I am not.* Barailles had been a married man. Her relationship with him was inappropriate at times, especially that fateful evening at his apartment when tongues caressed and hands massaged and —

She shook that thought from her head. She had ended up doing the right thing that evening, stopping the progression then and there before anything detrimental occurred. Jolene laughed at herself, pulling the driver's eyes to the rear view mirror for a moment. Her current situation was absurd. Was she actually trying to compare her years with Anthony Barailles to her day and a half with Jacoby Ratliff? There had definitely been built-up sexual tension between her and her former partner. However, at the moment, all there was between her and Jacoby was a dinner invitation, which, for all she knew, could have been solely to get to know each other professionally. A dinner invitation and her obvious extreme attraction to him.

The cab made several quick turns, shaking her brain waves loose from their internal struggle and forcing her eyes to the road ahead. "This is fine," she said to the cabby as he yanked the car to the curb. Jolene paid her fare and handed the man a nice tip, receiving a smile from him as he watched her exit and begin her trek to the corner restaurant several dozen yards ahead.

Jolene not only pulled the cabby's eye along with her, but several other by-standers as well, including a few of the same sex, mainly those who watched in horror as their significant others turned their heads as the beauty passed. The women began to protest until the detective came into view, realizing that, indeed, it had been worth a longer look. "That make your night?" Hartley heard one young woman ask her boyfriend. She did not wait around to hear the response, instead moving briskly towards the figure stationed outside the restaurant, the man who turned and smiled widely at her as she approached.

"Hey, Jo," James said, smiling down to her as he wrapped his arms around the detective, pulling her close and kissing her on the cheek as she embraced his slim frame.

"Hey," she responded. "Been here long?"

"Nope. Long enough to get us a table. Had a drink. Played some —"

"Yeah, yeah," she interrupted, tilting her head and glaring up at him, a smirk crossing her lips.

"Well, I did get us a table already though. Come on, let's get out of the rain." She smiled wide as he reached out and grasped her hand, leading her into the establishment as would an actual boyfriend. *Easy*, she thought. *Live in the moment.* They moved to a booth near the window, sidestepping waiters and busboys, as well as patrons. The restaurant was precisely the hectic mess they both had envisioned, full of boisterous hoots and hollers, constant movement and the never-ending aroma of over-used fryer grease.

Jolene wiped the rain from her brow and looked across the table to James. He smiled at her, his eyebrows rising as words formed behind his lips. Finally he let loose. "I have to get something off my chest," he said.

"Oh yeah? What's that?" Jolene asked.

"I made sure to be outside so I could walk you in here." Jolene stared to him with a half-grin, waiting for James to continue. He realized quickly that the statement did nothing but churn the residual tension that had filled their previous evening together. "What I mean is that I wanted this to start out better than last time, so what better way than to wait for you and lead you in by the hand and … " He closed his eyes and gently shook his head as his voice trailed off, the point he was trying to make lost amidst the aromas of the establishment.

Hartley stifled a chuckle before relieving him of his embarrassment. "I think I get it."

"I just figured last time was so awkward that I had to start differently right out of the gate."

"And you don't think this is starting awkward?" she chided.

He stared at her in mock disappointment, his mouth dropping open. "Ouch!" he responded.

"I'm kidding," she said, reaching across the table and grabbing his hand. "Much better."

"See, the handholding is all the rage right now," he laughed. Jolene rolled her eyes and laughed with him, letting go of his hand and removing her jacket just as the waiter approached.

"Hey, guys," the waiter said as he leaned into the table. "What can I get you to drink?"

James eyed Jolene who responded without hesitation. "A beer."

"Wow," James replied with a chuckle.

"Just feels like a beer night," she answered.

The waiter laughed. "What kind?"

"I don't care. Whatever you start pouring."

"All right," he said with a nod. "And you?"

"I'll do the same."

"Great," the waiter said, stepping back into the aisle. "I'll grab those and come back for your order. Menus are by the salt and pepper." He vanished into the constant motion of the floor, leaving the couple to themselves.

"So, how was work today?" he asked with an ear-to-ear smile.

"Shut up," she responded. "Just because you don't have to work doesn't mean you get to rub it in my face."

"I absolutely think that it does," he replied.

"Get out of here!"

"Hey, if you didn't have to work, I bet you'd still be a homicide detective, wouldn't you?"

She thought about it for a second before nodding her head. "Probably, yeah. So you think you know me in and out now?"

"Well," he said with a tilt of his head and wide eyes, "That's the goal, if you know what I'm saying —"

"Again, shut up."

They laughed as the waiter reappeared and placed two large pilsner glasses on their table. He hurriedly flipped open a pad of paper and took a seat next to Jolene. Hartley held her ground, unwilling to let their boisterous waiter or James's uncontrollable smirk best her resolve. "You guys have a chance to take a look at what you want?" he asked. They ordered their food in turn, each choosing a side of French fries to go along with their grease-filled, grilled onion-topped cheeseburgers. "Awesome," the waiter replied, standing and once again fading into the dizzying commotion.

"Seriously though," James said. "How's work?"

Jolene shrugged as she took a long sip from her beer. "Exciting as ever," she replied, noticing that James was content with listening to more. She smiled. "Paperwork and dead bodies. How about you? What's going on with your life?"

"With my life? Wow. Deep."

She laughed loudly. "Sorry."

"No, it's okay. Let's see." He paused and glanced to the table and back. "Friend in Jamaica wants me to come back for a few months to help him with his business." Hartley's eyes grew wider and her smile faded slightly. "I declined," James said hurriedly.

"Oh, yeah? Why's that? I'd rather be in Jamaica then Chicago when winter comes."

"True, but there's more to this city then the weather that keeps my interest." Jolene locked eyes with James as she lifted the beer to her lips. They held each other's gaze for several moments, both running scenarios in their minds of what to say next, James fighting the urge to invite her along while Hartley tried to gauge where to divert the conversation. "You said you're doing paperwork?" James finally asked, slicing through the tension. "Is it from our case?"

"*Our case*?" Jolene asked with a smile. "Since when did you become a detective?"

"You know what I mean."

"No, it wasn't from *our case*," she said in a mocking tone. "A much simpler and less stressful one. Just submitted it. Been working on a new case lately, though."

"About what? And don't say a dead body. That I already got."

She laughed. "Not quite sure yet. Guy was murdered on the north side. Worked for a financial magazine. Pretty well off." She shrugged. "That's about where we're at right now."

"We?"

"Captain Nolan assigned me a new partner."

"How's that working out for you? Is it true that most detectives like working alone?"

"Depends on the partner, I guess," she answered. "Barailles was good for a time. After *our case* —" she threw up two fingers on each hand to form air quotes, smiling the whole while "— it was nice to have no one to worry about. But he's a nice guy. Seems to be a good cop. We'll see how it goes."

"What's his name?"

"Jacoby. Jacoby Ratliff. Came from Narcotics." James nodded his head in understanding, listening intently as Jolene discussed how she ran her new partner through the mill before easing off and allowing him to be a detective.

"All right guys," came the waiter's voice from next to them. "Let me set these down here." He slid the plates in front of the two, each covered in a mound of fries and a cheeseburger as round as Frisbees. "You guys good on drinks? Okay. My name's Jason. If you need anything, just shout."

Jason left the two to their meals, each breaking conversation as they dove into the dripping, unhealthy plate before them, their taste buds erupting in delight at the flavors oozing from the greasy meat and salty fries. They smiled at one another, making a comment here or there that led to laughter, but mainly they remained silent, enjoying the food and company.

James glanced to his left as a bus boy collided with a waitress, a three-fourths eaten cheeseburger smothered in ketchup launching off a plate and splattering on the woman's white shirt. The crowd around the accident erupted in laughter as the waitress pealed the sandwich from her shirt and slammed it atop the busboy's head, the latter continuing to move through the throng of excitement towards the kitchen with his new hat.

James's attention was pulled to the diner bar and a man seated there, his intense eyes looking over a zigzagged nose to Jolene with a concentration that caused Graiser to do a double take. James grabbed a couple fries and brought them to his mouth, glancing to the table and back just in time to connect with the mysterious individual's gaze. The man held the link for a moment before turning to finish his drink in one large gulp. He rose and reached into his pocket, pulling out a wad of bills that he threw on the counter.

James turned back to Jolene, who was at the moment taking a large bite from her burger, mayonnaise and mustard oozing from the corners of her mouth. She laughed, despite the mouthful of food, bringing a huge smile to James's face as he turned once more to watch the man exit the restaurant and begin down the sidewalk with one last glance through the glass at the couple before he disappeared from view.

Jolene followed his gaze to the window. "What's going on?" she asked.

James pointed to the door quickly before shaking his head. "Just some guy eyeballing my date."

"Oh, yeah? Was he cute?" Hartley joked, lifting up in her seat and glancing around hurriedly.

"Ha. Ha," James replied. "Guess if we keep going on dates I'm going to have to get used to guys staring at you, huh?"

"I wouldn't worry about them," she replied. "I'd just worry about how you're doing."

"Is that right?"

"It is, Mr. Graiser."

"And how am I doing right now?"

She shrugged, raising her glass and downing the rest of her beer. She looked through the suds to him. "I'd say you're losing points for letting my drink go empty."

"Jason!" James yelled out, raising his hand in the air and turning as Hartley erupted in laughter.

THIRTEEN

Dane Hartley glanced to his watch as he strolled up to his apartment from the back alley. The light breeze that had accompanied the sporadic rainfall lifted the aromas circulating near the dumpsters and carried them into Dane's path, causing him to gag as he raced into the building. It was nearing nine-thirty in the evening and Dane was tired. After leaving the *State of Finance* offices, he had spent the majority of his day following up with sources on a number of projects he had in the works, each one nearing completion, yet now placed on the backburner due to the Reed job.

Bart Reed's story seemed important, that much was for sure. However, with the murder of his journalistic confidant, Dane realized there might be more to the story than Bart had given him. It was definitely worth a closer look.

That closer look, however, would have to wait until morning. All he wanted now was a cold beer and his seat in front of the television where, most likely, he would spend the remainder of the evening before moving to the couch to catch some shuteye.

Dane made his way to the elevator and up to the third and final floor, taking a right and walking the length of the hallway until he reached his unit located last on the left, overlooking the intersection below. As he inserted his key he heard a door open behind him and turned just in time to see a tall blonde step into the threshold, her left hand placed strategically on her hip as she leaned into the door frame, her naked body reflecting the fluorescent hallway lights.

Dane removed his hand from the doorknob and glanced at the woman before him. "Late night, Kel?" he asked, his eyes roaming over her skin.

"Depends on if you're going in there or in here," she responded.

"Guess that depends on what *in here* means," he retorted.

"Use your imagination." She smiled as he ran his hand across his chin.

"I really should just head inside. I've had a busy day and I'm exhausted." He reached to his doorknob and began to turn it.

"How about a nice massage? Maybe some wine?" Dane froze as the word *massage* crossed her luscious lips. He released the knob and it clicked back into position. Kelly Depler, although mildly attractive and extremely promiscuous, was, in Dane's mind, the best masseuse in the city. She was the healing hands behind some of the area's leading celebrities — as well as the local political ring — and came with a don't-ask-don't-tell mantra regarding after-massage horseplay.

"I *am* a little tense," Dane responded, retrieving the key from the doorknob and moving towards the vixen.

"I can tell," she replied, stepping back as Dane squeezed into her apartment. "Why don't we get that worked out for you?" She reached out and clamped on to Dane just below the belt, pushing the door shut with her free hand as the journalist removed his shoulder bag and jacket, realizing his much needed night of relaxation would have to wait until the following evening.

* * * * *

Dane felt awkward — and intrigued — as he lay spread eagle across Kelly's bed, his hands and feet tied to each of the four bedposts, his privates basking in the candlelight the masseuse had set around the room. Kelly had lived across the hall for five years, the last three of which included a steady boyfriend, although that did not mean their nights of passion had halted. If anything, they had increased. Her boyfriend worked on the medical staff for the Chicago Bears, a job that sent him from players' homes to the stadium to weekends away at a hosting venue on a consistent basis. Dane and her relationship was one-dimensional, having no room for — or want of, for that matter — anything more serious. Sex was all they needed. Sometimes it was straightforward, passionate lovemaking. Other times, it included Dane tied to the bed, or vice versa. This was the usual. Sometimes Dane would make it to his couch and crack open a beer, only to have it snatched away by a scantily clad Kelly Depler in exchange for a quickie.

Dane did not mind.

He opened his eyes and sighed, the candle flames flickering against the walls and ceiling, dancing seductively behind Kelly whose face rose from near his waist. "I've had enough of this," she said, crawling cat-like towards the headboard, her hips popping to the left and right. "I think it's my turn." She reached down once more and grabbed between his legs, smiling coyly as he lifted his head in response. "You have protection on you?" she asked.

"Check my wallet," he responded, setting his head back on the pillow as she leaned to the floor and retrieved his pants, diving into the back pocket in search of a condom. She turned to him with a shake of her head. "Uh ... All right. I've got some in the first drawer on the right in my kitchen. I ..." He stalled as he looked to his hands and feet and the knots around them. "Well, you're going to have to go get them. Door's unlocked."

"Don't go anywhere," she said, sliding off the bed and walking from the room with a seductive grin. Dane stared after her as she turned the corner and disappeared from view, wondering if she grabbed a coat before heading into the hallway or if the quick jaunt across the corridor with the possibility of being seen would add to the kinkiness of the night.

He would never know, nor would he ever see Kelly Depler alive again. The explosion as she walked into his apartment tore through the building, pulverizing Kelly and the furniture that Dane had collected over the years, killing her instantly as the blast ripped apart her body. Bricks and mortar and drywall flew into the intersection below in a fiery heap, landing on vehicles parked for the evening, drawing those few out for a late night jog to the scene in a panic.

The concussion that rocked the building was enough to destroy Kelly's living room and carry with it her La-Z-Boy recliner, hurtling it through the bedroom wall and into the bed frame where Dane lay. The collision smashed the headboard to pieces, the wooden frame collapsing under Dane's weight and falling atop his head, knocking him into unconsciousness, the building's fire alarm fading into the dizzying atmosphere that surrounded him.

* * * * *

The second call came to Jolene's phone just seconds after declining the first. She pulled the buzzing device from her jacket pocket as she walked arm-in-arm with James down the street, a leisurely stroll after consuming what must have been a pound of grease. She looked to the screen for several moments, running the number through her mind. She obviously did not know the individual so desperate to get in touch with her, else a name would have displayed.

"Really, you can answer that if you need to," James said, staring into the night sky as a slight drizzle began once more.

Jolene shook her head and placed the phone back in her pocket. "Don't recognize the number. If they really want me, they'll leave a …" She let the sentence drift into the night as two marked squad cars with flashing lights flew down the pavement, sirens blaring as they sped through the nearest intersection. Her phone began to buzz again just as another patrol unit zipped by, stopping the two in their tracks.

James glanced to Hartley as she retrieved her phone, his eyes shooting up as an ambulance followed the parade. "What the hell is going on?" He looked back to her. "Same number?"

She nodded, a confused look crossing her face as she put the phone to her ear. "Hello? Who is this?"

"Jo!" shouted Ratliff from the other end.

"Ratliff?" she asked. "What's going on? Why are you calling me this late?"

"Jo, listen to me," he said. "There's been an explosion at Dane's apartment. Where are you at?"

"Say that again?"

"An explosion at Dane's apartment." He enunciated every word. "Units are on their way over —"

"Is he okay?" she cut in.

"I'm not sure about the details —"

"Is Dane alive?" she pressed.

"I don't know," Ratliff repeated forcefully, yet with an air of comfort. "Where are you at? I'll come get you."

"No, don't," Hartley rushed. "I'm heading over to his apartment now."

"I'll meet you there."

She hung up the phone and raced to the street, James following behind her at a frantic pace. "Jo, what's going on?" he asked.

"There's been an explosion at my brother's apartment," she answered, making her way into the middle of the narrow street as another patrol unit approached, horn blaring for the woman to make way.

"Oh, my God!" James replied. "Is he all right?"

"I don't know," she said, holding her hand up to the cruiser.

"Get the fuck out of the way!" the officer yelled from the driver's side window as he came to a stop.

Hartley approached the front of the vehicle, squinting her eyes as the lights flashed before her. "I'm Detective Jolene Hartley with Area One Homicide," she yelled to the officer. "Are you heading to the apartment explosion?"

The officer opened his door and took a step out. "Yeah, we're heading that way."

"Give me a lift?" she asked, moving towards the officer before he answered.

"Hop in," he said, regaining his seat.

"James," Hartley began, "I'm sorry but —"

"I'm coming with," he interrupted from the rear passenger door. She looked up to him from the opposite side of the vehicle, ready to repudiate the offer until she saw the steadfast determination in his eyes. She nodded quickly and the two entered the back seat, the uniformed officer stepping on the gas and rocketing them towards the apartment building.

FOURTEEN

The scene spread out before them was chaotic at best as Hartley, James and the patrol officers exited the cruiser a block from what used to be Dane's apartment and sprinted down the pavement. Isolated fires, spread throughout the surrounding streets, burned in the night; a large chunk of what appeared to be an ottoman flickered orange with flames from atop a totaled Volkswagen Beetle. The upper corner of the apartment building overlooking the intersection was completely destroyed, Dane's unit non-existent save for the kitchen where the refrigerator leaned precariously against a smoldering countertop. The flashing lights of police cars gave the area a club-like feel, the officers working the crowds like uniformed bouncers corralling the masses as a second fire truck approached to assist with the scene.

"Jo!" someone yelled from the madness. Hartley dropped her wide eyes from the catastrophe of the building to the pandemonium below, searching for the source. "Jo!" came the call again as Ratliff burst through a crowd of firefighters, waving his hand to grab her attention.

"Did you find out what happened?" Hartley questioned, her eyes nervously scanning the area as she tried to compose herself into a business-like mold.

Ratliff shook his head. "They aren't sure yet. I asked the lieutenant when I got here but he didn't know anything. Team's up there now searching." They looked to the ground floor where a group of plain-clothes fire marshals gathered, radios in hands as they conversed with the team inside.

"What about Dane?" she asked.

"He's alive. There were remains found though. Female. According to the brief statement I got from the initial report, it looks like someone was in the apartment when it exploded."

"Do they know who it is?"

Ratliff shook his head. "They were too busy to question your brother about it, but they're guessing a girlfriend or something." Hartley looked to him quizzically, knowing, unless something had seriously changed, her brother was not one to keep a steady relationship. Ratliff continued, catching the look. "The victim was completely naked. And according to a lieutenant, so was your brother."

"Where's Dane now?" Hartley pressed.

"They took him to an ambulance in the alley behind the building." Hartley moved quickly, oblivious as to whether or not her partner or James followed.

"You been back there yet?"

"Nope. Figured I'd wait for you before sticking my nose where it doesn't belong."

They rounded the corner and passed through a group of bystanders. Hartley strode onto the street and pulled the caution tape over her head as she passed the uniformed officer holding the position. "Excuse me!" he yelled towards her. "Hey!"

"She's with me," Ratliff said, flashing the officer his badge as he followed his partner. He glanced over his shoulder to the man that had arrived with Hartley. "And him too."

The three of them made their way into the alley and rounded the ambulance, their eyes falling upon a battered and bruised Dane Hartley. "Dane," his sister said as she stopped at the bumper, unsure what to follow it up with.

He turned slowly and locked his eyes on her before forcing a grin and glancing back to the floor. "What are you doing here, Jo?"

Hartley set her jaw. "Are you okay?"

He nodded, though his eyes remained focused between his feet. "Kelly was … She was going into my place …" He grated his teeth and swung his head to the ceiling lights, fighting the emotions.

"Is Kelly the woman they found?" Ratliff asked.

Dane sighed and looked coldly to the detective. "Kelly was my neighbor. She's the one they found on the sidewalk. She's the one that died looking for a fucking condom!"

"Okay, Dane," Hartley said, holding a hand up.

"No, Jo, it's not okay!" he exclaimed. "Why are you even here? And who the fuck is that?" He pointed to James. "No, you know what, it doesn't matter. I don't give a —"

"Leave him out of this," Hartley replied sternly. "Regardless of if you give a shit about me or I give a shit about you, you're still family."

Dane's eyes moved from James to Ratliff, resting finally on his sister who had taken a step towards the ambulance. "Family," he repeated, shaking his head.

"Whatever that word means to you, I don't care," Hartley continued, the ever-increasing intensity emanating from her eyes. "I just came to see if you were still alive."

"You could have done that with a phone call," he replied.

"Fuck you, Dane," she retorted.

"Fuck me? Unbelievable! You're always just the little fucking baby —"

"Enough!" shouted Ratliff, stepping next to his partner, his voice rising above the siblings and quieting the commotion. "This isn't the time or place for this. Jo, take a step back," he said, arm going wide to show her the way. She glared at him for a moment before conceding and backing away.

"Yeah, do as you're told, like always —" Dane started, only to be silenced by a left hook to the jaw that sent him crashing to the ambulance floor.

Hartley jumped as Ratliff leaned into the vehicle and grabbed onto the blanket covering her brother, pulling his face close to the journalist and his now split lip. "You're going to shut the hell up or else we're going to have another problem, you understand me?"

"What the fuck are —" Dane yelled, struggling to release himself from the detective's iron-like grasp.

"Shut up!" Ratliff yelled, raising his hand once more. Hartley smirked to herself as Dane covered his face. She had been used to her brother taking control of situations from the earliest age, pummeling much older combatants with fists driven by pure will and determination. Now, as he lay motionless on the ambulance floor, the younger officer towering over him, she could not help but laugh at the turn of events. "Are you done?" Ratliff asked.

"All right!" Dane submitted. "Get your goddamn hands off of me!"

Ratliff released the fabric from his hands and stepped back, allowing the journalist room to regain his seat on the gurney. "Listen, man," Ratliff began calmly, "I don't know what the deal is between you and her, and to tell you the truth, I don't really care. But she's my partner and if you ever raise your voice again to her like that, we'll have serious issues, understand?" He waited for a response yet only gained a venomous glare. "And we're here because you're part of an ongoing murder investigation and your apartment just erupted in flames. I'm sorry about your friend. We all are," he said, pointing to Hartley and James, his eyes resting on Graiser for a moment. "Well, I don't know this guy, but I'm sure he is too." He turned back to Dane. "Maybe just be a little grateful that you have people who care about your well-being, even if you are a prick."

A paramedic carrying what appeared to be a charred canvas shoulder bag rounded the corner just then, eyeing the three cautiously as he walked to the opened ambulance doors. "What's going on here?" he asked as his eyes fell upon the blood dripping from Dane's lip.

Dane remained silent as Ratliff stared at him, pondering what use it would be to tell the truth. "I slipped," he answered, grabbing a piece of gauze from the shelf next to him.

"Who are you guys?" the paramedic asked, looking to Ratliff.

The detective flashed his badge. "I'm Detective Jacoby Ratliff and this is my partner, Detective Jolene Hartley."

"Detective Hartley, huh?" the paramedic replied. He pointed to Dane. "Any relation?"

"My brother," Hartley answered.

The man nodded. "Well, Mr. Hartley's lucky. We've got some minor scrapes and bruises to go along with a mild concussion, but that's about it." He turned his attention back to Dane, lifting the burnt bag to him. "This is the only bag the firefighters found. It was across the street. It doesn't look like much survived, but here you go."

Dane reached out and pulled the bag to him. "Thanks," he said, though soft and dispassionately as the paramedic rounded the ambulance once more and walked from view. He flipped open the sole surviving latch and pulled out a melted, dilapidated laptop. The papers inside the satchel were completely black, charred unrecognizable by the fire, yet not wholly consumed. "Shit!" Dane said, throwing the computer to the side. "Shit, shit, shit!"

"What'd you have in the bag?" Hartley asked from behind Ratliff.

Dane looked up to her and rubbed his hand across his face. "Stories. All sorts of stories."

"And the papers?"

"Am I being interrogated?" he asked.

"No," Hartley replied.

They remained silent as Dane sifted carefully through the pile, his eyes glancing from page to page of black paper that stained his fingers. He glanced up just in time to see the fire marshal approach Ratliff carrying a box full of burnt fragments and wires.

"Detective," the marshal said as he approached. "This was no accident. That explosion was set off by a motion detector within the apartment." He lifted the box to Ratliff as the detective reached in, tossing shrapnel to the side as he searched. "There were two ignition points that we've found so far, one near the entryway and another about a dozen feet beyond. The explosions were set to go off once you were positioned between them." The marshal turned to Dane. "I'm sorry, son."

Dane nodded as he stared to the ground with a puzzled look. "Thank you," Ratliff replied as the marshal left the group the way he had come.

"This fucking story," Dane said aloud to no one in particular.

"What story?" James said, stepping into view.

Dane remained focused on the vehicle floor. "Dane?" Hartley asked. "What story?"

Her brother shook his head, a smirk appearing for a brief second before vanishing into the smoky night air. "The Reed story," he said, creating a silence throughout the alley.

"What do you mean the Reed story?" Hartley asked with a toxic tone.

He chuckled. "Look, I know more about the Reed story than I told you —"

"I can't believe —" she began only to be cut off by Dane's raising voice.

"I needed to check things out before giving up on it!"

Hartley stepped forward. "You lied right to my face when I asked you about Reed. You said you had nothing!"

He shrugged his shoulders. "I'm a journalist, Jo."

"It's obstruction of justice, Dane," she rebutted.

"It's freedom of the press!"

"Don't give me that shit!"

"What do you want me to do?"

"Maybe answer my questions when I ask them!"

"I do that and there's no story!"

"Guys!" shouted Ratliff, stepping in between the duo once more and placing a hand on his partner's shoulder. He looked to James and cocked his head towards Jolene. Graiser caught the detective's drift and moved forward to gently take hold of her. Ratliff held his hands to both of them who steamed in their respective positions, each wanting nothing more than to tear at the other's throat. He turned to the journalist. "We need to know what Reed gave you."

"Why?"

"How about because if you don't, I'll take you in right now for withholding information on a homicide investigation."

Ratliff let the comment sink in for several long moments before shaking his head and reaching for his handcuffs, grabbing on to Dane's wrist before the journalist said, "Okay! Okay. The day Reed called me he said he wanted to meet. He sounded rushed. I hadn't talked to him in a while, so I agreed."

"Did you meet him at the Fairborne Club?" Ratliff questioned.

Dane shook his head. "No, like I said, he never showed. But he did tell me part of the story he was working on. Guess he wanted to wet my beak a little. Get me interested."

"What was it about?" Hartley asked from behind Ratliff.

"He said he had gotten a package at home with documents showing some sort of embezzlement scheme happening within Intervise Securities."

"What's that?"

"Intervise Securities? It's a sort of investment firm. Has some old clients, from what I understand."

"Who sent the package?"

Dane shrugged. "He didn't know. I haven't gotten that far. Apparently in researching it, Reedy found that the embezzling wasn't only in Intervise, but reached out to his magazine too."

"You mean Intervise was taking money from *State of Finance*?" Ratliff asked.

"No. I mean that someone at *State of Finance* was embezzling *with* Intervise. Whatever Reed was following included a member of his own team, which would make sense of him wanting to get the story to someone else. Someone outside of the magazine."

"So he called you."

Dane nodded. "And to tell you the truth, I wasn't thinking of taking it on except that Reed was killed."

"What does that mean?" James asked.

"He means that the dangerous stories are the fun ones," Hartley answered for him with more than a hint of disgust. "Who was in on the embezzling scheme?"

"Don't know. I don't know if Reedy even knew. The documents he'd received showed that there was just an influx of money, but he didn't give me any names. He did say that a large portion of the evidence pointed to Intervise's CEO, J. R. Francesco."

"I don't get it," Hartley said, stepping forward. "You pick up a story from a dead man. What did you plan on doing with it?"

Dane smiled. "I took it to the source. Someone that knew what Reed was working on at all times. I took it to Reed's editor, Seamus O'Dowd."

"Wait. You met with Seamus O'Dowd?" Hartley asked.

Dane nodded. "When?"

"This morning." Hartley and Ratliff looked at each other. "Why? What's wrong?"

Hartley looked back to her brother. "We went into Reed's office this afternoon and your name came up in small talk."

"So?"

"O'Dowd said he never met you."

Dane cocked his head to the side, wondering where she was going with all this. "I don't follow." Ratliff took a step forward, tossing the box the fire marshal had handed him near Dane's feet. Dane looked to the rubble before smiling. "You think this was set up by O'Dowd? That doesn't make sense."

"Why not?"

Dane reached to the blackened papers near the burnt satchel. "Because O'Dowd hired me to take on the story. He paid me a couple grand up front."

"To distract you," Hartley said. "The only reason to lie to me about having met you is if he knew it would never get back to me. If this bomb killed you instead of Kelly, we'd never know the story Reed was working on."

Dane thought for a moment before a grin formed across his lips. "Sure you would have. Even if they succeeded in killing me, there's still someone out there who knows about the embezzlement scheme within Intervise and the magazine. Whoever sent Reed the information in the first place is out there."

Hartley could not conceal the glimmer of excitement in her eye or the fact that a smile was beginning to form. "What do you need to find out what's going on?"

"Time," he responded. "I need time to either find out who sent Reedy those documents or time to follow up on the story. Maybe something will reveal itself."

"But won't you be worried someone will come after you again?" James questioned.

"That depends on if I'm alive or not," he replied, turning his attention to his sister. "Can you give me a couple days of anonymity?"

Hartley looked to Ratliff and smiled. "You know if anyone talked to the press yet?"

"Not that I know of," he responded. "What do you have in mind?"

"Go talk to whoever's in charge. Brief them on our case and let's get the word to the press that there are two confirmed deaths in the explosion. I'll talk to the medic and get him to move Dane to the hospital." She turned to her brother. "Get checked out and then vanish. You have any place where you can lay low?"

He laughed. "Many."

"Good. I can give you a couple days at least. Probably longer. Work on figuring out what was going on between Reed's magazine and Intervise Securities. We'll see if we can't shake up O'Dowd and his assistant. See if anything falls out of them."

FIFTEEN

They departed the scene together, walking slowly down the sidewalk, Ratliff following behind James and Hartley as they made their way to an intersecting street in search of their respective cabs. Moments before their departure, Ratliff had pulled the fire lieutenant to the side and requested they mislead the press, an act which would, no doubt, reach the ears of whoever was behind the murderous plot against Dane. He had briefed the lieutenant with as little information as possible concerning their current investigation, yet mentioned Dane as being not only the target of the bomb but also a person of interest in their case. The two could be connected and any advantage they had could prove useful in regards to their case.

The lieutenant had agreed, leaving Ratliff to watch as a mass of media personnel congregated around the rear of a fire engine. "Before the questions come," the lieutenant had said loudly over the reporters' voices, "let me tell you the facts." He had looked steadfast into the blinding camera lights. "An investigation is currently under way. There have been two confirmed deaths that we know of. A team is working its way through the building as we speak in search of any more victims as well as evidence on the cause of the explosion."

He had paused for a split second, enough for a question to dart through the air. "Do you know who the victims are?"

The lieutenant had held a hand up to the lights to look towards the source. "One of them, yes."

"Can you identify the victim to us?"

"Absolutely not."

"Did the victim belong to this apartment?"

He had nodded his head. "We do know that one of the victims lived in the corner apartment that exploded. The other we are unsure of at this time. Like I said, we have a team searching through evidence and walking the halls."

"Was the other victim a resident of this apartment complex?"

The lieutenant had shrugged. "We are unsure at this time."

"Is it true that the explosion was set off by a bomb?"

"Once again, we are unsure."

Ratliff had been surprised upon his return to the alley to see a steady flow of tears falling from Hartley's damp cheeks. James held her as she cried, each watching the ambulance pull into the adjoining street and head into the night. Ratliff was relieved to find out, however, that it was just for show, his partner not only a brilliant detective but also, it would appear, a decent actress. "Someone planted that bomb," she had said. "If they're watching the scene, I want to make it seem like he's gone." She realized the positions of the ambulance, patrol units and fire trucks left little to no room for bystanders to catch a glimpse of the alleyway, yet she wanted to be sure. They were already pulling the wool over the public's figurative eye. There was no need to cut corners.

"So, I realize I interrupted your night," Jacoby said now as they stopped at the corner. "How about I buy you and —"

"James," Jolene's date introduced himself.

"Right. James," Ratliff repeated. "How about I buy you two a drink?"

Jolene tensed as the offer was put forth, turning her eyes from the street to her partner, her heart beginning to flutter as he focused on her. "I don't think so," she responded.

"Come on," he pressed. "I'm meeting Kim out at a bar near your place."

Her eyebrows furrowed and she cocked her head to the side, stealing a glance at James and asking, "When did you meet Kim? And how do you know where my place is?"

Jacoby chuckled. "I stuck around the precinct for a while tonight. Kim just came up and introduced herself. We talked for a bit and she invited me to get some drinks with her somewhere by your place." He paused as a thought arose. "She doesn't really have much shame, I'm gathering, does she?"

"No," she replied. "No she doesn't."

"I wouldn't mind going for a drink," James added immediately, glancing at Hartley and shrugging. "After that craziness back there, I'm game for a few."

"There you go!" Jacoby rooted. "What do you say, Jo?" She moved her eyes from James and glared at him. "Hartley. Got it. What do you say?"

She thought about it for a minute before conceding. "Fine," she replied. "After tonight, I could use a drink too."

* * * * *

They caught a cab and rode in silence for the ten minutes it took to reach the bar, Hartley and James in the rear of the taxi while Jacoby sat shotgun, the driver whistling a tune none of them had ever heard.

Freddie's Candy Shop was an establishment a block and a half down from Jolene's apartment, a favorite hangout for the off-duty police officers in the area. Jolene found humor in the bar, mainly for the fact that the Candy Shop used to be a front for the speakeasy situated in the basement during the prohibition years. Now, as Jolene and James followed Ratliff through the door, the tavern teemed with a mixture of law enforcement and everyday patrons, all enjoying themselves as they watched the overhead televisions or threw darts or shot a game of pool.

"Holy shit!" came the yell from their left as Kim Banneau raced over. "How'd you get these two out?" The question was directed towards Jacoby, though Banneau ignored whatever response was about to come forth and moved quickly past him, wrapping her arms around Jolene who smiled widely. "Good to see you out, babe," she said loudly before whispering into

Hartley's ear, "Which one of these gents are you taking home?" She gasped for breath and moved away, mouth wide in surprise. "Both?" she asked louder, laughing boisterously as her friend rolled her eyes and smacked her on the arm.

Banneau led them to the corner of the establishment where she sat with Doc Hester and Mac, as well as several officers Jolene had never met before. Upon seeing Hartley, Mac jumped into song, his surprisingly raspy, well-balanced vocal prowess blasting lines of Ray LaMontagne's "Jolene" into the atmosphere. The pleasurable quality of the forensic guru's voice was cut off immediately by what equated to a tone-deaf mute finding his voice for the very first time. Jolene turned to see Captain Henry Nolan coming up behind her, the song escaping from his soul in a screech as he set a mug of beer in front of her.

"I didn't know you were going to be out, sir," Jolene said in surprise.

"Hell, I didn't know he listened to good music," Mac added with a laugh, winking to the captain as he continued to his designated seat.

"Regardless of the square you think I may be, Detective Hartley, Detective McLourey, rest assured, I do know how to have fun," he replied.

"Of course, sir," she answered, removing her coat and taking a seat at the tall table. James and Ratliff moved to either side of her, each standing and conversing with an individual nearest them. Jolene lifted the mug to her lips and stalled as her eyes met with Kim's, Banneau smiling coyly and glancing to each man hovering over Hartley. Jolene forced a confused smile as her cheeks flushed slightly. Banneau cocked her head to the side and mouthed the words, "We'll talk," to which Hartley nodded her approval.

* * * * *

"So how long have you two been together?" Ratliff asked James as he leaned in next to him at the bar. He pulled a silver money clip from his pocket and signaled the female bartender.

She came over and placed two drinks in front of James. "Nine fifty, hon," she said to him as her gaze switched to Jacoby.

"I'll get those," the detective said. "And another round please."

"Sure thing." She walked off, grabbing a serving tray as she headed to the opposite end of the bar.

"You didn't have to do that," James replied.

"No problem," Jacoby responded. "I interrupted your night. Least I could do."

"Well, thanks."

"So?" James took a sip from his beer as the question hung in the air, his eyebrows rising in confusion. Ratliff chuckled. "You and Hartley. How long have you two been an item?"

"We're not really an item," he answered. "This was our second date."

"No shit? Well, then I'm really sorry I interrupted."

"No, it was fine. I'm pretty sure family emergencies trump everything else."

"And you guys met through a case, is that right?"

James nodded. "Yeah. Her and her partner — well former partner — they showed up at my place and saved my life." He paused as he looked to her, watched her laugh with Kim Banneau, her smile radiating in the dim light, her eyes shining as they glanced around the room between words. She was an unbelievable sight, simply stunning and graceful in her beauty.

* * * * *

"So you're screwed, is what you're saying," Kim said with a laugh.

Jolene sighed, smiling wide. The alcohol was taking effect, yet she was still in control, her body beginning to tingle as she looked to her best friend. "What's wrong with me?" she said, her bottom lip sticking out as if she were a child receiving a punishment.

"Nothing's wrong with you!" Kim stated sharply. "Hell, I've been trying to get you in bed for years. That should tell you something."

Jolene laughed. "That's not saying much. You're a slut. You'd sleep with Mac if he had a vagina."

"Jolene Hartley!" Banneau yelled, crumpling up a soggy, beer-soaked napkin and tossing it in her direction. It landed with a soupy, thud against Hartley's shoulder. "That's an awful ... Ah, probably," she said with a shrug, glancing sideways to Mac as he danced in the corner with a homely patrol officer. "He is graceful on his feet. Imagine what he'd be like in bed!" She took a sip of beer and quickly added, "And with a vagina!"

"Oh, God!" Jolene gasped, bringing her mug to her lips once more.

* * * * *

"Don't take this the wrong way when I ask, but how'd you land a date with Jo?" Jacoby asked, pushing himself up from his elbow and turning to join James in facing the group a few yards away.

"Wow," James said with a laugh.

"I don't mean it like that," Ratliff added quickly. "I just mean she seems like a pretty independent person."

"I guess I just got lucky," James replied.

"Got any advice?" James removed his eyes from Hartley and looked to Ratliff quizzically. "As her new partner," Jacoby continued, catching the glance as he surveyed the tables before him. "I'm just trying to get in good with everyone. Regardless of what you've seen on TV, we're not all hard-asses. I enjoy getting along with people."

"Could have fooled me with the shot you put on Dane in the ambulance," James answered, glancing to the detective.

"Yeah, well, that guy's sort of an asshole."

"Yeah, he didn't seem to be the most likeable guy I've ever met." They remained silent as each drank from their mugs, looking upon the group of officers as they yelled and laughed and danced to the music pouring from the jukebox. James spun to his left to order another drink and caught sight of a man in the back corner huddled near a group of college-aged women. He had seen him before, yet could not pinpoint from where.

James leaned into the counter as the bartender approached. "Another one." He glanced to Jacoby who nodded, yet remained focused forward. "Two, please." James glanced up as the bartender moved back towards the kegs. His eyes once more settled on the man near the wall. It took a moment before the alcohol swirling through his system allowed his memory to lock onto what he was searching for, the recognition of why this individual registered with Graiser. James turned quickly back to the table of officers, realizing that the man near the wall amidst the college-aged women was the same person eyeing up Hartley at the diner.

James stepped closer to Ratliff. "Don't look, but that's the second time I've seen this guy tonight." Ratliff looked to James, confused. "There's a group of girls over my shoulder against the back wall. He's just behind them."

Jacoby shifted his weight and glimpsed in the direction given him. "Guy in the black jacket? Short, dark hair? Corkscrew of a nose?"

"Yeah," James replied. "He was at the diner tonight and kept looking at Jo. He got up and left after he saw me looking at him."

"Yeah, well, he's looking this way now," Jacoby said, following the man's line of sight through the cramped establishment and to his partner near the window. "He's actually looking at her now." He turned to James with a grin. "You think we should go teach him a lesson?" He pounded his fist into the palm of his hand.

"What?" James asked.

"Come on, man," Ratliff said, grabbing his glass from the countertop. "The city's not *that* big. You're bound to run into the same people at some point."

"But twice in one night? And him staring at Jo like that?"

"Is that jealousy I'm detecting?" Jacoby poked. James shook his head as if shrugging off the comment. "Look, if you see him again at some obscure place, then maybe. But let's face the facts: your date, my partner … She's not your average woman. Just be thankful she stepped into your life at the right moment." He tapped him on the shoulder and moved towards the tables, joining the crew in a fit of laughter as an off-the-wall, semi-inappropriate joke rolled off of Mac's tongue.

James glanced one last time towards the man and caught his eye. He remained seated and locked on James for several seconds before leaning back into the wall and hiding himself behind the women. James lifted his beer to his lips as he looked away and moved after Ratliff, smiling at Jolene as he rounded the table and took a seat next to her.

SIXTEEN

Nearly two hours later, with yawns and sluggish movement creeping into the group, goodbyes were beginning to take form. Jolene and James gathered their items and stood, watching as numerous individuals situated around them fled towards the door in an inebriated waltz. From across the table Kim's obscene gestures to Jolene continued as hugs and handshakes were passed around. Hartley smiled and rolled her eyes to her friend, leaning across the table to plant a kiss on her cheek. "You're awful, you know that?" she said to Kim, who, in turn, grabbed on to Jolene's face with both hands and planted a quick one on her lips. Shrieks and hoots were heard throughout the front of the bar as the group laughed, the male officers not in her precinct egging on the two women for more.

Jolene backed away laughing. "If that's how you always kiss, then I'm never switching to your team."

"Oh, you bitch!" Kim said through gut-wrenching hysterics. "Get over here!" she yelled, standing and pretending to fight through the crowd gathered around her.

"No, no. Thank you, but no," Jolene said, grasping onto James's arm. "Good night, everyone. Sir," she said to her superior who sat stoically in a dim lit corner. "Good to see you out." He offered his goodnight with a raise of his glass.

Jolene smiled and turned with one last wave. At that moment a group of officers surrounding Mac shifted their position, obviously reacting to yet another quip brought forth by the medical examiner. Hartley's heel caught one of the officer's boots and she began a spin to the floor, her balance already jeopardized from the sufficient amount of alcohol consumed. James reached out to her at the last moment, but she was already stumbling backwards, en route to rendezvous with the soiled tile floor of the Candy Shop.

Just before her unwanted collision with a puddle of muddied beer, her descent was halted. Jolene opened her eyes to see herself floating feet from the ground, her new partner bracing his body against hers. He lifted her up carefully, allowing her to regain her footing before backing away from his grip. Jolene was unable to pull her focus away from those light green orbs searching her face. His mouth opened to form words but it was James that broke the spell that had been set upon her. "You all right?" he asked as he came up behind her and placed his hand on her lower back.

"Yeah," she answered, nervously glancing over her shoulder at him and forcing a quick grin. She turned back to Jacoby, their eyes meeting for a fraction longer than intended. "I'll see you tomorrow?" she forced out, unable to conjure any other words.

"Absolutely," he answered. "Have a good night."

"I'm sure they will!" Mac yelled as he squeezed in beside Captain Nolan. The hollers and catcalls began again as they made their way to the door, Jolene's cheeks flushing as she waved her goodbyes, her eyes once more meeting Kim Banneau's. Their exchange was quick, yet Hartley immediately caught the gist: she was definitely screwed.

As they reached the front door, James stepped in front of Jolene, getting to the exit before her for two reasons: One, though the drinks had been flowing throughout the night, James Graiser was chivalrous, a caring, conscientious individual that knew opening doors for a lady was the correct thing to do. The second reason was to steal a glance past the group of young women near the back wall. James remained stationery for a moment longer before feeling Jolene's eyes on him as she stopped on the sidewalk. He forced a smile and moved away from the door, catching up with her and beginning their trek away from their second date. It had been perfect. The food was delicious, the beer had gone down like water and the company was far above anything he could have hoped for.

Yet as they walked away down the sidewalk, one thing tugged at him: The seat behind the young women had been empty, and he had not seen the man walk out.

* * * * *

Jolene fought an internal battle from the moment they reached the damp sidewalk outside of Freddie's Candy Shop. She knew she wanted company. Yet in that moment, she did not know if it was James's company she yearned for or that of any man. She considered a wild night in the sack with an imaginary lover, trying to determine if a random — as Banneau called them — would be as invigorating and enticing as James.

She shook the thought from her head when the imaginary random morphed into Ratliff, his green eyes peering into her, fingers gliding across her skin, lips falling on her neck and — *Stop!* she thought to herself. *What is going on?*

Jolene reached out and grabbed onto James's arm, pulling herself close to ward off the chill that had settled into the night. James smiled and reached up to grab her hand, though released it after a moment as he realized she was locked firmly onto him. "Thanks for bringing me out tonight," he said as they sauntered down the pavement.

"Like I had a choice," Jolene responded with a giggle.

"Ouch!" They made small talk about their evening as they continued along, each avoiding the sexually charged elephant hovering over their heads as they neared her apartment building. "So, what happens tomorrow?" James asked, shoving his hands in his pocket and glancing to the intersection as a car pulled through.

Jolene tensed up. "What do you mean?" she replied with a subtle hint of anxiety laced with excitement.

"With Dane?"

"Oh," she said, deflated and relieved in the same breath. "Not sure. I guess Ratliff and I will take a stab at Reed's bosses again. See if we can't find out why they lied to us."

"Makes sense," he answered quickly, the nervousness wracking his body. "What do you think of Jacoby?" he asked suddenly.

Jolene looked to him and forced an embellished shrug. "He seems to be a good partner. Why?"

"I don't know. Just wondering. He brought you up in the bar tonight."

"Really?" she asked, hoping her surprised tone hid the intrigue. "What did he say?"

"Nothing really. Just wanted to know more about you. Asked me for advice."

"Advice about what?"

James chuckled. "Mainly how to get in your good graces, I guess. Not really sure."

They remained silent for a minute before Jolene shook her partner from her head. "Look," she said finally after several moments, "I don't have any beer, but there is a bottle of tequila upstairs if you want to stick around for another drink."

He smiled wide. "Absolutely," he stated, reaching out and putting his arm around her as they turned and moved towards the door.

The two entered the apartment and threw their jackets to the couch, Hartley moving into the kitchen and flipping on the track lighting that hung above the countertop, illuminating the sparkling marble countertop and precise placement of scented candles. "Want to go into that cabinet and grab a couple shot glasses?" she asked, pointing to the cupboard just above and to the right of the kitchen sink. She moved in the opposite direction, retrieving a three-fourths full bottle of silver tequila and a saltshaker from next to the oven. "Unfortunately, I don't have any limes."

James shrugged it off. "Who needs limes?"

"Hey, I'm just worried about you!" she joked, moving around him to the couch where she took her place nearest the door.

James followed with the shot glasses and sat opposite her, placing the containers on the coffee table and rolling up his sleeves while staring at her with a scowl. Jolene laughed and sat up, unscrewing the tequila top and carefully pouring the drinks. She reached out and picked up the first glass, handing it to James who held it under his nose. "Glorious!" he said with a laugh.

"Didn't anyone ever tell you to not smell the shot before you take it?" she exclaimed, licking her hand and shaking the salt onto the moist area.

"No," he answered. "I never went to college to learn such things." He reached out and took the saltshaker from her grasp, following in her wake.

"Well, now you know. Cheers!" They clinked their glasses together and lifted their salt-covered hands to their lips, licking the crystals from their skin before sending the liquid down their throats. Each furrowed their brow as the flavor ran across their tongues.

"Whoa!" James howled. "That's going down a totally different street then the beer!"

"Baby!" Jolene said as she filled their glasses once more.

"Really?" he said with surprise. "Coming from the straight-laced cop? Don't forget, Ms. Hartley, I spend a lot of my time in the Caribbean drinking rum all day long."

"Stop talking," she said, downing the shot quickly, this time without salt. James smiled and followed suit, slamming the glass onto the coffee table in triumph.

The night continued on this way for a half hour more, each of them consuming several more shots, the alcohol coursing through their bodies, warming extremities and loosening inhibitions. They gazed at one another in the silences between the banter, each wanting nothing more than to let their reserves slide to the floor along with their clothes.

James lifted another shot to his lips and downed the tequila, exhaling and letting his heated breath escape into the room. "Sorry, but where's your restroom?"

Jolene pointed towards the kitchen. "Just past the fridge on your left."

"Great," he said as he jumped up. He suddenly stopped as he reached the end of the couch and turned, his eyes falling on Hartley as she looked up to him with a confused grin. He reversed his path and leaned down to her, the butterflies in Jolene's stomach working overtime as she extended her neck to him. Their mouths joined. She could taste the salt on his lips, the flavor of the tequila on his tongue. She reached up and placed her hand on his face, grasping onto him as if she never wanted the exchange to end.

It did, however, as he pulled away and gazed into her eyes. "Sorry, I just couldn't help myself."

"No, that was fine," she said. He came in quickly for another one, this time placing a peck on her soft lips before moving around the couch and towards the bathroom.

Jolene placed her thumbnail between her teeth and stared through the wooden table, her thoughts racing as a smile formed. The kiss felt good, if not slightly sloppy. She would give him the benefit of the doubt, however. A few beers followed by copious shots of tequila would no doubt make anyone a sloppy kisser. Her thoughts floated around the room and up the steps, weaving their way through the hills and valleys of her comforter, winding across James's legs and her naked hips as they rolled back and forth on her mattress, their bodies intertwining in a heap of sweat and passion and —

"Jo," came the mistimed call from the kitchen, pulling her imagination in a heap down the steps and back to the bottle of tequila before her. She turned to see James standing a few feet away from the kitchen window, his eyes focused through the glass and towards the street below.

"What's up?" Jolene responded, shifting her weight and pulling herself up to dangle over the back of the couch.

"There's a guy standing by the bus stop down there."

She laughed. "Are you serious? You plant a kiss like that on me and then go right to people-watching?"

He forced a smile and a glance at her before returning quickly to the window. "Yeah. Sorry. But I've seen this guy twice tonight." He looked to her. "Remember at the restaurant, I said there was a guy staring at you? Well, at the bar I saw the same guy. He was watching our group all night long. And now he's outside."

Jolene's smile faded and her brow creased. She stood from the couch and made her way towards James, staying far away from the windows lining the wall. She glanced in the direction of the bus stop, catching a glimpse of a man with short, dark hair, his large frame resting against a signpost as he sucked on a cigarette. "Are you sure?" she asked him.

"Positive," he responded. "That's the third time."

Hartley looked from the street corner to James and back, weighing her options, a detective at work while not on the job. She knew what she wanted to do, and it did not include standing in the kitchen staring out the window at a stranger. She turned her attention away from the man and to the intersection itself, glancing from building to building, her eyes scanning the area. On the opposite corner, pointed down towards the intersection, hung a black metallic box with a large lock on the side and a Plexiglas window on the front. A plan formed immediately in Hartley's mind, pushing away the jumble and haziness caused by a night of drinking.

She walked to the counter and retrieved her phone from her purse, selecting a series of options as James looked on. Hartley raised the device to her ear and glanced back to him.

From the earpiece he could here Banneau answer. "Aren't you supposed to be fu —"

"Emergency, Kim!" Hartley cut her off. James smiled. "We need your help. Are you still at the bar?"

"Just about to leave. Why? What's up?"

Hartley turned her attention back to the street. "There's this guy outside my place. James has seen him at the same places as us all night. Now he's just hanging out by the bus stop keeping an eye on my apartment."

"Are you guys naked in front of the window?" Banneau asked with a laugh.

Hartley rolled her eyes. "No. Want to help us out?"

"Sure," her friend answered. "Some of my girlfriends just showed up to take me to another bar. What can we do?"

Hartley thought for a moment before responding. "I've got a plan."

* * * * *

Kim Banneau and a group of scantily clad women exited Freddie's Candy Shop and crossed to the opposite side of the road, beginning their walk towards the man near the bus stop and Jolene's living space. They were loud, laughing and cackling from the number of drinks they had in their systems.

As they neared the man, Banneau reached out and pulled a short-haired brunette to her, her arms wrapping around the petite woman's frame as their lips locked in an intense exchange. The man, who had been backing away, stopped and watched the event, a creepy smile forming as he brought a cigarette to his lips. "Hey, buddy!" one of the women yelled to him. "You want to take our picture?"

He waved his hand in the air and glanced away. "Sorry," he said in a deep, raspy voice.

"No, not like that," the woman replied, walking towards him with her group, Banneau and her lip-locked partner now following behind hand-in-hand. "Serious. We haven't seen each other in ages and we need our picture taken. Would you mind?" The man thought about it for a minute, glancing at each of the women, his eyes wandering over exposed skin and low-cut tops before shrugging. "Great!" she exclaimed, turning towards her friends.

"Maybe more towards the corner," Banneau suggested, pushing the group right to the edge of the intersection. The man brought the woman's phone up and snapped several pictures, smiling all the while at his fortunes. "What do you think about one more?" Banneau asked the group. They all agreed, yet were surprised when Kim ran into the intersection. "Come on!" she yelled. The women shrieked in laughter as they made their way to her, each posing as they stood in the intersection, thankful that the late night brought no traffic their way.

The man moved with them, positioning himself directly opposite the black box that hung from the street corner, oblivious as the machine inside steadily took high-definition images of the jaywalkers. The women thanked the man with hugs and kisses on the cheeks as they made their way up the street, Banneau glancing up to Hartley's apartment and smiling.

* * * * *

They had turned off the apartment lights and made their way to the living room windows. Hartley watched as Banneau and her group approached, witnessed the intense, passionate kiss with the brunette woman and followed as they moved into the intersection, an illegal activity no doubt caught by the automatic recorder in the black box hanging from the light pole.

Hartley waved her thanks to Banneau and lifted her phone to her ear. "Yeah, this is Detective Jolene Hartley. There's a man standing outside my apartment that doesn't need to be there. I need a patrol unit to come by and see if they can pick him up."

"There's a unit a few blocks over, detective," dispatch answered.

"Great," Hartley replied. "Tell them I'll meet them when they get here."

* * * * *

The disappointment Hartley felt as the squad car came down the street with lights flashing was palpable. The man standing watch over her and James immediately took off as the unit advanced and did not regain his post that evening. Hartley spoke with the officers on the sidewalk momentarily, briefing them on what the man looked like and where he had been seen throughout the evening. They agreed to call in a surveillance request for her benefit, volunteering themselves for the first shift. Hartley thanked them, saying it was not necessary and knowing, even if they did follow her directions and leave the scene, the officers would not travel more than a few blocks before making their way back.

Jolene returned to her apartment and walked into the living room, her mouth open as words began to form, only to be silenced as her gaze fell upon her recliner and a sleeping James Graiser. She smiled and swore under her breath, knowing they had missed a perfectly good opportunity to take their relationship to the next level.

She pulled a couple blankets from the closet shelf and tossed one to the couch, throwing the other over her date before retiring to the sofa. She stayed awake for several minutes, her eyes watching James as he slept, her mind drifting from their kiss to the look between her and Ratliff in the bar moments before her exit. Banneau was absolutely correct: she was screwed.

SEVENTEEN

She had started the morning with a pounding headache, yet now, as she began her ascent of the precinct steps, it had lessened to the point of an annoying, dull throb, a pain she knew she was lucky to have with the amount of alcohol she had consumed the previous evening.

James, scrunched up on her recliner in the same position he had been the night before, was still asleep in her apartment. She had woken and showered, leaving a note on the kitchen counter before exiting the building and making her way to the coffee shop down the road. *Feel free to whatever you'd like. Shower's upstairs. TV remote's in the end table drawer. The bed upstairs is much more comfortable if you need a change of scenery.* She had blushed when writing the last line, but thought twice about crossing it out. It was a nice feeling to have that trust in someone, to let them mosey about your personal area without fear of what they may do. Plus, if he was still there when she returned from work, the invitation to her bed had already been put forth.

She proceeded to her desk and immediately picked up her phone as she sat, ignoring Ratliff as he turned to face her. She was upset. No, not upset. Something else. Infuriated? Intrigued? Hartley could not put her finger on it, yet there was something in the pit of her stomach that caused her some anxiety, something about the way he just assumed he could ask questions about her. And to James, of all people! It was a confidence she had not seen or been privy to since Ronny Debarsi.

Hartley pressed a button to retrieve messages before slowly turning her eyes to her partner, her face tight and expressionless as their gaze met. He remained seated, bent at the waist with his hands folded, elbows resting on his knees, eyes staring intently to her as his mouth cracked into a grin. *Stop with that smile!* she thought to herself as she faced forward once more.

"Detective Hartley," the voicemail began. "This is Lieutenant Abe Vargas. I spoke with your partner, Detective Ratliff, last night at the apartment explosion. He told me to give you a buzz if we figured out anything more. We took a look at what was left of the ignition devices and just thought I'd let you know that whoever did this was extremely good. The way these were built … I mean, you don't see this with your everyday bomb builder. This was crafted with care and diligence. If I had to guess, I'm thinking military or terrorist training. Someone that's been doing it for a very long time. Thanks, Detective. Give me a shout if you have any more questions."

The line went dead and Hartley returned the receiver to the base, leaning back in her chair and running her hands through her hair. "What?" she said sternly, feeling Ratliff's eyes upon her.

"Wow," he replied with a shocked tone. "You okay this morning?"

"I'm fine. I can just feel you staring. What do you want?"

"Um, okay. Just was going to tell you that I was looking into …" He paused before straightening up. "I'm sorry, did I do something to offend you in the last three minutes?" He looked to his watch as if he had been timing her.

"Would you just tell me what you were going to say?"

He held up his hands in submission. "Fine. I took the liberty this morning of looking into Intervise Securities, just to check up on what this company is into, and, without knowing much about the financial world, I'd say these guys are legit. They're a mid-sized organization owned by a man named J. R. Francesco, an Italian immigrant who's pretty much a ghost, albeit an extremely wealthy one. Intervise was started in the late seventies and grew into a mid-sized company within a few years. They've held onto that status ever since. No giant growth. No giant loss. Just a steady, always-there financial entity. As far as Francesco being involved in illegal activity, I haven't found anything yet, but I doubt they'd make that known in the media."

He paused and waited for some sort of comment, yet shook his head and continued when he realized it would not come. "So, there's a figurehead of the company that seems to be running the whole operation even though Francesco is the proprietor." He looked to his notepad. "Damian Verland, Intervise Securities Director of Operations and Vice President. Any mention of Intervise has Verland's name attached to it. I'm sorry," he said without pausing, tossing his notepad back on the desk as Hartley rose mid-sentence and grabbed her coffee mug. "Seriously though, what's the deal? Did I do something to piss you off?"

Jolene turned to face him, placing her mug back on her desk. She bit the bullet. "What are you doing talking about me with James last night?"

He leaned back, dropping his hands to his knees, eyebrows furrowing at the surprising route this conversation was going. "That's what you're pissed about?" Jolene stared at him. "Look," he continued, rising from his seat, "I was just shooting the shit with him. I'm sorry if me asking questions got you upset. I didn't mean to. I'm just trying to get in good with everyone. Tough being the new guy, you know?"

"It's just a little strange though, don't you think? You don't see me going to your girlfriend —"

"I don't have a girlfriend."

"Whatever. You don't see me questioning your dates, do you? Just doesn't seem like the right way to get in good with people."

"Why not?" he asked.

Jolene thought for a moment, picking up her mug and turning it over in her hands. "You can learn plenty about me by just being my partner on the job. Just seems like a waste of time — not to mention an intrusion of my privacy — with you going behind my back, especially to someone I'm seeing." She paused before adding, "Doing that makes it seem like there's an ulterior motive."

Jacoby smiled and dropped his hands to his sides. "And what if there is?" he asked, catching Jolene off guard and sending her nerves into panic mode.

"Excuse me?" she asked, taken aback.

He looked to the left and right stepping forward. "Look, I respect you as an officer. You're great at what you do. I could tell that the moment we met. Better yet, I respect you as a person. You're tough, smart, independent. You don't take shit from anyone." He smiled again as her focus began to falter. "And on top of that, you're not bad on the eyes." She quickly looked around, worried that others would hear the conversation at hand. "So, I'm sorry if I offended you by asking James questions. Believe me, that was purely professional." He took another step closer, the movement pulling Jolene's eyes to his. "But let me be clear, Detective: I don't need help from him to try and figure you out on a personal level. I don't play games like that. If I want to get to know you outside of work, I will, with your permission, of course. And if I'm interested in you, then I'd just ask you out."

He stopped talking then, standing feet away from an anxious Jolene, whose eyes could not pull away from his. Her mouth moved slightly, trying to form words in response to his comments. She felt bad after his response to her accusations, yet was caught up on his last sentence. *And if I'm interested in you, then I'd just ask you out.* Had he not already asked her out on the way back from the magazine?

Hartley jumped as Banneau cleared her throat to their right. The partners turned their heads in unison to look upon the chipper, smiling detective, her eyes glancing back and forth between them. "Am I interrupting?" she asked.

Hartley tried to form words, but still could not, instead choosing to shake her head and return to her seat. "No," Ratliff responded, turning to look at his partner once more. "Just telling Hartley about a new facet of our case."

"Well, I've got another one for you," Banneau said as she approached, pulling her phone from her pocket and pressing a series of buttons. "Open up the email I just sent you." Hartley woke her computer with the shake of the mouse. "I got in early today and made a call to Patrick Morton over at the Transit Authority. He got a series of images off the camera near your place of your stalker."

"What stalker?" Ratliff asked in a serious tone.

"Nothing," Hartley said.

"Was it that guy from the bar?"

"You knew about that?" Hartley asked incredulously.

"James mentioned something to me, but it just sounded like a guy sticking up for his girlfriend."

"I'm not his ..." She stopped as Banneau cleared her throat again. Hartley looked anxiously from her friend to Ratliff before turning her attention back to the computer screen.

The attachment opened and Hartley zoomed in, focusing above the group of women to the man's face. "That is definitely the guy from the bar," Ratliff said. "Think we can get a hit if we run that through facial recognition?"

"Worth a shot," Hartley responded. "Picture's crisp enough. If he's in the system, we'll get something."

EIGHTEEN

"Luke Moran," Captain Nolan said as he strolled from his office and crossed to Hartley's station. Ratliff removed his feet from the corner of his desk and wheeled over. Hartley glanced over her shoulder at her partner as he stopped just next to her, his knee grazing her leg. She leaned back in her chair and shifted positions, moving away from Ratliff as her eyes looked up to her boss. "We got a match on your stalker." Nolan tossed down a manila envelope with a smack onto her desk.

Hartley pulled the fastened image of the man from the front of the folder and glanced at it. He was a strong looking individual with short, black hair and a chiseled jaw sitting atop broad shoulders and a muscular frame. His face was littered with pockmarks, though Hartley leaned more towards violent altercations than a case of pre-pubescent acne, mainly basing her theory from the zigzag of his nose. "That's one ugly dude," Ratliff said aloud, though to no one in particular.

Hartley turned to look at her partner with questioning eyes as the captain chimed in. "Just because he's not as pretty as you doesn't mean we need to pass judgment."

"Thanks, Cap," Ratliff said in a chipper tone that was immediately followed by what Hartley caught as a wink and a flash of pearly whites from her superior.

She glanced from one man to the other several times, not believing what was happening, watching as her police precinct turned into a comedy club starring fraternity brothers. "Does this really help us?" she stated finally.

"Find any humor you can with this job, Jo," Nolan said. He was right and she knew it, yet at the moment she could not force herself into a hysterical situation with her partner. Nolan sighed and continued. "I took a look through the file and it seems your guy was a seasoned criminal in his youth. Made a career out of it. Back in the day his name was included as a suspect in a murder charge but nothing panned out. He was in and out of jail for a number of years in his teens. Did a three-year stint for aggravated assault just before his twentieth birthday, followed by a small run for weapons possession, but ever since then he's been clean."

"How long has he been clean for?" Ratliff asked as Hartley shuffled through the pages.

"About seven years," Hartley answered.

"Gets better," Nolan said with a smile. "Turn to the last page."

Hartley did as told and gasped. "Military EOD?" she exclaimed.

"You've got to be kidding me?" Ratliff said.

"That's right. Our guy was on the Explosive Ordnance Disposal unit," Nolan added.

Hartley skimmed through the background of Luke Moran's military career quickly before looking to her boss. "How much you want to bet he knows how to make motion-activated explosives?"

Nolan shrugged and turned back towards his office. "You two figure out what you're going to do. Fill me in."

"Yes, sir," Ratliff said.

"I don't recognize any of these names," Hartley said suddenly.

"What's that?" Ratliff asked, turning his attention from Captain Nolan's retreat back to his partner.

Hartley had moved forward several sheets and was now glancing at Luke Moran's known associates. "His friends," she answered. "None of these guys are ringing a bell with me."

"Here, let me take a look." Hartley handed over the list and Ratliff read through them, his eyes intense and his lips moving as he read each name. "Arland Landry," he said finally, tapping the page with his extended index finger. "I know Landry. He used to be a problem child in Narcotics when I was a rookie."

"And now?"

Ratliff shrugged. "Been clean for the last couple years as far as I know. We used to make visits out to him on a monthly basis. After a while he just seemed to give up on the life. Who knows though, right? Maybe he's just hiding it better."

Hartley thought for a moment. "Where's Landry at now?"

"Last I knew, he was running a grocery store on the west side owned by his father. What are you thinking?"

"I'm thinking that you should call one of your buddies over in Narcotics and make sure Landry's still at the grocery store. If he is, maybe we can take a ride out there and see what he knows about Luke Moran." Ratliff nodded and rolled back to his desk, picking up the phone and dialing in a series of numbers. Hartley followed suit as she continued to talk. "I'm going to put an APB out on Moran. See if someone can't find him and bring him in. I'd like to know why he's spying on me."

* * * * *

Landry Produce Market was situated in University Village, a neighborhood once known for hard-working Irish immigrants looking for a place in the American culture that surrounded them, as well as the violence brought by the Valley Gang of Chicago's Bloody Maxwell section. Grocery stores and bakeries popped up across the map alongside restaurants and local watering holes, each desperately clinging onto their clients as the population grew and new, larger establishments were erected.

The area was ripe for criminal activity just before Prohibition and the Irish gangs knew it, taking hold of the neighborhoods surrounding Landry Produce Market and infiltrating the walls of the grocery itself. Myles Landry became a key component within the Valley Gang, allowing the higher-ups to use his warehouse as the central point for their distribution throughout the city. Although Myles himself did not belong to the Irish mob, he knew the consequences of declining such illegal activity, instead choosing to let the warehouse and basement of the grocery store be infested with scum and miscreants while he himself pocketed a small fortune to keep his mouth shut. And he did. No sense in passing up an extra income in an era when one paycheck was hard to come by.

Decades later, the Valley Gang lessened its grip throughout the area, as had all the major organized crime outfits, only to see their streets overrun by hooligans of all sorts, each pushing a new product that benefited only themselves financially and poisoned the neighborhoods around them. There was no sense of self with the new gangs. No unity within the neighborhoods, even if that connection had once been brought by payment for protection.

Hartley and Ratliff pulled up to the produce market just before 10:00 a.m. and exited the vehicle, securing their firearms and tightening their Kevlar vests. They did not expect any resistance, however one could never be careful enough. "Let me talk to him first," Ratliff said as they approached the entrance. "Maybe he'll remember me from back in the day."

Hartley nodded as she followed him through the doors, eyes scanning her surroundings as they made their way to the right towards a young Hispanic girl working the register. The grocery store was nearly empty save for a worker in the far aisle to their left and an elderly woman in a motorized cart near the dairy section. Hartley could hear voices towards the back of the store, yet due to the layout of the place she could not get a visual.

"*¿Te puedo ayudar con algo?*" asked the girl with a smile.

Ratliff smiled back as he glanced to her. "*Si*," he responded. "*¿Hablas ingles?*"

"*Si*," the girl nodded. "Not well. But a little."

"Perfect," he said with a grin. "Is Arland Landry here?"

The girl nodded and pointed towards the back. "In back. I will call him."

"*Gracias*," Ratliff said as they moved to the rear of the store.

Over the intercom came the call in an echoing voice. "Arland to floor, please. Arland to floor." The detectives stopped near a pair of swinging doors next to the meat display, watching as the elderly woman drove straight into a rack of French-fried onions. Ratliff chuckled and turned to see a grin cross Hartley's face as well. She glanced up to him and quickly hid her amusement, bringing Ratliff's laughter to a halt.

"Can I help you?" came a gruff voice from behind them. The detectives turned and gazed over the meat display at a middle-aged man with black-framed glasses. He stood just below six feet tall and had light brown hair with a red tint. His face was chubby, as was his entire body, yet he radiated confidence.

"We hope so," Ratliff replied as the officers turned. He held up his badge for Arland to read. Landry nodded his understanding and wiped his hands on a filthy towel.

"Detectives," he said in greeting. "I've been out of the game for years. So if you're here for me, I'm going to disappoint."

"Does anyone really ever get out of the game though?" Ratliff asked with a grin.

Arland was not amused. "Usually, no. But I'm an exception to the rule, I guess. You believe that?"

"Not in the least," Ratliff answered.

"Well, then we're right where we left off last time you came in here," he replied, his eyes moving to Hartley. "Except you've got yourself better eye candy."

Ratliff's smile fell from his face. "Two things, Arland," he said, stepping closer to the display case and into Landry's line of sight. "First, I'm glad you remember me. That tells me you know I don't like to be jerked around. And second, that's my new partner, yes. And like you, I like her better than my old one. So don't go running your mouth, or I'll shove one of those pig hooves in it. Understand?"

Hartley could see the anger rising from Arland as he stared to her partner. In another time, she could imagine Landry reaching across the display case and pulling Ratliff's face through the glass before pummeling him with his fists. Yet that did not happen. Instead, Arland remained fixed on Ratliff as he wiped his hands once more. He glanced to Hartley again before answering. "Like I said, detectives," he paused for effect and locked eyes with the man before him. "I've been out of the game for years. Anything you want to talk about, we can talk. Anything in my past, you already know. Anything about my past that you don't know …" He shrugged, though his face remained emotionless.

Just as Ratliff opened his mouth to speak, the swinging doors flew open, causing him to jump and Hartley to instinctively reach for her service piece. To their surprise, however, two little boys came flying through, each with their arms wide as they ran towards Arland. "Daddy! Daddy!" the leading boy yelled, jumping into Arland's arms as he lifted him up, setting the child on the display case. Hartley removed her hand from her hip.

"Boys!" Arland yelled, reaching down to hoist the other child into his grip. "Whoa! Settle down!"

"Myles took my toy!" the child situated on his right hip exclaimed.

"It's mine!" the one on the display case yelled back. "Yours is on the table!"

"No it's not! That's mine!"

"Enough! *Tóg go bog é!*" Arland yelled.

The doors swung open again and a short, round attractive woman appeared, her arms outstretched to the children, eyes glancing between Arland and the officers. "*Imímis!*" the woman said in a heavy Irish brogue. Arland placed the children on the floor and they immediately rushed towards the woman who Hartley assumed was their mother. The woman glanced once more to the detectives before disappearing behind the doors.

Arland watched after them before turning his attention back to Ratliff. "Like I said: out of the game for years."

Ratliff's expression softened before he nodded his understanding. "You have time for some questions?"

"About what?" he asked.

"About a one-time associate of yours," Hartley said from over Ratliff's shoulder, drawing Arland's attention.

"Who?" he asked.

"Luke Moran."

Arland nodded his head slowly and seemed to be lost in thought as he wiped his hands once more before looking to Hartley. "Sure," he said, tossing the rag on a butcher's block behind him. "*Mícheál!*" he yelled towards the front of the establishment. "I'm going in back! Watch the store!"

The detectives followed Arland through the swinging doors and into a dimly lit storage warehouse. Boxes lined each wall as well as the custom-shelving units running the length of the floor. Imported Irish goods could be seen between cases of Nestlé hot cocoa and Barilla pasta sauces. A dozen yards in front of them Arland's two boys and wife sat with another woman in a kitchen lighted by overhead fluorescents. Hartley smiled at the boys as Landry turned left down a short hallway leading into an office.

Arland flipped a light switch and pulled an extra chair from an adjoining room, handing it to Ratliff and taking a seat behind the desk. "So, you want to know about Luke." He leaned back and folded his hands across his stomach.

"That's right," Ratliff replied, pulling out a notepad and pen.

"He's a douche bag, in my opinion," Arland offered.

"We have him listed as an associate of yours," Hartley said.

"That's right," he replied with a nod. "Back in the day we all used to run in pretty much the same circle. But that was back in the day. I was a douche bag, too." He laughed.

"You guys have acquaintances that the others didn't know about?"

Arland shrugged. "Sure. Those guys and me … We did jobs together. Did our thing. But some other things they weren't right for, you know what I mean? So instead of doing this with that guy, I would call on someone else. Sometimes we did jobs with a separate group altogether."

"How did you and Luke Moran meet?" Ratliff asked.

"How every young kid meets another douche bag," he answered with a smile. "We had a scene in an alley."

"What do you mean?" Hartley questioned.

He turned his attention back to her. "We got into a little scuffle. I forget about what, but days later everything was worked out and me and him were in cahoots."

"Mr. Landry," Hartley began, "can you identify this man?" She held up the printed picture taken the previous night.

Arland leaned forward and laughed. "That's Luke Moran, all right."

"What's funny?" Ratliff asked.

Arland pointed to the picture and a divot in Moran's chin. "That's from our scuffle." He leaned back once again and looked to Hartley. "What's all this about?"

Hartley locked eyes with him. "He's a person of interest."

"Who's got interest in him?"

"I do," Hartley responded, her eyes peering into Landry's, who did not back down. "He's been tailing a colleague of mine —"

"You mean you," he interrupted. Hartley remained silent. "I ain't the smartest man in the world, but come on. Word travels, and I know your partner here is a homicide detective now, which would make you a homicide detective, no? So what are two homicide detectives doing at my door? I ain't involved in anything like that. Like I said: I'm out of the game. So why not just be square with me?"

Hartley thought for a moment before conceding. "We're investigating a murder and Moran's a person of interest. He was seen following me last night and when running him through the system, we found a list of past associates with your name on it. My partner recognized you. Is that square enough?"

"Sure. Now what can I do for you?"

"Would you mind going over a list of names for us?"

Arland sat up and leaned into the desk. "Who's on the list? Let's hear them."

Ratliff flipped to a page in his notepad and began reading. "Michael Quinn. Jason Dunne. David Scott. Tommy Merlini. Eric Sheehan."

Arland nodded as the names were read aloud. He stared to the desk in front of Ratliff, his mind traveling through time to his younger days in the city streets. "Yep. I knew all of them."

"Do you know where they are?" Hartley asked.

"*Mícheál ó Cuinn*," he said in perfect Irish Gaelic, obviously proud of how deep his roots went. "Mike Quinn is out on the grocery floor." Hartley scrunched her brow. "Mike works for me. He got out of all the shit a year before me. Lived with his parents and tried to figure out his life. When my dad passed three years ago, I came in to run the grocery and hired Mike on. He's here every day. Open to close, like myself." He pointed to the list of names. "You mind?"

Ratliff turned the notepad so Arland could read it. "Jason Dunne. Fortunately, this rat bastard won't be messing in anyone's business anymore."

"Why's that?" Hartley asked.

"Because someone put a bullet in his fucking head two years ago. He got himself mixed up in some heavy drugs about five years back. From what I heard, he couldn't pay on what he owed. So instead of investing in something so worthless, they ended their agreement by ending him."

"You didn't like Jason too much, did you?"

"That prick started spreading my name around town as someone who could vouch for him. I had drug pushers and cops at my door non-stop. Guns put to my head. My wife's head! It was a blessing the day that motherfucker got killed."

"What about the next two?" Ratliff asked. "I remember hearing their names at the station from time to time."

Arland looked to the sheet. "Scott and Merlini. Two knuckleheads. Good guys though, if they weren't all hopped up on drugs. Both of these two are relaxing in the state hotel right now. Caught two years ago, if I remember correctly."

"What was the conviction?" Hartley asked.

"Intent to distribute. They had bought a couple kilos of cocaine and were pushing it pretty hard on the streets around here. Their over-aggressiveness got them pinched. Hopefully it'll keep them straight now, too." He leaned into the desk once more and glanced at the last name on the list, shaking his head. "*Eiric O'Siodhachain.* Sheehan I lost touch with years and years ago. He was a quiet kid. Pretty intense on the jobs we did. Last time I heard his name was from Jason. Said he was heading to Ireland. Had family there that would take him in."

Arland turned to the wall and a series of file cabinets that lined it. "I got a picture of us all when we were younger. As much as I hate to remember all that shit, it's still part of me, you know?" He rummaged through the contents for a minute before pulling out a worn and weathered picture frame with the glass cracked across the top left corner. He set the frame in front of them and pointed to each of the men shown. "There's Mike on the left here. That's me, David Scott, the Italian, Jason Dunne and Sheehan."

Hartley's eyes went wide as she went through the procession of men, landing finally on Eric Sheehan with her mouth open. She reached out suddenly and grabbed the frame from Arland's hand, pulling the image up to her face. "Ratliff," she said, pointing to the image. "Look at Eric Sheehan closely." She handed him the picture. He stared at it momentarily before turning to her with a smile.

"It's fucking Kyle Walker from the magazine!" Ratliff exclaimed.

NINETEEN

"That little shit!" Hartley stated as they made their way back towards the precinct. "I didn't like him when I met him and now he's really starting to piss me off. I'm guessing he has more of a role in this whole thing then just being an Assistant Editor to a dead man."

"He's an associate of an ex-military bomb expert who happened to be following you around last night while your brother's apartment was bombed." Ratliff laughed as he looked out the window. In their short time together as partners, Hartley had taken the lead on everything they had been through, which included the driving. Now, as he held the steering wheel firmly and moved through the Chicago streets, he felt elated that not only had Hartley allowed him to drive, but she had also let him take the lead with Arland Landry. As he thought about his progress with her, however, it did not go unnoticed that the phrase "she let him" was attached to his recent accomplishments.

"Let's not jump to conclusions though," she said from her position in the passenger seat. She was reclined slightly, her knees brought to her chest as her shoeless feet danced on the dashboard. "Let's go through what we have so far before we throw the guilty verdict at anyone." She shifted her position away from the window towards the interior of the vehicle. Ratliff could feel the excitement in the air. "Reed is murdered, presumably because of the story he was working on. The cover up within *State of Finance* and the missing briefcase and laptop point to that."

"Right," Ratliff added. "Questioning his bosses leads us nowhere except to a sneaking suspicion that Reed's desk was cleaned, if in fact there was any sort of evidence there at all."

"Which I'm sure there was. You can't be a reporter and have no notes or anything resembling information from what you're working on. It just can't happen. When Dane started out he was doing fluff pieces and he had Post-its all over. There's no way Reed had nothing."

"Agreed."

Hartley retrieved her phone and dialed a series of numbers. "Yes, this is Detective Jolene Hartley with Homicide," she said after a moment. "I need a unit to the *State of Finance* offices to bring Kyle Walker in for questioning. Let me know if he puts up a stink." She waited a moment for confirmation, thanked the dispatch personnel and hung up, placing her phone once again into her coat pocket.

"Dane," Ratliff began as if they had not halted for the phone call. "Dane visits O'Dowd and Walker at the offices and tells them what Reed has given him and, in turn, they hire him on as a freelance reporter. Only Dane isn't expected to continue with the story due to the fact that he was supposed to be the one to set off the explosives, not Kelly Depler."

"We have to figure out what role O'Dowd plays in this," Hartley said, bringing her thumbnail to her teeth.

"You think he's involved too?"

Hartley gave him a shocked look. "O'Dowd was the one who told us he had never met Dane, remember?"

"That's right!" Ratliff exclaimed, smacking the palm of his hand on the steering wheel for effect. "He figured that Dane wouldn't be around to tell us otherwise, considering you and your brother aren't on speaking terms."

"Exactly." They remained silent for several minutes while each of them ran through their thoughts. "What is confusing me though is how Luke Moran comes into this."

"How do you mean?" Ratliff questioned.

"Well, I know they were known associates from their past. But nothing within the last five or six years has them dealing with each other. Even Landry said that Walker took off for Ireland years ago to get away from the life."

"Still not following."

"Okay. If Walker leaves the country to get away from everything, why come back to it? Landry did it by not moving away from the same neighborhood that caused him problems. Walker leaves the country. Why would you make it back just to call on an old acquaintance? Especially if you worked your way into a good position within a respectable magazine. His days of running from the cops and jail time were behind him."

They remained silent for a moment before Ratliff added, "We'll just have to see once we get Walker in the interrogation room." He smiled to Hartley and she grinned back, unable to maintain her frustration with him from the morning.

"We still need to keep digging though. Hopefully Dane can get us something regarding the embezzlement scheme. In the meantime, let's dig a little deeper on Intervise Securities. I want to know everything about them."

"I'll take a look when we get back," Ratliff responded.

They continued towards the station, each of the detectives losing themselves in the city that passed by their windows. As they turned onto the precinct street Ratliff looked down to the clock. 11:52 a.m. "Hey, listen, Jo," he began, the sound of her first name coming from his lips sending a shiver of annoyance and anticipation throughout her body. "I'm sorry about talking to James about you behind your back. I wasn't trying to be disrespectful or anything. I hope you know that. I consider myself a decent guy, and I hope I didn't screw that up for you."

Silence filled the car for several tense seconds while Jolene built up the courage to speak. "Apology accepted," she said finally, relieved as Jacoby laughed aloud. She glanced to him nervously and caught his gaze.

"What do you say to lunch? My treat."

Her heart immediately jumped as she felt the blood rush to her cheeks. Jolene quickly looked to her window and weighed the options, knowing she should continue to the precinct to look into the case. Before she could muster up her rejection, she caught herself. What was the harm in having lunch with her partner? She had done that a hundred times with Barailles. *Look where that led,* she thought to herself.

She turned quickly to Ratliff and was surprised to see him waiting patiently, his eyes peering from the road before him to her and back. She grinned and said, "Sounds great." Hartley turned away hastily as the words passed through her mind once more. *Sounds great.* Great? Where had that come from? A simple *sure* or *yes* would have been fine. *Great* made it seem like she was really looking forward to it.

She brought her thumbnail anxiously to her teeth and bit down, closing her eyes and trying to free her mind from these thoughts as they made their way past the precinct and towards the restaurant of Ratliff's choosing.

* * * * *

"So what's your deal? Why'd you choose to be a cop?" The question stunned Jolene as she brought a piece of buttered bread to her lips. They had made their way to an Italian restaurant just north of the precinct that Ratliff favored above all others in the area. He was new to the precinct, but not to the city, and from his earliest days on the force the restaurant had been high on his list. It was a nice establishment, one that Jolene had heard of but never been to. The windows were crystal clear with two large curtains to either side made from thick fabric that alternated between green, white and red in proud display of the owner's heritage. The aroma of fresh bread floated throughout the rustic atmosphere, entwining itself with the low volume opera that pumped from speakers hidden near the ceiling or behind large-leafed plants.

They were seated to the right of the entrance, fourth booth against the window in a spot that overlooked a long, worn countertop. The hostess, a dark-haired, olive-skinned woman in her mid-fifties, smiled at the pair as they took their seats, seeming to hesitate on Jacoby as if she remembered him from his prior visits. Hartley understood completely. Individuals such as Ratliff, with his rugged good looks and chiseled frame, tended to stick in her memory as well.

She took a bite of bread in order to give herself time to think of a response. Jolene had never really been asked this particular question by another officer before, except for her oral examination prior to the academy. Plenty of civilians had posed the inquiry, yet other members of the force had just assumed, like them, she wanted to help people. Finally she shrugged. "It's just what I'm good at. I've always been good at looking at the bigger picture and finding out what fits and what doesn't. Some people are good at math. Some can play the piano. I'm good at being a cop."

"I get that," he responded as he buttered his own piece of bread. "Any family members cops?"

She nodded. "My dad was a cop. Sheriff in the town I grew up in."

Jacoby snickered. "Funny how it gets passed down like that. Like it's hereditary or something, you know?" She did not answer, assuming the question was rhetorical, instead choosing to raise her eyebrows slightly and sink her teeth into the roll between her fingers. He continued after a moment. "It's the same with me."

A sudden twinge of guilt immediately settled into her stomach as she realized she had not reciprocated the interest. "I was going to ask …" she replied quietly, letting her voice trail as he shook his head in forgiveness.

"Both my parents were cops. My uncle's still a cop. Got a couple cousins that are on the force down in Florida."

"What about your siblings?" Hartley questioned.

"My brother, Adam, is a branch manager at a bank in Lincolnshire. Leah and Bernie are both doctors in Hawaii, if you believe that." He chuckled. "They're a year apart and you couldn't separate them if you tried."

Jolene watched him as he talked about his family, saw the warmth and love cross his face as his siblings' names rolled from his tongue. She could not help but grin as she looked into his eyes, wondering what it must feel like to have such a close-knit group at this age. "Bernie?" she heard herself ask with a grin as she ripped a chunk of bread and placed it on her tongue.

Jacoby nodded and shrugged. "Bernadette. Bernie for short. She never liked the name. I'm not exactly sure why, but I'm guessing it's because we used to torture her when she was younger. She would get so mad! Leah would come running to her rescue and me and Adam would just keep on going. Finally my pop just told us to lay off. He said, 'One of these days you're going to need her help when you get shot.'" He laughed as Jolene's eyes widened.

"How old were you when he said that?"

"I don't know. Maybe sixteen or so."

"Seems like a weird thing to say to a sixteen year old."

"Probably, but he knew what I wanted to do. He knew I was going to follow in his footsteps."

The waiter approached the table and took their order, setting down a fresh basket of bread and a complimentary salad for each. They remained silent as they ate, Jolene catching herself glancing across the table to Jacoby and quickly away when she felt his eyes traveling to her.

"So is there any one point you can remember that made you say, 'That's it. This is what I want to do'?" Jolene asked finally after they had finished their salads. She knew she was going against the grain she had set earlier, yet she could not help but continue the conversation. There was an undeniable attraction to Jacoby Ratliff as a person that drew her away from keeping things completely professional.

Jacoby pushed his plate away and looked to the tablecloth, his smile fading and a seriousness settling into his face. "When I was about fourteen or fifteen. It was Christmas Eve and it was me, my mom, Adam and my sisters at our house. My old man was on duty, but he came home to surprise us with a couple gifts before heading back on patrol." He stopped and smiled to the waiter who brought fresh beverages to their table. "There was this girl in our subdivision that was a bit older than me. She had to be about twenty or twenty-one. Pretty girl. Blonde.

Kind of a free spirit. One of those girls you knew was good deep down, but went down the wrong path at some point. My dad always told me to watch out for her. He had picked her up several times for drug charges.

"Anyway, Christmas Eve, he pulls up and brings in the presents. We're all excited, you know, because we usually don't see him on that day. So as we're joking around in the living room, I see Courtney — that's the blonde druggie girl — I see her limping towards the house in the street. I went towards the door and could see she was all messed up. Not from drugs. Well, that too, but she was all bloody. Split eyebrow, broken nose, split lip. Her clothes were all torn. Blood was running down her leg. I called to my dad and ran outside."

"Where was she coming from?" Jolene asked, intrigued.

"Apparently from the park across the street," he answered. "It was a big space with a couple of well-secluded spots where the teenagers would go and smoke pot and drink and whatever. So, I run out there and Courtney immediately starts sobbing. She collapses into me and pulls me to the ground. My old man asks what happens. Apparently she had been shooting up in the park and nodded off. When she woke there was a man on top of her. She tried to fight back, but being high, she was no match for him. She ended up grabbing a broken bottle and stabbing him repeatedly in the side and neck. He got off and she bolted through the park and into some trees. She saw the squad car pulling up at our house and hobbled over." He paused, lost in thought for several moments before continuing. "Anyway, my dad called it in and took off towards the park.

The rest of the family stayed with the girl in the driveway until we could get her up, then we brought her inside. She wouldn't let go of me. She was in complete shock.

"I remember being furious over what happened. Courtney was older than me and I felt sorry for the way her life was going, but she didn't deserve what happened to her. In the end, it turned out to be the guy that sold her the heroin. He followed her and waited for her to nod off before forcing himself on her."

"Whatever happened to her?" Jolene asked.

He shrugged. "I don't know. My old man told me years later when I was in the academy that she had overdosed on a speedball. She was alive, but not in good condition. That's it. I told him not to tell me anymore. Sometimes we need good endings, you know? Even if we have to make them up ourselves." Jolene nodded and remained focused on her partner as the waiter set their food in front of them. She felt proud of Ratliff as she listened to his story, amazed that his passion for the job equaled her own.

Her phone rang from the tabletop then, causing her to jump and laugh. She looked down to the display and read the caller-ID. JAMES GRAISER. Jolene ran her thumb across the screen and paused as she hovered over the answer button, surprising herself as she pressed ignore. She had never ignored a call from James before, except for when she was in an important meeting. Yet this could hardly be considered a meeting. She was just out to lunch with her partner. There was no reason why she could not have taken the call.

Hartley glanced up to Ratliff and caught his eyes moving from the phone display to her, a slight grin forming across his face. She flushed and forced a smile before diving into the plate of pasta before her.

* * * * *

They skipped dessert yet ordered coffee, each content with dodging the hustle and bustle of their work at least for the time being. The silence of the moment enveloped them. Jolene could feel the tension hovering above their heads since the fateful phone call from James nearly fifteen minutes ago. Jacoby, on the other hand, looked calm, if not slightly more depressed from having told the story of Courtney, an episode, Jolene was sure, he thought of every day. Yet the physical act of speaking it aloud had brought with it a weight that he had not obviously experienced in quite a while.

"You could have answered that, you know?" Ratliff said finally. Jolene remained silent. "I don't mind. If you need to call him back, go ahead."

"It's okay," Hartley said. "I can call him back later."

"Okay," he replied, lifting his coffee mug to his lips. "He seems like a pretty good guy," he added. "Like I said, I didn't mean to go behind your back. But now that it's in the open, I like him. He's a decent guy."

"I don't remember asking for your approval," she said a bit too harshly, regretting the comment even as it fell from her lips.

"I didn't think you were looking for it," he answered with a firm, yet sensitive tone. "Just making conversation." He looked to the table. "You guys serious?"

She stared at him as she fought an inner battle on whether to curb the personal route this conversation now seemed to be taking. "Not that it's any of your business, but I like him, yes."

"That wasn't the question," he said with a smile.

Stop with that smile! she thought as she looked around the restaurant. "I don't see how this is relevant."

"It's not. I was just asking."

"Well maybe we can just focus on our case instead of James."

He nodded. "Sure. I get it." They stared at each other for a moment before he grinned once more, an action that caused Jolene to roll her eyes and relinquish her seat. "Hartley?" he called after her as she continued towards the exit. "Jo!" She turned and glanced at him nervously, angered at herself for her unsteadiness. "Where are you going?" he asked with his arms wide.

"I, uh …" She scratched her head, realizing they were too far from the precinct to make a stroll seem casual. She pointed to the door yet remained stationary. She felt unbalanced, out of control with the current situation. She needed stability. She needed something — anything — to divert the tempest of feelings that were battling within her body. And worse yet, she felt with each smile he displayed, he knew it as well. His confidence was infuriating, yet at the same time it was clouding her mind.

Ratliff nodded to her and wiped his mouth before standing and retrieving a wad of bills. He left a substantial tip for the waiter and followed, stopping directly in front of her as she looked to him with burning eyes, her lips tight across her exquisite face. She nearly reached up and grabbed his neck when he placed his hand on her arm, the image of her lips locking with his sending a tingle throughout her body. "Come on," he said finally, extending his arm past her towards the exit. "Let's go to the station. I won't pry anymore." She blushed as she turned, nodding her head and making her way to the unmarked vehicle in the parking lot, thinking to herself that she was definitely screwed when it came to her men.

TWENTY

The APB out on Luke Moran turned up nothing. Several patrol units had reported back to the command center that they were in pursuit of an individual that fit the description of Moran, yet all were unsuccessful in either contacting said person or locating the correct man.

Hartley and Ratliff were excited to learn that Kyle Walker had been brought into the precinct roughly forty-five minutes prior to their arrival and sat contained in the interrogation room with nothing but his thoughts and a small cup of room temperature water. Hartley was surprised when Captain Nolan told her that Walker had not requested his lawyer present upon arrival, seemingly hoping that whatever they needed him for would be short and sweet. Twenty-five minutes into his wait he had grown impatient and began a quick pacing session in front of the one-way mirror. Thirty minutes into the debacle, Jane Flannery, Walker's attorney, had contacted Nolan stating that she had been made aware of Walker's situation, however, she was indisposed and that no one was to question her client until she was present.

"Are you serious?" Hartley asked incredulously.

"About what?" Nolan replied as he made his way back to his desk.

"About what you just said. About not being able to question him."

"I don't know what you're talking about," Nolan responded with a shrug of his shoulders. "I've been waiting for you to get back for a while. It's not my fault I didn't see you go directly into the interrogation room without stopping to check in." He smiled and turned, closing the door and blinds of his office.

Hartley smirked and directed Ratliff to follow her towards the interrogation room. "Let me lead," she said. Kyle Walker sat cross-legged with his hands folded neatly on the table before him. As soon as the door opened to the room, his face softened, his anger being put behind the façade he now threw before the detectives. Hartley made her way to the far chair on the opposite side of Walker without looking to him, instead reading a file that contained some of the aspects of her current investigation, along with Walker's past discretions.

"Hope you haven't been waiting too long," she said as she sat, Ratliff eyeing the assistant editor as he took his place next to his partner.

"About an hour in this room with nothing to read," he responded lightly. "Been a great start to the day. Not like I have a magazine to run or anything."

"You don't," Ratliff said as he shifted in the hard, metal chair. "Mr. O'Dowd's the Editor." Walker turned his attention from Hartley and glared at him. "Technically it's his magazine."

"Thank you for clarifying for me."

"Mr. Walker," Hartley interrupted. "What's the deal with Bart Reed working on fluff pieces?"

Kyle Walker looked to her yet remained silent. He shrugged and said, "I don't understand the question."

"Seems like a pretty simple one to me," Hartley answered as she folded her hands on the open file folder and gazed up to him, her intense eyes locking onto his. "You told me Mr. Reed was working on fluff pieces."

"That's right," he stated matter-of-factly.

"Why?"

"What do you mean why? We told you that's just what he was working on."

"Cut the shit, Mr. Walker," she said firmly. "We know he was working on something bigger than mediocre filler content."

"I assure you he wasn't —"

"And I assure you he was," she quickly added, her face taut, lips pursed.

Walker studied her for a moment before shrugging once more. "If he was, it wasn't for us, which would be unfortunate."

"Why?"

"Because we hired him on as a full-time reporter. Freelancing for another magazine wouldn't be the best thing for a man in his position."

"Be enough to get him killed?"

Walker laughed. "Come on, detective. You really believe that going behind our backs with another story to another agency would be grounds for murder? Maybe termination of his job, but not his life. Reedy was a great journalist, making good money —"

"Which keeps me coming back to a single question: why have your great journalist writing fluff pieces?"

"How would I know why he's —"

"You should, Mr. Walker," she interrupted yet again, her stone-cold gaze never leaving him. "According to you and Mr. O'Dowd, you know everything that's going on with your reporters. It's your job to know. So I'll ask you again: why have Bart Reed, your award-winning reporter, do shit pieces on things no one cares about?" Walker remained fixed on her with his hands folded, yet said nothing. Hartley caught his lower jaw shift downwards as if he were running his tongue across his teeth, a movement she had witnessed a hundred times with suspects trying to come up with an answer.

She decided to keep the flow of conversation going instead of listening to a lie. "Melinda — Bart's wife — she said that there was definitely something going on. Bart was one hundred percent working on something. Do you know about that?" Walker slowly shook his head. "Of course, you said he wasn't working on anything major." She looked down to the files in front of her, shifting through papers as she spoke. "Did you know that when they found Reed's body, there was something that had been taken from inside the car? Would you happen to know what that was?"

Walker shrugged. "Why would I know —"

"Well, after meeting with Mrs. Reed at her recently robbed home, there were a couple things missing there too. One of them was a briefcase he kept under a chair in his office. The other was his personal laptop." She looked back up to him with her icy eyes. "He never went anywhere without them. Which leads me and my partner to believe that what was taken from the car were those two items." She remained silent for several seconds as if trying to coax a response from Walker. He said nothing. "Do you see where I'm going with this, Mr. Walker?"

"Not in the least, detective," he responded calmly, yet with a hint of anxiety that Hartley had been keen on perceiving. "Like I said, if Reedy was working on something, it wasn't for us."

"That just doesn't make sense, though," Hartley continued. "Reed made good money at your magazine, right?" Walker stared to her, tight-lipped. "Mr. Walker, I can have a warrant for Mr. Reed's financials drawn up. It'll take a while, though, which means you'll be sitting here all day. Or you can just answer the question and make this whole thing go much quicker. I'll ask again. Did Bart Reed make good money?"

"Award-winning journalists usually do," Walker responded.

"So he had a good, steady paycheck coming in. This is what doesn't make sense to me, and maybe you can help clear it up. You say Reed's doing freelance. Mrs. Reed says otherwise. With a solid income and knowing that if he gets caught doing outside work there's a possibility of termination, why would Bart Reed even put himself in that situation? Why risk it? And why not tell Melinda that he was doing freelance, if that was indeed the case?"

Walker smirked and shrugged, unfolding his hands as he shifted his weight and crossed his arms. "I don't know. Maybe he was lying to her."

"Maybe," Hartley repeated quietly. "Or maybe you're lying to me." She stared at him with the intensity of the burning sun.

Ratliff watched the proceedings from next to her, actually feeling himself grow slightly nervous as Hartley worked the man across from him. Walker's face had become expressionless, which, in most cases would have benefited him. Yet when dealing with Jolene Hartley, a woman Ratliff had begun to respect on a whole new level within the last ten minutes, Walker's demeanor did nothing but show his hand. Ratliff watched as the smirk slipped off his face and crashed to the floor. He witnessed the arms retreat from the table to form a protective barrier around his body.

Finally, Walker spoke, a decision that only fueled Hartley's fire. "I've told you the truth, detective."

"Is that right?" Hartley said with more force. "And does that truth happen to include *not* meeting my brother, Dane Hartley, yesterday regarding the story Bart Reed was working on?" Ratliff watched as Kyle Walker stared to his partner, saw his upper lip quiver ever so slightly as tiny beads of perspiration began to form across his brow. "Why did your boss blatantly tell me that he did not know Dane when in fact he had met with him earlier that morning?"

Walker thought for a moment before responding. His voice, Ratliff noticed, was not as strong as it once had been. "You'll have to ask my boss that question. If I had to guess —"

"Please do," she added.

He glared at her before continuing. "I'd guess that Mr. O'Dowd told you that to protect your brother." Hartley's eyebrows furrowed as she tried to make sense of the comment. "Sometimes we at *State of Finance* like to protect our writers' identities by keeping them confidential."

"Does that include when there's been a homicide?"

"I didn't know your brother was part of the Reed investigation," he responded quickly.

"You didn't know he was part of the investigation," she repeated. She leaned into the table towards him. "Did you know someone put a bomb in his apartment last night?"

"I think I read about that in the paper this morning," Walker said without emotion.

"Mr. Walker, do you know a man by the name of Luke Moran?"

Ratliff watched as Kyle quickly set his jaw and shifted in his chair. "Doesn't ring a bell, no."

Hartley smirked before turning her eyes back to the files before her. She halted briefly before looking back up to him.

"Moran was following me the other night. We got a hit on him in the database. You know what he's really good at?" Walker shook his head slowly. "Building and dismantling bombs. Picked it up in the military. Before that —"

At that moment the door to the interrogation room burst open and a blonde-haired woman in her early fifties burst through. Hartley's gaze remained fixed on Walker as both the assistant editor of *State of Finance* and Ratliff shifted their eyes to Jane Flannery. She made her way hurriedly to the table and positioned herself over her client's left shoulder. "This session is done!" she stated firmly, pulling Hartley's eyes to her. "My client has nothing more to say. Unless you have reason to arrest Mr. Walker, we will be leaving now."

Walker shifted in his seat before rising slowly, his hands smoothing out the suit he had chosen for the day. He looked to Hartley with a smirk before saying, "I'm sorry to hear about your brother, detective. It's a shame. The story he was looking into would have been something."

Jane Flannery led Walker towards the door as the detectives remained seated. Just as the assistant editor passed through the threshold Hartley spoke. "Mr. Walker," she said, stopping both attorney and client in their tracks. "Thank you for your condolences. Dane was a great writer." Walker nodded and began to turn. Hartley continued as she rose from her seat. "And I'm sure whatever he was looking into will find a home with another reporter." Walker stopped and stared to her. "Dane and I weren't really on speaking terms, as he told you. But before the explosion at his apartment, we had somewhat patched things up. Enough so that he gave me the files regarding what Reed had given him. He thought it could help out the investigation."

Walker stared at her with fire in his eyes, visibly shaken before Jane Flannery grabbed his arm and pulled him towards the exit. Hartley watched after them with a smile as they disappeared down the stairwell, seeing her partner from the corner of her eye look to her, an expression of awe across his face. She could not help but crack a mischievous smile and glance at him. "I'm *that* good," she said and walked out of the room.

TWENTY-ONE

Hartley sat facing her computer with Ratliff rocking back and forth in his chair, their thoughts collectively twisting through the proceedings moments before with Kyle Walker. She was pleased with the way things had gone. They had technically not received any information from Walker other than he and Seamus O'Dowd indeed had met her brother, as well as the fact that they believed Dane to have perished in the explosion the previous day. "I'm confused on one thing though," Ratliff said. "Why didn't you mention him being Eric Sheehan? Seems to me that his alter ego would be the thing to get him riled up the most."

Hartley shook her head. "Walker's not a dumb guy. If I would have played that card he would have trumped me by clamming up and not giving us anything."

"Didn't really seem like he gave us all that much in the first place," Ratliff replied.

"Yeah, but leading with that would have set his mind racing right in the direction we don't want it to go." She paused, catching a glimpse of Ratliff's confused face. "Okay," she began again, leaning towards him. "The way I see it is that we've lit a fire here. You say the name Sheehan and immediately Kyle Walker is connecting the dots. Sheehan and Moran are connected. People tend to zip their lips once you start putting two and two together. Right now, in Walker's head, he's running through the scenarios of where we are in our investigation as well as can he be connected. Moran, in his mind, is just a coincidence. It's a coincidence that a military bomb expert just happens to appear when Dane's apartment blows up. Add into the mix that I make no point of hiding that I think Walker's a jackass, and asking about Moran just seems like we're grasping at straws. In Walker's mind, we have no proof of a connection to Moran. Hell, there wouldn't even be a connection except that you happened to recognize Arland Landry."

"You're welcome," Ratliff said, legs wide and hands clasped behind his head as he took the theory in. Hartley could see from her periphery the smile across his face as he stared to the ceiling. She stole a glance at him and quickly looked away as he stopped moving and sat up straight, his shirt bunching at his muscular shoulders and his eyes moving to her. "I'm going to grab a coffee. Can I get you one?"

"Sure," she said in a chipper tone.

"Okay," he said and stood, weaving his way towards the kitchen. "Sugar? Cream?" he yelled back. She shook her head as he disappeared.

Hartley woke her computer with a shake of the mouse and stared at the monitor as she collected her thoughts. Save for the most recent activity with the *State of Finance* Assistant Editor, she felt as if the investigation was moving at a snail's pace. Nothing had jumped out at them and she needed to dig deeper into the potential players. When Ratliff returned she looked up to him with determination. "We need to set a game plan."

"What about going to rattle O'Dowd's cage?" Ratliff offered.

She thought about it for a moment before shaking her head. "Let's let them stew for a little bit. By the time we'd get over there, Walker would have already tipped O'Dowd off. We'll figure them out soon." She paused and thought before continuing. "We need to dig a little more. Take a look into Intervise Securities. We need to know what's going on with them and how they tie into this whole thing. We need to work the angle that whatever Reed was trying to hand off to Dane is the reason he was killed."

"Have you heard from your brother?" Ratliff asked.

She rolled her eyes. "No. He's supposed to get in contact with me, but who knows?"

"He didn't leave you a number?"

"I didn't know where he was going," she replied with a shrug. "Dane's not the most trusting person. This may be a murder investigation, but he's still working on a story. I really doubt he's going to be checking in with every lead he gets."

"How are we supposed to know when he's found anything useful?"

"Who knows? I'll give him the benefit of the doubt that he'll eventually get in touch with me. But for the time being, let's keep working off what we have so far."

"Okay. I'll dig into Intervise and see what I can come up with. What are you going to do?"

"I'm going to try and find more on our friend Eric Sheehan. I have a hunch that a change of name and location in his youth didn't alter his character all that much. I refuse to believe Moran's appearance and Dane's apartment are a coincidence. That just doesn't sit will with me. Regardless, we need the proof."

* * * * *

Eric Sheehan had had a troubled youth, Hartley found out. He had been born into an Irish Catholic family led by an alcoholic father who mentally and verbally abused his mother and siblings on a daily basis. His mother, Brenna — no saint herself — had taken to drugs as a teenager and tumbled into a cesspool of a life at the age of sixteen, separating her time between the back alleys of sketchy neighborhoods and guest rooms of family members and friends. She had met Sebastian Sheehan at the age of nineteen through mutual friends, connecting with him from time to time when she needed money to support her habit and he had the desire to satisfy his sexual urges. On one such occasion they conceived their first and only son, Eric. It was a less-than romantic affair, Brenna bent over a snow-covered garbage can in an alley, a wad of money clutched in her hand and her pants around her ankles as Sebastian took control.

The two, though their problems with drugs and infidelity continued, were nonetheless Irish Catholics, and a child born out of wedlock was enough to garner them a one-way ticket out of their respective communities, let alone families.

Eric Sheehan grew up in a loose knit family, never being that close with either of his parents or three sisters. A file, which Hartley now read, stated that an investigation into a shooting at the Sheehan household that left Sebastian in critical condition never amounted to much and was shelved after several weeks. The investigating officer noted, however, "the fierceness of the fourteen year old Eric" and a mother that seemed "less than worried about her husband and more proud of the young male." All signs pointed to an altercation that ended in Eric putting a bullet in his father's spine.

The rap sheet on Eric Sheehan followed quickly after the family dispute. Hartley read through a series of crimes, many of which included probation, house arrest and jail time: assault and battery; domestic violence; public intoxication; resisting arrest; theft; trespassing; blackmail; larceny; fraud. Each item on the list gave a detailed account of what transpired and who was involved. Hartley made note of Luke Moran's name on several occasions.

* * * * *

Ratliff sighed deeply in frustration as he clicked with his mouse. He could find nothing in regards to fraud or any other misgivings when it came to Intervise Securities and its CEO, J. R. Francesco. He ran across the same information as before when rummaging around the internet earlier in the day.

Intervise Securities was a small corporation when compared to other financial firms, yet had a strong, loyal customer base that had grown with the company. Started in 1977, Intervise was the brainchild of an Italian immigrant by the name of Jacomo Rafaele Francesco, a graduate of *Sapienza – Università di Roma*. Francesco was a lifelong academic until starting the company at the age of fifty-eight, holding multiple degrees, masters and doctorates in economics, finance and business.

Francesco had been blessed with brains and wealth at the moment of his birth. His family came from money. Each of his living relatives had some major function in a booming industry within the Italian borders. Besides Francesco, only a handful of his relatives seemed to have exported their talents to countries around the globe. He had a cousin who had made a name for herself in Russia, buying up plummeting companies only to restructure and turn them into industry leaders before selling them off to the highest bidder. Another cousin had ridden the coattails of his father in the automobile industry, buying up a scooter manufacturer in Finland and planning out a diverse line of motorized vehicles that was sure to garner attention in the United States. Unfortunately his cousin also inherited a drinking problem from his father and was killed in an automobile accident six months before the line of scooters was to launch. The company fell into disarray and never recovered.

* * * * *

The paperwork on Eric Sheehan ended abruptly in the early '90s. There were no more notes on his whereabouts or what he and his associates were involved in. All arrests halted. In questioning individuals he tended to run the streets with, it seemed Sheehan had taken initiative of his life finally and escaped what would inevitably end in a jail cell or a grave.

Hartley clicked around on her desktop and searched through the files once more. She stopped on a mug shot of a young Eric Sheehan, smirking as she looked upon the face of the Assistant Editor of *State of Finance*. "How'd you get to the magazine?" she asked aloud, yet quiet enough where no one heard.

She leaned back in her chair and crossed her arms over her chest. Hartley had hit a standstill in her research into Eric Sheehan. Things had been well documented in his youth and through a multitude of arrests as a teenager and twenty-something. He had been accounted for most of his life, thanks in part to his parents' mishaps. Then, in his late twenties, Sheehan seemed to vanish from the radar. *Most likely to Ireland like Landry said*, Hartley thought.

She leaned forward again and minimized the file on Eric Sheehan, instead turning to his parents, Sebastian and Brenna. Arland Landry had stated that Sheehan had family that would take him in, yet nowhere in her research did she find any connection to Ireland. For all she could tell, Sheehan knew no one in the motherland.

* * * * *

Ratliff was stunned when he found an article on J. R. Francesco in *The New York Times* from 1999. He had located Francesco's name in virtually every instance where Intervise Securities cropped up in an article, yet all of them briefly mentioned him as the company's CEO and nothing more. *The New York Times* article seemed to be an exposé of Intervise's owner and the deconstruction of his mental capacity.

Francesco, along with battling cancer for a number of years, had suffered a stroke and had had three minor heart attacks. The stroke, though trivial in regards to memory and verbal skills, had left him with a limited sense of mobility, which only emphasized his deteriorating social abilities. Ratliff was in awe to find out that Jacomo Rafaele Francesco, head of a twelve billion dollar corporation, was following in the footsteps of Howard Hughes.

* * * * *

She smiled to herself as, after nearly an hour of searching, Hartley had found the connection she had been looking for, though she did not know what it meant in the grand scheme of things. Eric's father, Sebastian Sheehan, had been born in the states, though Sebastian's father, Aedan, had not.

Aedan Sheehan, Eric's grandfather, had been born in a rough neighborhood in Tralee, County Kerry, Ireland, a gritty town situated at the eastern end of the Dingle Peninsula. Aedan had immigrated with his family to New York and from there had spread out across the nation. Aedan's sister, Regan, had, after a time, decided to return to her home country and settled in Dublin, where, upon arrival, had met and married Padraic Leary. The Learys, as far as Hartley could surmise, had remained in Dublin from that time until present.

Hartley exhaled deeply, drawing Ratliff's eyes to her. She glanced at him and shook her head in apology before standing and making her way towards the kitchen and another cup of coffee. "No thanks," she heard her partner call after her with a sarcastic tone. "I didn't want any more."

* * * * *

"So what did you come up with?" Hartley asked as she placed a new mug of fresh, hot coffee in front of her partner.

"Ah, thank you!" he said excitedly, lifting the aroma into his nostrils with a wave of his hand.

"No problem," she replied.

"Not much more than before."

"Why don't you recap for me?"

"Okay. Intervise Securities. Established late 1970s." He paused and clicked around the computer screen. "1977, to be exact, by Jacomo Rafaele Francesco. J. R. was born in 1919, fought for *Il Duce* in World War II, and immigrated to the States in the early '60s."

"Born in 1919? And he's still alive?" Hartley asked with surprise.

Ratliff nodded. "Alive, but according to what I could find, not well."

"How so?"

"Well, the last full-fledged article I could find about him where he actually took part was from 1999. He's had cancer, heart attacks, strokes, brain tumors. A whole mess of things that are bad enough by themselves. And on top of that, he's apparently well on his way to becoming the Italian version of Howard Hughes." Hartley's eyebrow rose quizzically. "You don't know who ...? Nevermind. He's a hermit. There's been no contact with the outside world — well, at least the media — in a little over a decade."

"So, for all intents and purposes, J. R. Francesco could, at the moment, be dead?"

"Could be."

"So where does that lead us now?"

"To Damian Verland, Director of Operations and Vice President of Intervise Securities. I'm hoping we can get in touch with him and see what he knows about all of this."

"Have you tried to reach him?" Ratliff shook his head. "Maybe give him a buzz in a bit. See if we can't meet and ask him a few questions."

"What about Walker? Find anything else?"

"Typical bad boy youth. Horrible upbringing. Not a lot of authority figures around — well, other than cops. Disappeared from police records in the early '90s. Matches the timeframe that Arland Landry said he got out of the country." She leaned back in her chair and swiveled back and forth. "I found a connection back to Ireland through Walker's grandfather on his dad's side. The whole family seems to have stayed in the States except for a sister. She headed back to the motherland and ended up in Dublin where she married. Last name Leary. Ring a bell?"

Ratliff shook his head. "Not at all. So we think that Walker headed to Dublin to get out of the limelight?"

Hartley shrugged. "Who knows? There could be other connections I haven't come across yet. It's the only one I got though."

Ratliff chuckled. "Hate to say this, but I don't think our databases cover Ireland."

"I know," Hartley said with a smile. "But I think I have someone in mind that can help us out."

"Who?"

Her smile faded as she looked to her computer. "Someone that works on a bigger scale then the Chicago Police Department."

TWENTY-TWO

From the corner of his eye he watched as Hartley fiddled with a dusty Rolodex situated on the corner of her desk, her graceful fingers gently swiping the aged grime from the plastic cover before bouncing to a stray pencil inches away, an item she utilized as a stress-relieving drumstick as the eraser emitted a low, steady *thump-thump-thump.* She seemed slightly anxious to Ratliff, like the call she was planning to make was a dreaded event. He asked her if she wanted him to do it and received a scowl followed by stern directions. "Just call and get a meeting with Intervise."

He picked up his phone and dialed, immediately connecting with a surly receptionist that stated Damian Verland was currently indisposed and could not be bothered. Between annoyed sighs she assured the detective that the Director of Operations and VP at Intervise Securities would be in touch as soon as possible, however she could not give a timetable as her superior was a very busy man.

Ratliff took several moments to concoct his next plan, one that Hartley — now staring blankly to her screensaver — had not given him. He picked up his receiver and made the necessary calls to request the financial movements within accounts for Kyle Walker, Seamus O'Dowd and J. R. Francesco. The last he was unsure would be possible, due to the fact that there was no probable cause to look into the old man's personal funds. Besides, Ratliff had thought to himself, the amount of money the man pulled in each week would probably hide anything that was coming from the suspected embezzlement scheme.

He hung up the phone and turned in his chair to speak to Hartley, halting once he saw the receiver perched between her ear and shoulder. Her eyes were vacant and she was chewing on her thumbnail, her free hand holding down the button to link the call.

"Jo?" he asked.

He was surprised when she answered quickly, obviously not zoning out completely. "Don't do it again, Ratliff."

He laughed nervously. "Just making sure you're there. Do you need me to make any calls?" he prodded. She remained silent, unblinking. "Okay. Well, do you need me to get some smelling salts or something? I'm worried that you may have just fallen asleep with your eyes open."

"I'm thinking," was the only answer he received.

"About —"

"Shut up." She moved quickly then, her eyes darting to the phone base and her finger rising from the button, dancing across the keypad as she punched in a series of numbers that she no doubt had dialed dozens of times before. She leaned forward in her seat and waited, her eyes glazing over once more as the line began to ring.

Ratliff leaned back in his chair and crossed his legs, folding his arms across his chest and staring towards his partner, an action she caught from the corner of her eye. Hartley thought of turning and ordering Ratliff to go make coffee or fetch the mail, but she did neither. She was apparently destined to have an audience. She caught her breath as the call connected and the familiar voice on the other end spoke.

* * * * *

He stood in a conference room adjacent to his office, staring at a whiteboard with photos of known criminals plastered to every square inch. Things had not gone as planned recently, with a spree of criminal activity running rampant throughout the city, everything from domestic disturbances to robberies to murder.

He rubbed his hand over his face, feeling the stubble run across his palm. He had not shaved in three days. Hell, he had not been home in four, working such late hours that he found himself curled up on the waiting room couch just down the hall. He could not remember the last time he took a shower. Yesterday morning? Two days ago? The days were beginning to blend together.

A chiming began to ring in his ears, very faintly, drawing his attention from the whiteboard to the hallway to his left. He turned quickly to the conference table behind him and eyed the phone sitting there, watching and waiting for the ringing to begin again. It did not, at least not from this room.

He reached down with both hands to either pocket of his dark gray jeans and realized at once he was not carrying his cell phone. The ringing chimed again and sent him scuttling from the room, taking a quick right and moving to his office ten feet down the hall.

He turned into the threshold and immediately noticed his cell phone vibrating hazardously near the edge of his desk. He reached out and snatched it up, lifting the display to his face and squinting his eyes into focus. A smile formed wide across his face at the name crossing the screen.

Jolene Hartley.

He pressed his thumb down on the answer button and put the phone to his ear.

* * * * *

"Hey, Jo!" came the response from the other end of the line.

Jolene leaned forward with a slight smile and responded. "Hey, Ronny," she said to her ex, the soothing sound of his voice dissolving whatever tension she had built up within the last several minutes. "How's everything going?"

"Good, you know. Living the dream," he replied with a weary laugh. Jolene could envision him rubbing his eyes the way he did throughout their relationship when things were tough.

"You don't sound too convincing."

"Didn't even convince myself. Been up for way too long."

"Yeah? Rough night?"

"Rough couple of nights. When's the last time you saw me with a beard?"

Jolene could not stifle her laugh. "Can you even grow a beard?"

"Of course I can grow a beard! Not saying it doesn't look strange, but yes. When we're done, I'll take a picture and send it to you." They laughed together for several seconds before he continued. "How's everything going there? How are you?"

"Doing well. Everything's good," she answered, feeling Ratliff's eyes on her.

"Good. The ribs heal up yet?"

"Yeah."

"Awesome," he replied. They remained silent for a moment before he spoke again. "I'd like to think this was just a pleasure call, but I think I'd be wrong."

"Unfortunately, yeah," she responded. "I've got a favor to ask."

"Shoot."

"I need your resources to track down someone."

"What did they do?"

"Not sure yet. We're trying to piece that together now."

"We?" Debarsi asked with intrigue. "They finally stick you with a new partner?"

Hartley turned and faced Ratliff. "Yeah. Homicide rookie. Real piece of work." Ratliff smirked and nodded his head, glancing around the room as he took the ribbing with humor. Hartley remained straight-faced and turned her back to him.

"Well, I can see what I can do. I'll have to pass it off to someone else here, though. What do you need?"

Hartley proceeded to spew out the information on their case, everything from the murder of Bart Reed and attempted killing of her brother. "This is where it gets tricky. Kyle Walker's real name is Eric Sheehan. In the early '90s, this guy takes off and we believe he went to Ireland. That's where we lose him."

"Doesn't really seem like you lost him if he's Assistant Editor at *State of Finance*."

"Right, but we lose his connections. I want to figure out what he was doing over there. Who he stayed with? Did he continue his criminal activity? That sort of thing."

"Sure," Debarsi said as he wrote down the information. "And I'm assuming asking would get you nowhere?"

"Yeah," she responded. "He's been pretty tightlipped about everything so far. I doubt he'll start talking now. Plus, I don't want to give him any clue as to how this investigation's going. Into the murder or the embezzlement."

"Since when are you handling cases on fraud?" Debarsi said with a laugh.

"Since I'm pretty sure the two are related. Do you think you can help me out?"

"I can definitely see what I can do. Like I said, I'll have to pass this along to someone with Interpol connections. We agents assigned to bank robberies don't really dabble much in international topics. Give me a day or so?"

"Great, Ronny," she said. "Thanks a lot for this."

"Anything for you, Jo. You know that."

TWENTY-THREE

The phone call from Intervise Security occurred at the exact same moment Hartley ended her conversation with Debarsi. The receptionist Ratliff had spoken with previously suggested the detectives come meet with Damian Verland as soon as possible. "He's a busy man. But he insisted I cancel his next hour's meetings and pencil you in." Ratliff smirked at the phrase "pencil you in," knowing full well that if he needed to, he could cancel the VP's meetings himself, although repercussions were inevitable when dealing with someone in such a position as Verland's. Instead, Ratliff thanked the woman very much and said they would be over as soon as they could. She hung up as he said his goodbyes.

Ratliff looked to his partner as she drove the unmarked squad car into the city streets, her steady gaze locked onto the world outside, a thumbnail resting against her bottom teeth through parted lips. Ratliff had come to the quick conclusion that, visually, Jolene Hartley was extremely pleasant on the eyes. It was hard not to notice her external gifts. Yet with each passing hour, with each event that occurred, that beauty rose to a whole new level. She was not only an angelic face underneath goddess-like flowing brown hair. She was also a driven, humorous individual with a tenacity that was beginning to overshadow her exquisite exterior.

At that moment, lost in his thoughts and eyes glued to his partner, Hartley glanced sideways to him, catching Ratliff with the start of a smirk on his face. He did not mind much that he had just been caught checking her out, though he quickly conjured his next move to sidestep her wrath yet again. "So who is Ronny?" he blurted out.

She remained silent for a moment before answering. "Ronny Debarsi used to be a detective at our precinct. He's an FBI agent in Philly now. Works on a unit assigned to bank robberies."

"How long has he been in Philly?"

"Just under a year," she responded matter-of-factly.

Silence filled the car as they drove on, though Hartley could feel her partner looking at her with a grin from time to time. Finally she glanced to him with a scowl. "What?" she asked.

He smirked before responding. "You and Ronny were close, huh?"

"Why do you always have to bring up shit like this?"

"Hey, you're the one that made the big deal out of it!" he answered. "Should I call him? Should I wait? What should I say?" he said with his hands mimicking a scale, the tone of his voice rising to a more feminine pitch.

Hartley glared at him yet could not help but find the humor in his display. She shook her head and ran her fingers through her hair as Ratliff laughed. "I hate you," she finally replied, a smile forming on her lips.

"I know," he rebutted, looking to her.

She thought for a minute before giving in to him. "Ronny and I were an item for four years, okay? He left for Philly and we went our separate ways."

He nodded his understanding. "And it's still a little weird, I'm guessing."

"A little. It's a little weird. But then again, I don't ever call on him for police favors." She caught herself as a wide smile crossed his face. "Or any favors! God, you're a child!"

"Hey! You're the one that said it. I was just going to say it gets easier."

"Oh yeah? You have a lot of experience with things like this?" she prodded.

"I've had my fair share of weird breakups. None with a coworker, but weird, nonetheless."

"I don't go dating coworkers all the time," she added, suddenly feeling the need to clarify her situation with Debarsi.

"But you made an exception though," he said, nodding his head in understanding.

"Yep," she agreed. "I made an exception."

He glanced out his side window before turning to her and saying, "Well, it's nice that you make exceptions in that regard." He smiled before focusing his attention once more to the road, reaching up and grabbing the handle above the door as they made a turn. Hartley thought about the comment for a moment before realizing he had once again thrown out another hint in their growing relationship, this time surprising herself when she smirked and glanced to the street.

* * * * *

"Kobayashi," Ratliff said quietly as they stood in the waiting room and watched a man approach from the other end of the hall.

"What?" Hartley asked, completely perplexed at Ratliff's utterance.

"He looks like Kobayashi from *The Usual Suspects*," he replied. Hartley gave him a questioning glance. "Come on. *The Usual Suspects*? Kevin Spacey? Gabriel Byrne? Benicio Del Toro?" Hartley shook her head, yet smirked. "Tell me you haven't seen that movie."

"I haven't seen that movie," she repeated, trying to hide her amusement. "Is it good?"

Ratliff turned his attention from Damian Verland's approach to his partner. "*Is it good*?" he said, his voice raising enough to grab the attention of the receptionist. He apologized and leaned towards Hartley. "Once this case is over —"

"I've seen it. Shut up," she said, cutting him off and bringing silence to the room once more.

Damian Verland walked into the room with a swift saunter, his appearance a dead ringer for a Pete Postlethwaite clone. His hair was picture perfect, the part on the left edge of his head clean and straight as it folded into a tidy combover to the right. Serious, yet kind eyes peered from beneath bushy brown eyebrows and around a bulbous nose that separated prominently high cheekbones. He was a thin man of less than average height, yet immediately Hartley could tell he was a man of power within Intervise Securities. "Detectives," he said. "My apologies for not being accessible before. I'm Damian Verland. You must be Detective Ratliff."

"Thank you for your time," Ratliff said to the man, taking his hand firmly. "This is my partner, Detective —"

"Jolene Hartley," Verland interrupted, grasping her hand delicately. "I've read about you in the papers."

"Have you now?" Hartley said. "A man in your position getting a lot of free time to read surprises me."

"Well, everyone needs an escape from his or her life," he responded. "Mine just happens to be the newspaper." He smiled delightfully. "The pictures in the paper don't do you justice, my dear."

"Thank you," Hartley replied with a grin.

"Now, what can I do for you?"

"We happen to be investigating a murder that happened several days ago," Ratliff said.

Verland raised his eyebrows in surprise. "Who was killed? Please tell me it wasn't someone I know."

"I guess that depends on if you know Bart Reed?" Hartley asked.

"Bart Reed? The reporter, Bart Reed?" Hartley nodded. "No, I can't say that I do. Bart Reed was murdered? By who?"

"That's what we're trying to find out," Hartley replied. "So you didn't know Mr. Reed?"

Verland shook his head. "Never met him before in my life."

"How'd you know he was a reporter?" Ratliff questioned.

Verland looked to him. "Like I said, I tend to bury myself in newspapers and books in my free time."

"With all the reading you do, how didn't you know Bart Reed was murdered? He's somewhat in the same industry as you."

"Indeed," Verland responded. "Unfortunately my hobby of being a bookworm hasn't been that productive as of late. We've had a minor crisis over the last several days that's taken my attention from anything but the job."

"What sort of crisis?" Hartley prodded.

"I'm sorry, detective. I'm not at liberty to discuss that at the moment. Not until the crisis is over and the legal team has said it's okay. I assure you, however, it has no bearing on your investigation."

"That's the thing, Mr. Verland," she continued. "I'm not sure that it doesn't."

He looked at her with a frown. "How do you mean?"

"Like my partner said, we're investigating the homicide of Mr. Reed, yet we have reason to believe that his murder was due to a piece that he was working on, either for *State of Finance* or as a freelancer."

"Oh, dear," Verland replied. He thought for a moment before continuing. "Pardon my being blunt, but how does this concern Intervise Securities?"

Hartley looked to Ratliff for a moment, weighing her options of either letting Damian Verland in on part of their investigation or not. She decided to go for it. "We have reason to believe that what Mr. Reed found and was in the process of working on at the time of his murder dealt with an embezzling scheme."

"With an Intervise client?" Verland asked.

"With Intervise itself," Hartley responded plainly. "It points to your CEO."

"Signore Francesco?" he exclaimed. "That can't be."

"And it may not," Ratliff added, stepping forward. "But what we have points to your boss embezzling money from Intervise clients. If we can prove otherwise, great. It's one less person on our list then."

Verland thought for a moment and raised his pointer finger. He opened his mouth to say something then shut it abruptly, lowering his hand and smoothing out his Armani suit. Hartley noticed his fingers rubbing together as the silence continued. "Mr. Verland," she interrupted, causing his eyes to jump to her. "If you have something, I need to know."

"Yes, of course," he replied, then remained silent again, glancing to the receptionist just out of earshot. He took a step closer and lowered his voice. "Intervise is a well-established corporation. Old business with old money. We've staked our reputation on being a credible entity in the eyes of our customers." He paused again, glancing once more to the woman behind the desk several yards away.

"Mr. Verland," Hartley pushed. "Spill it."

He nodded. "The minor crisis we were facing ... The people in Finance have noticed a large sum of money withdrawn from within our client accounts. Little bits here and there. Nothing that would send our clients into a tailspin or anything, but enough that the account it's going into is growing exponentially."

"What account is it going into?" Hartley prodded.

Verland looked at each detective in turn before responding. "It's being deposited into an account under the name of Isabella Bartollo."

Hartley glanced to Ratliff with a furrowed brow, noticing that he too could not make heads or tails of the name. "Who is Isabella Bartollo?"

"Isabella Bartollo is J. R. Francesco's daughter. She's been dead for nearly thirty years."

* * * * *

"How does a dead Isabella Bartollo have an open account?" Ratliff asked as he slid into one of Damian Verland's expensive, plush office chairs.

Hartley took a seat next to him as the VP of Intervise Securities took his spot behind his desk. "The fact that Isabella has an account open does not surprise me," he stated. "Many of Signore Francesco's relatives have had or currently have accounts open within Intervise. The strange part is that the only activity in nearly thirty years has occurred within the last couple days."

"How can that be, with Isabella deceased?" Hartley asked.

"I'm not sure. The finance department is checking into it now. There's a possibility that before her death, Isabella set up an end date for all of her assets to be transferred over." He put his finger to his mouth and thought for a moment, losing himself in the shine of his mahogany desk. "No," he continued, almost as if to himself. "That doesn't make much sense either."

"Why not?" Ratliff questioned, pulling Verland's attention back to the detectives.

"Well, I shouldn't say that. There's a possibility that before her death Isabella lent money to other investors with a deadline to draw her funds back at a given date. That I wouldn't know about in-depth, however."

"Why's that?"

"Because that all happened before my tenure began here. What I can tell you for certain is that some of the accounts that are being withdrawn from and showing up now in Isabella's were set up well after she had passed."

"Which means that there was no possible way for those clients to borrow from Isabella's account, due to her not being able to give the okay," Hartley chimed in.

"Precisely."

"Was there anyone else linked to the account? Someone that had access to Isabella's funds? Maybe, like, her father?"

Verland shrugged. "Not sure. Finance is checking into everything now. But I doubt it. Signore Francesco hasn't been in the best health for quite some time, as I'm sure you've read."

"Unfortunately, in our line of work, ill health doesn't necessarily carry a get-out-of-jail-free card," Ratliff added.

Hartley thought for a moment, deciding to turn the magnifying glass on the VP himself. "Do you mind if we ask you some questions?"

He nodded. "Please."

"Thank you," she replied, pulling out a notepad and pencil. Ratliff followed suit. "How long have you been working for Intervise Securities, Mr. Verland?"

"Oh, let's see," he said, trailing off in thought. "If memory serves correct, I've been working for Signore Francesco for thirteen years now. I came aboard just as his health began to decline."

"What is Mr. Francesco like?"

Verland sighed. "From what I've heard, he is a decent man. Not overly friendly, but not a pain in the ass, either. He seemed to be on top of his game when it came to the business."

"From what you've heard? What do you mean?" Hartley pressed.

"I've never met J. R. Francesco in person before," Verland said matter-of-factly. He stared at the two detectives as they glanced at each other with confused looks. "Allow me to explain," he began after a moment. "I *was* hired by Signore Francesco and I, to this day, work for him, although I have never seen him outside of old press clippings and such."

"How were you hired then?"

"In a series of phone interviews conducted by Signore Francesco."

"What were you initially hired on as?" Ratliff asked.

"Same position I am in now. Director of Operations and Vice President."

"Isn't that odd? I mean, coming into an extremely successful corporation from the outside and being placed into such a high up position?"

Verland shrugged. "I assure you, I'm no slouch, nor have I ever been. I came into this position knowing fully what needed to be done to make a successful corporation that much more powerful."

Ratliff held up a hand in submission. "Apologies," he said. "I didn't mean to insinuate you don't know what you're doing."

"No need to apologize, my boy. I didn't take it that way. I came from a background in finance. I've owned several of my own companies in the past. I'd like to think that Signore Francesco believed I was capable of running his corporation because I was good at what I do, although with this week's fiasco, I'm starting to doubt that myself."

"Does Mr. Francesco know what is going on at the moment within Intervise?" Hartley asked.

Verland shook his head. "I'd rather try to fix the matters at hand with the resources I have than scare an elderly man into another — possibly fatal — heart attack."

"How often are you in touch with Mr. Francesco?"

He thought for a moment. "He calls every couple of months or so. I'd say probably once every quarter he will get in touch. Signore Francesco is a ninety-two year old man and a powerhouse of business genius. If it weren't for his physical and social hindrances, I'm sure he would be here running the company himself."

"When was the last time you spoke with him?"

"I'm sorry," he said, leaning into the desktop and shaking his head. "I understand the questioning, however, to clarify for myself. Do you think Signore Francesco is at fault in the murder of Bart Reed?"

Hartley looked at him for a moment. "In truth: no. Like you said, Mr. Francesco is ninety-two. I seriously doubt he's running through the city shooting people. But as you stated, he is a cunning businessman, so we can't rule him out of the embezzlement scheme that has come up. Which in turn doesn't allow me to release him as a person of interest in my investigation."

"I understand," Verland replied, folding his hands and leaning back in his chair once more. "What was the question again?"

"When you spoke with Mr. Francesco last," Ratliff repeated.

"Ah, yes." He was silent a moment as his face grew long, his eyes peering out the side window into the sunlight. "I spoke with him a couple months back. A conversation that I wish had never come about."

"Why's that?" Hartley pressed.

"Signore Francesco called to make his usual check-ins. See how his accounts were doing and all that. Then he broke the news that his cancer had come back and spread to his brain. He said that he was dying and was in the process of selling off Intervise Securities to the highest bidder. He wanted to warn me that I would need to take some time to tell the staff and eventually help them find new positions elsewhere."

"Why not just let the company continue without him?"

Verland smirked. "That's what I suggested. Let me or someone in his family take over."

"What did he say to that?"

"Nothing. Like we've discussed, Signore Francesco is not of sound mind and body these days. Intervise is his brainchild. If he wants to it to leave this world with him, that's his prerogative."

"Have you begun to tell the staff?"

Damian shook his head. "As of yet, I have not been given the go-ahead to tell my employees."

"What about you?" Ratliff asked. "Where do you go from here once that happens?"

He shrugged. "Detective, I've made plenty of money to not work another day of my life. I'll be fine with whatever happens. It's just the principle of the matter. I've spent the last thirteen years of my life in this building. This company — these people — have become like family to me. Whatever happens, one thing is for sure: I'm going to miss walking through those doors day after day."

TWENTY-FOUR

They left Intervise Securities moments after their discussion with Damian Verland had ended. They felt no need to tour the vicinity or resume questioning with another member of the staff that would, no doubt, know less of the goings-on than the VP himself. Verland had seemed genuine and helpful when questions arose, and Ratliff, as well as Hartley, left the building feeling much more at ease with the direction their investigation was heading.

"Let's give him a day or so before issuing a warrant for their finances," Hartley replied as they made their way back towards the precinct, Ratliff behind the wheel as his partner scrunched up in the passenger seat next to him, her toes stretched to the windshield, a fog forming on the surface beneath her socks.

"What? You don't believe him?" Ratliff asked.

"It's not a question of belief," Hartley explained. "It doesn't matter what I believe. It's what I can prove."

"That doesn't sound police-like at all," Ratliff laughed. "'It's what I can prove.'"

Hartley looked to him and rolled her eyes. "Shut up," she replied, removing her feet from the dashboard and sliding on her shoes. "There's been plenty of times that I believed someone couldn't have done something. I remember there being facts that said so-and-so wasn't even around the scene. Turned out video evidence proved otherwise. Regardless of how nice I think someone is, it doesn't make them innocent."

"So what *do* you think of Mr. Verland of Intervise Securities?" Ratliff pushed.

Hartley laughed and shook her head. "You don't give up, do you?"

He looked at her with a grin. "Not when I want something."

She kept his gaze for a moment before turning her eyes to the windshield and the city before her. "I think Damian Verland is doing what he can to help our investigation. And I think that regardless of how old Mr. Jacomo Francesco is, he seems to be dirty in this whole scheme. And no," she added quickly, silencing her partner before he began, "I don't think Francesco killed Reed. Or Kelly Depler. But the evidence right now says he stinks."

They rode in silence for a while before Hartley spoke again. "Check into getting a warrant for Intervise Securities finances if we don't hear from Verland within the next day and a half. And while you're at it, check on Verland's and Francesco's finances too. I'd like to cover all our bases."

"Already got Francesco's in the works," Ratliff answered, causing Hartley to turn to him. "While you were waffling about calling your ex in Philly, I made a call to get Walker and his boss, as well as Francesco."

Hartley nodded slowly before turning her focus back to the windshield. "Good thinking," she said finally.

"Thanks," he replied, smirking at her before putting his eyes back to the road before him. They remained silent the rest of the way to the precinct.

* * * * *

Hartley and Ratliff walked up the stairs to their floor together in silence, each lost in thought on the day they had just gotten through. To Ratliff's dismay, however, his was not over, as Hartley assigned him one last task. "Check and see if anyone has come across Luke Moran," she said as he made his way to his desk. He held his arms wide. "It'll take two minutes, you baby!" she exclaimed and reached down to turn off her computer monitor, glancing to her phone to make sure there were no new voicemails pending. "I'll see you tomorrow."

"Where are you heading?" Ratliff asked as he took a seat and lifted his desk phone to his ear.

"To the gym," Hartley responded, surprising herself with her willingness to open up her agenda to him. "I'll see you tomorrow."

"Yeah," he said, watching as she moved to the end of the pit and turned down the hallway.

* * * * *

Her tanned skin glistened with perspiration, her shoulder muscles tensing and releasing underneath her Under Armor rib tank top as she struck the punching bag with quick, succinct jabs. Her silky, brown hair was pulled into a tight ponytail near the back of her head, although strands now clung to her forehead and cheeks. Her breathing came in short, rapid bursts, perfectly syncing with the movements she was now performing.

Jolene was not power training at the moment, though she had thought intently about doing some lifting to tone up, an idea any other officer that witnessed her in the tight workout attire would have laughed at. She had settled for the sparring bags instead, a mix of cardio and combat training that always freed her mind from whatever investigation she was currently working on, a release that she desperately needed at times.

She pounded the bag for nearly half an hour straight before pausing and making her way to the water fountain, releasing the Velcro straps of her sparring gloves and refilling her plastic container with the cool liquid. She took a long sip from the bottle, water spilling from the sides of her mouth as she rushed to get the hydration back into her system.

She moved away from the fountain and set her water bottle and gloves on the flat, blue mat in front of a mirror hanging from the wall opposite the sparring area. Jolene looked at her reflection for a moment, happy at the intensity she was able to put forth in today's workout. She was drenched in sweat and her muscles had a tingle to them, yet she still felt good.

She took a seat on the ground and wedged her feet underneath the metal clasps holding the mirror in place, shifting her weight so her legs were bent before her. She lay back onto the mat and folded her hands underneath her chin as she breathed in deeply, immediately diving into a regiment of sit-ups, varying the degree to which her torso rose as well as the twist in her waist. The rib injury she had received from her case with Taylor Thames felt good, nearly healed through, though once in a while a slight twinge of pain coursed its way sluggishly up her side. It did not stop her.

At fifty-two sit-ups her mind began to wander, shifting from her workout routine to James and her call to him moments before descending into the heart of the precinct. She was supposed to meet him for either dinner or drinks in the early evening, though at the last instant she had decided against it, canceling their plans for the moment and saying she would call him later after her sparring session. He had understood and said he would be around and available if she were to change her mind, as he hoped she would.

James had been on her mind recently, mainly due to the fact that he brought a childlike, carefree feeling out of her that she had not felt since she was a teenager. She had been so much about her job that it seemed she had neglected the fun side of life. Her time with Ronny Debarsi had been good, yet both of them were officers fully focused on their current investigations. Four years together had proven no match for the intensity brought on by the silver star they carried. They had parted ways amicably when he set off for Philadelphia and a career in the FBI.

She had been hurt, although understood what needed to be done for the advancement of his career. She, however, was not the type to drop everything and follow, nor would she ever be. Jolene Hartley was a beautiful, driven, independent woman who wanted to share her life with someone that could accept her as she was, not depend on her to be around at every beck and call. The truth of the matter was that her life as a homicide detective sometimes required her to work late hours. On many occasions Jolene had not even seen her apartment for three days straight, instead falling asleep in the break room — or not at all. Many instances saw her powering through the nights on a mixture of adrenaline and caffeine.

Then Benjamin Ochoa had been killed, and with the investigation into his murder came a web of unsolved homicides that pulled in one James Graiser, a young, quirky traveler of the world who had inherited a wealth that allowed him the freedom to do as he chose. James, through connections in his past, helped identify and track down the killer of Ochoa, and in turn had swindled his way into a date with the lovely detective. She had accepted, feeling a certain tingle in her stomach that she had not felt since her crushes in high school.

Jolene lifted her torso up one last time and wrapped her arms around her knees. She titled her head to the ceiling and breathed deeply, tasting the saltiness of her sweat upon her lips. She leaned to the side and retrieved her water bottle, unscrewing the cap and guzzling the remaining liquid before focusing her eyes on her reflection once more.

Her stomach was tense from the workout she had just endured, yet she did not feel quite ready to throw in the towel. She reached over and slid the sparring gloves over her hands once more, readying herself for round two with the punching bag. Jolene stood and raised her hands over her head, stretching the tension from her abdomen as she leaned from the left to right repeatedly. She stopped suddenly as she glanced to the mirror and caught sight of Ratliff coming up behind her in his workout clothes. His eyes were fixed on her rear.

She could not pass up the opportunity to call him out. "Etch it into your mind, Ratliff," she said, remaining still as her eyes focused on her partner.

He looked up to the mirror and caught her gaze, surprising her with a grin. "One more second and it would have been." She turned and glared at him momentarily before moving to the water fountain where she filled up her bottle once again. "Hey, were you about to do some sparring?" he asked, turning towards her.

She stared at him before answering. He was stretching on the blue mats, his toned, muscular arms in full view underneath his sleeveless t-shirt. She forced her eyes away and brought the bottle to her lips. "Was about to get back on the bag, yeah."

"What do you say to some sparring practice?" he said, pointing to the padded gloves resting against the far wall.

"No thanks," she replied.

"Come on," he said with a grin. "I'll go easy on you."

She smiled and shot him a cold, calculating look, thinking quickly before stepping forward. "I'm not worried about you taking it easy," she said confidently. "I'm worried about having more competition with the bags over there. I don't want to neglect my workout to make time for you."

He smiled as she set down her water bottle and lined up opposite him. "Good. I wouldn't want you to."

* * * * *

As she moved in a circle around her opponent, Jolene was distracted. She knew what she needed to be doing. She knew she needed to strike furiously and back away, dodge the sparring pad swinging towards her and sidestep the rush Jacoby threw from time to time. Yet for some reason she could not explain, her mind was not completely focused.

And then it happened, and she completely understood her lackadaisical motions.

Jolene found herself focusing on her partner's shoulders and face, glancing to his eyes and losing herself in the green orbs. She dispassionately jabbed with her left then right, the initial strike glancing off the edge of the sparring pad. The second missed altogether. She was preoccupied with his looks, the way he moved, his eyes being intently focused on her.

Bottom line: Jolene was smitten with him, and there was nothing she could do about it.

Jacoby swung the pad in a downward arc and watched as his partner ducked under the attempt at the last possible moment. He grazed her shoulder blade before she bounced back several feet and gave him a look that would have stopped most men dead in their tracks. "Watch that," she said fiercely, knowing as the words fell from her lips she was the one who needed to pay closer attention.

Ratliff smiled at her. "Move faster," he suggested. She came at him with a rush, working the pads furiously. He could feel her determination, sense the passion that led to her becoming the exceptional officer that she was.

Jolene caught the grin form on his face and immediately felt her adrenaline race as she envisioned wiping the smirk off herself. She parried a jab to the torso and countered with a right hook followed by her left. Jacoby stumbled backwards as the last blow grazed his chin and landed on his shoulder.

Hartley dropped her hands momentarily and smirked at him, her beauty apparent even from underneath the sweat and perseverance coating her façade. Ratliff glared back to her, surprised — and intrigued — by the strike she had delivered. He took a moment to switch from the sparring pads to his own set of gloves, tempting her into some one-on-one combat. She did not back down, instead raising her fists in acceptance.

He came at her just under full speed, swinging his hands wide as she rose up to block and counter, neither one seriously attempting to land a blow that may do damage. "So," he said between blocks, "did you ever call your boy back?" He smiled as the words fell from his lips, knowing that his partner had a difficult time opening up personally and that the suggested conversation just might get under her skin.

"Is that how you talk shit? By bringing up James?" she responded, ducking an attempted hook and responding by jabbing his exposed ribs with a left. "It may be better for you to stop fighting like a sissy." She stepped to the left and quickly sent a series of jabs towards his midsection, a melee that caused him to jump back on the defense.

Jolene looked to his eyes and grinned again, noticing the nod of his head as he silently congratulated her for the attack. "Hey, you're a formidable opponent," he said. "I was just wondering how he feels about you staying late after your shift to spar with your new partner?" She did not answer, yet stared at him as he approached. "One, who I might add, is ruggedly handsome and a joy to be around."

Jolene lashed out with the goal to yet again knock the smile from his face. Jacoby sidestepped the blow easily, reaching out to grab onto his partner's exposed right shoulder. Hartley realized she had overextended and spun quickly around, feeling his hand slide across her back. "You're cocky, you know that?" she asked, bouncing on the balls of her feet.

He advanced slowly with a shrug. "I'm confident is all," he replied. "So are you. I'm just more vocal about it." He jumped back as Jolene swung her leg up to his torso. "You telegraphed it."

"Next time I won't," she replied.

They circled for several moments, each eyeing the other and running possible attack scenarios through their minds. After a bit, Jacoby continued. "And you can't possibly think I believe you're not a confident woman. Not with impeccable looks like that."

Jolene paused for a brief second at the compliment and stared at him. Without hesitation he jumped forward and threw several quick jabs that caused her to veer to the side. Two shots landed near her right ribcage as she tumbled to the ground, swearing under her breath as she rolled to her feet. "The only difference between my confidence and yours is I'm not afraid to tell you that you're gorgeous and that you're messing around with someone who isn't a good match for you."

Jolene's heart raced as the words fell from his mouth. She was flattered and aggravated at the same instant as she looked upon him, the grin forming across his face yet again, the sweat soaking into his shirt and clinging to his body. At last she made her move, dancing to the right and beginning a kick that would inevitably take out her partner's knee. His hands dropped towards the ground in an attempt to block it.

Jolene was too quick, however, pulling her foot hastily back and bouncing to her left. She threw a punch into Jacoby's exposed right hip, causing him to buckle away from the assault, giving her room to lock her arms around his neck and wedge her right foot behind his unbalanced frame. With a quick jerk she had him tumbling backwards, colliding against the mat with his leg pinned between her thigh and calf. Her right forearm lodged under his chin and as she reached out with her left hand and pinned his arm to the mat. "Don't run your mouth about who's a good match for me. You don't know what I'm looking for. And it's horrible trash talk. You're better than that."

Jacoby looked up to her. "It may be, but I do know one thing though," he said.

"Yeah? What's that?"

He smiled wide before reaching his free left hand across Jolene's neck. She swore aloud as the realization that she had not secured his left arm hit her fully.

In one quick motion he pulled her head back, causing her to swing over him. He used her falling weight to propel himself into the air, grasping onto her arm and pinning it under her own body, his other hand locking onto her wrist above her head.

Jolene landed on her back, her arms forming an S shape starting above her head and ending between her torso and the blue mat. Jacoby had somehow maneuvered his frame enough to lock her legs together with one of his and had positioned himself atop her. She tried to struggle but it was no use. He had the upper hand.

She calmed herself and through heavy breathing focused on his intense, yet soft eyes hovering above her. Their faces were no more than a few inches apart and as Jolene and Jacoby stared at one another, they each caught the other glancing at the set of lips opposite them. Jolene's heart pounded. She was teetering on a precarious ledge. On one hand she was bothered that he had mentioned James yet again. He should have known that her personal matters were exactly that, regardless of if she happened to let him in to her sacred space earlier. Yet on the other hand she was fighting the intense urge to place her mouth against his, to feel the passionate kiss she was now envisioning.

From inches away he opened his mouth, his lips parting as he looked upon her face. She suddenly heard herself speak. "It's time for me to leave." He remained stationed over her for several moments, Jolene in no hurry to remove herself from under his body.

Finally, he released her hand from the mat and pushed himself up, unlocking his legs from around hers. She slid her arm from behind her back and stopped, laying still for nearly thirty seconds as Jacoby propped himself up next to her. They stole glances at one another. *What is happening?* Jolene thought to herself.

The tapping of shoes coming from the stairway woke her from the trance, sending her into action as she stood and grabbed her water bottle. She glanced at Jacoby who remained seated. His eyes were locked on her. "I'll ..." she began, though stopped as she glanced towards the locker room. "I'll see you tomorrow." She turned and walked down the open hallway, Ratliff following her with his eyes as she turned to steal one last glance at him before disappearing into the adjoining room.

"See you," he said quietly, unable to move, realizing there was definitely something special about Jolene Hartley.

TWENTY-FIVE

Jolene stood under the showerhead in the women's locker room and let the warm water fall upon her head and stream down the length of her body. Her eyes remained fixed on the row of blue tiles before her, though her mind was still pinned underneath Jacoby Ratliff's body on the sparring mat in the other room.

She understood fully what had happened, though for the life of her she could not see why. The last thing she wanted was another partner loaded with potential problems. She had gone down that path with Barailles and had promised herself she would not do so again. Then why was she suddenly drawn to him, as if just being his partner brought forth some forbidden lust from deep within?

Jolene leaned her face into the warm streams flowing from above and let the rejuvenating liquid wash over her, the water droplets rolling across her shoulders and down her back for several more minutes before reaching up and turning the knob to the off position.

She dressed and made her way slowly to the city streets, flagging down the first cab that crossed her path. She rode in the silence of the rear seats with eyes peering half-heartedly through the window at the blur of buildings, pedestrians and headlights zooming past. She sent a text to James to say she was heading home and would call him later, though she was not sure how she would be able to entertain the thought of speaking with him, especially not after what had just happened between her and her partner. She was confused, to say the least.

"Actually, this will be fine," she said to the driver, pulling his attention from untangling a knot of necklaces, rosaries and ornaments that hung from the rearview mirror. "I'll walk the rest of the way."

"Yeah? You ask for stop ... uh ... you stop just there," he said in broken English, pointing to her corner just a block ahead.

Jolene nodded. "Yeah. I need to walk a little. Thanks." She exited the vehicle and waited on the corner as the driver made an illegal U-turn and headed the way they had just come from. She crossed the street and made her way down the block, her shoes clicking against the rough concrete sidewalk near her Lincoln Park apartment. She pulled her jacket's zipper to her chin, shivering off the chill that was being carried on the cool night breeze.

Jolene was relieved when, after walking several yards, James and Ratliff exited her mind, instead being replaced by equally frustrating thoughts regarding her current investigation. Things had progressed slightly with the interviews of Walker and Verland, but aspects still seemed to be hidden in the background. What she knew was that Bart Reed, journalist at *State of Finance* magazine, had been killed three days earlier in what appeared to be a murder-robbery. An item had been taken from Reed's car after the fatal shot had been delivered, most likely a briefcase containing his laptop.

According to Melinda Reed, Bart's widow, her husband had been working on something important that seemed to be taking most of his time and had left the reporter — in the words of his daughter, Kaley — "preoccupied" and "a little jumpy." O'Dowd and Walker denied this aspect of the case, stating he, in fact, had not been working on anything of significance, and if so, it was being completed as a freelance assignment not from them.

Hartley had connected the proverbial dots and came up with the conclusion that whatever Reed had been working on must have been a big enough story that he had thought his job, maybe even his life, was in danger. Why else would he contact her brother and try to pass the story off? Journalists in Reed's position — and Dane's — thrived on stories that pushed the envelope. It was how they made their name in the business.

Their investigation had led them to Reed's place of work, *State of Finance* magazine, and his superiors, Editor in Chief, Seamus O'Dowd, and Assistant Editor, Kyle Walker, the latter having had a past filled with criminal activity and associates now either in prison or dead. He had left the states in the early '90s for Ireland and come back at some point with a new identity and what seemed like a legitimate career in the media world. However, something seemed fishy about the heads of the magazine, and Hartley was focused on figuring out exactly what that was.

In the midst of commencing their investigation, Luke Moran had been identified — with the help of Arland Landry — as having a connection with Walker's pre-Ireland transformation. Moran had, at one point, been on the Explosive Ordnance Disposal unit during his military service, leading Hartley to the assumption that he had something to do with the placement of the motion-activated bombs in Dane's apartment. Dane had gone to O'Dowd and Walker with Reed's project the morning of the explosion, the head of the magazine hiring her brother to a freelance contract to continue the work. Hartley and Ratliff had made their second appearance with the magazine's head personnel and received the information that Dane Hartley was unknown to O'Dowd, a blatant lie, as the detectives would find out later that evening. They had come to the conclusion that due to Dane and her strained, almost non-existent relationship, the fact that O'Dowd had hired him was supposed to have died with Dane in the explosion.

Now, as she made her way slowly back to her apartment, Hartley could not help but wonder about the missing pieces of the puzzle: mainly, was there any sort of connection with regard to Walker going to Ireland? Who had he stayed with? Who were his connections while there? And most importantly, why had he come back with a different name and an obvious base of knowledge in the media realm?

Another question that was also posing a problem for her materialized in her thoughts: who had Reed's source been? Dane had told her and Ratliff that someone had indeed fed Reed information in connection with the embezzlement scheme between *State of Finance* and Intervise Securities, though this had been something that Dane himself was supposed to be checking on.

Which brought on a final question: when was Dane finally going to get in touch with her?

Jolene shivered as she reached her apartment building and made her way inside, opening her mailbox and pulling out several envelopes. She went through them one by one, quickly discarding each into the recycle bin near the elevators.

She made her way up the steps to her floor and turned down the hall, walking slowly to her apartment door and sliding the key into the lock. She entered and tossed her bag containing her workout clothes, badge and firearm on the floor near the closet before moving towards the kitchen where she flipped on the light and turned into the room, stopping immediately as she looked upon opened cabinets with their contents spilled across the countertop.

Hartley had no time to react as the arms wrapped around her upper body, the muscles of her assailant squeezing her to the point where she had difficulty taking in a breath. She struggled to slide free but to no avail, her intruder lifting her off the ground and turning her towards the living room. Hartley's eyes adjusted to the darkness and noticed a second, much larger man moving from the shadows near the wall.

"Hold her still," the man said as he approached. Hartley could see a bulge from underneath the black shirt near his hip, a telltale sign of a firearm.

She looked upon the man's masked face as he made his way closer, bracing for whatever was about to happen, her mind racing as she thought of her next move. The individual holding her was obviously too strong for her to free herself by struggling alone. However, her main focal point at the moment was his partner, whose hands were not busy lifting a full-grown woman a foot in the air.

As he stepped closer, Hartley reacted, lashing out with her left foot towards the man's groin. His hands were quicker, however, and both shot down to catch her attempted strike. She could see a smile form across his face as he looked up to her, his hands holding her foot firmly. "Nice try," he said with a chuckle.

The last laugh belonged to her, however, as she had planned out her attack with his reaction in mind. Using the stability with which he held her foot, she pushed off and swung her right foot hastily through the air, connecting with the man's left cheek bone with such force that it sent him spiraling into the back of the couch and onto his knees.

Her momentum propelled her backwards, causing her assailant to stumble into the corner of the wall with a crash, his grip loosening enough to allow Hartley to reach the floor. She grasped the man's forearm tightly and leaned forward before shooting her head back into his face, immediately feeling the warmth of his blood on the back of her neck as his nose shattered. He released her immediately and fell to his knees, hands reaching up to his face as he groaned loudly.

It took Hartley's mind only a split second to decide that her firearm in her workout bag was just out of reach. By the time she could have reached it and unzipped the bag, the man with the gun would have had time to take aim and fire. Instead, she turned her attention to him as he regained his feet and glanced her way.

Hartley raced towards him, lowering her shoulder into his side with such force it caused him to topple over the couch. "Bitch!" he managed to yell, the last part of the expletive cutting off hastily as he hit the floor between the sofa and coffee table, the air shooting out of his lungs with a disgusting exhale.

Hartley felt a hand grasp the left side of her shirt and pull, bringing her away from the living area as she spun to face her initial attacker, his masked face covered in blood, his broken nose obvious even from underneath the black fabric. "Fucking bitch!" he yelled, raising his fist high and lashing out. The blow was thrown with an energy that the faster detective was not able to completely dodge the assault. She leaned back, the man's grasp on her clothes keeping her from falling to the ground. Hartley felt the wind from his fist pass just under her chin and connect with her collarbone above her right breast.

She groaned in pain, yet retained the air in her lungs while spinning to her left, pulling the man closer as she attempted a jab to his ribcage. She connected, though knew the damage was minimal. As he turned to face her, Hartley reached out and grabbed the nearest object she could find: a Waterford crystal vase atop a small, mounted shelf. She swung it with all her might and brought the beautifully designed piece crashing down into the man's cheek. The vase was thick, nearly a quarter of an inch, yet the weight the detective put behind it was so much that, upon impact, it shattered into a dozen pieces. The man crashed to the floor again, this time grasping at what Hartley thought would be a fractured cheekbone.

She bounced around him and was about to turn when a hand grabbed firmly onto her ponytail and pulled with a strength that caused her to yelp. Her head was wrenched skywards and she threw her hands up in surrender as a gun barrel pressed against her right jawbone. "Don't fucking do anything!" the man with the gun yelled in her ear. "Stop moving!"

"All right!" she yelled back, eyes wide as she looked to the ceiling. "All right. I'm not moving. I'm not moving." She thought quickly, trying to get a grasp on the situation at hand, her adrenaline running high. "I'm a detective with the Chicago Police Department and you really don't —"

"Shut up!" he yelled, turning his attention to his partner. "Get up! Check her bag!"

Hartley watched the man on the floor slowly get to his knees, shaking his head as he reached out for her workout bag. He unzipped it shakily and dumped the contents onto the floor, his unsteady hands sifting through the items and nonchalantly tossing the badge and firearm to the side. He turned to his partner and shook his head.

"Where is it?" the man asked in a fierce tone, yanking back on her hair. The sudden strain on her neck caused Hartley to have a flashback of the moment when Taylor Thames, the murderer of Benjamin Ochoa, had bested her in the warehouse. At that moment, for the first time in her life, she knew her destiny was completely in the hands of another individual. She had survived, though with both intense physical and emotional damage. She did not intend to allow that destiny be in the hands of another individual ever again.

"Listen, I'm a police officer. You don't want to —"

"I said where is it?"

"Where is what? What do you want?" Hartley asked, watching as the man she had clobbered with the vase tentatively get to his feet, his bloody hands pressing against the wall to balance his drooping frame.

"Don't play stupid with me, detective," the man said into her left ear. "I want the information you have from Reed."

Hartley caught her breath as she realized her attackers were in search of the fictitious files she presumably had on her, a lie she had told only one man in order to get a reaction: Kyle Walker. She also came to the realization that, unless incredibly stupid, these men were not going to keep her alive. It would be counter-productive if she were left to spread the information that Kyle Walker undoubtedly was behind this assault.

She reacted immediately, allowing neither one of the men in her apartment any time to think. With catlike speed, Hartley simultaneously reached for the man's wrist and shot her left elbow into his ribs. As he doubled over, she tried to twist the firearm from his grasp. His grip on the piece was strong yet she was successful in freeing her ponytail from his other hand. Hartley twisted to face him and sent her knee into his groin. He groaned and almost went down to a knee, instead stabilizing himself and throwing an open-palmed slap that connected with her exposed jaw.

Hartley held fast to his wrist as the blow spun her into the back of the couch. The man near the door made a move towards them but stopped abruptly as his unsteadiness forced him to lean back against the wall, his eyes wandering the room as he tried to focus. Hartley blocked another strike meant for her body, taking the assault fully on her bicep before lashing out with the base of her palm. She made contact with his eye socket, diffusing another attempted punch intended for her face, the blow instead connecting just below her neck and pushing her up and over the couch with such force that she sailed through the air and crashed into the coffee table, two of the legs snapping under the weight of the impact.

The gun the man had held under her chin was sent flying through the air, landing with a thud just behind Hartley and the now splintered table. She turned quickly and reached for it, spinning to her back with the firearm raised towards where the man had just been. Realizing where the weapon had landed and that the female detective was nowhere near incapacitated, her assailant retreated quickly, grabbing the man near the door and helping him out of the apartment and down the hall.

Hartley remained still, gun raised to the doorway in the chance the men returned. She finally moved as the adrenaline subsided and a pain began to grow in her midsection, caused, no doubt, by her collision with a sturdy coffee table. She tasted blood on her lips from the slap she had received moments before.

She rose to her feet and remained fixed on the doorway as she made her way to the emptied contents on the floor near the closet, retrieving her cell phone and entering in a series of digits. "9-1-1 dispatch. What's your emergency?"

"This is Jolene Hartley. I'm a detective with the Chicago Police Department. There's been an attack and I need officers and paramedics immediately."

"Okay," dispatch responded, a series of clicks heard in the background as the operator began typing quickly on the keyboard. "Are you on the scene right now, Detective Hartley?"

"Yes. I've been on the scene the entire time. I was the one attacked."

TWENTY-SIX

Hartley leaned into the hall with the intruder's firearm still in her left hand, her right arm draped across her midsection with her palm massaging her once again aching ribs. She raised the firearm to the end of the corridor, waiting for the men to turn the corner and finish the job that she had refused them. The door across the hall suddenly opened and an elderly woman appeared, her tiny frame enveloped in a soft, fluffy robe. Hartley lowered the weapon to her side as she leaned into the doorframe, panting heavily as the blood from her lip continued to drip down her chin.

"Oh, my word!" the woman shrieked. "Are you all right, my dear? What happened?" she asked, staring at the disheveled, gun-toting detective before her, noticing for the first time the blood-soaked, torn shirt and the sparkle of hundreds of shards of glass within the apartment.

"I'm fine, Mrs. Habernath," Hartley responded, taking a deep breath and wincing in pain, her face contorting slightly as the elderly woman took a step closer. "Please," Hartley said, raising the hand from her side. "I need you to stay in your apartment. There's been an attack and the police are on their way now. It's best you stay inside."

Mrs. Habernath nodded vigorously. "I was just going to check my mail."

"I can have one of the officers get it for you, Mrs. Habernath," Hartley replied. "Please, just go back into your apartment."

The elderly woman disappeared as Hartley shifted positions against the doorframe. She felt battered, though could not tell if it was more from the intense workout after her shift or the beating she had just received. She was certain she had broken a toe kicking her intruder in the face; her hand was bleeding and stung fiercely, no doubt caused by fragments of the Waterford crystal embedded in her skin; and her bicep had begun to turn an ugly shade of purple.

What hurt most, however, was her chest and midsection. The punch she had taken in the chest had collided powerfully with her collarbone, sending her flying over the couch and onto her sturdy, wooden coffee table. Hartley had landed on her back, yet rolled onto her left side as the table collapsed, her ribcage slamming into the edge of the surface.

She knew neither her collarbone nor ribs were broken, yet they ached incredibly, causing her to slide down the doorframe into a sitting position, her eyes down the hall, firearm still held firmly in her left hand. Hartley sat still for several minutes before once again bringing her cell phone to her ear. She had made the important call to the authorities, knowing that she had bits of evidence that needed to be accounted for. Now she needed her support team. Hartley was undoubtedly a tough cop, yet she was also human and needed comforting from time to time.

Her first call was to Banneau, the phone ringing a number of times before being answered by a male obviously in a crowded environment. Tears instantly formed in Hartley's eyes as the sound of Ratliff's voice came to her ear. "Hey, Jo," he said in a calm, soothing voice. "I'm out with Kim right now. She's in the restroom but —"

"I need you guys," Hartley said quickly, fighting the emotions.

Ratliff could tell something was amiss. "What's going on?" he asked hurriedly. "Are you all right?"

"Come to my apartment," she replied as a tear streamed down her cheek.

"What's going on, Jo?"

"When I got home there were men in my apartment. I fought them and they ran. Please. I need you guys to come here."

"Oh, my God!" he interrupted, his voice rising with an angered, worried tone. "Are they gone? Are you okay? Jo, what did —"

"Ratliff, stop," she said. "I'm okay. Police are on their way. Just you and Banneau come now."

"We'll be there as soon as we can."

Hartley hung up and was about to dial another number when a rustle from the stairwell caused her to raise the firearm once more. Her breathing became rapid, causing her chest to rise quickly and collarbone to ache more intensely. As the footfalls drew nearer Hartley yelled down the hallway. "Police! Identify yourself!" The noise stopped abruptly. Hartley listened to the sounds of whispering. Again she made herself known. "I'm Detective Jolene Hartley with Homicide! Identify yourself now or —"

"Detective Hartley," came the response from the stairwell as a large, solidly built uniformed officer appeared with his hands raised. "It's Train, detective." Hartley lowered the weapon as the officer stepped from the stairs. "Are you alone?"

"Yeah," Hartley responded. "They went down the stairs a little while ago." Train rushed over and knelt beside her as several other officers went into the apartment, stepping over the contents of her bag with guns raised.

"What happened? Are you okay?" Train asked.

Hartley nodded. "Yeah," she replied. "Can you get me up?"

"Sure." He grabbed underneath her arms, gently pulling her to her feet and leaning her against the doorframe. He retrieved a towel from the kitchen and dampened it with water from the sink before handing it to her. "You really took a beating, huh?"

Hartley laughed. "Yeah, well, I gave a couple good beatings out too."

"By the looks of your apartment, I wouldn't disagree." Hartley's phone rang then, both the detective and uniformed officer glancing down to the device in her hand. Hartley sighed and looked up to him, indicating her need to take it. "I'll be in the kitchen." Train moved off and convened with the other officers as Hartley limped into the hallway.

"Hey," she said.

"Hey," James answered. "What would you say to a late night snack? My treat."

"Sounds great, but I think I'm not going to be able to," she replied.

"Oh," he said, defeat in his voice. "Is everything all right?"

Hartley remained silent for a moment as her emotions once more rose up from the depths. Finally, in a shaky voice, she said, "Can you please come over here?"

* * * * *

A pair of paramedics worked on Hartley's wounds as Banneau and Ratliff entered the scene, the latter's eyes widening as he took in the destruction and chaos of his partner's living room: the blood-smeared wall to his right; the carpet splattered red; the couch turned askew next to a destroyed coffee table.

Banneau hurried to her friend's side and put a hand on her shoulder. Hartley smiled back, though her eyes locked on Ratliff as he slowly made his way into the room. "What happened?" she heard Banneau ask, though she did not respond. Ratliff glanced up from the shards of crystal strewn about the area and met his partner's gaze, their eyes connecting, an unspoken bond solidifying at that moment.

From over his shoulder James appeared, immediately being stopped by an officer. "Hey!" Banneau yelled, getting the uniform's attention. "He's with her." The officer released James and he came through carefully towards Hartley, his face a mix of emotions as his eyes followed the path of ruin.

"Are you okay?" he asked worriedly as he came to a stop behind Banneau.

Hartley nodded her head and smiled at him, grasping his hand as he reached to her. Her eyes lifted as a medic drew near, yet continued to swing through the crowded space until finally coming to rest once more on her partner. They eyed each other from afar, Hartley wondering what exactly was going through his mind as he looked back to her. What was he trying to process? That he had nearly lost his partner? Or that he had nearly lost *her*?

She blinked quickly and turned her head as Train approached, grateful for the distraction the large officer bestowed upon her. "All right, detective," he said as he passed by James and Banneau, coming to rest in front of her. "Do you have any idea why these men were in here tonight?" Hartley nodded. "You do?" he asked in a shocked tone. "Why?"

"To look for something that doesn't exist," Hartley responded with a smirk, glancing from Train to Ratliff.

The uniform looked at her for a moment. "Are you sure she doesn't have a concussion?" he asked to a paramedic, who was busy wrapping her bicep in an elastic bandage.

"Not a chance," the medic replied. "Not sure about the guy she hit with that vase though." The medic turned to her hand, holding it steady against a knee and using a pair of tweezers to gingerly remove three small crystal splinters embedded in Hartley's palm. The detective grimaced as the pieces came out, yet held the tears back in front of the crowd before her.

"I can't share everything," Hartley continued after a moment as Ratliff approached to listen, "but I interrogated a man involved in my current investigation. When he was leaving I bluffed to get a rise out of him and said that I had the information that may interest him. The men that were in here were looking for that."

"It was Walker's guys?" Ratliff asked. Hartley said nothing, though remained fixed on him. The silence between the two was anything but.

"All right," Train spoke up, looking down to a pad of paper in his hands. "Most important thing: are you okay?"

"Yes," Hartley responded, focusing on him.

"Good. Second: they're going to take the gun to the lab and do some forensic mumbo-jumbo on it. See if we can't track where it came from. There's enough blood on your floor and walls that I'm sure the lab techs can get some DNA. Maybe we can find out who exactly was in here tonight."

They remained seated for a while longer while the paramedic completed her work, fixing Hartley's split lip and wiping the blood that had dried to the back of her neck. After nearly an hour Train approached. "You're free to go if the medic clears you," he said. "Lab techs are going to be here for a while longer and we're going to post surveillance outside so no one can come back in here. I'm sure you'll be able to get back into your apartment tomorrow." Hartley nodded her thanks. "Do you have someplace you can stay at tonight?"

For whatever reason, Hartley looked at Ratliff for several seconds, their eyes connecting briefly before she turned to James. He smiled at her and answered, "She can stay with me for as long as she needs."

Hartley smiled weakly, turning to thank the medic before looking to Banneau. They hugged, Kim whispering to her, "Any other night and we'd have to talk."

They separated. "I know," Hartley replied. As they made their way out the front door, Hartley retrieved her bag and its contents, glancing one last time at Ratliff before they disappeared down the hallway, her partner's green eyes following her the entire way.

TWENTY-SEVEN

Train arranged for a police escort back to James's home, and Captain Nolan, after word of the attack reached him, called in a favor to the precinct near Graiser's residence to set up an overnight watch for his prize detective. They rode in silence, Jolene slouched in the seat next to James with her eyes closed and fingers massaging her temples, a headache beginning to set in as the night lurched on. James kept a watchful eye on her, giving directions to the chaperoning officer as to the quickest way to the apartment.

When they reached his residence, James walked her up the steps, giving Jolene no more than she asked for, which happened to be only an arm to hold onto. For having just been attacked by two large men, she moved pretty well, James thought. She obviously showed signs of the brutality that her attackers had dealt, yet he knew this woman was beyond tough. She had a determination that defied reason.

The first day he had laid eyes on her, Hartley had been assaulted in a warehouse by a conditioned killer, taking a metal pipe to her midsection as well as the butt of a pistol to her head, the latter injury knocking her unconscious. Most officers of the law would have been undoubtedly taken off the case, or at least set up in the background as a form of consultant. Not Jolene Hartley, however. She had stated to Captain Nolan that she was not quitting the investigation. It was her case and regardless of what had occurred, she was not going to abandon it. Nolan had agreed, which proved to be the right move, although Hartley inevitably became the recipient of several broken ribs.

James got her up to his apartment and closed the door behind her, locking it as Jolene moved to the kitchen table and removed her coat, the discoloration of her bicep beginning its exodus from underneath the elastic bandage. James looked at her cautiously, not sure how to proceed. She turned to him and forced a smile. "I need a bath," she stated with a sigh.

James smiled. "Well, you're in luck," he replied. "This place isn't much, but the one thing management did right was to install a top of the line bathtub. Come on. I'll show you."

Jolene followed him down the hall, turning into a room that was completely out of place in his small, cozy apartment. The bathroom was big, though not overly so. A large countertop held a massive, deep sink with an enormous hanging mirror lined with shelves and cabinets. Directly in front of her was a tub that made her smirk. It was a deep, whirlpool style bathtub with jets running the length of each side that dispensed a frenzy of water and air for a relaxing massage when needed. And right now it was exactly what Jolene needed.

"Towels are right here," he said, walking to the left and opening a skinny, floor-to-ceiling closet door. "And here's a washcloth." He handed them to her and smiled.

Jolene stepped up to him before he could exit and pinned him against the door, their eyes locking momentarily before she put her lips to his. She did not know why she kissed him, though deep inside she realized the need to feel something different then the confusion and pain she had been dealing with for the latter half of the day.

James kissed her back, though reluctantly at first. It had been such a surprise exchange that it caught him off guard. After several seconds Jolene backed away, her eyes downcast as she hugged the towels he had handed her moments before. She looked up to him. "I'll set you up in my bed just across the hall," he said. "I'll take the couch." She nodded as he reached out and rubbed her arm, their eyes locking for an instant before he turned and shut the door, leaving her standing in front of the oversized mirror to look upon her battered body.

* * * * *

She soaked in the bath for a little over an hour, draining portions of the cooling liquid from time to time as the faucet pumped steaming hot water near her feet. Hartley had started with a massive amount of soap to produce what was possibly the largest bubble bath in human history. Yet after the third time refilling the tub she had opted to use just the jets, deciding that the comfort of lavender was no competition for the massaging streams working their way over her skin.

Jolene opened her eyes after a while and stared to the ceiling. She took a deep breath and sunk into the liquid, completely submerging herself and lying still for nearly a minute before reappearing and wiping the water from her face. She rested her arms on edge of the tub and glimpsed the bicep where one of her attackers had landed a punch. It was a disgusting purple, yet, after such a long soak and the pain relievers the medic had given her, she would survive.

She thought back to the kiss with James just before he exited as well as the night when they had been fueled by beer and tequila. She definitely felt a tingle in her stomach when she thought of him, yet she could not quite make out what that was. She knew she felt for him, though could not determine where she wanted their relationship to go. Part of her was leery about jumping into anything at the moment. She had been enjoying herself in the recent weeks. Yet she also could see herself with him, going to dinner or drinks, cuddling up on the couch to watch a movie. It was a comforting thought, though there was something undeniable getting in the way.

Jacoby Ratliff.

Jacoby's expression in her apartment gave her the feeling that more than just a professional partnership was driving him. His eyes had been teetering on the verge of tears and she was pretty sure he had not approached her because the emotions would have gotten the better of him. Though she did not want to admit it, she had caught herself worrying about her partner more than James or Banneau while the medic worked on her, and for a reason she could not quite put her finger on. Hartley's attention had been drawn to him, and his to her.

She shook her head and ran her fingers through her long, dark locks, sighing loudly. She was utterly confused. On one hand she had James, an easy-going, hassle-free individual that cared for her deeply and whom she cared for as well. He was fun and childish in a way that brought her to a place she had not been in at least a decade. And to top it off, he accepted her for her. He had never complained when she needed to stay at work late or cancel evening drinks and dinner, for that matter. He was easy.

Yet he was immature compared to people Hartley had dated in the past, probably due to the fact that he had not really needed to work his entire life. Sure, he had picked up jobs here and there during his travels that had gotten him by, yet since meeting Jolene, James had remained in the city, which meant he was now dipping into his wealth. Fortunately, it was an endless bucket for him to dip into. However, Jolene had begun to feel guilty, thinking of herself as an unworthy reason for his hiatus in numerous trips abroad, something he had done on a regular basis since he was young. The bottom line was that she definitely liked him, though did not know how far she was willing to take it.

On the other hand there was Jacoby Ratliff. He too had an easy-going side, though Jolene thought it had come about more to win her over rather than a natural, carefree attitude engrained in his being. He was tough, opinionated and had no problem disagreeing with those around him, yet those disagreements were such that after a debate drinks could be bought and chips shrugged off shoulders en route to an enjoyable evening.

He was extremely good-looking, a fact that, regardless of Jolene's fair and accepting nature, she could not deny. She had witnessed him being cocky about it as well, which should have been a negative against him, however the manner in which he did it had brought butterflies to her stomach. The only thing he had going against him was that, like it or not, he was her partner, and she had refused to ever get herself into that situation again.

Jolene sighed loudly and leaned forward, pushing the lever to drain the tub. She stood and stepped into the middle of the bathroom, turning to the mirror and looking at her wet, naked body through the steamed sections of the glass. Her arm and lip were by far the worst looking injuries, though it was her collarbone and toe that were causing the most pain. She thought for a moment as she ran her hand over her side, gingerly pressing her ribs where she had landed on the coffee table, her mind traveling out of the bathroom and to the couch where James was set up for the night.

She grabbed a towel with anxiety-laden hands and wrapped it around her body, the bottom edge stopping halfway down her thighs. She steadied herself and inhaled once more before opening the door and turning into the hallway, making a right and walking away from her room and towards James.

She stopped as she entered the living room, the only light coming from above the kitchen sink to her right. James was on his back on the couch, his left arm tucked under his head as he lay with eyes shut.

Jolene nervously approached the couch and grabbed onto the blanket, pulling it down to his knees, her towel swaying as she bent over him. His eyes popped open and he jumped, nearly cracking heads with her, calming as his gaze fell on his guest. Jolene looked into his eyes and forced a nervous smile. James rose to his elbows, a look of confusion on his face as she straddled him. They sat in silence for a few seconds as he waited for her next move, not wanting to overstep his bounds with her. Hartley's mind emptied as she allowed her spontaneity to take control.

She grabbed the towel from underneath her chin and pulled the corner from where she had secured it, the fabric sliding down her back and resting near her rear. Her skin erupted in goose bumps as the chill of the apartment enveloped her damp, naked body. His eyes remained focused on hers for a moment before traveling downward, taking in her curves as if she was a priceless piece of art.

Jolene pulled him to a sitting position and wrapped her arms around him, planting her mouth on his as his hands gently slid across her back. She shivered at his touch and immediately reached down to pull his shirt over his head. He raised his arms as she threw the top to the ground, staring into his eyes for a long, drawn-out couple of seconds before she made any move.

Jolene pushed away from James then, moving slowly to the opposite end of the couch, her eyes steadily locked with his. When she reached the end she laid down, her head on the armrest, her flawless body facing the ceiling. James leaned forward and removed his sweatpants and boxers in one motion, moving up her long, tanned legs and flat stomach, stopping as he hovered over her immaculate face.

Jolene looked at him for a moment before reaching up and pulling him to her, their lips locking yet again in a heated, passionate exchange. James stalled for a moment, lifting his head to say something. He did not get the words out as Hartley leaned up to meet him, pulling him back down to her as her hand worked its way towards his pelvis. They moaned in unison as the act they had both envisioned since their first date became a reality.

TWENTY-EIGHT

The orange glow of the sun was just beginning to creep lazily over the horizon, meandering ever higher to work its way between the slits in the blinds. It was 5:36 in the morning when it finally began to shine down upon Dane Hartley's face, causing him to stir and curse as he wiped the sleep from his eyes. He tried to roll over and fall back to sleep, a successful maneuver until his phone began to purr from the bedside table, rousing him once more.

He hated this motel. He wanted nothing more than to curl up in his own bed within his own apartment. That was not to be, however. His apartment and bed now lay in a thousand shredded and burnt pieces somewhere in a dumpster or in a city police evidence locker waiting to be glanced at nonchalantly before being tossed aside.

Dane reached over and picked the phone up, placing it to his ear and answering. "Hello?"

A grainy, feminine voice spoke from the other end, its robot-like tone causing Dane to question if he had actually woken up or was in the midst of a futuristic, artificial-intelligence dream. "Who am I speaking with?"

Dane looked to the clock and sighed audibly. "Who am *I* speaking with?" he responded in a vicious tone. "It's fucking five-thirty in the morn —"

"Who am I —"

"This is Detective Escobar," Dane lied. "Who the fuck —"

"It's not important who I am, Mr. Hartley," came the reply, shocking the journalist and forcing him into a sitting position. "You can call me Amy Thorpe if you need a name."

Dane smirked. "Amy Thorpe, huh? I'm assuming you're in the game of espionage then. Am I —"

"Mr. Hartley, please just listen to my instructions," the voice interrupted. Dane sat silently. "Get to the nearest payphone and call back this number." The voice gave a series of digits for Dane to contact, the journalist rushing across the room to etch them onto a piece of motel stationary.

"What's this about?" Dane asked as he stood in the center of the room in his boxers. The line went dead.

Dane looked at the receiver as if for an answer to his question and sat down on the corner of the bed, his eyes glancing to the phone number he had just written down. He debated about his actions, whether to call the number or not, wondering if indeed the voice on the other line had something interesting to say or was just another crackpot trying to make something out of nothing. Then again, it was not every day that a caller used an audio processor to mask the sound of their voice. And it was definitely intriguing that the mystery person had used the name Amy Thorpe, a supposed American spy during World War II that worked for the British Security Coordination.

Crackpot or no, Dane decided that it was worth a look. Besides, he needed coffee desperately and he had seen a payphone just outside the Starbucks down the block.

He did not take the time to shower, brush his teeth or comb his hair. The voice on the other line seemed to be that of a punctual entity. He threw on his clothes and an oversized stocking hat and exited his room, walking to the adjoining street and veering left towards the coffee shop.

Within ten minutes he had his mocha in hand and was inserting coins into the payphone. He dialed the number and waited as it rang. The voice answered with a question. "What is my name?"

"What?" Dane asked.

"What is my name?"

"I have no idea —"

"What name did I give you?"

"Amy Thorpe, but I'm sure that's not really your name."

There was a pause before Amy continued. "Mr. Hartley, I have the information that you are looking for."

Dane remained silent as he chose his words carefully. "How do you know I'm looking for information?"

"I know," was all she said.

"Yeah, you know shit," Dane responded, slightly annoyed at the game that was being laid out before him.

"I know that the journalist Bart Reed contacted you before he died to hand off a story."

Dane froze. "Who is this?" he asked quietly, looking around as if the voice would be standing on a street corner. "Are you Reed's source?"

"I'm someone who knows things," came the response.

"Were you working with Reed?" Dane pressed

"Yes," she answered.

"Did he know who you were?"

"No, and neither will you. Now, do you want the information or not?"

Dane ignored the question. "Whatever information you have got a man killed. Why not go to the police with it?"

"Because if I go to the police, those that are involved will disappear and Reed's work will have been for nothing. This needs to be finished."

"And you think I'm the one to finish it?"

"You're already involved."

Dane thought for a moment. "Was my apartment blown up because of Reed getting in contact with me?"

"Yes."

"Are Walker and O'Dowd in on it?"

"Yes."

"How do you know?"

"I know," she answered sternly.

"You don't know anything unless you have proof," Dane whispered angrily into the phone.

"I have proof," she said matter-of-factly. "I have documents that Reed returned. They are in a locker at the train station waiting for you to pick them up."

"You think I'm going to waltz right into a train station and pick up some mysterious documents? You're fucking nuts!"

"If you don't get the documents then this story disappears, along with Bart Reed, Kelly Depler and you."

"Are you threatening me now?"

"No, Mr. Hartley. I'm telling you the facts. The embezzlement scheme is real. O'Dowd and Walker are involved, though I don't know who the third party is. Reed was on the verge of finding it out when he was killed. And unless you live under a rock, you should see that you and those around you are being targeted as well."

Dane's brow furrowed in confusion. "What do you mean?"

"Your sister was attacked last night in her apartment."

"What?" he replied.

"And it's bound to continue until everything and everyone is swept under the rug. Now do you want the information or not?"

Dane settled himself for a moment, his eyes scanning the surrounding area as he thought. Things had definitely gone south from the start. First Reedy, then the attack on him which killed his friend and occasional lover, Kelly Depler. Now his sister, a city police officer with an impeccable record and a certain amount of fame. Where did it stop?

"Okay," he replied finally. "I want it."

"Good," Amy replied. "Get to the south end of Ogilvie Transportation Center. There's an employee-only door with a row of utility lockers just inside. Number 4503. That's where Reed put the documents for pickup."

Dane wrote down the number. "Why didn't you pick the documents up yourself?"

"If they come back to me they could be found by the people behind all of this. And I could be the next one to wind up dead."

"Fair enough. I assume there's a key to this locker someplace."

"That I do have," Amy replied, pausing as if in thought. "Is there someplace I can send it to?"

Dane considered his options and smirked. "Send it to my sister at the precinct."

"We can't turn this over to the police without —"

"Don't worry about that. This won't be made public just yet. Send the key to her and I'll get the documents."

"Fine. I'll send it via messenger this morning."

"Great," he said, pausing. "Amy, how'd you know you could reach me? I mean, I'm dead to the world right now."

He was surprised when he heard a laugh. "You are," she agreed. "But you cashed the advance for Reed's story given to you by Seamus O'Dowd after your apartment blew up."

"Guess that will get around to them sooner or later."

"Possibly," she replied and hung up.

Dane smiled as he walked out of the booth, realizing at last he had a lead, something solid that he could share with his sister, after, of course, he himself glanced through the material. And on top of that he found something much more intriguing: Dane had made a mistake when depositing the check the day after he was supposed to have perished in the apartment blast. *State of Finance* would eventually see he had survived, if they were indeed looking into it. Yet if he had not made that mistake, he would still be in limbo as to who Reed's possible source was. At this moment, he had a pretty good clue.

* * * * *

Dane walked from the payphone to a diner two blocks down the street, taking a seat near the window to watch the early morning commuters begin their day. He ordered his breakfast and sipped his Starbucks, having hassled with the hostess to allow him to smuggle it in. After nearly twenty minutes he picked up his phone and found the name he was looking for.

"Jo, it's me," he said into the mouthpiece. "I've got a lead."

Hartley sounded lethargic. "Dane? What time is it?"

"Time for you to get to the precinct," he responded. "I got a call this morning. I'm heading to the precinct now and I need you there."

"Why are you —"

"Just get up. A messenger is bringing a package over and I need you to give it to me. I have to pick something up."

He could hear her shift and clear her throat. "Pick up what? I'm not doing anything illegal for you —"

"Shut up," he interjected. "I'll tell you about it when I get there. You have to leave now though."

"Okay, okay," she answered. "I'll be there in a little bit. Can't you tell me —"

"No," he said and hung up, knowing that would piss off his sister to no end. He smiled and bit into a piece of bacon, savoring the flavor as he pondered what he would find in locker 4503.

TWENTY-NINE

Jolene swore under her breath and rubbed her eyes, her vision blurred as she glanced around the room, making out deep, dark forms that morphed into a dresser or an open closet as she stared at length.

She was naked, her legs swung over the side of the bed, toes wiggling on the carpet. There was a chill permeating the room that sent goose bumps running up the contours of her torso. She glanced to the window and vaguely recalled James opening it before returning to her at some point in the early morning, sliding his sweaty body up hers until they were once again embraced in passion.

They had moved from the couch after only fifteen minutes, Jolene's knees either falling from the sofa or wedging between the cushions and James, both creating a dilemma with the back and forth motion she was trying to settle into. They had made it to the bed in a rush and began anew, each taking turns with the majority of the work as they rolled and played throughout the early hours of the morning. Jolene had been pleasantly surprised with James and his abilities. *What else do you do in the Caribbean for a month other than drink and screw?* she found herself thinking.

Jolene stood and made her way into the bathroom, gliding on catlike feet to not wake James from his slumber. She closed the door quietly and grabbed her clothes from the bathroom floor, dressing hurriedly before glancing to the mirror. She looked like hell, although ex-boyfriends from her past would most likely disagree: Jolene Hartley, in the morning, after minimal sleep, with bruises and a busted lip, was still like waking up next to the winning lottery ticket.

She splashed some water on her face and ran her fingers through her hair, pulling it back into a ponytail before leaning in closer and eyeing her split lip. It had grown to double in size since the previous evening, though that could partially be due to her and James's heated kissing. Her chin was beginning to form a yellowish-green bruise and the whites of her eyes were bloodshot.

Jolene rinsed her mouth with water and a shot of Listerine, deciding the first thing she would have to accomplish once at the precinct was a thorough brushing and shower. She pulled her shirt up over her bra and turned, running her fingers gingerly over her injured ribs before moving on to the collarbone. She leaned forward, causing her right foot to roll from the ball to her toes, cringing slightly as a pain ran to her ankle. She nodded, coming to the conclusion that the toe was actually not broken as previously thought, instead maybe badly jammed, an injury she could live with and fight through. She felt good, relatively speaking. Definitely better than the previous night, though she realized she had not let her muscles cool down to the point of allowing a steady ache to set in.

She stretched her arms high and rolled her neck. Her better judgment told her to take the day at an easy pace, yet there was something that seemed to be calling her to the precinct gym to continue her workout routine as if nothing had happened, and she intended to listen to whatever beckoned from deep within.

She opened the bathroom door and hobbled back to the bedroom, her mouth agape as she began to form words, stopping suddenly and tightening her lips as she looked down at James, his chest rising and falling smoothly as he slept.

At that instant she knew whole-heartedly that the previous evening — and early morning, for that matter — had been a mistake. She had forced herself to move the relationship along quicker than the universe had intended, wanting to feel something different than their occasional awkwardness and her recent physical pain, needing to test the waters to see if she could catapult herself into that next phase. Yet she had not succeeded in doing any of those things and now felt herself tumbling further into confusion, no closer to a resolution than she had been previously. Instead, she felt abysmal, as if she had wronged someone that did not deserve it. Jolene looked upon James and sighed, turning down the hall and exiting without confronting her nighttime lover and friend.

* * * * *

The cab dropped her off at the precinct fifteen minutes later. Hartley was surprised to see her brother already positioned on the steps, a large Starbucks coffee in his hand and another between his feet. She approached and he reached down, hoisting the cup up to her and smiling. "Thought since I woke you, I at least owed you coffee." His grin faded and he stood, his eyes focusing on her split lip and bruised chin. "Holy shit," he said softly, as if to himself. "You all right?" he asked, nodding towards the injury.

"Yeah, I'll be fine," she said, taking the cup and bringing it to her lips. The liquid warmed her as it traveled down her throat. "Thanks," she said.

"Yeah," he replied.

"Come on," she said to him, taking several steps up the stairs.

"We need to wait here," he answered, turning his focus away from her as he resumed his seat.

Hartley stopped her ascent and glanced back to him. "It's freezing out here, Dane," she pleaded. "The messenger will come into —"

"We're waiting out here," he said sternly, cutting her off and taking a long sip of coffee, not bothering to turn to her and thus missing out on the exasperated expression that crossed her face.

Hartley rolled her eyes and moved to the large, concrete wall that doubled as a handrail, taking a seat on the cool surface. "What's with the rush to get here?" she asked with a hint of annoyance.

Dane peeked at his watch. "I got a call from Reed's source this morning."

"What?" she asked out of surprise.

He glanced to her and smirked, giving that smug, self-assured look she had seen on numerous occasions in their youth, as if to say, "That's right. Leave it to me." His focus returned to the streets as he continued. "The source is shipping over a key to a locker in the train station."

"Who's the source?" Hartley questioned, knowing she was grasping at straws.

He shook his head. "Nice try."

"You know who it is though," she added, more of a statement than an inquiry.

"I have a good idea who it is."

"Then why not help me out?"

"I'm going to," he replied with a grin.

"You keeping a source from me that could help with my investigation is not what I consider helping. Giving me something to go on would be helping." She waited momentarily before realizing he was not going to speak. Finally she decided to continue the conversation. "What's in the locker?" He eyed her as he pulled a pack of cigarettes from his pocket and lit one. "Come on," she said, feeling her blood pressure beginning to rise. "You owe me at least —"

"I don't owe you shit," he interjected with a sideways glance to her.

Hartley's eyes narrowed and she set her jaw. "Right now, you owe me everything," she said, stepping in front of him and drawing his attention. "You don't give me something right now, I swear to God, Dane, I'm going to bring you into the station and —"

"All right, all right," he said, his palm raised in submission. He stood and looked to her. "I won't give you the source though. Not yet. After I figure out what I need to, I'll tell you who I think it is."

"But you don't know for sure."

"I have a pretty fucking good idea."

"How?"

"Because of certain circumstances and things that were said."

"Was it a man or a woman?" He shrugged. "Dane, come on."

"I don't know," he replied. "They were using some sort of audio processor as disguise."

Hartley took a step back and followed Dane's gaze down the street to the left, her eyes focusing on a bike messenger making his way alongside a taxi. "What's in the locker, Dane?" she asked, still staring down the street.

"Supposedly documents proving the embezzlement scheme and who's involved. To a certain point."

"What does that mean?"

"I was a little leery about getting a call from out of the blue when I'm supposed to be dead. So I asked if certain people were involved. People like Seamus O'Dowd and Kyle Walker."

"Are they?" Hartley asked.

Dane nodded. "Said there was a third member of the embezzlement team too, though the source didn't know who it was. Said Reed was on the verge of figuring that out when he was killed."

"How much you want to bet Reed had found out who that person was?"

Dane glanced at her as the bike messenger pulled up to the curb and dismounted, securing the front tire to a signpost with an oversized lock. "I thought the same thing. And I bet that's why he was killed."

"You think that information will be in the documents?" she asked, knowing the answer before the question fell from her lips.

Dane shook his head. "Seriously doubt it, but who knows. My guess is whatever was on Reedy's computer was the most recent information. Whatever's in that locker will probably be just proof of the fraud."

They paused as the messenger reached into his bag and began up the steps, nodding to Hartley and Dane in turn as he made his way towards the precinct doors. "Got a package for Jolene Hartley?" she asked, slowing the man down as he turned towards the pair, his eyes glancing down to the sealed package he was carrying.

He held it up and eyed the attractive woman before him. "You her?" he asked, to which he received a nod. "Sorry, but got to ask for some ID." Hartley retrieved her badge and identification card, signing the clipboard as he handed the package over and retreated with a smile and double take to the detective.

Hartley held the package in her hand for several moments, thinking over her options as Dane stared on, his mind working as well. "You'll get what's in the locker in a couple hours," Dane said, "as well as who I think the source is."

Hartley handed the package over and Dane immediately ripped it open, upending it and catching the orange-topped key that fell out. "Dane, if I find out you withheld anything from that locker, I will arrest you and make sure they prosecute you to the fullest. Regardless that you're family, I won't hesitate."

He smirked at her, an expression that emanated complete understanding and utter contempt at the same instance. "You'll get it. Give me a couple hours, at least. I'm going to make sure this isn't a set up."

"*And* go through the documents," Hartley added.

"And go through the documents," he repeated in agreement. "I'm still a journalist and I'm doing this story. So unless you want to become part of it by interfering with freedom of press, then I suggest you trust me and get off my back a little. Understand?"

They stared at each other for several moments before Hartley nodded. "Meet me back here when you're through. If I don't hear from you by noon I'm putting an APB out on you."

Dane bobbed his head before turning and moving to the curb, flagging down a taxi and disappearing down the street into the waking Chicago morning.

THIRTY

Hartley made her way into the precinct and took a seat at her desk, reaching out her hand to flip on the monitor, the screen buzzing to life with a technological growl. From the corner of her eye she saw a flash of red, the calling card of at least one awaiting voicemail. She dialed her passcode and listened. "Jo," came Debarsi's voice through the receiver. "I got something for you on Eric Sheehan. You were right: he did take off for Ireland. Rhonda, my associate, found some other stuff too. Give me a call back. I'll be in the office early. Or you can always get me on my cell. Talk to you."

Hartley saved the message and returned the receiver to its base. She leaned back in her chair and sighed, glancing around the pit with tired eyes to the surrounding empty desks. Eventually she leaned forward and woke the machine with the shake of her mouse, setting the cursor in motion and double-clicking the desktop icon to open her email client. She waited until the program loaded and immediately scanned her inbox, running through the items one by one, deleting those she deemed unimportant and leaving the rest for a later hour.

She stalled as she came to a correspondence from her partner, staring at his name in bold, black letters and the subject line associated with it. *Need to talk.* Her brow furrowed and she glanced back to the phone, debating if she should try Debarsi or not. She knew he would be up, though did not expect him to be at the office.

In the end she did not call, though the verdict came not from a conscious thought regarding his whereabouts at this early hour but rather the sudden realization that Ratliff's desk lamp was on and screen saver activated. Her eyes shot back to his email and noticed it had been sent roughly twenty-five minutes before she had stepped foot in the precinct.

Jolene peered around quickly, expecting Ratliff to appear before her, something she was unexpectedly nervous about. Hartley had always prided herself with being able to confront difficult situations that arose, and, up to this point, she had been mostly successful. Now, however, combining her uncontrollable lust for Jacoby as well as the current circumstances with James, Jolene was feeling more and more anxious about her personal life. *Why can't things just be easy?* she thought.

She determined her partner was not in the near vicinity after several tense moments of glancing across the floor in either direction. Her nerves calmed as she pictured him at a diner down the street, sipping on a cup of hot coffee and eating whatever breakfast he was privy to. Her heart began to race again when she thought of another scenario: Ratliff in the precinct gym, working the bags she herself was set to confront.

She leaned back in her chair and sighed deeply, debating on whether to proceed to the lower levels to work the sparring bags as she had planned or retreat to the coffee shop down the street and sink into a booth near the rear of the establishment. There was a chance either way she would run into him. She laughed and shook her head, becoming conscious of the fact she would no doubt have to confront him at some point during the day. He was her partner after all. It was beyond realistic to assume she could avoid him for an extended period.

Jolene rose quickly and moved to the elevator, deciding that, regardless of Ratliff's presence in the gym or not, she was going to continue with her plan. She had dealt with difficult situations in the past and was too proud and too driven to let this one get the best of her. Plus, a lengthy time behind her desk would most likely drive her mad.

* * * * *

Jolene walked quickly through the gym and to the women's locker room, relieved to have not caught sight of Jacoby, or any other soul for that matter. The idea of working out alone within the precinct confines was cathartic. She was elated at the notion of working the bags or doing sit-ups or jumping-jacks without having random officers checking her out or hurrying her along by setting up shop in anticipation for a spot on the mat. Sometimes it was just nice to work up a quality sweat without a pair of eyes on your ass.

She opened the locker she used to store her equipment in and retrieved the spare Under Armor athletic gear she kept in the rear of the compartment, cringing slightly as the whiff of mildew floated to her nose. The outfit had not been worn — or washed, for that matter — in weeks and had taken on the scent of the locker room and her sparring gloves, a combination that was not pleasing to the senses. Jolene thought for a moment before settling on a humorous solution. She sidestepped to Banneau's locker and opened it up, reaching in and retrieving a small, crystal vial of perfume. She laughed. *Nothing like getting done up before sweating profusely.*

Jolene changed quickly and made her way out of the locker room and into the hallway, stopping in her tracks as she suddenly caught a glimpse of Jacoby in the wall-mounted mirror across the room, her partner's back in full view as he removed his shirt and tossed it to the ground. He had definitely not been in the room when she had passed by minutes before, yet his sweat-soaked shirt stated loudly that he had been there for at least a little while.

She watched as he began a series of stretches, the muscles in his back compressing and relaxing with each movement. He was facing her, yet Hartley's spot on the opposite side of the wall made her invisible to him, a position she retained as her eyes ran across his torso, her vision dancing along the contours of his muscular frame. She vaguely noticed herself leaning into the wall, edging her way closer to the mirror in order to get a better view, a fingernail between her teeth as she anxiously nibbled.

Jolene's heart was pounding in her chest and for the first time since she had met Ratliff, she did not seem to care. Her actions with James the previous night had solidified in her mind that she was not looking for anything more serious with him at the moment, though for the life of her she could not conjure up one solid reason why. She had begun to open up more after her relationship with Ronny Debarsi had dwindled, thanks in large part to James. Yet ever since she and Graiser had begun seeing each other, something had definitely started to tug at her, whispering to her that the relationship would not fulfill her needs and desires, physically or emotionally, though the flashback of James's performance last night did give her cause to reconsider.

Just then she caught her breath, and for two reasons. One: the solid reason she had been looking for as to why she could not fully commit to James was, in fact, Jacoby Ratliff. She had been intrigued by his looks, his confidence and, possibly the most important aspect to her, the way he interacted with her, as if she were his equal, or he was hers. His fierce, green eyes, the sound of his voice, the way his lips moved and, of course, that smile, had all contributed to the fact that she had become completely infatuated by him. Add to it that she had witnessed an over-abundance of emotions well up within her partner the previous night after her attack, and it proved that he indeed thought of her as something more than a personal conquest.

The second reason she caught her breath was equally shocking: while lost in her thoughts, Jolene had neglected to react as her partner turned and caught sight of her in the mirror, watching as she stared at him progress through his routine. Their eyes locked yet neither one moved, both lost in each other's presence and the build-up that had occurred since their last meeting.

Jolene felt the uncomfortable eruption of blood coursing through her veins as the realization she had been caught checking Jacoby out smacked her fully in the face. She wanted nothing more than to flee, tuck tail and run in the opposite direction, hide in the confines of the women's locker room until the tension and embarrassment had passed. Yet she remained adamant. She forced herself to deal with the situation by moving away from the wall and into the room with him. She walked past him and nodded her greetings, courageously determining to call herself out for being caught eyeing him up. "Now we're even," she said, pulling a slight grin from him as he recalled the episode a day earlier where his eyes were glued to her bottom.

"How're you feeling?" he asked.

Jolene only nodded and situated herself in front of the mirror and dove headlong into a round of cardio, working her muscles into a state of readiness. She repeatedly glanced at her reflection and that of her counterpart, watching as he continued with his routine, catching his eye from time to time before quickly glancing away. After several minutes she went to the mat to begin her regiment of sit-ups, plowing through them with an intensity that surprised even her.

After a time she stood and made her way to the water fountain, filling up her bottle and downing half the liquid before repeating. Hartley moved back onto the pads only to notice Jacoby positioned next to her, his back to the ceiling as he knocked out a dozen pushups in just about the same amount of seconds.

She paused and wiped her brow, watching as he continued his vigorous workout and debating her plan of attack. As she turned towards the sparring pads he spoke. "Did you get my email?" he asked, causing her to stop in her tracks.

Jolene suddenly felt herself flush with anger, a reaction, she thought, that was due to the ups and downs she had been faced with over the last twenty-four hours. "I saw it," she said, taking a swig from her bottle and continuing to the punching bags. "I didn't read it yet, though."

He continued on the mats without pause for several minutes as Jolene strapped on her gloves. They went about their business and ignored the elephant in the room until finally he stood and looked at her. She could not help but react to his stare, looking him over once again as her eyes slid up his bare torso.

Ratliff smirked. "Want a partner?" he asked, pointing to the pads.

Hartley dropped her hands to her sides and shook her head. "No, I think I'll be fine," she said and began a distracted series of jabs.

Jacoby walked towards her and stopped just shy of her striking point. "Come on. I'd like to talk to you." She continued unabated, her eyes focused on her target. "Look, we're both here doing our thing. Why not do our thing and talk?"

"Because I'd rather spend this time for me," she responded, her voice a bit harsher than she intended.

He shook his head and stepped back. "Fine," he said, walking several feet before turning back to her. "You know what? It's not fine," he replied, his voice determined enough that it caused her to stop jabbing at the bag, though her feet continued to move. "I'm your partner, and regardless of you being the lead on our team, I deserve to be heard."

She smirked at him, though it came from a place of contempt. "Why?" she said, striking with such force that the impact almost drowned out the question.

"Why what?" he asked.

"Why do you deserve to be heard?"

Jacoby's smile was laced with exasperation as he tried to determine why she was now coming across with such loathing towards him. "Why?" he repeated.

"Yeah," she said, standing still and dropping her hands to her sides. "Why? Why do you deserve to be heard? Why should I listen to you? What makes you so special that I should take a break from trying to forget about being punched in the face and whipped across my living room?" She was becoming enraged as she moved towards him, though both parties knew it was coming from an emotional overflow rather than a hatred for him.

"Because," he answered boldly, taking a step towards her, "I did my time in the Marines. I've seen people get killed. But that's expected there. I grew used to that as much as I could." He paused with his eyes locked onto her. "But I've never had a partner attacked in her home before. It scared the shit out of me." Jolene continued to stare, her anger faltering as she tried to hold onto it for a reason she could not put her finger on. "Regardless of what you think, James wasn't the only one worried about you last night."

"Oh!" she exclaimed, taking the opportunity to boil over. She came upon him quickly and attempted a jab to his chest, an attack that caught him by surprise. Ratliff ducked to his left, barely getting out of the way of the blow. "And now you bring up James. Imagine that!"

"Hey," he replied, raising his hands in defense. "I don't care if you like me bringing up James or not. In all honesty, he's a good guy. I like him."

"I'm glad I have your approval," she hissed, taking a step towards him and sending a barrage of shots to his midsection, connecting on several to his ribcage before he sidestepped and brought both palms up, grasping onto her forearm and spinning her into him. She reacted quickly, kicking her heel up in an effort to connect with his groin. Jacoby reached down with both hands and caught her foot before it made impact, though the move left his upper half vulnerable. Jolene spun and caught him with an elbow to the jaw, jumping away from

Ratliff as he straightened up and rubbed his face with a gloved hand, his cool green eyes staring at her.

"I notice you hit harder when I've struck a nerve," he replied with a smirk. He raised his hands and sank into a defensive posture, circling her as he continued. "As I was saying, I have no problem with James. What I do have a problem with is you lying to yourself."

"How am I lying to myself?" she asked, sending a right hook that was easily deflected.

"How aren't you?" he questioned back. "You're hanging on to something that's not right for you. But you use it as an excuse not to let yourself open up to something that could be."

"Very cryptic," she responded. "You always talk in code? Why don't you just say what's on your mind, Ratliff."

He halted, dropping his arms to his sides and standing up straight. "You really want me to? Because I'm not sure you can take hearing it out loud."

"I asked, didn't I?" she said, her heart pounding at what she knew was coming.

"Fine. You're not owning up to the fact that you know James isn't what you want. You're denying yourself the feelings that have obviously crept up between you and me, and you're scared to deal with it because you don't want to hurt anyone's feelings —" He had to halt conversation as Hartley flew across the mat with catlike speed, her leg extending towards his knees to take him out. Jacoby rolled and popped up, bolting forward and wrapping his arms around her torso, his right leg bracing against the back of her knees as he fell to the floor, his weight pulling her down in a heap. The collision of their bodies against the mat caused him to lose his hold of her and she immediately took advantage, hopping to the side as he began to rise. She wasted no time in attacking once more, feigning to the left and spinning in the opposite direction, catching Ratliff off balance and sending a shot to the gut.

As he tried to dodge the blow, he once again left his jaw open. Jacoby swore under his breath as he watched his partner's right hook connect with his chin. He immediately tasted blood from the impact but did not slow down in the least, grabbing onto her extended wrist and yanking her towards him, spinning his body along the length of her arm and pushing her into the nearest wall.

She collided with the wall with a force that caused her to lose some of the air in her lungs. Jolene would have been forced to take a knee to recover, yet Ratliff was there against her, holding her right arm between her own body and the wall, her left held firmly in his grasp.

She breathed deeply as the air rushed back to her, her eyes lifting to his and connecting from a mere couple inches distance. "Let me go," she said, though the determination in her voice was no longer apparent.

"Tell me you don't feel something for me," he replied. She stared at him and tried to free herself, though both of them knew her attempt was half-hearted. "Tell me," he repeated.

She looked at him sternly. "I don't know what I'm feeling," she finally said, catching herself off guard with her willingness to open up yet again with him. "I have feelings for James. I definitely —"

"I want to know about us" he interrupted.

"You're my partner."

"So?"

"So, I've made the mistake of doing this before."

"With a partner who had baggage," he replied. "I don't have baggage. I'm a good guy. I treat people right and give respect where it's due. And I know for a fact that I want you —"

"But it doesn't change the fact that you're my partner and —" She was unable to finish the sentence as Jacoby moved forward and placed his mouth on hers, kissing her passionately as he held her to the wall. Jolene was taken aback by his sudden boldness, yet could not have stopped him if she wanted to.

But she did not want to. She stood there and saw him move towards her. She witnessed his eyes closing and felt his lips part as they careened with hers. She wiggled her body against the wall, but realized after the fact that she had done so only to free her left arm to bring up and grasp onto his neck, pulling him closer to her as she closed her own eyes and vigorously kissed him back. Her mouth parted and their tongues met, their breathing heavy and loud as they lost themselves in the moment.

Jolene arched her back and freed her other arm, wrapping it around his shoulders and pulling herself up his slightly taller frame. She could not remember the last time she felt such intensity from a single kiss, such forbidden ecstasy from the touch of another human being. The entirety of her body tingled as his hand pulled her closer from the small of her back, their bodies touching and rubbing and —

The clearing of a throat from behind the two caused Jolene to break their connection, pushing him away slightly and glancing over his shoulder to the source of the disturbance. She was relieved and mortified at the same instance to see Kim Banneau standing in the entrance to the sparring room, her shoulder resting against the wall as she stared at the two with a mischievous smirk across her face. "I'd be lying if I said I was surprised to see this," she said with a chuckle.

Jacoby took a step back and quickly glanced over his shoulder to Kim before connecting with Hartley once more as she rubbed the back of her neck nervously. "I, uh," she began, leaving the sentence hanging as she pointed to her friend. She forced a smile and retreated across the room and past Banneau, turning into the hall and disappearing into the locker room.

Jacoby turned and looked to Kim, both of their eyes following Jolene until she was out of view. Banneau glanced to him and nodded with a grin. "I'll talk with her," she said, following after her friend and leaving him alone in the room with the sparring pads and his thoughts.

* * * * *

"What am I doing?" Jolene said as she opened her locker and gazed inside. "What am I doing? What am I doing?" She placed her fingertips on the bottom of the cubbyhole and leaned her sweaty forehead against the cool metal above the opening, staring blindly into the alcove as Banneau came up behind her.

"From the looks of it, you're getting yourself all mixed up," she answered with a chuckle, taking a seat on the bench between the two rows of lockers.

Jolene turned to her with a blank stare. "You have no idea," she replied.

"Oh, I'm sure I have some," Kim responded. "Remember who you're talking to here."

"This isn't supposed to happen again. I can't do this —"

"Relax," Banneau chimed in, standing and stepping forward to place her hands on Jolene's arms. "Just relax. Breathe deep." She demonstrated her best calming inhale followed by a slow, easy release. Hartley stared into her eyes and obliged, feeling the need for anything to take her mind off of the matter at hand. "See," Banneau continued with a smile. "Everything's better when you just relax and —"

"I slept with James last night," Jolene blurted out, the words flying from her mouth and seeming to pick up volume as they sailed through the damp locker room air. She nervously caught her breath and glanced around to make sure no one besides Kim Banneau was within shouting distance. She lowered her voice. "I slept with James and then kissed Ratliff. Within hours of each other!"

Kim cringed before shrugging her shoulders. "Sounds like a good stretch to me," she joked, trying to make light of the situation before focusing more intently as Jolene shot death rays from her eyes. "Sorry," she replied. "Look, it's not that bad."

"How isn't this that bad?" Jolene asked cynically, throwing her arms in the air.

"It … just isn't," Kim answered calmly, stepping to her own locker and retrieving her black shower bag and towel. Jolene's face contorted as she tried to determine why her friend was being so nonchalant about the idea of her sleeping with her friend and kissing her partner within a day's time, wondering exactly how many times Banneau herself had been faced with a situation like this. She instead followed Kim's lead, walking with her towards the rear of the locker room and pulling back the curtain of a shower, cranking the lever to hot and immediately producing a steaming cauldron that beckoned her to enter.

They remained silent for several minutes, Banneau using the precinct showers as her own personal bathroom due to a busted hot water heater in her condo rather than the typical post-workout rinse that Jolene now employed, standing motionless as the warm streams fell upon her head and body. "I have to ask," Banneau said finally. "How was James?"

"Kim," Jolene exhaled, knowing the question was coming out at some point.

"Come on!" she replied. "You're going to try to tell me something like you slept with James and not expect to share the details? Spill the beans!"

"I need your advice on what to do," she stated. "I don't need you to pry into every aspect of my life right now."

Banneau halted her scrubbing and stepped out of her shower, pulling aside Jolene's curtain and pointing to her. "Listen," she said, causing Hartley to jump and cover herself with her arms.

"Kim!" she yelled, her cheeks flushing red.

"Please," Banneau said, waving a dismissive hand. "It's nothing I haven't seen before. Well," she continued after glancing to Hartley's rear, "*better* than any I've ever seen, but regardless ..." Jolene turned to the side and raised her leg as she tried to cover her valuables, her arms draping over her breasts as she glanced to Banneau. She caught her eye as Kim continued. "You want my advice? I want an answer to my question. That's how this works."

"Fine!" Jolene yelled. "Just go back to your shower!" Kim disappeared without saying another word, resuming her morning routine while Hartley shook her head and grabbed her loofah, squeezing a large dollop of moisturizing soap into it.

"Waiting —"

"He was fine," Hartley said as she began to scrub.

"Just fine?" Banneau pushed.

"No. He was good. He was ... He was actually very good."

"Then what's the problem?"

"Ratliff's the problem!" she said sternly. "Ratliff's been the problem since he got here!"

Kim laughed. "Oh, I wish I had your problems! An extremely good-looking, muscular cop that isn't a dick as my partner would be such an issue!"

"You don't get it," Hartley said.

"What is there to get? You start something up with James because you like him."

"That's only part —"

"And then along comes Mr. Universe who rattles your entire foundation because he's actually exactly what you've wanted since Ronny took off."

"Yeah, but —"

"But you've already started something with James and you'd feel bad breaking it off for Jacoby because he's your partner." She stopped and waited for a moment. "You're right. I probably don't get it."

"Maybe you can stop being a smartass and give me some advice," Jolene replied after several seconds.

"You're not looking for advice. You're looking for someone to tell you what to do. I can't do that, babe. You'll have to figure it out on your own."

They remained silent for the remainder of their showers, Banneau finishing her rinse and exiting before Jolene had turned off the water. She toweled off and dressed, parking herself on the bench where their conversation had begun. Hartley appeared after a time to dry herself and dress quickly, sliding into a pair of dark gray slacks and a white blouse. Kim remained stationed on the bench, calmly checking her emails from her cell phone as Hartley wrapped a scarf around her neck, finally lifting her eyes to meet her friend, a signal for their conversation to continue.

Kim stood and reached out to Jolene, resting her hands on her friend's arms. "If you want the complete truth from me, then I'll give it to you, but it's not going to make anything easier."

Jolene smiled and nodded. "Please."

"James is a good guy. Ratliff's a good guy. But they are two different types of guy. I'm not sure how serious you are about getting into a steady relationship, and I couldn't say one way or another about either one of them. But I do know for a fact that each of those guys is into you." She paused for a moment. "When we showed up last night I asked you a couple times if you wanted to stay at my place." Jolene's brow furrowed as she tried to remember the conversation. "You didn't respond because you were across the room with Jay."

"Jay?" Hartley asked with an amused tone.

"Are you going to listen?"

"Yeah. Sorry."

"You didn't respond because you were across the room with Jay. Figuratively. I noticed it. Jay noticed it. And I hate to tell you, but James noticed it too." Hartley's eyes rose quickly from the floor to meet with Banneau's. "But it said a lot to everyone that you chose James to go home with."

Jolene took a seat on the bench and rubbed her temples. "What does it say that I couldn't stop thinking about Ratliff?"

Kim knelt before her and took her hands in hers, smiling gently at the flustered Jolene Hartley. "I think you know. Just be honest with yourself. You'll figure it out." She rose and pulled her friend with her. "Come on," she said, wrapping her arm around Jolene and pulling her towards the hallway. "Let's get to work."

THIRTY-ONE

They ascended the stairs briskly and turned into the hallway leading to the pit, Hartley attempting to focus on anything other than her personal life as the office buzzed with activity. Banneau remained fixed on her arm as they turned into the floor's chaos and froze, Hartley's eyes locking onto the group congregated around her desk.

Banneau bit her lip and patted her friend's arm. "Just doesn't seem like your day, does it?" she asked, both their gazes extending through the hustle and bustle of officers milling about the pit and coming to rest on Ratliff, James and Dane.

"Oh, God!" Hartley whispered to herself, causing a sympathetic smile to cross Banneau's face.

"Looks like it's time to face the music."

Hartley shook her head, retrieving her cell phone and glancing quickly around. She spotted an office the precinct had been using for storage for the past six months and moved away from Banneau. "No music just yet," she said, tapping Kim's arm and glancing to her. "Thanks, Kim. I need to make a call. I'll deal with that in a minute."

Banneau nodded and sauntered off in the direction of the kitchen. "How about dinner tonight?" she asked. "Give you an excuse to say no to every other invitation I'm sure will come your way."

"You're on," Hartley said, pushing a series of numbers and lifting the phone to her ear. "I'll call you later," she said as she watched Banneau throw a wave over her shoulder.

Hartley closed the door to the office and shut the blinds, not bothering with the light switch as the overhead fluorescents had long ago been removed and transferred elsewhere. She zigzagged through the towers of cardboard boxes until she reached something that resembled a desk, pushing a smaller stack of papers out of the way and taking a seat as her call was answered.

"Jo," Debarsi replied. "How's it going?"

She guffawed as a response. "I haven't been shot," she said. "I got your message this morning. What do you have for me regarding Sheehan?"

"Right to business, huh? That type of morning?" he asked, the smile apparent across the wire.

"That type of week. What did good ole Rhonda find out about my boy?"

"Well," Debarsi began, "to give you an answer before you ask: no, we don't have a solid ID on who he stayed with in Ireland. Seemed to bounce around a lot in the first year or so.

Got a couple hits on random hotels and one halfway house. But other than that, nothing so far. We'll keep looking."

"Did he get into any trouble that was tracked?"

"Yeah, little things," he answered. "Nothing of significance that gave him a long stay in an institution or anything. Spent a couple nights in town jails here and there, but that's it."

"What did he do for work?"

"As far as Rhonda could find, he did odd jobs wherever he landed. Worked as a deckhand on a fishing boat for two or three seasons. Couple auto body shops."

Hartley sighed, waiting for him to continue. When he did not she shrugged and lifted a hand in the air, realizing her actions were going unnoticed within the storage room. "That's it? Ronny, you said you had something good for me. Right now it looks like you've done nothing but tell me the history of an average teenager."

"Give me a second," he said on the other end of the line. "I'm coming to it." She could hear him shuffling papers as he began again. "After those first couple of years things went silent with Sheehan. No police records of any kind. Didn't get in any sort of trouble it seems."

"How is that possible for a lifelong criminal?" Hartley prodded.

"Because he was enrolled in University College Dublin."

"Walker's a college graduate?" she asked, surprise evident in the inquiry.

"Not Walker at the time," Debarsi answered. "He was still Eric Sheehan. And yes, he graduated from UCD School of

Business. It wasn't until he came back to the States that he changed his name to Kyle Walker, probably to get away from the criminal aspect surrounding him."

"Hold on, hold on," Hartley said, standing and rubbing her hand across her brow. "How is a broke kid able to afford something like college? I've seen criminals trying to get out of the life that can barely afford their apartments, let alone full-time college tuition."

"I thought the same thing, so I had Rhonda look a little deeper. Seems at some point Sheehan came across old family ties in his stay in Dublin. Does the name Leary ring a bell?"

Hartley's mind immediately traveled back to her research into Kyle Walker and the name Leary attached to his father's side of the family tree. "Yeah, it does," she said. "Leary is the family Sheehan's great-aunt married into."

"Right," he replied. "Well, it seems some of the Leary family grew into upstanding citizens while others ran with a different crowd. Either way, the entire Leary family had money."

"Let me guess: Eric Sheehan's tuition was paid for by someone in the Leary clan?"

"Correct. Seems there was an uncle or a cousin that paid for it after meeting with Sheehan on a couple occasions."

"Do we have a name?"

"Not on such short notice, but I'll see if we can dig a little deeper. There seemed to have been some sort of commotion raised by the university as to having a known criminal from the

United States enrolling, but whatever happened between the relative and the Dean of Students, he was admitted."

"Seems like you'd have to have a lot of pull to get that done, doesn't it?"

"I would think so. Either pull or money."

Hartley thought for a moment before continuing. "What type of degree did he graduate with?"

"Economics and Finance from the School of Business," Debarsi answered.

"And after graduating?"

"Pretty much right back to the states and a job within *State of Finance*. Had his name legally changed to Kyle Walker before taking the position at the magazine."

"See," Hartley cut in quickly, "doesn't that seem strange to you? He takes off from the life he's leading here, bums around Ireland for a while and then all of a sudden meets a mysterious relative who pays for him to get into a prestigious university. Then as soon as he graduates he gets a name change and a spot in the city's most reputable financial magazine?"

"It's very strange," Debarsi agreed.

"I mean, most companies run background checks on prospective employees. How could his past discretions be overlooked? His change of name was done legally, right?"

"Right."

"That means everything in his past could have been tracked. How do you get that spot at *State of Finance* if you have a rap sheet like Sheehan's?"

"I don't know," Debarsi answered. "Maybe it was overlooked." Hartley laughed. "Maybe it was taken into account but *State of Finance* was willing to give the guy a shot. Or maybe he was placed there to keep an eye out in the media for the embezzling that you're looking into. Of course, that would suggest there was a connection between Walker and Intervise and that the embezzling had been ongoing since at least the early 2000s."

"It's possible," Hartley answered. "Maybe whoever paid his way in college got him into the spot at the magazine. Maybe that connection is the third embezzler."

Hartley sighed and looked to the ceiling, trying to process the information her ex had just given her. "Is everything okay, Jo?" he asked from the other end of the line.

"Yeah, it's ... confusing. Just a confusing time," she answered.

"You know I'm always here for you," he said.

"Yeah, I know," she replied. "Thanks, Ronny. For the information and being there."

She could imagine him smiling. "Any time. Let me know if you need anything else."

They said their goodbyes and Hartley placed the phone in her pocket. She looked to the wall and took a long, deep breath, thinking about her next move and cringing as she realized it was leaving the storage room and confronting the three individuals she did not want to see at the moment.

* * * * *

Hartley felt like a human magnet the moment she stepped from the storage office, the eyes of her fling, her partner and her brother all honing in on her as she took small, slow steps towards her desk, her own pair scanning the three briefly before casually glancing to the floor. James forced a shy smile. Dane remained stalwart, leaning against her desk. Ratliff — Jay, as Banneau had called him — was seated in his chair, leaning back and swiveling to the left and right with folded hands.

As she approached, they moved closer in unison, hustling into position to be the very first to get her attention. It was Ratliff who spoke up first. "We got a hit on the guy you jacked up in your apartment. It's …" He was silenced as she raised her hand to him. "What?" he asked.

Hartley glanced to James and Dane quickly, extracting a chuckle from the latter. "Come on now," her brother said. "I find out everything eventually."

"Not right now you don't," Hartley replied.

"Listen, what I got for you is solid gold here," he said. Aggravation laced his words as he held up a large manila envelope. "Maybe a little —"

"Don't start, Dane," she interrupted. "You don't deserve —"

"I deserve what —"

"Stop," Ratliff interjected from his desk with a voice that silenced them both. "We're not doing this again."

"I've had enough of taking shit from you," Dane replied, turning to Ratliff and pointing a finger in his direction.

"Guys," James tried to mitigate, only to be given a silencing look from Dane.

"Jo," came Captain Nolan's voice from behind her. "Where are we at with this Reed thing?"

Hartley did not turn to him. "It's coming along," she replied.

"Coming along?" he repeated from his doorway. "We need something soon to —"

"Enough," Hartley whispered, her voice barely audible over her superior's question and the duel happening before her.

"What?" James asked, seeing her lips move.

"Jo, just give me —"

"Enough," Hartley repeated. "Quiet!" The shout was enough to make those around her freeze in their tracks, officers not even part of the happenings between the dysfunctional crew stopping on a dime or slowly backing away as they looked to her.

"Excuse me?" Captain Nolan said, standing straight and sticking his chest out. He deflated as Hartley glanced over her shoulder.

"Sorry, captain, but I need some form of control right now. I'll get you something solid when I have it." She turned her attention away from the retreating Captain Nolan and focused on Dane, who smirked at her stoic glare and tried to match it. "Let's not forget who's holding the key to you being able to continue your work."

"Please. You need —"

"Another fucking word and I'll confiscate that envelope and throw your ass in a holding cell, Dane. I'm sick of you trying to play things to your benefit. What we have here is a murder investigation that we — as officers of the law — are allowing you to tag along on. So stop with the shit and get it through your head: you give us what you've come across and I may decide to forget the fact that you deliberately obstructed my investigation. Or don't, and you can spend the next year or so in prison followed by Big Brother watching your every move and stomping on your toes. Got it?"

She did not wait for him to respond, instead turning to James who remained as still as a deer in headlights as he watched her business side take over. She shook her head slightly and turned her palms up. "What are you doing here?" she asked, not meaning for her true emotions to ride out with the words.

The color drained from his face. "I'm sorry," he replied, clearing his throat and glancing towards Ratliff, who had begun to swing in his seat once more. "I just thought maybe you'd like to get a bite to eat. I didn't realize you had a big meeting planned." He stepped into the aisle. "Maybe just give me a buzz later?"

He smiled and turned, making it only a step or two in the direction of the exit before Jolene called after him. "James," she said, moving towards him, sensing her partner's eyes following her every movement. He halted as she approached and felt relieved when she rested her palm on his arm, directing him to the far wall and out of earshot of Dane and Ratliff. "Look, I'm sorry," she said. "I didn't mean to … I'm sorry. Just a hectic case, you know?"

He nodded. "It's okay," he said. "I understand. I still shouldn't have shown up unannounced though."

"No," she said with a shake of her head. "It's fine. Really."

"Listen," he said after a moment of silence between the two, "I've got some running around I was planning to do. Maybe I'll do that now and, you know, if you're up for it, we can do dinner …" He stopped as Jolene glanced into his eyes with an apologetic look. "I'm guessing that's a no?"

She nodded. "I've got plans tonight," she replied, adding, "with Kim," when he seemed disappointed.

"Well, maybe lunch or something?"

"Lunch sounds good. I can't promise anything, but I'll call and let you know."

He smiled wide. "Sounds good enough to me. I'll see you later." He walked down the hall and descended the stairs, disappearing from view as Hartley watched after him, the eyes of the two remaining men drilling holes in the side of her head.

She turned to them with such intensity in her eyes that it caught the pair off guard. "You two," she said over passing officers moving about the pit. "Break room. Now."

* * * * *

"Spill it," Hartley said to the men taking their seats on opposite couches in the break room. The directive was focused more on Dane than her partner, though Hartley had definitely not forgotten Ratliff mentioning they had found something on her home invader.

Dane slid the large, manila envelope onto the coffee table and placed his boots next to it, stretching into the couch and making himself comfortable. Ratliff glanced to each sibling, half waiting for another torrent of pent-up expletives to shower from his partner's mouth. They did not, however, and she seemed to not care about his shit-eating grin or the fact that he was treating their break room like his own personal living space.

"Ann Carroll," Dane said matter-of-factly, as if the name of the *State of Finance* receptionist was a topic they spoke about daily.

"What about her?" Hartley asked, crossing her arms and leaning into a nearby table, obviously not taking the bait to play the guessing game she no doubt realized Dane was fishing for.

"That's the source," he replied, looking at his fingernails. "Well, who I believe to be the source, anyway."

"Why do you think she's the source?"

"Because of what was said on the call this morning."

Hartley waited for a moment before reaching up to the bridge of her nose and shutting her eyes. "Dane, listen to me carefully. I'm not going to pry every answer I need from you. It's either share or don't. You know the consequences."

"Take it easy," he said, throwing his palms up to her. "I understand your threats. I told you I'd give you what I have and I intend to." He sat up and put his feet on the floor, his elbows resting on his knees as he bent towards the table. "The call this morning came from Ann Carroll. I'm sure of it."

"How sure?" Hartley prodded, stepping forward and standing at the end of the coffee table with arms folded. "You said they were using an audio processor."

"They were," he agreed, holding up a finger. "But it was what was said and how she got in touch with me that makes me sure of who it was. When I met with O'Dowd and Walker that day to bring them what I had gotten from Reed, two things happened that led to both a mistake on my part and hers. First, I received an advance from them in the form of a check. In the aftermath of almost being blown up and moving from the hospital to where I'm at now, I made the poor decision to deposit that check in my account."

"When was that?"

"Sometime the next day. I just wasn't thinking. Anyway, when I was leaving the magazine that day, I gave my cell phone out to three people: O'Dowd, Walker and Ann Carroll. Given the fact that the caller knew where to reach me after I was supposed to be dead, and based on that they knew I had cashed the check, that led me to Ann Carroll."

Hartley thought for a moment. "Why wouldn't that lead you to O'Dowd or Walker?"

Dane smirked. "I figure if it was them behind the call, a packed train station wouldn't be the chosen destination."

Hartley walked the edge of the room slowly, her mind beginning to focus entirely on the case before her, banishing whatever thoughts of James and Ratliff that had been consuming her as of late. "How would Ann have all this information?" The two men glanced at one another before returning their eyes to Hartley. She stopped and turned to face them from the opposite side of the coffee table. "Ann Carroll, from my understanding, was just the secretary of *State of Finance*. She greeted visitors and took calls. I don't see how she could've come across anything regarding the embezzlement from her position behind that desk."

"But you're pigeonholing the secretary position," Dane replied. "*State of Finance* is a successful magazine within the Chicago city limits and surrounding areas. It has a small foothold nationwide, as well, but it doesn't come close to the distribution of, say, *Forbes* or *Money* or those types. And because of that it doesn't have the typical structure of the bigger circulations, which have Human Resources and Public Relations departments. *State of Finance* wasn't one of those corporations. From my understanding, they did have one or two people that looked after the finances, and another couple that did the PR. But nothing in terms of a designated division or department. But Ann Carroll had a hand in all of it. She *was* the greeter and call taker, like you said, but she was also pretty much the office manager. That gave her an in to every aspect of the business, including the finances."

The eyes within the room turned to the manila envelope screaming from the coffee table. "What's that say?" Hartley asked, moving around the couch and taking a seat next to Ratliff, who shifted to make room as he threw his arm on the tops of the cushions.

"That says everything you need to know," Dane replied cryptically, getting a glance from both detectives simultaneously. "The embezzling had been going on for at least a decade, according to that," he added, leaning forward and pulling the stack of papers from the folder and tossing them back to the table. "It seems like Ann kept copies of everything that was going on. First one starts just over ten years ago."

Hartley picked up the stack and shuffled through them, spending a decent amount of time sifting from one page to the next, though not enough to gather in all the information from a single sheet. "Why would she keep all of this?" she finally asked aloud, though the question was meant to be rhetorical.

Dane shrugged, rubbing his hand across his grizzled chin. "That's what I'm wondering."

"And why didn't she report this in the first place?" Ratliff added. "Ten years of solid proof of an embezzling scheme that includes your bosses ... Seems like something you don't want to be holding on to."

"Unless you were part of it to begin with," Hartley added. She looked up at the two men who both shrugged at the possibility. "Can't rule that out now. At some point within a decade's worth of scheming and defrauding, you have to realize you become an accessory to it. The only other reason to not come forward is that you are more than an accessory."

"I'd say that's possible," Ratliff added. "But maybe there are other circumstances that we don't know about."

"I'm sure there are," Hartley said, tossing the stack of papers back to the table. "But we need to keep everything in the foreground as we proceed. Nothing can be out of our line of sight." She paused momentarily before leaning back into the couch and raising her eyes to Dane, who looked back intently to her. "Give me the rundown of what these papers prove."

"Aren't you going to just look through them anyway?"

"Yeah," she replied, "but I'd like your take on it. We're going to scrutinize them under a very powerful microscope. Get some people that deal with fraud on it. But let's face it: being a journalist gives you more of an objective view at things."

Dane leaned forward, extending his hands and tapping his fingers on the documents. "After glancing through the documents, my opinion is this: for the last decade O'Dowd, Walker and an as-of-yet unknown third party have been skimming money from client accounts within Intervise Securities and placing the funds into offshore holding companies."

"Are there names listed in here?" Ratliff asked.

"For the holding companies? Yes. You'll have to skim through and find them, but what it essentially shows is that a large amount of money is being lifted from client accounts, passed into some offshore holding companies, rerouted in smaller chunks into other corporations and eventually ending up being withdrawn from there. The names of the guilty individuals don't show up within the documents, but two of them are definitely Seamus O'Dowd and Kyle Walker."

"How do you know that if the names aren't there?" Hartley asked.

Dane gave her an *are-you-joking* glance. "I may not have a badge but I also have ways of getting things."

Hartley nodded, directing her attention to Ratliff. "How much you want to bet the separate amounts withdrawn from the holding companies shows up as deposits in O'Dowd and Walker's personal accounts?"

Ratliff smirked. "We'll have to compare these pages to the financials that were just sent over, but I'm guessing it's to the penny."

THIRTY-TWO

They took a small break for everyone to warm up their coffees, grab a bagel or, in general, stretch their legs. Dane declined the offer for a pastry from Ratliff, instead remaining in the break room and pulling out a pen, skimming through the papers and writing down a list of nearly two dozen companies found throughout the documentation.

"From what I've come across since you two left," he began as the detectives made their way back into the room, "there are twenty-two companies that are in some way connected with the rerouting of funds."

Hartley and Ratliff took their positions on the couch opposite him and leaned into the table, their knees grazing slightly and causing each to cast a sideways glance to the other. Dane caught the anxious look between the two but wisely said nothing. "Delaney Holdings. West Palm Subsidiaries. New Wales Financial Assets. The list goes on and on."

"What do these companies do?" Hartley asked, her brow furrowing as she glanced up to her brother.

He shrugged, his eyes never leaving the papers. "I looked a few of them up on the way over here. Some seem to be legit. Some I couldn't find. I can get a few of my sources to look into the validity of them —"

"That's okay," Hartley interrupted. "We can get our people to do that." She looked up and connected with him. "Did you come across amounts?"

"Yeah, and they're pretty hefty, to say the least." Dane shifted through the papers once more and came to one of the sheets he was looking for. "For instance, this is a summary for West Palm Subsidiaries for the last 5 years. In all, over six million has gone through West Palm. Shows the transfers in small increments from a grouping of what I would assume to be Intervise clients. Money goes in. Money comes out."

"Where to?" Ratliff questioned.

"To the other businesses. From there they are eventually withdrawn, though the documentation doesn't provide who's making the withdrawal."

"I think I can help there," Ratliff said, picking up a stack of papers he had brought back with him after their break. "I got the financials for our people of interest."

"Which includes who?" Dane questioned.

"O'Dowd, Walker, Verland and Francesco. Now, if we can match the sums that are being withdrawn from the holding companies to these people, that would prove they are mixed up in all of this."

The group started with the *State of Finance* crew, Hartley and Ratliff each holding the respective sheets for the magazine's upper echelon while Dane worked his way through the never-ending combinations of numbers within the Reed documentation. The process was slow going, one of the detectives rambling off a corporation name and waiting as Dane skimmed through the pages. Several times they would cross an item off the list only to have Dane stumble upon the name twenty minutes later.

After nearly two hours of searching and highlighting the material before them, Hartley stood and stretched, her eyes tired, yet the fiery glow of progress lit behind them. They had what they needed to pull O'Dowd and Walker in for the embezzlement that had transpired for the past decade, yet they were still missing the third member of their criminal team. "What about Verland and Francesco?" Hartley asked, looking to her partner.

He flipped through the pages for several moments before responding. "Verland seems clean. There isn't anything that I see that's out of the ordinary. May want to get another pair of eyes on it, but from my point of view, everything's copasetic. Nothing outrageous. Well, besides his salary, that is." He chuckled and was surprised to pull a smile from Hartley as well. He continued. "Francesco is another story."

"What do we have on him?"

"Besides being a shut-in with extreme health problems? We have an account that has grown by about twelve million dollars in the last sixteen hours."

"What?" Hartley asked, walking over and snatching the paper from his hands. Her eyes grew wide as she looked to the financials of a successful, ninety-two year old man in the twilight of his life.

"According to the rest of his financials, Francesco's loaded. I have no other details on that twelve million. Don't know where it came from or where it was going. For all I know, it could be normal. Guy that rich may have twelve million just floating in and out of his account. It just struck me as odd that that amount of money is moved at this point of our investigation."

She handed the paper back to him just as his phone began to chime in his pocket. "Could be from his own accounts," Hartley agreed. "Who knows? We better follow up either way."

"Agreed," Ratliff said as he stood, signaling he would take the call in the pit. He left the two siblings in the break room and walked to his desk, taking a seat before his computer monitor. Hartley watched as he departed, her mind trying to connect the dots within her investigation, her eyes honed in on her partner's rear as he sauntered to his desk.

"You're more scandalous than I thought," came Dane's reply from over her right shoulder. "Your other little toy know you're in the market for your partner?"

Hartley turned to him with wide eyes, yet her face softened as she looked upon her brother, a playful smile crossing his face. No matter her feelings of dislike towards him, Dane was the one person in the world — besides Kimberly Banneau — who would not pass judgment on her for the way she was dealing with her current predicament. Indeed, he had been involved in an affair with Kelly Depler while she was in a serious, long-standing relationship. And as for Banneau, she just had no shame.

"Shut up," she finally said to him, moving away from the door and back into the room. Her arms were crossed as she looked to the floor, finally speaking while she walked along the length of the couch. Dane remained fixed on her, hanging on every word as she began to spout the details of the investigation, not knowing if it was to include him or to just voice her train of thought aloud. "Okay, so Reed gets handed these documents, probably because of his ability to investigate whatever topic thoroughly. We know he was an above average journalist. Both O'Dowd and Walker have attested to that."

"He was," Dane added, though his sister did not seem to hear him.

"He starts to get in over his head. Learns too much about it and needs to pass it off, which is where you come in. He sets up a meeting with you at The Fairborne Club but never shows because he's gunned down near his neighborhood. Whoever the killer is takes his briefcase and computer from the car and then rolls it down the hill with a deceased Bart Reed in the driver's seat."

The two glanced up as Ratliff made his way towards the printer. Hartley's train of thought was racing, however, and she looked past Ratliff, through the precinct, and into the files zipping around her mind. "The killer, or someone associated with the crime, ransacks Reed's home, presumably looking for the documents we now have before us."

Dane chimed in, feeling the adrenaline rush. "Meanwhile, the only other person to know about what Reed was working on was me. I head to *State of Finance* and meet with those assholes. I'm a thorn in their sides, so the only reasonable thing to do is knock me out of the picture. If I'm gone, the story's gone."

"And the embezzling can either continue or disappear. So, Walker hires his old buddy, Luke Moran, to build one of his motion-activated bombs and puts it in your place, although it goes off when Kelly walks into the apartment instead of you."

"So we can link Moran to Kelly's murder?"

"There's not a lot there, so it'll be tough," Hartley added. "I'm guessing there are hundreds of veterans in the city that worked with explosives. Really, you could build a case against any one of them. But with the ties to Walker, it gives us some solid ground to stand on. In addition, Walker was the only one that thought I had these documents, so he's the only one that could have sent those men to my place."

They remained quiet for a moment, each lost in thought. "So what now?" Dane asked as Ratliff opened the door and entered, a piece of white printer paper held between his finger and thumb.

Hartley lifted her gaze to her partner and their eyes connected. "There's already an APB out on Moran. With what you have here, I think it's time to go and pick up O'Dowd and Walker for their involvement. One of these assholes will have to break at some point. I just wish we had something a little more solid to press them with."

"I think I can help with that," Ratliff added, smiling and walking forward with the paper extended. "That was the lab with the ballistic results on the gun from your place. The bullets match those that were pulled from Reed's body and car."

"We have an ID on the owner?" Hartley asked.

"Not yet. I asked them to push hard on it and get back to me as soon as they have a hit."

"So we have the murder weapon," Dane said aloud, feeling his heart pump excitedly.

"Better than that," Ratliff added, glancing from him to Hartley and smiling yet again as their eyes met. "They were able to pull prints from the gun. I ran them through the system and got a match from military processing."

"What's that mean?" Dane asked.

Ratliff answered without taking his eyes off his partner. "Before giving your oath to serve, you go through MEPS. It stands for Military Entrance Processing Station. One of the things they do is take fingerprints for an FBI check."

"So the guy in your apartment was a military man?" he asked.

"And one we all know too well," Ratliff said, handing the sheet to Hartley who looked at it intently for ten seconds before tossing it on the table, the black and white image of Luke Moran staring up at them.

"It's time patrol finds this shithead," Hartley said. "Put another APB out on him. Light a fire under their asses. Let's pay another visit to *State of Finance*. O'Dowd and Walker's days of being free are about to come to a close."

THIRTY-THREE

Before they left, Jolene and Dane came to an agreement: he was able to make copies for himself and remain in the break room to go over the details of the documents with a fine-toothed comb, an option he was glad to accept. He had agreed to the fact that if anything new presented itself he would report it to Captain Nolan — who was keeping a watchful eye on the journalist — as well as the pair of detectives. They were working together on the case and each needed the other to be fully cooperative. Hartley needed Dane's source and the material that had been bestowed upon him, and Dane needed the protection the police had given him, at least until this thing was over with and he could return to the normality that was his existence.

The car ride to *State of Finance* was wrought with obstructions from the get-go. As Hartley and Ratliff entered the precinct garage they were confronted with a rear wheel that had gone flat overnight. Ratliff made a call upstairs and procured a new vehicle located a floor and a half above their current position, causing the detectives to hike it and be in the moment with each other for a decent amount of time.

To Hartley's surprise, however, her partner did not mention anything that had transpired between them, obviously focused on the task at hand. It made her smile as they walked side by side to the tan, unmarked auto. If he had been Barailles, the entirety of their stroll would have been wholly consumed with inquiries into their personal relationship and what their future could hold. The hiatus her and Ratliff now put on their extracurricular activities that morning was refreshing. Maybe he *could* separate his work and personal life.

The next obstacle they faced was late morning traffic. Cars were stacked bumper to bumper throughout the interior of the city, the result of an early morning accident involving a bus and an undersized, speedy, economical vehicle. Ratliff switched on the emergency lights momentarily before dimming them again, realizing nothing would move the congestion along save for the hand of God.

"So," Ratliff began, the sound of his voice stirring Hartley from the passenger window. "Did you want to know about what was found regarding the dude from your apartment? You know: the guy whose face you broke against that vase?"

Hartley turned to him with a puzzled expression that vanished almost immediately. "That's right," she replied. "You did mention that before. I'm sorry. I've been a little distracted this morning with ..." She stopped short as her temperature rose and she realized she had nearly walked right into the conversation she had wanted to avoid. Ratliff glanced to her and chuckled before returning his gaze to the parking lot in front of him.

"Korhan Karaca," he continued.

"Excuse me?"

He laughed again. "Korhan Karaca. He's the misfit son of an elderly Turkish couple from Norwood Park."

"An elderly *criminal* Turkish couple?"

"Not from what I got. No priors on the parents. Seems Korhan just ran with the wrong crowd from day one. Rest of his family is straight-laced, upstanding citizens with careers. Korhan must have been the bad apple."

"What's the connection to Moran and the *State* guys?"

Ratliff shrugged. "No clue. Didn't have time to look into it."

Hartley thought for a moment. "How'd we tag him? No way forensics could get DNA that quickly."

"DNA *is* underway, but no. Dumbass decided to not wear gloves to the scene, just like Moran. Left a paw print on the wall in his own blood. Technicians were able to pull from that and ran it."

"Do we know where Mr. Karaca is today?"

"Evidently he didn't hit up a hospital or clinic. My guess is he's licking his wounds someplace. He'll show up though. Shattered glass embedded in one's face tends to need some type of treatment. Either that or it'll leave one hell of a scar."

Hartley's phone rang just then and she looked away from her partner and to the display, her brow furrowing at the unknown number. "This is Detective Hartley."

"Detective," came Damian Verland's voice from the other end. "I hope I didn't catch you at an inconvenient time."

"No, Mr. Verland," she replied. "Just checking in on a few things. What can I help you with?"

"Actually, I was thinking that maybe what I have could help you." His voice was laced with tension, though had an unmistakable tone that bordered on excitement.

"How's that?" she inquired, pressing the speaker button and holding the phone aloft.

"Well, we were taking a look at the accounts early this morning, trying to come to terms with what exactly has been happening. You see: we're going to have to send out a correspondence to our clients soon to let them know of what has occurred. It's unethical to keep this from them."

"Understandable," Hartley replied.

"Well, moments ago I took a look into Isabella Bartollo's account and noticed that the funds that were present just yesterday have been removed."

"Do you know who made the withdrawal?"

"Officially? No. But there's only a couple people that have the authority to distribute large sums of money like that."

"Tell me this first," Hartley said, wanting to avoid any speculation at the moment. "How much was moved?"

Hartley could hear the VP of Intervise shuffling papers before he responded. "Just under twelve million dollars. $11,876,582, to be exact."

Hartley smiled. "Thank you, Mr. Verland. I think we can take it from here."

"Don't you want my opinion on who made the withdrawal?"

"At this particular moment, no. Kind of in the middle of something. I'll shoot you a call if I need anything."

"I will be available."

They hung up without saying another word, Hartley immediately hoisting the two-way radio to her lips and pressing the button. "This is Detective Jolene Hartley. I need a patrol unit to the *State of Finance* offices."

"Copy that, detective," came the grainy response. "Patrol to *State of Finance* building."

"Have them wait outside until I get there."

"Copy that, detective."

She tossed the two-way on the floor and turned her attention to the congestion surrounding them, looking for an escape of any kind that did not require them to walk. Ratliff fell in line and began to seek out an alternative route as well, settling on an alleyway thirty yards up the street on the left. "Hold on," he said, flipping the lights on once more and inching forward. As he edged closer to the bumper of the car in front of him, he let loose a series of alerts from the cruiser, causing the man in the vehicle to jump and raise his arms. Ratliff waved to him to inch forward, following the vehicle ever so closely until he had enough room to work his way onto the sidewalk.

Bystanders jumped out of the way of the cruiser as the detectives made their way slowly down the sidewalk, siren blaring and pulling in looks of amusement and consternation from those witnessing the scene. As they approached the alley Ratliff made the sharp turn, nearly clipping the brick building to their left. He looked to Hartley with raised eyebrows and an amused look. She could not help but grin and shake her head. "Nice work," she replied. "A few more of those and we should be there in no time."

* * * * *

The tension he felt as he paced back and forth behind his office desk was, to say the least, palpable. Seamus O'Dowd, in his entire life, had only been in trouble with the law once in college, arrested for underage drinking and possession of marijuana. He had spent the evening in the university police drunk tank and was released the following morning with a court date, a large fine, and an even heftier headache.

Now, as he made tracks on his office floor, he could not comprehend how things had unraveled so quickly. He should have never listened to Kyle Walker all those years ago. The scheme his partners had conjured up was foolproof, yet here they were, fools with the noose growing tighter around their collective necks.

And to make matters worse, Kyle seemed to not be that worried about it. He tended to display a calm, if not hesitant, demeanor when faced with the recent issues of their scheme going public, as if something or someone would grant their wish and make it all go away.

And then it did, in the form of a murdered Bartholomew Reed, a man that had helped modernize the *State of Finance* brand within the city and, to a much lesser extent, nationwide. Seamus had almost succumbed to a heart attack that morning when he had found out of Reed's downfall, though Kyle assured him it was the right course of action. He was already involved up to his ass in fraud and embezzling, his associate had said. He would hate to have to make a decision regarding O'Dowd's future.

Seamus had walked away with his tail between his legs, knowing that, in the grand scheme of things, his lust for money had resulted in the direct demise of his best reporter.

When Dane Hartley had shown up with the tainted story he knew what needed to be done, though in his own heart he did not have the courage — or connections — to see it through. He had brought Kyle into the meeting to listen while he acted as the respectable Editor in Chief he was. The story *was* sensational, and had he not been a central figure within it, he would have printed it in a flash. However, he was certain, with the investigative capabilities Dane had, his name would surface at some point, an outcome which he could not have. They had done the only thing they could: hired Luke Moran to remove the looming threat.

Dane was none the wiser when accepting the check and leaving the offices. Seamus had tried to curb the murderous appetite his associate was so eager to dish out, yet, in the end, there was no other way. Even if they were able to tarnish Dane Hartley's reputation to a point of no return, his accusations into the embezzlement would be scrutinized and O'Dowd's name would eventually be brought into the light.

Seamus knew his situation was not something that would only smear his name. He was facing a substantial amount of jail time. The amount of swindling he had been involved in would no doubt consume the remainder of his time on earth, and that was something he was unwilling to let go of. Freedom meant the world to him. He was against the killings that came so easy to Kyle and his associate, Luke Moran, however, if that was the only way to solidify his freedom, then so be it.

The door to his office swung open and in stepped Kyle Walker. His anxious face said it all: they were screwed. Kyle made his way to the window and stopped in the path Seamus had been treading for the past forty-five minutes. "We need to decide what to do," Seamus stated nervously, his arms crossed over his chest as his finger tapped rapidly against his slim biceps.

"Calm down," Kyle said, gazing through the glass to the streets below.

"Calm down?" Seamus said in a high pitch voice. "All this is crumbling around us and all you have to say is calm down?"

"Yeah," Kyle replied, stepping to Seamus. "I said calm down. We'll take care of it."

"Right," the Editor in Chief said. "What are you going to do now? Kill the detectives and storm the station? You've already managed to piss her off by killing her brother."

"Fuck you, you piece of shit," Kyle replied with venom dripping from his tongue. "I don't remember anyone holding a gun to your head when all this started. In fact, I remember you being quite willing to join in on getting rich."

"But I didn't sign up for the killings."

Kyle Walker smirked. "Comes with the territory."

Seamus eyed him cautiously. "No, it comes with you." He watched as Kyle shrugged and moved away, rounding the desk and taking a seat in one of the chairs opposite his superior.

Seamus followed suit, leaning back and rubbing his forehead. "What are our options right now?"

"Depends."

"On what?"

"On whether you want to get involved with some —"

"No more killings. What are our other options?"

Kyle crossed his legs and thought for a moment, rubbing the fabric near his knee. "First option is to run. Pull your money and get out of the country. We've both got plenty saved up to disappear and start new lives."

O'Dowd shook his head. "I can't live like that. I can't run like some felon."

"You are a felon." The comment brought forth a hate-filled gaze from the editor, though it faded after a moment. "Option two is dealing. Take what we know to the cops. Give yourself up. We can give them the head honcho and hopefully get a lesser sentence. Personally, prison doesn't sound like a good plan to me."

At that moment the door to the office opened and in stepped Luke Moran. Kyle turned and nodded briefly before returning to his spot. "Shut the door," he said. Moran did as directed, turning to glance quickly into the mayhem of the floor as he pushed the door closed quietly. He reached up and grabbed hold of the plastic rod of the blinds and began to twist, slowly narrowing the spaces to keep peering eyes from catching a glimpse of the impromptu meeting of the higher-ups.

It was at that moment Seamus O'Dowd noticed the gloves on Luke Moran's hands. He was not privy to the wardrobe of the man, yet gloves worn inside the building was something that struck him as odd.

It was not until Moran finished closing the blinds and turned into the room that O'Dowd completely understood. In his outstretched left hand, held tight and steady, was a black pistol with what appeared to be a silencer attached. The severity of the situation did not completely envelope Seamus until the first shot was fired and Kyle Walker's blood and brain matter splattered across his desk, the Assistant Editor falling forward and colliding with the solid wooden surface before collapsing to the floor in a heap of death, uprooting the chair as he went.

He did not have time to react, however, as the second shot zipped through the air and pierced his chest, embedding itself in his right lung. The third and fourth shots came in rapid succession, each connecting with his torso and sending him hurtling to the ground. He tried to breathe but was unsuccessful. His vision became blurry and he rolled onto his back, glancing up just in time to see Luke Moran step closer and aim the barrel at his forehead.

THIRTY-FOUR

Luke Moran remained stationary over Seamus O'Dowd just long enough to watch the life within his eyes extinguish for eternity, his lids making it three-quarters of the way shut before halting. He had been sent to complete a job and, as a military man, he always made sure that job was finished to the best of his ability.

The hole in Kyle Walker's head, in addition to the amount of blood now pooling on the office carpet beneath him, told Moran that his old friend was beyond this world, most likely tumbling through the bowels of hell for all his past transgressions. It was unfortunate to have ended their longtime relationship in this way, yet business was business. The payment he was to receive for today's act would far exceed what Walker and O'Dowd had handed out to him.

Luke Moran turned on his heels and began towards the door, sliding the silenced pistol into his jacket pocket as he reached for the knob. He exited the office through the narrowest of spaces, standing tall in case there happened to be another employee waiting to meet with the two men. Fortunately for him, there was not. The floor seemed to have gone unfazed by the commotion in the Editor in Chief's office, no doubt busy with the latest financial news coming out of the city.

Moran closed the door quietly and turned into the hall, glancing around quickly before making his way back towards the stairwell to his right. He nearly made it to the exit sign and adjoining stairwell, slowing as a sense of turbulence rose from where he had just departed, causing the hair on the back of his neck to stand tall. Something was not right. His objective was to use the keys Walker had given him to access the floor on which his old friend and the Editor in Chief resided. He was then to terminate both men, leaving no living witness — other than himself — as to who their third partner was in the embezzling ring. After, he was to return to the hallway and leave the premises, catching the first flight into Canada and from there someplace in Asia.

All had gone to plan, yet as he slowed, he could feel something behind him, something unaware of his presence, but just on the verge of identifying him. He halted quickly and glanced over his shoulder, catching sight of the two detectives as they approached Seamus O'Dowd's office door and knocked. Luke Moran sidestepped into a vacant office and walked to the corner where he would be hidden from view, his mind trying to grasp why the officers were there. He smiled to himself, coming to the realization that his murderous assignment had been carried out at the last possible moment.

* * * * *

Detectives Jolene Hartley and Jacoby Ratliff met the uniformed officer near the entrance of the building. His duty was to follow them to the appropriate floor and escort Ann Carroll to the precinct where she would be detained for an indefinite period in connection with the fraud that had played out for the past decade. In actuality, Hartley wanted to get Ann out of harm's way, making it seem that the receptionist was heading to the station against her will, a ploy she thought necessary in case of retaliatory actions against her. Charges against the supposed mole could eventually arise, yet the detectives did not see that occurring at this moment. Plenty of questions still needed to be answered and the Reed documentation scrutinized by financial experts before anything could be set into motion.

Ann Carroll did not seem too surprised when they stepped from the elevator, standing and forcing a nervous smile as she looked to Hartley. The detective explained herself and made it known that she was wanted for questioning, the uniformed officer stepping in and reading Ann her rights before placing handcuffs on her slim wrists and directing her to the elevator. Hartley watched, pulling her hair back into a loose ponytail that draped between her shoulder blades, confident that the receptionist was keen on the detective's friendly demeanor.

As the elevator closed and began its descent, the detectives made their way through the doors and onto the floor, very nearly taking out a running intern as he flew across the aisle, a stack of papers cradled precariously in his arms, a scowl on his face. They made their way to the far left wall and walked to Seamus O'Dowd's door, stopping and glancing over their shoulders as the room full of journalists rose to watch the officers, a din growing as both Hartley and Ratliff readied their handcuffs.

Hartley raised her hand to the door and knocked loudly. "Seamus O'Dowd," she said loudly through the wooden door. "Chicago PD. I have a warrant for your arrest and need you to come out here, please." They waited momentarily before she knocked again. "I'll give you five more seconds, Mr. O'Dowd. Then we're coming in." They waited, each ticking off the seconds in their minds. Hartley looked up to Ratliff. "Ann did say he was in here, right?"

Ratliff nodded. "Yep. All morning."

"Okay," she replied. "That's it." She turned away from her partner and reached out for the knob, twisting her wrist and pushing the massive door inward.

The instant it opened Hartley knew something was amiss. The smell floating in the air resembled that of the firing range she frequented several times a week and, at first glance, the office seemed unoccupied. A split second later Hartley's mind registered the overturned chair and Kyle Walker lying in a large pool of what appeared to be blood. She instinctively placed her hand on her firearm as she made her way across the carpet and to the body, Ratliff following behind her and pausing momentarily before noticing a heap behind the desk.

He took two steps before his eyes came to rest upon the mess that was Seamus O'Dowd's lifeless corpse.

"O'Dowd?" Hartley asked anxiously.

"Gone," Ratliff replied, bringing his portable two-way to his ear. "This is Detective Jacoby Ratliff. I'm at the offices of *State of Finance* magazine. I need backup. I have two civilians down. Repeat: two civilians down. Both appear deceased."

There was a crackle from the radio speaker. "Copy, detective. *State of Finance* building. Sending an ambulance and patrols units."

Hartley stood quickly as Ratliff hooked the two-way back onto his belt. She glanced around the room before turning and making her way towards the doorway, her partner following close behind with a last glance to the pool of blood consuming Kyle Walker. A small crowd had begun to form outside the office, men and women moving into place to watch the detectives arrest their superior. They fell back into one another, grabbing onto cubicle walls as the gravity of the situation kicked them squarely in the face.

Hartley pushed through the gathering group and looked down the hall to her right, watching as several men in suits made their way hurriedly towards her, a look of concern spread across their faces. "Please, go back to your offices or cubes," she said aloud. "We have units en route. I will need you all to please remain at your stations."

"What is going on?" one of the men said loudly from a dozen yards away.

"Please, sir, just go ..." Hartley froze as, from a short distance behind the suits, a large man in a black coat exited an office and turned quickly away from the commotion, making his way briskly towards an exit sign and the stairway to the ground floor. The man glanced over his shoulder for an instant and Hartley caught her breath, immediately recognizing the crooked nose of Luke Moran. She retrieved her service piece and held it at the ready.

"Move!" Hartley yelled to the suits, each one of them ducking or moving into the closest opened office or cubicle. "Luke Moran! Stop where you are! Chicago PD!" The detectives, as well as the suits and swarm of reporters, glanced in the direction of Hartley's gaze just in time to see the large man in the black coat remove a pistol from his jacket pocket and turn towards them.

"Down! Down!" Hartley shouted, pulling the nearest group of crying women to the floor as she fell. The concussion was not that of a typical gun blast, yet the bits of drywall and shattered glass from hanging picture frames gave way to the realization that bullets were indeed heading in their direction. Ratliff fell to the floor, rolling into O'Dowd's room and pulling his service piece from its holster. He looked up to see a *State of Finance* employee leaning against the wall in direct fire, his arms covering his head as he screamed. A moment later he crumpled to the floor with a guttural groan, reaching to his hip and rolling manically to the left and right. Ratliff reached out, listening to the whizz of bullets strike the drywall behind him, grasping onto the man's blue-collared shirt and pulling him to safety.

Hartley leaned into the aisle cautiously, sighting Moran against the corridor wall with his gun raised. She ducked back just in time as a bullet penetrated the cubicle wall, ricocheting off the metal construction and into the hall window of the far office. "Jay!" Hartley called to her partner.

"You okay?" he responded.

"Yeah. You?"

"Fine. You got a shot?"

"No. Can you?"

"Not from where I'm at." He paused for a few seconds before continuing. "I've got an idea. When he turns, shoot!"

Ratliff edged closer to the doorway, ducking his head out quickly to gain perspective as to his target's position. The man was moving backwards towards the exit sign and stairwell, gun still held to the officers, his head jerking over his shoulder and back as he tried to keep both the detectives and his escape route in sight.

"Ready?" Ratliff said.

"Go!" Hartley yelled, watching as her partner shifted half his body into harm's way.

The movement produced the result they were looking for, however dangerous it was. From the end of the hall, Luke Moran halted briefly, aiming the pistol at the exposed detective and squeezing the trigger. Ratliff anticipated the reaction and ducked back into the room, the loud *ping* of the projectile striking the metal doorframe and careening somewhere into the chaos that was *State of Finance*.

The seconds it took allowed Hartley to complete her plan of attack. She dropped to her right shoulder and aimed at the murderer down the hall, pulling the trigger and letting a bullet lose. A roar escaped Moran's lips as the slug struck the gun and proceeded to embed itself in his right hand, the firearm dropping to the floor in a broken metallic clang as he brought his wounded extremity to his chest. He spun quickly to the exit and flew through the opening, his momentum sending him flying headfirst down several steel and concrete steps before regaining his footing and bounding towards the ground floor.

Hartley regained her feet, her partner grabbing an elbow and assisting her up as the two began down the hall with weapons raised. Ratliff moved swiftly behind her, two-way again in hand. "Detective Jacoby Ratliff! Shots fired! Repeat: shots fired! I need that backup as soon as possible!"

"Copy that, detective. Patrol units are en route."

"Have them seal off the building and get a three-block radius set! Our suspect is on the premises but making his way towards the exit!"

"Do you have a description of the suspect?" the dispatcher questioned.

"Affirmative. Our suspect is a tall, dark-haired Caucasian male. He has a wounded right hand. Name is Luke Moran." He ended the conversation as the pair approached the stairwell, slowing up and positioning themselves on either side of the door. Hartley nodded and stepped square with the doorway as

Ratliff pushed it open, each raising their weapons immediately for the ambush that was not there. They passed through the opening and into the stairwell, peering over the side for their suspect and noticing the bloodstained handrails heading to the ground floor.

The detectives took off, each clearing two or three steps at a time as they corkscrewed their way down, pausing slightly as they rounded each corner until they reached the ground floor. Hartley nodded to Ratliff and they burst through the door to an empty hallway, the duo glancing left and right with raised weapons.

"Go check the front," Hartley directed her partner. "See if the guard saw anyone go past."

Ratliff turned and ran cautiously down the hall, disappearing from view as Hartley remained stationary near the stairwell, her breathing rapid as the adrenaline pumped through her veins, a feeling she had not had since the fateful day at Navy Pier when she had confronted Taylor Thames.

After nearly thirty seconds, Ratliff reappeared. "Guard's posted near the door. Our guy didn't come through there. Said there's an exit on the far side of the building, but it's tied into the central alarm system, which hasn't gone off. The only other way is through the printing warehouse that leads to the back alley. Guard says all the doors should be locked though. Press isn't running today so the warehouse is locked up and empty."

"Makes the perfect escape route for our guy then," Hartley replied, beginning her way towards the warehouse. They weaved through the interior of the building, following the zigzag of the off-white hallway until it finally opened up to a straightaway. A loud clang from the end of the hall and to the right brought the detectives to full alert.

The pair proceeded cautiously in the direction of the disturbance, Ratliff shadowing Hartley with his firearm lowered as she continued with hers extended before her. As they neared the corner Hartley caught sight of Moran heaving himself into the door, his massive shoulder connecting with the surface and rattling the solid metal frame like a caged animal looking for an escape to freedom. "Moran! Police! Freeze!" Hartley yelled, halting a dozen yards away with her piece pointed to the door, an ample amount of room to fire several shots if the need arose.

Moran turned and glanced at the detective with a sneer, backing away from the door quickly and disappearing behind the corner of the wall. "Moran! I said freeze —" she began to yell again, the latter half of her directive cut off as his enormous frame barreled through the sturdy, metal door with a thunderous clamor.

From sheer power, Moran was able to break the lock from its housing, the jamb bending inward as he flew through the opening and into the warehouse. The door swung in with such force that it crashed into the connecting wall, the handle rattling as it hung limply. Moran's momentum carried him so rapidly through the entrance that Hartley was unable to determine if he had stayed on his feet or not. She charged forward, halting next to the opening as she allowed her eyes time to focus into the gloom. "Stay close," she said to Ratliff.

The warehouse beyond was dark. Light from grungy ceiling windows fought its way through in broken, pitiful rays, shining down on inactive, dusty machinery from an era long ago. A clatter from the end of the warehouse tipped Hartley off as to Moran's location and she once again began her hunt, passing through the threshold and into the room ahead of her partner.

At that moment, from the gap between the door and wall, Ratliff caught a glimpse of their suspect, the light from the hall shining onto him as he dropped his shoulder and ran full speed towards the opening. "Wait!" Ratliff yelled, jumping forward just as Moran barreled into the door. Hartley turned at the last instant and braced for the impact, the door rocketing towards her and sending her airborne, her firearm dropping and skittering among the machinery. A grotesque exhale escaped her mouth as the air from her lungs rushed out. She slid across the warehouse floor and came to rest against a stack of wooden crates with a thud.

Ratliff, in his haste to help his partner, had jumped into the door from the other side just as Hartley went flying. He reached for her but came up empty, instead colliding with the metal panel and sliding forward until his wrist entered the room, the door crunching bone and tendons against the twisted jamb. He let out a scream and dropped his gun in the hallway, reaching up to yank his broken wrist from the vice it was now in. He collapsed in agony within the hallway and listened to their suspect slam the door shut, the metal of the jamb screeching in the process.

ON THE EDGE OF GREED

As he tried to regain his feet, left hand tucked beneath his right armpit, thoughts switching from the excruciating pain of his broken bones to his helpless partner, he heard the one sound he dreaded: the metal-grating lock of a deadbolt sliding into place.

THIRTY-FIVE

The jarring sound of the deadbolt was echoed clear to Hartley as she struggled to capture her breath from her crouched position on the cold warehouse floor, her hand resting on a pallet stacked with hundreds of reams of computer paper. She scanned the floor while working her lungs, searching for the gun that had been wrenched free from her grasp when Luke Moran bull-rushed her at the entrance.

The scream that emitted from Ratliff's mouth as she flew through the air had caused the hair on the back of her neck to stand tall. She could not imagine what had brought forth the eruption from her partner, though she was certain that he was in definite pain. Now, with the deadbolt set in place and Ratliff's calls muted beyond the divide of the warehouse wall, Hartley mentally checked off another negative on her ongoing pros and cons list.

She could always tell who was holding the better hand, and at the moment, hers was well below par. Locked in a warehouse with a murderer of stature much larger and more powerful than her own was not the ideal situation. Yet she had been dealt these specific cards and, as an officer of the law — and a human being — she needed to make the most of her current, abysmal predicament. The odds of beating Luke Moran hand-to-hand were astronomical, even with all the training throughout her career, which, in the end she decided, would just delay the inevitable. She needed to even up the odds, take hold of the upper hand.

She needed her gun.

Hartley was yanked from her reveries as a muffled cry seeped through the walls. "Jo!" Ratliff yelled, the distant words tinged with pain and concern. Hartley turned to the sound of his voice just in time to see Luke Moran closing in, a look of determination spread across his bruised face, a reminder of the last time the two had met.

She moved quickly, rolling across her right shoulder and popping up into a crouched position a few yards away. She rose to her feet and took off around the stack of paper, Moran reaching out and taking hold of the bottom of her jacket and yanking the fabric towards him, pulling the detective into the pallet. Hartley reacted instinctively by throwing her left elbow up with a sudden jerk and connecting with his exposed throat, the shot causing him to stagger, though his grip on her leather jacket did not lessen.

As Moran composed himself, pulling the coat with his left hand, Hartley wriggled free, shedding the garment and running along the locked wire cages of printer inks and toners in her short-sleeved white blouse, her eyes scanning the ground for her service piece or any other item she could employ against him.

* * * * *

"Jo!" Ratliff screamed from the hallway, his body doubled-over as he tried to curb the excruciatingly painful throb that had begun in his broken left wrist. He winced as he retrieved the firearm laying an arm's length away and drew himself up, instantly taking aim and kicking out at the warehouse door with the ferocity of a caged animal, his foot ramming into the surface with a thud, rattling the fractured doorknob hanging down on either side.

The deadbolt, however, did not budge.

His wrist ached fiercely and he could have sworn his shoulder had been dislocated from bouncing off the door, though upon further inspection he realized this was not so. The thought of his partner trapped in the warehouse with a mass murderer clouded his mind, acting as a sort of painkiller to his brain for the moment, keeping him moving as he raised his foot once more and lashed out.

He kept at it, his boot again and again striking the surface, only to be thrown back each and every time. He took large breaths between hits, his ankle colliding with a jarring action that sent an increasing amount of discomfort shooting up his leg.

"You're not getting through that," the guard from the lobby said suddenly as he turned the corner. Ratliff stopped mid-attack with weapon raised to the approaching figure, perspiration evident across his brow as he set his boot back on the floor.

He lowered the firearm and turned back to the door. "I need a way in," he said, leaning his weight into the opposite wall as he caught his breath. "How many doors lead into this warehouse?"

"Two," the guard replied, stepping closer to the detective as he eyed the bent doorjamb with astonishment. "This one and another in the back alley. There's also a small loading dock, but I don't have keys to that. Only the warehouse manager."

"Who's the manager?" Ratliff questioned.

"Simon Lesh," he responded. "I didn't see him come in today though. Usually doesn't when the presses aren't running."

"What about the door to the back alley? How do you get to it? You have keys?"

"Yeah. At the front desk. The alleyway is just to the left outside the front lobby, but the city blocked it off a few months ago with a wrought iron gate. Goal was to keep the homeless out."

"So you can't access it is what you're telling me?" Ratliff said, an irritated tone creeping into his voice.

"Not unless you wrap around the parking garage to the block just behind. You can come through the alley that way and —"

"I don't have that kind of time," Ratliff said as he limped slowly down the hallway, eyes searching. "What's on the other side of this?" he asked, pointing his firearm at the wall separating the warehouse from the rest of the building.

"Metal cages."

"How high?"

"It's a warehouse. They go up to the ceiling. About eighteen feet or so."

"Shit!" Ratliff whispered under his breath. Eighteen feet meant that the warehouse ceiling was much higher than the one above their heads. Ratliff had hoped to climb into the paneled ceiling and maneuver his way into the warehouse by following the air ducts and dropping in on the other side. With the higher ceilings Ratliff would be forced to climb, an option he did not have with a busted wrist. It also made the plan of going through the wall impossible. Even if he were able to pull down the drywall on either side, he would be forced to remain in the hallway due to the metal grating, which would be fine if their suspect was sitting in the open for a clean shot. If he were not, however, Ratliff would risk creating a panicked scene within, something that would definitely not help his partner in the least.

"Wait," the guard said with a finger extended before him, eyes focused elsewhere. "The metal grating covers these two walls here," he replied, pointing to the surface adjacent to them, as well as up the hall. "But there's a portion that was removed to fix some pipes a couple years ago. It was never replaced after that. The printing crew put up some pegboard and a desk instead."

"Where?" Ratliff asked hurriedly.

The guard grinned. "Come on. I'll show you." He led Ratliff down the hall and to the left, continuing for nearly twenty yards before stopping near a red-painted pipe jutting from the wall, the valve pointing to the floor as the rest of the tubing turned skyward and disappeared into the ceiling tiles above.

* * * * *

As she moved among the wooden pallets and metal crates filled to the brim with inks, toners, paper reams and random office supplies, Hartley kept her ears open for signs of movement, her eyes still scanning the floor in search of her firearm. She had not seen or heard anything of Luke Moran since striking him in the throat and hoped he was incapacitated — if not dead — on the cold floor with a crushed larynx. She did not, however, have the gall to backtrack and check. Not without her gun.

She reached the end of the aisle and lowered to a knee, dropping her head to the floor to gain a visual underneath the shelving unit. It was the wrong time to be off guard. She at last heard feet shuffle across the floor and rose up just in time to catch Moran's bloody knuckles across her right cheek, the backhand thrown with a force that sent her spiraling into an empty cubbyhole across the aisle.

Hartley collected herself quickly, realizing any stall would, no doubt, end in her lifeless body being shoved into an alcove to be found at a later date. She bounced up and stood her ground, setting her body into a defensive stance as he came at her once more, his right arm hooking towards her ribs with a speed that caught her off guard. Hartley was unable to dodge the assault completely, instead dropping her left arm and taking the blow fully on the elbow. She cringed, but pounced on an opportunity of her own, striking out with her right hand speedily and connecting once more to his exposed throat.

Moran tried to dodge at the last minute, overcompensating and losing his balance slightly as the detective spun and began in the opposite direction. He reached up in time to clasp a fistful of Hartley's long, brown hair, pulling it forcefully towards him and bringing forth a groan from her lips as she came to rest against his body. He swung his injured right arm like a club, connecting with blistering strength into her lower back, the pain dropping her to her knees.

She was vulnerable in her current position: on her knees, head tilted to the sky, Moran standing tall behind her with a strong hold on her ponytail. She needed to act, and quickly.

Without hesitation, Hartley wrapped her right arm around Moran's thigh, grabbing on so tightly he was unable to regain his balance with both feet, instead teetering precariously on his left leg. With her other hand she clasped onto her own ponytail just below Moran's vice-like grip, setting her hand closer to her head in an effort to cause as little pain as possible as she dropped her full weight to the floor.

The sting as dozens of strands of hair simultaneously tore loose from her scalp was insanely intense, yet the move was utterly necessary. Moran could have easily held her aloft for hours, yet the sudden drop caused him to shift towards her, allowing Hartley to spin clockwise and swing her raised legs into his, buckling his knee and sending him collapsing in a heap.

He released his grip on her hair as he tried to catch himself. Hartley reacted without delay, leaping up and kicking into his midsection, her toe connecting just under his ribcage and extracting a grunt from her suspect. In the attempt to curb the blow, Moran threw his hands to his stomach, grasping onto her foot loosely as she retreated, catching her boot and causing her to stumble backwards.

She squared him up again. Moran had regained his feet and was inching towards her, arms down, a toxic grin spread across his face that set a fire within her. From the corner of her eye Hartley caught sight of an object she could employ, something that could, if used properly, afford her the breathing room she so desperately needed.

She reached up to the shoulder-high shelf and retrieved a red Swingline stapler from a row of random office supplies and unhinged it, bringing it to the ready at her side. The object, on any other given day, would have brought forth thoughts of Milton from the movie *Office Space*, his magnified glasses and extreme, hilarious quirkiness a favorite of the detective's as she ate popcorn and drank wine on her long nights in.

Moran chuckled at the stapler, her desperation evident to him as he threw a left jab to her chest. The humor faded fast as Hartley jumped back a half step and brought the mechanism up to meet his outstretched fist, the pressure from the strike triggering a two-pronged staple to eject from its chamber and embed itself into the meaty area straddling a knuckle. "Fuck!" he yelled as he pulled back, shaking his hand briskly in a failed attempt to free the fastener.

Hartley took the opportunity to strike again, this time swinging the stapler sidearm like a tennis racket, connecting just above Moran's left eyebrow. He went down to a knee as a staple sliced through flesh, the prongs scraping against bone and pulling another expletive from his mouth.

Her advantage disappeared immediately as she felt the blood-covered palm of his right hand grasp about her throat, the pressure enough to cause the detective extreme discomfort, yet the embedded bullet not allowing him to close off her windpipe completely. He pulled her to him, pinning the stapler between their bodies, his breath passing over her face from inches away. "You're getting on my fucking nerves, detective!" he growled just before jerking his head forward to collide with her left eyebrow, splitting the skin and forming a river of blood that ran down her cheek and turned her white blouse red.

The gash stung like hell as her pain receptors sparked to life, yet it was the blunt force of the hit that shook her. Her head immediately ached. Her ears rang and vision blurred as she watched through a haze as Moran raised his left fist to strike out again. Hartley was sure the outcome would knock her unconscious and, ultimately, end in her inevitable death. She suddenly felt her right arm swing free, the stapler still held fast in her palm as her suspect cocked his arm back.

With a quickness and accuracy that surprised even her, Hartley unleashed the stapler again, the mechanism's chamber colliding with Moran's cheekbone and ejecting a fastener into his eye socket. "Shit! Shit!" he screamed as the staple prongs sliced into the sclera of his eyeball. He dropped his fist and reached to cradle the fresh wound, fingers gently running along the fastener as it moved wherever his gaze fell.

Moran, incensed, turned his attention back to Hartley, curling his fingers into a tight fist and connecting fully with her ribs. She collapsed, looking up just in time to receive yet another backhand, the blow spinning her to the floor to land as if ready to take on a round of morning pushups. She opened her eyes wide and exhaled, watching as droplets of blood fell from her split brow to pool beneath her.

It was at that exact moment, eyes to the floor, Moran shuffling towards her little by little as he tried to pry the collection of staples he now wore as facial piercings from his skin, that Hartley realized for the first time she was going to die. Nothing seemed to stop him. Not punches. Not kicks. Not even a staple embedded into the white of his eye had halted his progress, though it had indeed slowed him for the moment. She was hurting as she lay on the cool, dusty floor, visions of another warehouse where Taylor Thames had held a gun to her head filling her mind.

What is it with warehouses? she caught herself thinking, shaking the inner dialogue from her brain and trying to draw her attention to the here and now. She lifted her head and nearly burst out laughing with excitement as her eyes came to rest on her service piece a dozen yards away, half-hidden by a large, blue tarp hanging loosely over a mound of recently printed *State of Finance* issues.

Hartley began to push herself up, her body shaking as if she had completed her very first marathon. All she needed was a moment, a singular instant to propel herself forward and take two — maybe three — unsteady bounds before diving towards the gun.

Luck was not on her side. Before she could even take that initial stride, the instep of Luke Moran's foot collided with her ribs, rolling her onto her back with an intense pain spreading throughout her stomach. She looked up and watched him approach, the staple still hanging from his eyeball, though the one attached to his forehead had successfully been ripped out, leaving two fresh drops of blood to begin their slow decent down his face.

He towered over her for a moment, looking upon the detective with utter hatred, though a definite respect. She had taken a beating that most human beings would have succumbed to long ago, even lashing out and causing him an exuberant amount of pain as well. She was a worthy opponent. Unfortunately she was not one he could allow to live another day.

THIRTY-SIX

Hartley had planned to take a quick shot at either his injured eye or, if he refused to protect it yet again, his throat. Yet Luke Moran did not allow the opportunity to arise, turning her away from him as he yanked her from the floor, grabbing tightly to her shirt collar and belt.

She felt her body flying away from him, helplessly flailing her arms and legs as she sailed through the air and towards a metal work desk with a thick glass top stacked high with papers and random office utensils. Hartley knew the landing was going to hurt. Pens and steel rulers and large metal plates littered the three-quarter inch glass surface, and the only option she could think of was to raise her arms and protect her vitals, hoping the sharp objects would not puncture any arteries.

She slammed into the desk with such force the glass top cracked and split, breaking into dozens of large and medium size shards that tumbled several inches onto the steel plating separating the upper workspace from the lower shelving units.

Hartley miraculously missed the steel rulers and metal plates, however, connected fully with a slim, six-inch glass dagger that sliced through her pants and into her upper thigh, embedding itself into the muscle nearly two inches deep.

Hartley yelled in pain as she tumbled to the ground with her hand clasped around the wound. Cautious fingers tested the makeshift dagger protruding from her thigh, massaging the area with gentle fingertips in an attempt to will herself to pull the shard from beneath her flesh. She opened her eyes and zoned in on Moran, the behemoth of a man standing stationary as he yet again flirted with the idea of pulling the staple from his eye. Hartley glanced back to her leg and wrapped her hand around the piece of glass loosely, breathing deeply as she readied herself for the pain that would unavoidably come with the removal of the protrusion.

Just before she pulled she glanced up. Ahead, equidistant from Luke Moran and herself lay her firearm. Hartley released the crystal splinter and thought quickly, coming to the conclusion that if she moved hastily, there was a definite possibility she could reach the gun with just enough time to spin and fire. Moran seemed distracted with his wounds, giving the detective reason to believe she could get even closer to the piece before he realized what was happening.

Hartley rolled to her hands and knees and stole a glance to Moran once more before setting her heel and springing forward, diving at the last moment with her arm extended in a desperate attempt to retrieve her firearm. She caught her breath as, from her left, Moran charged and collided with her, stopping her progress just feet from the weapon. Moran rolled Hartley to her back and straddled her, surprised as she lashed out, gifting him a glancing blow to the chin that jerked his head viciously back and to the right.

Enraged, Moran showered blow after blow down upon the detective, Hartley raising her forearms up in a defensive posture as each strike connected with little to minimal damage. She was in dire straits and knew it. Moran's weight atop her body did not allow Hartley any leeway to move, let alone escape and reach the gun. From her spot underneath the man she had no quick access to a red stapler or Waterford crystal or any weapon, nor had she strapped on an extra piece to her ankle, a normality when she was expecting trouble. Her trip to *State of Finance* was supposed to be free of obstacles. Everything that had happened within the last twenty minutes had not even crossed her mind on the ride over. It was something she would have to remember in the future, if she indeed had a future.

Hartley was brought from her thoughts as, from between her raised forearms, Moran's fist passed through, colliding fully with her left cheekbone and forcing her head back into the concrete floor with a thud. Sparkles formed behind her eyes and she struggled to keep her arms raised, her body feeling heavier than it had moments ago, her mind clouded as she tried to remember where she was and what she was doing.

Moran raised his hand once more yet halted, realizing the last blow had done its job. He looked to the gun before focusing on the attractive, battered officer pinned below him, smirking as he ran his fingers across her forehead, brushing the blood-soaked hair back from her eyes that fluttered open and shut. "You think it matters?" he asked, bending towards her and wincing as the staple attached to his eye moved a little too much. "You think those two bastards mattered in the grand scheme of things?"

Hartley listened to the distant voice as she tried to center past the flickering stars in her vision to the man hovering above her. She opened her mouth to speak but the words failed her. Moran laughed, bringing his fingers down her cheek. "No," he continued. "They don't matter. They were pawns. Just like me, I'm sure you're thinking. Sure, you're right. But I'm still walking this earth. And I'll continue to walk this earth. You and your partner out there think this is about a dead journalist, but it's not."

"What's it about then?" she forced out in a rasp, blinking rapidly.

"Money," he said blatantly. "Lots of money."

"We'll catch you," Hartley replied, extracting a laugh from him.

"No, you won't. Believe me. The amount of money I'm getting will allow me to disappear. No trace."

"There's always a money trail."

"Not the way it's been done for me, detective. This isn't like someone writing a personal check. This will never be traced. Not the way my employer is moving it." He stopped as his eyes passed over her in a controlled, manipulative way, seemingly oblivious to the fact that patrol units were now on their way to secure the building, if not there already. His demeanor seemed steady, and Hartley immediately came to the conclusion that Luke Moran was sure of his escape from the premises, regardless of the amount of time spent in combat with her. The thought bothered her, and she decided at that moment that, along with securing her safety, Luke Moran must not be allowed to leave.

With her arms already at her side, Hartley gritted her teeth and grabbed hold of the glass shard sticking from her thigh, feeling the ragged edges cut into her palm as she yanked it free and brought it flying up towards Moran's neck. She heard him curse loudly as it pierced the skin and buried into his flesh, the makeshift dagger pulling free of her grip as he toppled backwards onto the ground, his hands reaching up to the protrusion sticking from his body.

Hartley rolled onto her side and nearly doubled over in pain as her hip burned fiercely. The stars reappeared within her sight as she tried to repress the urge to vomit, her equilibrium still off from the blow she had received moments ago. She shook her head and forced herself to focus. She needed to clear her vision. She needed to gather herself to make her next move. She needed to reach her gun.

* * * * *

The crash that reverberated along the wall Ratliff and the guard, Andrew, now stood in front of caused enough of a jolt to make both men jump. Something was happening, and that something was no doubt Hartley fighting to stay alive. "I need your help," Ratliff said as he stared to the wall, his voice tinged with anxiety.

"Anything," Andrew replied.

"Go back to the door and keep trying to get through."

"It's pointless though," the guard said with raised palms. "With that deadbolt, no one's getting through there. I can help you here. I'm assuming you're going through the wall?"

"Yeah, but I need you to keep at the door."

"Detective, like I said, with the —"

"I know, I know!" he interrupted. "Just keep kicking the door. I need a distraction. I need the guy in there to keep his attention focused at the door while I get through the wall." The guard nodded as the misdirection began to sink in. He turned and darted back the way they had just come, rounding the corner and sprinting down the hall where he set himself in front of the battered door.

Ratliff waited, his eyes looking to the surface of the wall, his ears listening for any sound coming from the other side. It had gone silent, and Ratliff's worry increased ten-fold as he waited for Andrew to get into position. Within several moments a loud clang began to rush down the hallway, the sign Ratliff had been waiting for as Andrew began his assault on the warehouse door, pausing a second or two between each kick.

Ratliff holstered his weapon and glanced around, searching for anything to help him through the wall and realizing, even if he had found an item such as an axe or fire extinguisher, he would be unable to swing it with his wrist in shambles. Instead, he waited for a moment, listening to the repetitive sound of the guard's banging before timing his own kick to match. The drywall beneath his footfalls began to give way in small chunks, the inner plaster core flaking off in miniscule amounts and floating on the air, catching onto his clothes and skin as he mimicked the pattern of Andrew's repeated attacks.

* * * * *

Hartley moved on all fours as quickly as she could, teetering back and forth as she tried to keep her eyes on the prize — the Glock 19 lying on the floor in front of her. A series of concussions had begun to rise from the warehouse door and spread quickly throughout the building, rumbling off the walls and falling upon Hartley's ears in an obvious sign that someone was trying to come to her aid.

She made it nearly a foot and a half before feeling a tug at her pants leg, the yank bringing her flat to the floor. She was flipped to her backside and saw the hazy silhouette of Luke Moran glaring down at her, his face beet-red with anger, the glass shard sticking out from the grotesque laceration Hartley had inflicted upon him.

She determined she had missed an artery — however, not by much — as blood oozed down his neck instead of spurted, soaking into his shirt and jacket. She made a mental note that if he were to draw her to him again, she would need to bury the object deeper.

From his knees Moran reached out and tugged on Hartley's left thigh, slowly reeling in the detective like a fish that was no match for his superior size and strength. She was at a severe disadvantage and had learned through training that when confronted with the bleakest of situations, one could not discount cheap shots and dirty play, something that could enable her freedom, if just for a moment.

Using the force generated by his latest tug, Hartley kicked her free leg towards him, driving her heel straight into his crotch with a sickening crunch. Moran grunted as the veins in his face popped out, his arms growing shaky as he tried not to vomit from the blow. His hand, however, remained locked on her pants as he leaned forward and propped himself up, trying to work his way to the detective as well as give himself some stability.

Hartley took advantage of his positioning, kicking out with her heel once more and sending the large man crashing to the ground as his knee was knocked from under him. He landed across her legs, however, pinning them as she tried to make her escape. The detective leaned up and shot her right fist towards the glass shard but fell short as he rolled to the right, her arm grazing his elbow. Moran came to rest near a crate full of tarps and quarter-inch thick white rope, an obvious necessity for a warehouse with a leaky roof.

Hartley flipped over quickly and reached out for the gun, knowing she had left herself utterly vulnerable even before the white rope passed over her head and in front of her eyes, the scratchy material coming to rest across her throat and tightening. She twisted to her back, realizing the action may allow her to wedge her fingers between the noose and her flesh.

Moran jumped forward, straddling her yet again as she turned to face him. Sensing the roll, he swung the rope to her back, the noose wrapping tightly around her neck as he pulled her into a sitting position, his weight fully on her kneecaps as he bear-hugged her, pinning her arms to her sides.

This is it, she thought, feeling the rope tighten over her throat, her breathing completely cut off as she stared up to him. She was utterly at his mercy now, something she understood he would not show her. With her face beginning to turn red and tears streaking down her cheeks, Hartley forced herself to shift back and forth, wiggling in a desperate attempt to free her arms from his grasp.

"Sssh," he whispered to her, bringing his face in close. "It'll be over soon."

The truth of the statement hit her fully as she looked up to her killer. Her life had been good, if not slightly skewed away from a personal one and more towards her career. She wished she had focused a little more on her social life. Nights out with Kim Banneau. Vacation days. Longer lunches. All seemed to have more appeal at this particular instant.

Moran's face was calm, though Hartley could see the pain she had inflicted upon him in the form of a staple in the eyeball and a bloodstained glass knife protruding from his neck. There was no overpowering him, no miracle that would allow her to free herself from his grasp. The shard, possibly millimeters from an artery, tempted her from inches away, teasing her to reach up and plunge it deeper and cause an inevitable, catastrophic event for Luke Moran.

She could not manage that, however, and her focus began to falter as the pressure inside her head increased. She lifted her eyes past him, not wanting her last memory to be of her killer's amused face. She wanted something better. A sunny day in a park. A steaming hot bubble bath.

Ronny Debarsi on his motorcycle.

James Graiser at the dinner table.

Jacoby Ratliff with a gun hanging through the wall.

Anything would be better than —

Wait. What? she thought, fixing her gaze over Luke Moran's shoulder to the shattered workbench she had crashed into moments before. She could not fully comprehend what she was seeing. Her dreams seemed to be transforming into reality before her eyes as she was slowly dying. *But where are Ronny and James, then?* She forced her eyes wide and saw her partner's form morphing from the wall, the solid surface changing into a living, breathing human being aiming a gun at the back of her attacker's head from a distance.

The object waved the barrel of the gun sideways, obviously requesting her to alter her current location. Little did he know, she could not move anywhere. Moran was holding her fast, the noose about her neck scraping and burning away flesh, the veins extruding as they tried to pump much needed blood to her brain. She could not move her extremities in the slightest. The only leeway she had at the moment was her head and neck, which was also the cause of her inevitably slow and painful demise.

Her eyes popped open as a thought came to her. She moved her head to the left and right, feeling the burn of the rope against her skin as she tested her range of motion. Then, without a second thought, she jerked forward, her forehead connecting squarely with Luke Moran's nose in a bloody crunch that whiplashed his face away from her.

He did not lessen his grip on the noose in the least, but that was not Hartley's intention. The shock of the impact of bone on cartilage caused him to shift back slightly, which in turn allowed her to wriggle a leg free, bending at the knee and forcing his rock solid torso away from hers. She tilted her head back until she was staring at the opposite wall, the cold, concrete floor at the top of her vision. The motion allowed the noose to grow tighter, however, and the world around her began to fade at an alarmingly rapid pace.

A split second later she heard the gun blast, knowing the small amount of room she had given herself had been more than enough for her partner to release a shot. The bullet entered the back of Moran's head and exited just over his right eye. His arms immediately went limp as he fell with a thud onto Hartley. She gasped for breath as his full weight rested over her, the blood from his wound running to the floor and pooling beneath the combatants. She remained still for several long moments, letting the pounding and pulsating inside her head recede into the distance. After a time she set her heel and tilted her body, freeing her arms as she pushed her attacker over and stared into his lifeless eyes.

Hartley sat up and looked to Ratliff, his breathing deep and hair frosted white with plaster as he stared back to her. He forced a smile before pushing into the drywall, the plaster cracking as the rest of his body tumbled in. He yelled in pain as his wrist connected with the concrete, the blue-green hues of bruising and dried blood visible to Hartley from where she sat.

She rolled to her knees and began the slow, short crawl to her gun, picking it up and scooting to the nearest backrest she could find: the plastic-wrapped crate of thousands of *State of Finance* issues ready for distribution. Ratliff limped around the body of Luke Moran and fell into place beside her, their bodies leaning against one another, their eyes on the dead man feet away. Ratliff set his gun between his legs and reached out, placing his hand on his partner's thigh, letting her know he was there for her and not leaving.

Hartley thought for a moment, eyes never leaving their suspect, gun raised to him even though she knew he was no longer with them. She was surprised when she reached out and grabbed Ratliff's hand, squeezing it tight as they waited for backup to arrive.

THIRTY-SEVEN

Three minutes after the bullet passed through Luke Moran's head, the warehouse and *State of Finance* offices were teeming with police activity. Units had been deployed to all areas of the building and forensics rode their coattails, dusting for fingerprints and collecting evidence from the multiple crime scenes. Interviews were being held in every office, every conference room, every nook and cranny that law enforcement could find.

The gunshot that had ended Moran's life also caused the echoing collisions with the warehouse door to come to a halt. The lobby guard had appeared in the manmade hole where Ratliff had slipped through minutes prior to save Hartley's life. The guard was disheveled, his work uniform drenched in perspiration and a stricken look spread across his face. Ratliff had waved to him from their position on the floor, glancing sideways to Hartley as she lowered the gun.

From Andrew's vantage point he could see the two officers leaning into a pallet, their shoulders resting against one another, hands intertwined as they stared to a mass several feet in front of them. It had taken several seconds to register with the guard that the large object before them was a man. A lump caught in Andrew's throat as he looked upon the scene, having never witnessed an individual extinguished from the world in such a manner as this, staring with lifeless eyes towards the ceiling above, the dark, crimson pool underneath him silhouetting his frame.

Ratliff had forced himself up from next to his partner and signaled to Andrew, pointing to the warehouse door and watching the guard disappear back into the hallway. The detective had made his way to the shattered entrance and retrieved a metallic paperweight from a shelf, employing it to hammer the deadbolt out of the locked position with his good hand. Andrew, after hearing the detective's assault subside, had barreled into it with his shoulder, popping the door back into the warehouse with a metallic grind and sending the broken doorknob rattling to the floor.

Moments later a team of officers arrived with weapons drawn, flowing through the door like a blue river to surround the detectives and the deceased suspect. "I need a medic!" Ratliff called down the hallway before moving back into the room towards his partner. He knelt down beside her and looked into her eyes, noticing a fire still burning behind them as the pain started to settle in. He reached down and removed the gun from her hand and placed it atop the pallet. "Can you move?" he asked, receiving a nod in return.

Ratliff reached out and slid his arm underneath hers, cradling her frame as he pulled her to a standing position. He led her away from the scene and set her near the door on top of a blue, dust-covered Igloo cooler he retrieved from one of the shelving units. "Paramedics are on their way," he said, kneeling in front of her with his face close to hers, their eyes locking for several moments before he glanced away to a team moving around them. "Follow my finger," he directed, raising his hand directly in front of her as he moved it to the left and right. Hartley obliged with some difficulty, her left eye but a sliver as the swelling set in from the blow Moran had gifted her.

The paramedics eventually made it into the warehouse and worked on the pair for several long minutes as officers questioned them about the occurrences of the day. Ratliff filled in the details of Walker and O'Dowd, including the chase down the stairwell and up to the point of his and Hartley's separation. "At that point I started kicking at the door until Andrew showed up," he said, lowering his head as the medic strapped on a sling, sliding the detective's broken wrist into the opening as gently as possible.

"You'll have to get a cast when you go to the hospital," the paramedic informed him. Ratliff nodded his thanks before stepping back and allowing the medical team full access to his partner.

Hartley answered questions as best she could, though her responses came slowly and with an obvious effort. Her head throbbed and her left eyebrow, just above the bruising of her cheek, was aching more fiercely than any other part of her body. The assessment from the medic was that she had possibly suffered a concussion and that, while her cheek seemed to have only sustained a deep bruise, her left supraorbital ridge most likely had a hairline fracture, the result of Moran's forehead colliding with her face. She would need a full workup when she reached the hospital as well.

"Not yet," she said, seemingly waking slightly from whatever daze she had been floating in moments ago.

"Detective," the medic said, "you've received some substantial injuries that need to get checked out —"

"And they will," she interrupted, grabbing her gun and placing it back in its holster. "But right now I have to make an arrest."

"Who?" Ratliff said as he stepped forward to help her up.

"Our third embezzler," she replied with a smile. "Give me your phone." Ratliff fished it out of his pocket and handed it to her, Hartley waking it and typing in a series of digits before switching the audio to speaker.

"Hey, Jay," came the voice of Kim Banneau from the other end. "What's shakin'?"

"Kim, it's me," Hartley said.

"Jo? Don't you have your own phone? Or are you two —"

"No," Hartley stated. "Listen, are you busy?"

"Not really. Just going through some paperwork. Going to grab a bite to eat in a little bit. Why?"

"I need you to do me a favor."

"Sure. What's up?"

"Dane's at the precinct — probably at my desk — going through some documents. I need you to tell him to make another copy and leave the originals on my chair."

"Okay. You need me to drop him someplace?"

"No. If you're not busy, I actually would prefer if you drove us to where we're going."

"Sure. But why can't you or Ratliff drive?"

"Let's just leave it at we're not really capable of that right now. Besides, I wouldn't mind having some more backup." There was silence for a moment as Hartley rubbed her forehead gingerly. "You'll see what I mean when we get back there. Just meet us outside in about twenty minutes. Tell Dane it's time he came back from the dead."

* * * * *

Hartley rode in the front passenger seat as their chauffeur, a uniform who had pulled up to assist with closing off the street, drove her and Ratliff in their unmarked squad car back to the station. The ride was silent, Hartley even turning off the almost inaudible radio as soon as they started forth. Ratliff rode behind the driver, his eyes passing between the city outside the vehicle and his partner's battered existence. He was obviously worried about her, knowing full well her injuries needed a thorough examination and at least a few days' rest. He also knew she would not submit to anything until her duty was fulfilled, and at the moment, their current assignment was driving both of them through their separate pains.

Hartley could see her brother and Banneau standing near the curb as they neared the precinct, Dane carrying a familiar manila envelope beneath his arm. The car slowed and Banneau waved from the sidewalk, unable to see past the glare on the window to the bruised left side of Hartley's face.

"There you go, detectives," the uniformed officer said as he put the vehicle into park, smiling forcedly as he opened the door and stepped out to the pavement.

"So where are we headed —" Banneau began as she slumped into the car, halting abruptly as her eyes fell upon Hartley's wounds. Her hands rose to cover her mouth. She looked over her friend's façade, the bruising and swelling of Hartley's cheek pulling Banneau's attention away from the blood-soaked bandage covering her eyebrow. Hartley's hair, though damp from what must have been an impromptu rinse, was tinged red as well, and the white shirt beneath her jacket looked as if the detective had tried to tie-dye it unsuccessfully only moments before. "Jo —" she began, only to be cut off as Dane stepped into the remaining back seat.

"I got the copy you wanted. I can't wait to see the look on —" He stopped dead in his tracks as he looked around, Banneau's stare never leaving his sister in front of him. Ratliff glanced his way momentarily before looking once more to his partner. "What's going on?"

Hartley sighed before turning to stare at him through a narrow slit that was her left eyelid. "Give me the folder," she said, reaching over the seat.

"Yeah. I — uh," Dane stammered, lifting the documents to her as his eyes swept across her face. "What — what happened?" he finally asked.

"Luke Moran happened," she replied, opening the folder and peering inside. "You copy everything?"

"Yeah," he answered, glancing to Ratliff and back quickly. "Are you okay?"

Hartley chuckled from the front seat and shook her head. "Dane, I have a concussion, a swollen eye from being punched in the face and what was described as an intensely painful fracture of my left eyebrow. So, no. Thank you for asking, but no, I'm not okay. I'm having trouble focusing on anything right now and I just want to finish this day before I go to the hospital and pass out."

The assembled team remained silent for a moment before Dane opened his mouth. "When you make it to the hospital you should check to see if they can find the rod sticking up your ass too. Getting that removed may make you feel a little better."

They all froze, Ratliff eyeing Hartley as she stared out the front window and set her jaw. Banneau stole a glance at both siblings, waiting for an eruption to rise from her friend. Instead — and to the surprise of everyone — Hartley turned to Dane and smirked, looking at her brother for a long moment before responding. "Fuck you."

* * * * *

They pulled up to their destination slowly, Hartley reading the addresses along the wide street carefully as they passed through the neighborhood. The houses in this suburb of the city were massive, each set upon its own large plot of land that would have consumed an entire inner-city block. Yards were pristine, grass trimmed to a specific height that complemented the surrounding floral arrangements set up by the most expensive landscapers money could buy.

Banneau idled their vehicle towards a bend in the road before Hartley spoke. "That's it. Straight ahead." They worked their way on up a brick driveway that swung to the right before looping around a large, majestic fountain, the water spraying up from the feet of what appeared to be a Roman soldier. Banneau stopped the car near the entrance, purposely blocking any easy access to the street.

"You sure this is it?" Ratliff asked from the back seat.

"It's the address they told me," Hartley replied, taking a moment to look around the yard and at the towering structure before them. "Okay. Let's go. Dane, you stay with Kim until I signal you in. Got it?" She did not wait for an answer, exiting the vehicle and walking with Ratliff towards the front door, both detectives glancing to the left and right at the exquisite features offered by the property.

As they approached the door Hartley turned, her eyes pulling Ratliff's into the garage to their right and the silver Aston Martin DBS Coupe with its rear end open, a suitcase lying neatly in the cubbyhole. The car purred as it awaited its exit from the enclosure and Hartley could not help but peer at Ratliff and smirk. "That's pretty," she said as he nodded.

Their attention was drawn to the door leading into the mansion as Damian Verland stepped through, his eyes catching sight of the officers as he wheeled another suitcase behind him. "Detectives," he said with a nod, picking up his luggage and placing it gently next to the other. "This is a surprise. To what do I own the honor?"

"I didn't know you were heading on vacation," Hartley replied, ignoring the man's question.

"Yes, well, with everything that has been going on, I figured it's finally time to set up a personal meeting with Signore Francesco and fill him in." Damian took several steps towards them. "Can I offer you two —" He stopped as he finally noticed Hartley's face, the bruising obviously grotesque to the man as he noticeably cringed. "Oh my word!" he exclaimed. "Are you all right, my dear? How did this happen?"

Hartley remained fixed on him. "You tell me," she replied, causing Damian to steal a quizzical glance in Ratliff's direction.

"I beg your pardon?" he said finally.

Hartley took a step towards him. "I paid a visit to Seamus O'Dowd and Kyle Walker today, Mr. Verland. Have you ever heard of these men before?"

Damian thought for a moment before responding. "I can't say that I have, no."

"That's hard for me to believe. O'Dowd and Walker were the heads of *State of Finance*, the magazine that Bart Reed — our murder victim — worked for."

"Okay," Damian said as he crossed his arms across his chest.

Hartley paused and glanced to her partner. "Mr. Verland, you are the acting head of a securities company and an avid reader. I find it really hard to believe that you didn't know who Seamus O'Dowd — Editor in Chief at *State of Finance* — was." Verland remained silent as he looked between the two detectives.

"What do you mean *was*?" he finally asked.

"By the time we got to the offices to take O'Dowd and Walker in on charges of embezzlement and murder, they were dead."

"Oh my!" Damian said, raising his hand to his mouth.

Hartley smirked. "They were killed by a man named Luke Moran, who was a past associate of Kyle Walker when he went by his given name, Eric Sheehan. Have you ever heard of either of them?" Damian shook his head. "Well, Moran is dead also," she added, looking to the ground and beginning her advance towards him once more, stopping just outside the garage door. Ratliff moved forward as well, taking position at the end of the opening closer to the street.

"You said you were going to arrest these men," Verland began after an uncomfortable silence.

Ratliff nodded. "For their participation in the embezzling of Intervise Securities' customer accounts. The murder of Kelly Depler. Attempted —" he paused as Hartley shot him a glance. "Conspiracy. There's a long list."

Verland's brow furrowed. "But how was that possible? I mean, I know everything that goes on at Intervise. How does something like that happen right under my nose?" He paused, looking to the ground and letting the question hang on the air. He brought his eyes up to Hartley after realizing his questions would not be answered. "This Moran ..." Verland said, pointing to her face.

"Yes," Hartley answered. "But not before he decided to give me a little bit of information."

Verland glanced to the detectives' car, watching the subtle movements of its unrecognizable inhabitants before leaning back into his own vehicle. "About what?" he asked.

Hartley began to pace back and forth in front of him, drawing his eyes as she limped a path along the opening of the garage. "About how he planned to disappear after disposing of me. He told me that the amount of money he was going to get for erasing O'Dowd and Walker would be enough to allow him to fade into the world. Never be heard from again. Problem with that is money always leaves a trail." She stopped and looked at him. "Want to know what he said to me?"

"Sure," he said with a shrug.

"He said it doesn't leave a trail the way his employer was doing it for him. He said he would be scot-free, with no chance of ever being found." She smirked at him before pacing once again. "That stuck with me, you know? Even as that bastard started choking me with a rope." She pulled down her collar to reveal a burn mark across her neck. "And you know who popped into my mind while all this was going on?" She stopped and smiled. "You."

He frowned and glanced nervously between the detectives. "I don't think I follow."

"Neither did I. Not until this morning when I got a call from …" She halted, bringing her fingers to her lips. "No. I'll wait on that." Hartley stepped forward, squaring herself up to the Director of Operations at Intervise Securities. "All of this embezzling and siphoning of money from client accounts — I don't understand it. I'm a homicide detective, as you know. Finding murderers is what drives me, not thieves. But the way Reed's murder and this embezzling scheme intertwined with Intervise and O'Dowd and Walker at its center … I have to say it was kind of intriguing."

Verland glanced to his watch. "I apologize, detective, but I need to catch a flight soon. Is there anything I can help you with at the moment?"

Hartley's face turned cold, her good eye glaring at Verland and making him unsteady. "You're not catching a flight today, Mr. Verland," she said sternly.

"Excuse me?" he said with a challenging tone.

"I said you won't be flying anywhere today," she repeated, accepting the challenge. "Did you hear me that time?" She glared at him, her swollen eye staring from between the slit that had become her line of vision.

"Detective, I have been nothing but helpful with regard to your investigation. I think that warrants some form of respect.

I've been patient up until now, however that patience is wearing thin. I would suggest —"

"Ten years," Hartley interrupted, the tone of her voice silencing the VP. "Ten years the embezzlement has been going on." She watched as his eyes grew slightly wider, a tell he could not suppress as she let loose a bit of information that could have been found nowhere except inside the Reed documents. "That's a long time to skim pennies off client accounts. We're talking about a lot of money over a decade. And like I said, I don't really care about that. What I care about is Bart Reed. I care about Kelly Depler. And as much as it puts a bad taste in my mouth to say it, now I care about Seamus O'Dowd and Kyle Walker."

"Detective, I really don't think —"

"I don't give a shit what you think right now," she said with a growl that caused Verland to close his mouth forcefully. "What I think you should do is listen to what I have to say." Hartley stepped forward and eyed Damian Verland up. "This morning when you called you gave me a number regarding the Isabella Bartollo account. Do you remember?" She waited for a response briefly before continuing. "There was roughly twelve million dollars unaccounted for that was there just yesterday. Now, you said you had a guess as to who moved the money."

"Precisely, yet you didn't want to hear —"

"Mr. Francesco." Hartley said it with a conviction that brought Ratliff's eyes to her. "Is that your guess?"

"He's the only one who could move that money! It's his daughter's account, for Christ's sake!"

"That's true. But like you said: Mr. Francesco is an elderly, sick old man. He's living a life of a hermit in Italy and has had no activity on this account other than this twelve million dollar withdrawal and automated monthly deposits within the last six years. You, on the other hand, have all the power that Francesco has given you, and that includes the supervision of Intervise Securities' clients, which, if I'm not mistaken, also incorporates Francesco's personal accounts." She paused and set her eyes to his, taking several steps forward before continuing. "To be blunt, Mr. Verland, you're the only one that knew how to siphon money from client accounts this way. You're the only one with the know-how to skim pennies from Intervise and reroute them through Delaney Holdings. Or West Palm Subsidiaries. New Wales Financial Assets." Damian Verland swallowed hard. "The list goes on and on."

"This is outrageous!" he exclaimed. "You're pulling at straws, detective. Everything you have is speculation."

Hartley smirked at him before turning her attention to the car they had arrived in and directing her brother to exit. As the rear door to the vehicle opened and Dane stepped out, she looked back to Verland, watching as his eyes widened ever so slightly and his jaw muscles grew rigid. "I don't think you've ever met my brother before, Mr. Verland," she said as Dane drew nearer, extending the manila folder to her. "You see, he was the real threat to you after Reed's murder. When Walker had Reed killed, this story was supposed to be swept under the rug as well. I can't imagine what a mind blow it was when Dane showed up at *State of Finance* with the exact same story two days later. You see, Dane didn't know it at the time, but what he did by going to the magazine that day was walk directly into the lion's den; throw fuel on an already burning fire. He went to the only place that would kill to have that story — these documents — go away." She lifted the envelope high and watched as Verland's eyes settled upon it.

Damian's gaze rose to meet with Dane's, his demeanor obviously shaken by the sight of the journalist. "I swear I didn't —"

"Didn't what?" Dane interrupted. "Didn't try to kill me?"

Hartley waited momentarily before proceeding. "That's the first bit of truth you've said today. The attempt on Dane — and Kelly Depler's murder — was all Kyle Walker. He decided to have Dane knocked off before he was able to bring anything to light. Kelly was just collateral damage."

Hartley paused, letting the story sink in. Verland remained stoic, yet the detectives and Dane could definitely see there was a change in him, a shifty, anxious alteration in his mood that Hartley had seen on way too many occasions to not stay alert and focused. She shifted her jacket to the side, revealing her firearm poised on her hip and within reach. Verland glanced to the weapon and back to the detectives.

Hartley took the opportunity to continue. "Walker was foolish when he sent Moran to my apartment. I bluffed him. I didn't have any documents, and the best part was Dane didn't have them either. But they didn't know that. And neither did you. But the chance that Reed's story was still in the open was something that none of you could afford. And with the heat on your associates growing, you had to make a choice. The odds that they would deal with the DA and get what equated to a slap on the wrist, while you spent the remainder of your life broke and in jail, was definitely something you couldn't chance. So you hired Luke Moran. You hired Kyle Walker's own associate to put a bullet in each of their heads. They were the only ones who knew you were in on the embezzlement and the only ones to connect you with it."

As Verland weighed the narrative laid out before him, flashing lights from down the street pulled the group's attention away from the garage. Banneau, still behind the wheel of the unmarked vehicle blocking the driveway, watched as a half dozen police cruisers approached. She put the car into gear and crept forward, setting the front wheels just into Verland's pristine grass, glancing over her shoulder as several vehicles passed by and stopped in the drive.

Hartley turned back to Verland and extended the manila envelope to him. He took it and stared to the detective, his eyes glaring at her momentarily before turning down to the papers and beginning to sift through them. "There's a money trail in there that starts ten years ago," she continued. "We have the financials for you, your employer, and Walker and O'Dowd. We have a warrant to search your home." Verland raised his eyes to her quickly, a look of consternation spread across his face. "There's already a team at Intervise taking stock of the company's financial records. It's over, Damian."

Hartley watched as a uniformed officer approached with handcuffs ready, patiently waiting for the detective to give the sign. Hartley glanced back to Damian Verland and held her hand out. He looked from her to the uniformed officer and back, before finally speaking. "You don't know what you're dealing with, my dear," he said, handing back the manila envelope before raising his arms together for the uniformed officer to shackle.

"Damian Verland," Hartley said as the cuffs were placed over his wrists, "you are under arrest for the financial fraud against Intervise Securities clients, the murders of Seamus O'Dowd and Kyle Walker, and conspiracy. You have the right to remain silent. Anything you say or do can and will be held against you in a court of law ..."

EPILOGUE

The doctors tending to Hartley's wounds were amazed, to say the least. The fact that she entered the ER under her own power and directed the nurses to take care of the broken wrist of her partner before treating her was impressive. Once the examination commenced, it was nothing less than inspirational. She refused to take any sort of painkiller, citing her need to be rational when she made it back to the precinct to be questioned regarding the goings-on at *State of Finance*. While stitches were being sewn into her eyebrow and fragments of glass removed from her thigh, she maintained a steady, focused gaze ahead with little more than a topical anesthetic, all the while answering questions put forth by the attending physician.

In the end, Jolene was the recipient of a variety of wounds, none too pleasant to deal with. She received fifteen stitches to close the gap in her thigh caused by the glass shard that ended up in Luke Moran's neck; seven more were placed in her eyebrow. After much poking and prodding, the attending threw out the idea of a broken cheekbone, instead agreeing with the much earlier assessment of the paramedic on scene that it was nothing more than a deep bruise. She had suffered a broken pinkie finger, most likely from striking Moran in an attempt to free herself from under his weight. Through a series of tests the attending also determined Jolene had suffered a mild concussion, a combination, she assumed, from the strike that split her eyebrow, the punch to the cheek and her head slamming into the hard concrete floor.

Before they allowed her to leave, the attending scheduled a quick MRI, which allowed the physician to conclude a hairline fracture of the left supraorbital ridge did exist. There was nothing they could do about it other than allow time to heal the wound, something the detective would need plenty of in the coming days.

Kim waited for Jolene and Jacoby to emerge from their respective exams, hugging her friend as she hobbled forward. "So I'm guessing dinner's out of the question for you tonight?" Banneau asked.

Hartley smiled. "I'm thinking a bottle of tequila will do just fine," she laughed.

"I second that," Ratliff agreed with a smile. "You okay?"

Jolene looked to him and smirked, her good eye gleaming in the fluorescent overhead lights. "I'll survive," she replied, reaching out to touch his sling. "Thank you."

"Anytime."

Kim laughed and jingled the keys. "This is getting to be too much of a common occurrence. Maybe we try to stay away from the hospital for a while?"

* * * * *

"Where'd Dane end up going?" Jacoby asked from the backseat as they drove towards the precinct.

Kim shrugged, looking to the green glow of the digital clock before her that read 4:52 p.m. "Came to the hospital with us, obviously. Saw him hop outside for a cigarette and he never made it back in."

"Figure he's hiding someplace with a copy of those documents," Jolene added, rubbing her forehead.

"Hanging in there?" Kim asked her friend.

Hartley forced a smile and nodded. "Just a nice solid headache."

"What do you think Verland meant when he said we didn't know what we were dealing with?" Ratliff asked after several minutes.

Hartley shrugged. "Not sure. But I figure once we dive into the documents and financials we'll figure it out. Man like Damian Verland probably comes with some high profile lawyers."

"Yeah, I guess," Ratliff responded as his phone began to ring. He searched for it quickly and put it to his ear. "This is Detective Ratliff." He listened intently, pulling a notepad from his pocket and beginning to write. "Yeah," he said. "That's right. Just looking for the trail." He paused again, his pen scribbling a mixture of doodles and actual notes. He suddenly stopped and glanced up, the notepad and sketches fading from his mind completely. "Are you positive? Okay. Thanks."

He hung up the phone just as Hartley turned to face him, noticing the serious expression. "Who was that?" she asked. "Everything all right?"

He looked to her, locking eyes. "That was forensics. They got a name on the owner of the gun Luke Moran left in your apartment."

"Great. Who else do we need to go question?" she asked with a sigh. She glanced to Banneau who shook her head with a smile. After a moment Hartley turned her attention back to Ratliff, surprised to see him staring at her as intensely as before. "Jay?" she heard herself say.

* * * * *

James was ecstatic to receive a call from Jolene asking him to meet her for an early supper. She had suggested a restaurant relatively close to his place, a joint that served cold beer and greasy burgers, bringing him back to their date several days ago. Things were shaky when he left her earlier in the morning after showing up to the precinct at what seemed to be the worst possible time. Regardless of the circumstances of the previous evening, James could tell that his relationship with Hartley — on an emotional level — was struggling. He did not understand why, yet knew something was amiss.

It had not gone unnoticed that her anxiety rose whenever her partner, Jacoby Ratliff, entered the room. James did not hold that against either of the detectives. He knew Jolene was out of his league, though their mutual interest in one another gave him the confidence he needed to continue his pursuit of her. He was also not stupid. He could tell a good-looking man when he saw one, and Jacoby Ratliff was indeed a good-looking man. James was comfortable with his own sexuality to know that her new partner was a better fit aesthetically with Hartley. It just made more sense to the public to see two exceptionally flawless beings in unison rather than her on James's arm.

So when Jolene called for him to meet her, he jumped at the opportunity. He needed every possible chance to show her he could be the man she was looking for. He ordered two beers and made his way to the tables lining the sidewalk. The late afternoon had remained humid, a rarity as of late, and James thought the ambiance of the city streets would be a soothing backdrop for the two as they drank and ate to their hearts' content.

It was confusing to him when a cruiser pulled up and Ratliff exited the rear door, forcing a smile and nodding to James as he sat at the table, raising his hand in acknowledgment. His heart caught in his throat as Hartley emerged from the front passenger seat, a stunning vision that looked as if she had been through a war. He rose quickly, mouth agape as he glanced from her to Ratliff and back several times, the look pleading with either one to explain what had happened.

Hartley forced a smile before turning to her partner to whisper something. Ratliff nodded and leaned against the vehicle, watching his partner move away from him and towards James. "Are you okay?" he asked, his voice draped in worry. "What happened?"

"A lot," she answered, stopping in front of him and staring up with her good eye. "Thanks for meeting me."

"Sure," he replied, glancing to Ratliff.

"Can we sit?" she asked, pointing to her leg.

"Oh. Yeah. Absolutely." James rounded the table and pulled the chair out for her, his eyes scanning every inch of Hartley as he took his seat once again. "I got you a beer. I thought …" He looked back up to Ratliff. "Does he want to join us? He can —"

"No, James," Hartley said, holding her hand up and reaching out to him. "He's fine. Really." She held on for several moments before releasing his hand and leaning forward, resting her elbows on her knees.

"What happened, Jo?" he asked quietly.

She thought for a moment, debating on whether to tell him the brutality of what had occurred since he left the precinct earlier in the morning. "James, I need to ask you something."

He sat back in his chair and focused on her, the seriousness of her statement catching him off guard. He finally shrugged. "Anything."

She glanced to her fingers before returning her gaze to him. "What do you remember of your parents' murders?" The question fell from her mouth like a ton of bricks, pulling with it the wind from James's sails. His brow furrowed as he tried to assess the situation before him.

"I, uh … What does this have to do with …" He stopped, unable to conjure up another word.

"Please, James," she replied with a sweet, sincere voice.

"They were killed on a business trip," he answered, the past rushing back to haunt him once more. "My father was stabbed to death in the boathouse and my mother was beaten and raped. I told you this before. Why? What's going on?" he asked, leaning into the table.

Hartley held his gaze for several seconds, processing the words she was about to say. "James, listen to me. Last night — the two men who attacked me in my apartment left a gun behind. Forensics tested the bullets and it came back as a match to the bullets pulled from Bart Reed's body." James nodded that he was following the flow of conversation. "Luke Moran — the man killed in the *State of Finance* warehouse today — he was carrying that gun yesterday, and there's a strong possibility he was the guy who killed Bart Reed."

"Okay," James said. "What does this have to do with my parents?"

"Ratliff had forensics trace the weapon to its original owner." She paused, eyes locked on her friend. "That owner was Michael Graiser. Your father."

James shook his head. "That can't be. My father didn't own a gun. I don't think he ever held a gun."

"The officers at your parents' lake house found a lockbox in your father's closet opened with the gun missing the night of the murders."

"He didn't own a —"

"The date of purchase was three days before they were killed, James. Do you know of any reason why he would buy a weapon before heading to a business meeting? Were they in any kind of danger?"

"No," he said, shaking his head and staring to the table. "No, this — I don't understand."

"I'm not sure what any of this means either, James," Hartley said. "All I know is that this gives us our first lead into your parents' murder in nearly a decade. This could be the break we need to find out who did this."

James ran his fingers through his hair as he glanced around. He looked upon Hartley's beautiful, battered face before reaching for his beer and downing half of the contents. He set the bottle down and sighed deeply. "Who was the other man?" he asked.

"I'm sorry?" Hartley replied, unsure of what he meant.

"Do you know who the other man in your apartment was?"

"Uh, yeah. A Turkish kid. Korhan Karaca, I think his name was."

James's mouth dropped wide as he stared to her. "Karaca?" he asked.

Hartley nodded. "Yeah. Why? Does that name mean anything to you?" James looked around before standing quickly. His face displayed no emotion. His eyes grew glassy yet no tears fell. He was the epitome of a lost soul. "James," she said, rising up in front of him. "Do you know who Karaca is?"

James peered at her with serious eyes. "Korhan Karaca is the son of Ahmet Karaca."

"Who is that? Who is Ahmet Karaca?"

"My father's personal assistant. A man he trusted with his life."

James excused himself, apologizing as he fought back emotions. He left the restaurant hastily, Hartley waving off Ratliff as he began to follow, the two instead watching Graiser stumble blindly down the sidewalk and into the night, his past chasing after him in the form of his murdered parents.

AN EXCERPT FROM THE FORTHCOMING

ON THE ROAD
THROUGH CHAOS

THE HUMANITIES SAGA
BOOK THREE

A Jolene Hartley Novel

RYAN JENNINGS PETERSON

PROLOGUE

JANUARY ...

The air was humid, more so than earlier in the day thanks to the combination of a late-afternoon thunderstorm rolling slowly across the Caribbean and the above average temperature that had settled in over northern Jamaica and refused to budge. The weight of the atmosphere in Ocho Rios was palpable. It was as if one could reach out a hand and pull back with a fistful of sweaty heat, like a snowball made from tropical dew.

It was a change of pace that James Graiser welcomed. He had checked the weather patterns in the United States a time or two since being back in the Caribbean, noticing the mercury for the winter had remained far above average in Chicago than previous years. Yet other than a quick glance to stifle his meteorological inquiries, he forced his life in the States out of his mind. There were things there he did not want to remember. He had no intentions of heading back to his home base. He was even considering making Jamaica a permanent fixture in his life. Desmond Brown, his longtime friend, had even offered a room in his quaint, comfortable shack until James could find a pad of his own.

Like that was a problem for James. Graiser's financial limitations lacked one major thing: limitations. Finding a shack, tent, hut or beachside mansion was not something James needed to worry about. His bank account — or rather the funds in his hand-me-down account — was astronomical. Working at Desmond's small fruit plantation was by no means considered a job in James's mind. It was an activity to pass the time.

Graiser lifted a bottle of Red Stripe to his lips and continued down the beach, the darkening sky blending into the evening sea, millions of stars reflecting off the shifting surface of the ocean. The illusion of a never-ending sky before him made his already compromised equilibrium that much more unsteady. He turned his focus away from the sea and glanced over his shoulder at the raucous party underway a hundred yards back.

It was Desmond's friend's place, though for the life of him, James could not remember his name. Cortez? Curtis? Kirk? Either way, Desmond's pal was gracious with all he had. James was well beyond inebriated. He and Desmond had worked earlier in the day, walking through his fields and picking ripe fruit that they later sold at the market in town, a business that produced just enough to allow Desmond a spot in the tropics. They had retired in the late afternoon to Brown's abode to a meal of Ting soda and saltfish, followed immediately by several Red Stripes and an abundance of marijuana.

James had smoked pot before in his earlier days but had never found it to be his thing. His spirit was more aligned with that of a backpacking tree-hugger than a joint-rolling pot-smoker. Yet in recent months, he had fully embraced the drug, smoking with Desmond every chance he could. He got used to the feeling of paranoia until eventually he could comprehend what was happening around him, even shrugging off the inability to carry on a conversation in fear of saying something completely off the wall. He learned to function, if only to thank those passing him a smoking pipe or spliff. Within the six months he had been in Jamaica, James Graiser became a new man altogether.

James lifted the bottle of Red Stripe to his lips once more before tossing it among a grouping of palm trees. He stretched his arms high over his head and spun in a circle, feeling the much-needed breeze cross his sweaty face. His hair was longer than it had been while in the States, the wavy curls draping just below his eyes, a shag look he had not worn since his high school days. *Funny,* he thought. *That's the last time I smoked pot, too.*

His arms went wide and he continued in a slow spin, knowing full well that the motion would test his limits of balance as well as his gag reflex. He stopped after a moment and was surprised to see a vision before him, a hallucination obviously created by the past he wished to flee from. The brilliant white light silhouetting a woman's frame shined brightly against his face. He tried to focus his vision to her, tried to decipher who now stood before him. His eyes darted up her frame, sliding along the curve of her hips, meandering over the side of her breast and into the wind-blown, shoulder-length hair. James could judge against the backlight the jaw line, the high cheekbones underneath soul-penetrating eyes.

He fell to the sand, dropping ungracefully into the billions of grains below his feet and toppling to the side. He remained still, forehead resting on the coolness of the beach as he forced the vision from his sight. After several long moments he opened his eyes. All was dark, the light and silhouette once again replaced by the never-ending sky and the millions of stars reflecting off the sea.

* * * * *

James. Hey, it's me. Listen, we need to talk. Give me a call when you get back. I'll be around all night.

* * * * *

He sat there for a time, elbows resting on his knees as he cradled his head, uncontrollable thoughts swirling in the recesses of his mind like they always seemed to do while intoxicated. He glanced around, realizing his refreshment had run out. He really did not want to make the walk back to the party just yet. To his left, about a dozen yards away, sat an ATV packed with garbage cans and a red Igloo cooler, most likely leftovers from a reception or company outing that had long since called it a night.

James was not ready to follow suit. He stood, gathering himself for the short walk, steadying his legs and taking a deep breath before proceeding towards the vehicle. He smiled as he opened the cooler and eyed a dozen or so Real Rock Lagers. He grabbed one and popped the cap off, taking a long, slow sip from the bottle before turning and making his way towards his spot in the sand once again.

* * * * *

Hey, it's me again. I just wanted to make sure you're okay. I haven't heard from you yet and I need some rest. I'll have my phone by me all night, so please call when you get this. I'm not going in tomorrow. Or for a few days at least, so I'll be around if you want to talk. Okay. Bye.

* * * * *

James's mind began to race again, his thoughts flooding his vision, memories rushing to the surface with reckless abandon. His eyes glazed over as he stared to the sand, each of the grains before him spinning and morphing into a thought he tried to push away unsuccessfully.

He traveled back, swirling to a time just as chaotic and misplaced as the present. He looked out a window in an airplane somewhere over the Atlantic, the blackness interrupted by the intermittent red blinks from the light on the wing. He had been contacted the previous day via satellite phone by Daniel Vincent, a family friend, telling him he needed to end his excursion and fly back immediately. James had pushed the subject, knowing that Vincent calling meant only one thing: something had happened to his parents. He did not know if it was his mother or father. He played scenarios in his mind. House fire. Car crash. Heart attack. Nothing stuck, yet he knew without a doubt his return to Chicago was necessary. Backpacking would have to wait.

* * * * *

Where are you? It's been a week and I haven't heard from you. I'm thinking about having someone stop by your place. Guess that would be abusing my powers though, right? Can you please call me back? I'm going back to work tomorrow. I just … Please call. We need to talk.

* * * * *

He was vacant. Emptied completely. Sounds had crammed together to form what equated to an extremely slow motion record player, the polar opposite of the Chipmunks singing Christmas songs. Movements from those around him had trails, lagging entities trying to keep up with the present. He stared to the white carpet of Daniel Vincent's living room floor, not comprehending the words that had just passed from his parents' friend's mouth. "James, I'm sorry to tell you, but your parents are dead." *Your parents are dead.* James would have thought it cruel the way those words just fell from Vincent's tongue, yet the tears that dripped with them softened the blow. He appreciated Daniel. He appreciated the way Daniel spoke to him as if he were an equal. *Your parents are dead.* Just like that. No need to sugarcoat it.

* * * * *

Presently, James lifted the Real Rock to his lips again. A movement from his right caught his eye, pulling him momentarily from his reveries. He watched as Mattie moved towards him, unaware James was seated to her left fifty yards ahead. She was a pretty girl originally from Kingston, having moved to Ocho Rios to work at the tourist hotels in the area as a teenager. Her long dark legs reflected the moonlight and James watched her hips sway back and forth in a pair of khaki shorts. Mattie had a beautiful smile and blonde-tipped dreadlocks that fell just to her shoulders. He was unsure of her age but knew she could not be more than twenty-two or twenty-three.

* * * * *

James. It's me again. I'm not really sure if I did something to make you not take my calls, but we need to talk. Not about us, if that's what's worrying you. We need to talk about what I brought up the last time I saw you. It's important. Please call me back.

* * * * *

He was catapulted back to his parents' murders, the malleable sand beneath his feet transforming into a hard concrete floor. He sat in a morgue in Wisconsin next to Daniel Vincent and Ahmet Karaca, his father's business assistant. James did not bother to look to them, knowing each was thinking the exact same thing. They had repeated on numerous occasions on the flight into Rhinelander that he did not need to be here. They could identify the bodies. It was not something he needed to witness. James repeated himself each and every time. "I'll do it."

* * * * *

I stopped by your place a couple times over the last week or so. I'm assuming whatever's going on with you at the moment doesn't involve me personally. So until I hear back from you, I just want you to know that I'll be here for you. No matter what. I've got to go. Bye.

* * * * *

The bright lights over the silver tables reflected into his eyes as the Medical Examiner stood to his left, waiting for James's sign to pull back the white sheets. He breathed deeply, feeling as if he was caught between reality and a dream. No: a nightmare. The lab smelled of cleaning agents. The floors were spotless. Instruments lined perfectly organized tables. The eyes of the man to his left weighed heavily upon him, though, at a glance, held comfort. James gave the man a slight nod and waited as he pulled back the sheets.

* * * * *

"There you are," Mattie said, stepping towards him and stopping with a jutting hip, her sleek legs crossed. "You had me worried," she said with a smile and a cock of her head, the Caribbean accent heavy on her words. James forced a smile and sipped his beer, his eyes never leaving Mattie. "You all right?" she asked. He nodded and looked to the sea.

* * * * *

Are you all right? I don't know what to say anymore. Merry Christmas? Happy New Year, maybe? I don't know. I checked with the post office and they said you have them holding your mail. No forwarding address or anything. At least your disappearance seems to be on purpose. Gives me a little piece of mind, I guess. Happy New Year, James.

* * * * *

He remembered nodding to the medical examiner for each. They were definitely his parents, though his mother's face was badly bruised and swollen. The small, blue dove tattoo behind her right ear, however, was the calling card. He floated out of the room then, exiting the lab as the medical examiner spoke, the voice fading into the distance and two objects rising from chairs before him as he collapsed onto the linoleum floor and into darkness.

* * * * *

"I said where'd you get that?" Mattie asked again, nudging his knees as she knelt in front of him. James stared into her eyes before nodding his head in the direction of the ATV to his left. She chuckled. "Stealing beer from a wedding, huh? How about you give me a sip of yours?" She reached her hand out and grabbed onto the bottle, brushing her delicate fingers across his. She kept her eyes on him as she sipped the beverage, holding his inebriated, jumpy gaze as best she could.

Mattie leaned forward and put her lips to his, kissing him with a drunken lust as their tongues danced against one another. She pulled him up to her, wrapping her arms around his head and threading her hands through his wavy hair, her body pressed against his, their sweaty skin gliding together. She moved away and looked down to him, his lazy eyes opening and locking onto hers, her beautiful, sensual face and blonde-tipped dreads pulling him into the moment.

* * * * *

I won't call again, but I just wanted to let you know that you know where to find me. I hope you're all right. I'm sure you are. I miss … I won't call again. Bye, James.

* * * * *

Mattie laid James down into the sand and unzipped his pants. She removed her khaki shorts and unbuttoned her thin, linen shirt, pulling James's hand up to cup her breast while she worked him into readiness. She leaned forward and kissed him again, this time James taking initiative to reach up and grab a fistful of Mattie's hair. He pulled her mouth into his, working frantically as this young beauty slid him into her and began to rock back and forth, the Caribbean night embracing them, the sea lapping onto the beach providing the soundtrack to their union.

ONE

LATE MARCH ...

The financial waters had swallowed Intervise Securities completely. Newspapers across the city — and even the nationwide journals — had descended upon the streets of Chicago in search of any juicy tidbit they could scrounge up regarding the company's unprecedented scandal. All the major media outlets were reporting the largest investment debacle in decades. And it was all thanks to a freelance investigative reporter by the name of Dane Hartley.

> *The rumor-mill has been buzzing since last September of an alleged embezzlement scheme gone seriously wrong. Now, as the year rolls along in what appears to be a citywide financial crisis, those indignities reported by Chicago's own Dane Hartley seem to have been confirmed by local authorities and money gurus alike.*

Intervise Securities, a once well-maintained and established financial entity in Chicago's fiscal realm, was rocked in the latter half of the year amidst a fraud scheme that reached out to encompass one of the cities most established magazines, State of Finance. And in the wake of what allegedly spanned the better part of a decade, five people are now dead, and thousands more left to wonder if they were indeed victims of financial fraud.

It was some of the best work Dane Hartley had ever done, though he treated it — and the media personnel now surrounding his everyday life — as nothing more than child's play. He had been thrust into the story through one of the murder victims, Bartholomew Reed, a man who worked for *State of Finance* at the time of his demise. Reed had been handed the evidence via a ghost, a source that hid in the shadows and lurked behind every corner, copying files and keeping a keen eye on the happenings between *State* and Intervise.

That ghost, it turned out, was a mole within the magazine, a woman by the name of Ann Carroll, who, over the years, kept the monetary ledgers in her sight and a Xerox machine at her fingertips. The jury — along with public opinion — was still out on Ann's role within the fraud, however, with the death count as it stood, an older woman blowing the proverbial whistle on the current scum of the financial world would hardly garner a mention in the bylines, much less a lengthy legal battle. Ann had been — and continued to be — a key part of the mounting story. Yet her cooperation and willingness to throw others under the bus had placed her in protective custody, at least until her day in the limelight.

Bart Reed, however, had not been so lucky. After learning of the connections to his bosses, *State of Finance* Editor-In-Chief, Seamus O'Dowd, and Assistant Editor, Kyle Walker, Reed hastily shoveled the mess to Dane. It had pulled Hartley into what would become, up to this point, the defining piece in an otherwise somewhat-successful career.

Dane had enjoyed writing the piece thoroughly.

Who knew that chaos and greed shared such a volatile edge? The line on which some individuals walk baffles me. As a journalist, I will be the first one to admit that corners need to be cut at certain times. Information needs to be disseminated on a timely basis to let the general public know the inner workings of the beast.

Yet, the minds that conjured up this lust for money, this murderous rampage that would stop at nothing to fill already over-abundant bank accounts – these people are the epitome of trash. I know from first-hand experience. I was the intended victim of a motion-activated bomb that killed a dear friend. She was the

second person to be murdered in regards to this
influx of greed.

Kelly Depler. The name resonated throughout his mind as he wrote the follow-up article to the Intervise-*State* scandal. She had been blown to bits in his apartment, a wrong-place-wrong-time individual wearing nothing but her skin. She had been Dane's neighbor, a lovely woman with a serious appetite for strings-free sex. Dane had been happy to oblige.

He had not attended her funeral, however, yet it was not something that pulled at his heartstrings too much. At the time of her burial, Dane had taken residence in a grimy motel room on the west side, lurching through file after file of the Reed documentation he had received from Ann Carroll. The documents had cast a shining light upon major players in the embezzlement scheme, yet there were definite holes. Seamus O'Dowd and Kyle Walker, however, had been slam-dunks.

Upon receiving the documents from the
late Bart Reed, I weighed my options: take on
the work of a great journalist or let the story
fade into the abyss? In the end I chose to stand
on the shoulders of Reed, to continue his trek
into the dangerous underbelly of what would
become the financial crime of the decade. The
headquarters of State of Finance beckoned.
Little did I know I was walking blindly into the
line of fire, happening into a realm of greed and

murder that encompassed not only O'Dowd and Walker, but also Mr. Damian Verland, former Vice President of the Chicago-based firm, Intervise Securities.

* * * * *

Damian Verland sat back on his leather couch and threw his feet onto the oversized ottoman before him, his eyes staring blankly to the muted television on the other side of the room. He was tired. His days had become monotonous, to say the least. There was not much to do when you were unemployed, on house arrest and readying a defense for what equated to the rest of your natural life.

He had been arrested on numerous charges: murder, conspiracy and fraud, to name a few. The list was long, and he knew his freedom was something that was dimming with each passing day. His bond had been set at a ridiculously high price, a death sentence for the average citizen. Yet Damian Verland was hardly that. The amount was pocket change for him, a slap on the wrist. He walked out that night, though not before that bitch detective recommended house arrest, a decision that was backed completely by the higher authorities.

Verland had already gone through his preliminary hearings, yet the trial was still not set in stone. He had faced the detectives in the courtroom and set a plea of not guilty to the judge. The battle for his freedom was on. His passport had been revoked and his name smeared across the tabloids as the next Bernie Madoff.

He sat up and leaned to his left, grabbing onto a crystal tumbler of scotch set near the base of the couch. He drank from the glass, savoring the taste as the liquor swished around his mouth. His eyes scanned the room. Stacks of papers loomed on every surface. Boxes upon boxes of financial documents cluttered the den, overflowing onto the dining room table.

Verland began to rise, yet retained his seat and turned the volume up as the news reporter began to interview Dane Hartley. The journalist was exiting a high-end restaurant, his aviator sunglasses out of place in the darkening night.

"Mr. Hartley, your publication has stirred up quite a controversy," the reporter said, her voice strong and flowing. "Is it true that Damian Verland was connected to Seamus O'Dowd and Kyle Walker of *State of Finance* magazine, and that they were siphoning money from Chicagoans for the past decade?"

"According to the documents from my source, absolutely," Dane said, removing his glasses and setting himself in the cameras light.

"Who is your source?"

Dane laughed. "Nice try."

"Is there any —"

"Look, look. You can read the piece. Everything is factual. The documents I have — the documents I gave the Chicago Police Department — prove it. I've fabricated nothing."

"Some people in the media world have looked down upon your report as being biased," the reporter pushed.

"Absolutely I'm biased," he replied, his brow furrowing slightly at the woman who shifted nervously. "Doesn't mean it isn't fact. This isn't like a normal investigation. This wasn't like me catching an interview from someone stepping out of a restaurant. I was targeted. I had my apartment bombed by a psychopath that left bodies throughout the city. How could I not be biased? I was targeted to be killed. Tell me how I'm supposed to look at that with an objective view."

"I read in your publication, as well as the reports last year, of the explosion at your apartment that killed Kelly Depler."

"That's right."

"Can you tell me what Ms. Depler was doing in your apartment?"

"Baking cookies," Dane answered quickly.

The reporter halted briefly, unsure how to follow up. "Cookies?" she questioned, stumbling.

"That's right. Cookies. What's it matter? Kelly Depler was a good woman. And she's dead now. She was an innocent bystander that was murdered due to the greed of a few people."

"Those people being Seamus O'Dowd, Kyle Walker and Damian Verland?"

"That's correct."

"Is it true —"

"Listen. The fraud that was perpetrated upon the clients of Intervise Securities is awful. Absolutely horrible. They deserve to have their day in court against Verland. But let's not forget the people that won't have their day in court. Let's not forget Bart Reed and his family. Let's not forget Kelly Depler. Those are the real victims, not some millionaire trust-funders that lost the keys to their second Lamborghini."

"Mr. Hartley, don't you —"

"Thank you, but that's it." Dane turned and walked away, waving to the camera one final time before lighting a cigarette and disappearing down the street.

Verland took another long drink from the tumbler, watching as the news program switched from the live feed back to the studio, the face of an attractive black woman filling the screen. "That was Monica Alvarez in Roscoe Village with investigative journalist Dane Hartley. Thank you, Monica." The anchorwoman turned to a new camera. "Hartley has experienced a sudden amount of fame over the last six months with his exclusive knowledge into the Intervise Securities scandal that shook the financial world here in Chicago. As he said just moments ago, the embezzlement scheme has taken center stage due in part to a string of killings that has followed it. Bartholomew Reed and Kelly Depler were two of the victims. Reed was allegedly murdered due to the documents he had in his possession, and Ms. Depler was mistakenly killed in an explosion at Mr. Hartley's apartment.

"Three other individuals were killed in connection with the Intervise scandal as well: Seamus O'Dowd, Editor-In-Chief of *State of Finance*, and his Assistant Editor, Kyle Walker, were both gunned down at the magazine's headquarters in a brutal slaying within O'Dowd's office. The gunman, Luke Moran, was later shot and killed in the magazine's printing warehouse by Chicago police. Moran had a record as a youth before joining the military and excelling as a soldier. He was killed while assaulting Detective Jolene Hartley, who, as we first reported, is the sister of Dane Hartley."

Again, to a new camera, a flashing smile welcoming the viewers to a new perspective. "Jolene Hartley, herself, has gained a decent amount of fame in Chicago since her inception into the police force. Detective Hartley's first case as a member of the homicide unit garnered national attention for the Chicago Police Department with the hunt and subsequent takedown of a well-known serial killer. Hartley's more recent escapades on Navy Pier at the end of last summer, and her latest attack in Lakeview, have garnered much attention in the media. Our investigative team learned of Hartley's involvement in the Korhan Karaca assault months ago, though no arrests have been made.

"Last year, Detective Hartley ended up shooting and killing Taylor Thames on Navy Pier, sparking an investigation into the murders of three Chicagoans, one of those being Alderman Daniel Vincent, who was found murdered in a parking garage five years ago. Taylor Thames, as you may have heard us report, has been linked with embattled Congressman Harold Johnston. Johnston is currently facing a number of legal issues, including being connected to the murder of Vincent. Authorities believe the Congressman to have ordered the hit that ended in Vincent's death."

Verland's eyes panned across the television while the anchorwoman spewed out her report, a collage of photographs displayed on the screen showing the bodies of Seamus O'Dowd and Kyle Walker as they were pulled from the *State of Finance* headquarters on gurneys, the black body bags shimmering in the Chicago sun. The images faded into the background as the mugshot of Luke Moran filled the area. Damian glared at the face, cursing under his breath at the man who led the detectives to his doorstep.

His blood began to boil as the collage slid stage left, immediately replaced by the still photograph of the lovely Detective Jolene Hartley. It was an image that had been taken before his time on her radar, though not by much. Detective Hartley was seen walking away from Navy Pier, her hand up in a defensive posture as the paparazzi flashed away at a maniacal speed. She was escorted by several medics and other officers, and followed by a man that looked as if he had been through a battle alongside the beautiful detective.

Damian lifted the tumbler to his lips and halted as he stared to the man, his eyes searching the face before returning to the female officer. He grumbled at the sight of her, downing the remaining scotch before turning the television off and tossing the remote on the ottoman before him. He sighed and glanced around, taking in the mountains of paperwork strewn through his once pristine home. His eyes traveled down the hallway and locked onto a wooden paneled wall and the notch just large enough for his pinky to slip into. He thought of rising and walking towards the section, a vision forming in his mind of him bending and pulling at the board until it popped off, revealing the mysterious contents within. He no longer had the strength, however. He was tired. Tired of the trial preparation. Tired of searching for the freedom he knew he would not find. The search was in vain, even with the information he still had up his sleeve.

* * * * *

The amber glass from the shattering beer bottle thundered throughout the garage, echoing in a singsong chime as the slivers rained down upon the concrete floor. He resumed his pacing, lifting the cigarette to his lips and taking a long, drawn-out drag before moving to the ancient refrigerator against the wall. He opened the door with a piercing squeak and retrieved another beer, popping the top and tossing it into a corner. His eyes fell to the television once more and he took a swig.

Things seemed surreal at the moment, like he had been transported into the past and was once again dealing with individuals he wanted nothing to do with. The image of the Graiser kid splashed across the TV was one thing. He had checked up on him from time to time, though not in the past several years. He hardly seemed to be any sort of threat. Yet the fact that he followed the young, pretty detective away from Navy Pier was something altogether different. It immediately raised a red flag. There were too many connections that led back to him.

The main one being Korhan Karaca.

Word on the street was Karaca — the fucking invalid junkie Turk — was wanted for attacking a police officer. There were things a criminal just did not do, he remembered thinking to himself. Messing with the cops did nothing but bring the heat on you. "Better to let the police do their thing and you get the fuck out of sight."

The quote was from his past as well, and, at this exact moment, his undeniable future. He took another drag from his cigarette before bending down to place the bottle of beer on the ground. He stood facing the television and pulled his cell phone from his pocket, eyeing the display and the numbers that stared back to him like a bad dream.

He did not have the number programmed into his phone, yet, for the years between the duo's last rendezvous, he had not forgotten the digits, or the hideous scar that graced his associate's left eyebrow, leaving a drooping lid over an evil orb. He punched them in and placed the phone to his ear, listening as the ringer chimed loudly, as if to remind him of what was about to happen. He was seconds away from connecting with the most dangerous man he had ever come across, a man that —

"What the fuck do you want?" a smooth, monotone voice answered from the other end of the line. The calmness sent a shiver down his spine. The last thing he had wanted in his life was to rekindle any form of relationship with this man. He was terrified of him. The things he could do, places he could reach. He was more than happy to rid himself of the dread that he had associated with in his youth.

That was not to say he was a saint these days. Far from it, in actuality. He ran with a crew that stayed in the shadows, lurking just beyond reach of the Chicago Police Department, ever present in the mind of a select few, yet wholly overlooked by the collective sum. On several occasions he had had to flee the city, taking shelter in the far south suburbs until the heat dissipated, relinquishing unto another guilty party that he, without hesitation, let take the fall. His name was out there, yet no more than any other common crook.

Yet these altogether new happenings had forced his hand. He had been required to make a move. The past decade had been beyond lucky. He knew that. Things had played out in their favor more than they could have ever hoped for. But their luck was running thin.

"You got your TV on?" he asked, his gruff voice trying unsuccessfully to hide the anxiety that spread throughout his body like wildfire.

"I'm watching it," came the response, followed by silence.

He waited briefly before continuing. "Well, did you see the picture?"

"There are a lot of fucking pictures." The humor in his tone was nothing but eerie.

"The one from Navy Pier."

"What about it?"

"Come on," he answered, pleading and bending for his bottle. "Tell me you don't recognize him."

"I'm not an idiot. But I am still wondering why the fuck you called me about it."

"Why I'm ...?" He let the phrase hang in the uncomfortable air. "You know who the woman is?"

"Let me guess. Someone you're looking to hook up with. Tell me: you going to turn on your charm? Or use your fists?" The comment hit home hard. Apparently their time apart had done nothing to ease the tension that had built.

He chose to ignore the remark, changing the subject away from himself and back to the detective on TV. "Come on, man. It's the same cop. It's the one that they attacked."

"So?"

"So? *So* ... She's the one that was there at the magazine." Another uncomfortable pause. "I'm hoping I don't have to explain it further."

"What do you want me to do about it?"

"I don't know. Maybe care a little fucking bit!" He tossed his cigarette to the floor and lit another. "Look," he began again, reigning in his irritation. "That fuck Karaca is unhinged. He attacked that cop and is running from every badge in the city. It's only a matter of time before he's caught and deals."

"If he's still in the city."

"My guess is he's still here. He's a fucking junkie. He's got to get his shit somewhere. Why start in a new place?" The question was rhetorical, yet the quiet that followed brought goosebumps. "What do you think we should do?"

"Look for the Turk," came the soothing voice. "If you find him, end him."

"What about the Graiser kid?"

"What about him?"

"Well, he's obviously talking to the cops."

"You don't know that. Don't go assuming anything until you know for sure. Killing Karaca is one thing. That fucker will do anything to get out of a lengthy jail sentence. You're right about him dealing."

"So we just leave the Graiser kid alone?"

"For the time being. Look, I'm out of town. I got shit to take care of and will be back in Chicago in about a week."

With that the phone went dead, leaving the man staring at the television screen as he lifted the beer to his lips once more. His hands were shaking.

ACKNOWLEDGMENTS

A sincere thank you to everyone who, once again, took the time to proof this manuscript. My wife, as always, was on the front line of editing, and I appreciate all the feedback you gave me.

I am grateful for the usual suspects on this book …

Mom and Dad.

Aunt Lynn, the title of this book was created from the suggestion you gave for *On the Ladder of Humanity*. If it wasn't for that, I'm sure I'd still be trying to think of one!

Angie Berglund, editor extraordinaire.

Sean, for your insight into how good looking Jolene Hartley did or did not need to be.

Sam, once again, your words of encouragement made writing and editing and editing and editing fun.

Mrs. Jean F. For your interest and our talk in the kitchen at your granddaughter's birthday party. It made my day.

Thank you.

RJP